FALLING FOR THE
Unexpected

LIFE *Unexpected*
BOOK 1

Terri,
Some of the best things
in life are unexpected!
♡ Rachel Lyn Adams

RACHEL LYN ADAMS

Acknowledgements

Cover Art by Kellie Dennis at Book Cover by Design

Photography by Nathan Hainline

Content Editing by Underline This Editing

Copyediting & Formatting by Carolyn Pinard

Cover Model: Nathan Hainline

FALLING FOR THE UNEXPECTED

Prologue

Kyle

Two Years Ago

$\mathcal{I}$ had just finished getting dressed in jeans, a gray T-shirt, and black Chucks when I heard my sister's ringtone blaring from my phone. Knowing her flight was due to take off shortly, I rushed over to my nightstand to grab it.

"Hey, Addie, what's up?" I asked, answering the call just before it was sent to voicemail.

"Hi, Kyle," she greeted. "My flight is about to board, but I wanted to make sure you were still able to pick me up from the airport."

"Of course," I answered as I headed out of my room. "You think I'd *not* pick up my little sister from the airport?"

It was spring break and Addie was coming home from college to spend the next two weeks finalizing the details for her summer wedding. She was marrying her fiancé, Brad, as soon as she graduated in a couple months. Brad was the younger brother of one of my best friends, Trent, but that didn't mean I liked Brad or thought he was a good match for my sister. At twenty-two, I thought Addie was too young to get married and Brad's lack of ambition was worrisome. Add to that his arrogant and entitled attitude — well, you could say I wasn't his biggest fan.

"Are you sure?" she asked again, hesitating. "I could just call a cab — "

"Hey, relax," I interrupted, not wanting her to worry. "The guys and I want to be there when you get off the plane. I think they've missed you as much as I have."

The guys I referred to were my closest friends: Trent and Erik. There was actually one more, but Ian was stationed across the country in South Carolina so he was going to miss out on this visit and the wedding. I'm sure he didn't mind since he disliked Brad just as much as I did. I knew Addie was disappointed he wouldn't be there since she and Ian had been super close growing up. I'd never told her, or the guys, but I had a feeling Ian was using his job as an excuse to get out of having to witness one of his best friends marry an asshole. Unfortunately, I couldn't do the same.

The four of us had met in kindergarten and had been best friends ever since. We had gone to school together, played sports together, and continued to be a huge presence in each other's lives. In fact, Trent and I were attending the same law school with the intention of us both joining his father's law firm once we finished next year.

I checked the time when I reached the bottom of the stairs, grabbing my wallet and keys off the side table near the front door. It was only a twenty-minute drive to the airport, but San Diego traffic — on a Friday, mid-morning — was going to be hectic. Plus, I had a couple errands to run before I picked up Trent and Erik.

"All of you are coming to pick me up?" she asked, sounding a little surprised, but pleased as well.

I smiled. "Trent is skipping a couple classes and Erik is taking the afternoon off from his shop to come with me," I said.

"Well... I can't wait to see all of you. I've missed everyone *so* much," she said, a slight tremor in her voice.

2

I knew it was hard on her being away from all of us. Growing up, there was hardly a time where we could escape Addie following us around. Sure, it annoyed us at times, but the guys knew that things at home weren't the best so they never made her feel unwanted. Instead, Trent, Ian, and Erik had become quite protective of her like she was their own little sister.

"Remind me why Brad isn't coming with us to pick you up?" I inquired, only half-heartedly masking my irritation. I didn't usually bring up her fiancé because it often resulted in an argument. At the same time, someone had to point out his obvious flaws. "I'm assuming you asked him to come to the airport?"

"I already told you," she huffed. "Brad has to work this afternoon."

I rolled my eyes. "Addison, he's a waiter. Are you telling me he couldn't get the afternoon off to come pick up the fiancée he hasn't seen in four months?"

"He said the restaurant has been super busy," she quipped back.

I took a calming breath because now we were both annoyed, but it ticked me off that she continued to defend Brad's lame excuses for everything. Trent and his parents were hardworking, kind, and humble people, which made Brad's obnoxious demeanor all the more baffling. I decided to opt for diplomacy because in a few months' time, the asshole was going to be my brother-in-law. Exercising some restraint, I suppose, should start now. But it wasn't going to be easy.

I rubbed my forehead, trying to erase the headache that Brad always brought on and tempered my own attitude. "Okay, fine, whatever," I eventually mumbled but

3

continued, "I'll see you soon, little sis. Travel safe."

"Okay..." she said, pausing for a second. "And thanks. I love you."

"Love you, too," I said and hung up.

Finally leaving the house, I ran my errands and picked up my buddies. Two hours later we were waiting near baggage claim for my sister. It would be easy to find Addie. At five-foot-nine, she was a few inches taller than most women. We both got our height from our father's side of the family, along with our light brown hair and green eyes. I was thankful it was only *physical* attributes that we'd inherited from him.

The minute she came off the escalator, she came running over to hug all of us. "I can't believe you're all here!" she exclaimed, grinning from ear to ear.

She hooked her arm through mine as we walked toward the carousels. "Hope you boys are ready! There is *so* much to do for the wedding and this is my last visit before the big day."

I might not have been thrilled about her upcoming nuptials, but hearing the excitement in her voice convinced me to remain positive. Our grandmother and I were the only family Addie had left and she needed to feel supported by us.

Erik and I grabbed her bags from the conveyor belt and we all headed out the automatic doors. The April sun was shining and a cool breeze was coming off from the ocean. I put on my sunglasses, looking around the busy airport and pedestrian traffic, and guided our group to the parking lot. We loaded her bags into the trunk of my old Jetta and piled in to start the drive home. The conversation in the car was filled with crazy college and law school stories and catching up with each other's lives. There was never a dull moment when we were all together.

*****

Two days later was Easter Sunday, and we had just returned home from church. 'Home' was where Addie and I grew up, at our grandmother's house. I continued to live here while completing school since the University of San Diego was close by and I wanted to help take care of our grandmother. It was the least I could do for the woman who did everything she could to make sure Addie and I were provided for.

Addie and Grandma quickly made their way to the kitchen to start preparing the Easter dinner we would be sharing with Brad, Trent, and their parents. I could hear the two of them chattering on about the upcoming wedding. Any time plans were discussed I could detect a small hint of sadness in Addie's voice. We were lucky to have our grandmother, who basically raised us, but it still hurt that our parents weren't part of our lives anymore. Our mother had died eight years ago, but the reality was that we had lost her a long time before that. Our father left immediately after Addie was born. I was two years old so I don't remember much about him and we never heard from him again. Grandma had essentially acted as both mother and father, and while we were forever grateful for everything she did for us, when it came to milestones like birthdays, graduations, and now this wedding, it felt like we were missing something or somebody.

Not having parents around had bonded Addie and I close together. I spent a lot of my childhood feeling responsible

5

for her, but the truth was, she took care of me just as much as I took care of her. Even with her getting married I would have to continue to watch out for her. Maybe more than ever before.

A short while later, our guests had arrived and everyone was speaking excitedly about the wedding. Well, everyone except Brad. I watched him every once in a while, a little disgusted by his attitude, like he'd rather be somewhere else. He was a complete douchebag, barely spending any time with Addie since she had arrived home. I wanted to call him out the moment he'd walked in the door, but I didn't want to upset my sister. He was her choice, and while I found him difficult to be around, he must have some redeeming qualities if Addie was going to marry him. But if he hurt her, all bets were off.

"Everything smells delicious, ladies," Trent said as soon as we all sat down at the dining table. After a quick prayer, everyone started filling their plates with prime rib and mashed potatoes. We all settled into comfortable conversation, enjoying the time together.

As the meal was winding down, the doorbell rang. I got up, walked to the front door and opened it, expecting to see Erik on the other side. It wasn't unusual for my friends to stop by for one of my grandmother's famous desserts, especially on a holiday. But instead of Erik, I was greeted by a gorgeous vision with long, black hair and dark chocolate brown eyes. I was rendered speechless, completely distracted by her killer curves. She was young, definitely not older than twenty.

"Hi," the mystery woman finally said, slowly eyeing me. She was fidgeting, nervously looking at me and then around me into the house, and then back to meet my gaze. "I'm looking for Bradley Thompson. A friend of his told me I

6

might find him here?"

"Who's at the door?" I heard my sister ask from behind me.

It took me a moment to realize I hadn't said anything since opening the door. "Brad, there's someone here to see you," I yelled over my shoulder toward the dining room as Addie moved in next to me.

Addie was standing there silently observing our visitor as we waited for Brad. It had to be awkward for her to have another woman here who none of us knew, asking to speak with her fiancé.

"What do you want with Brad?" I finally asked, letting my curiosity get the better of me.

She licked her perfectly plump lips and swallowed hard. "Um," she started, only to be interrupted.

"Simone, what the fuck are you doing here?" Brad shouted as soon as he came into the living room. The air was immediately filled with tension as everyone collected behind him, watching with frowns and looks of concern.

I glanced back at the mystery woman, Simone, since it was obvious Brad knew her. I didn't have a good feeling about any of this, but like a traffic accident, I couldn't look away.

"Brad, you wouldn't answer any of my calls or texts the last couple weeks and I *really* need to talk to you," Simone answered lowly, as though she was trying to keep their conversation as private as possible.

I could see the confusion on Addie's face as she watched the conversation between her fiancé and Simone very closely. Like the rest of us, she was trying to process what was occurring in front of her. I looked between Simone and

Brad, trying to get a better idea of what was happening. Simone's earlier nerves were now replaced with a sense of urgency and the pleading look in her eyes was hard to ignore. And yet, Brad's contempt for this woman was evident.

"We don't have anything to talk about. You need to leave," Brad stated bitingly. He turned away quickly, dismissing her.

I stood there, taken aback. That was beyond rude, even for Brad.

"I'm pregnant!" Simone blurted out, and Brad stopped mid-step.

Addie gasped, stumbling back. I reached out, to make sure she didn't fall. Her eyes were wide with shock, pain, and hurt. I watched as Simone put her hands over her mouth, her gaze meeting mine briefly. Horror and fear was evident on her face and then she glanced at Addie, whose expression wasn't much different. I found myself staring at Simone's stomach. She was in jeans and a loose-fitting tank top, but now hearing her announcement, I could make out the unmistakable roundness to her belly. I was no baby expert, but I knew enough to know she was probably in her second trimester.

I looked back into the living room. Everyone was frozen with the same stunned looks on their faces, but my grandmother recovered first. She moved toward Addie who all but collapsed in her arms, sobbing.

Brad had turned around by then, hands on his hips and observing the scene impassively, like he was bored with the whole thing. Trent glared at his younger brother, appearing as pissed as I felt. His parents looked both embarrassed and disappointed. My hands balled into fists at my side. For once, I didn't check my anger.

"Oh, hell no," I growled and charged toward the asshole without a second thought. No one broke my sister's heart and got away with it. A lesson Brad would learn the hard way.

Simone

It had been a few days of radio silence since I showed up at what turned out to be Brad's fiancée's house. I had run back to my car as soon as I heard the guy who had answered the door yell at Brad for cheating on his sister.

I had sent multiple texts and left him numerous voicemails since then. Each attempt at contacting him had gone unanswered. I figured that was his not-so-subtle way of letting me know that I was truly on my own with our baby.

The fact that Brad had a fiancée was a complete shock. I would never have guessed he was involved with anyone, let alone getting married. We had never defined what was going on between us for the past few months we'd been seeing each other, but the moment I realized he was engaged, it'd rocked my world. I was not only pissed at Brad for doing that to me, but to the other woman as well. From her reaction, she'd been devastated by Brad's deception. Even though I hadn't known about her, my guilt was overwhelming. I was not the type of girl who went after unavailable men. I hoped that one day I would have the opportunity to apologize to her, but I wasn't sure if that would ever happen.

Even with Brad's deplorable behavior, I still wanted to give my child a mother and father who were both involved in their life. My baby wasn't even born yet, and I already felt like a failure. I had no one in my life to model how to be a good parent. I was born to parents who had cared more about their next high than me. When I was finally put in foster care, the abuse and neglect I'd suffered didn't stop, but was instead delivered by complete strangers. It'd caused a host of issues, which included never developing a bond with anyone in a parental role. The moment I'd turned eighteen, just a few weeks after I'd graduated from high school, I'd been on my own—with no one to turn to. When I met Brad at the beginning of my sophomore year at Beachside Community College, it'd felt right, like perfect timing, but we'd only just started getting to know each other when I got pregnant. We were still new and I was still reeling from the thought that we'd forever be connected, regardless of what he did, or didn't do.

There was no guarantee that Brad would help us out, and that scared me. He had suddenly cut off all contact a few weeks ago. At the time, it'd shocked me, but now I assumed it had something to do with him getting married soon. During Brad's disappearing act, it was finally confirmed that I was pregnant. I had suspected it for weeks, but I had been too scared to find out for sure. Once I knew, I'd wanted to tell him right away, but I was worried about how he would react. Obviously, I hadn't been wrong in assuming the worst. Still, I wanted to provide for my child but every day, it seemed more impossible. There was no way I could juggle college, my part-time job, which I needed more than ever, and a baby. My baby deserved so much more than what I'd had, and I was determined to not fail as a mother like my own had failed me.

Sitting cross-legged on my dingy couch, I looked around my tiny studio apartment knowing I would need to figure out another living situation soon. This wasn't any place to bring a baby home to. As soon as night descended, so did the drug dealers and prostitutes who lived in the neighborhood. The mad dash I made from my car to my front door each night was a testament to how unsafe I felt here. As bad as my living situation was, I wasn't sure how I was going to be able to pay the rent for a nicer place, especially if I was going to have to pay for daycare as well. There were so many unknowns and the stress was starting to take its toll on me.

The one positive thing that kept me going was the baby growing inside me. Two days before I had gone to confront Brad, I'd had my twenty-week appointment and learned I was having a girl. That was part of the information I was going to share with him, but nothing went as planned that day. I hadn't expected a houseful of people, never mind Brad's fiancée and her family. Then the looks on all their faces... It was the most mortifying experience of my life.

And the good-looking man who had opened the door, with his tall build, light brown hair, and green eyes that were so much like the other woman's features... it was obvious they were siblings. I had felt his eyes on me the whole time, wondering who I was, what I was doing there. He probably hated me just as the rest of them did now.

I may not have had everything figured out yet, but I knew I loved my daughter more than anything and I was going to do whatever was needed to take care of her. That still didn't change the fact that I would love to have someone here with me to share this experience with.

While I was sitting in my dark, drafty apartment and contemplating my future, I heard my cell phone ding with a text notification. I wasn't interested in talking to anyone at the moment and chose to ignore it. Instead, I went into my kitchen in search of dinner, praying whatever I ate would stay down. I opened the refrigerator, but it was almost completely empty, just a carton of milk, some lunchmeat, and a jar of pickles. Again, I heard my cell phone ding. Deciding it could be important, I went to grab it off the foldable card table that was acting as a dining table and looked to see who the sender was.

With utter disbelief, I clicked on my text app to read the message from the one person who had been ignoring me.

Brad: *We need to talk.*

I felt like a lead weight had planted itself firmly in my stomach at those four simple words. Of course we had to talk, but what did he want to talk about? Had he decided he wanted to be involved with our baby? Did he want to finally confirm what I had feared this whole time, that he was done with me and our daughter and I was truly on my own? Or worse, did he want to try to take my child away from me? As much as I feared his intentions, I had to know what was on his mind.

Me: *Ok. Do you want to meet in person or talk on the phone?*

Brad: *In person. Can you meet tomorrow?*

Me: *I have to work at 3 so anything before that is fine.*

Brad: *Noon at your apartment?*

Me: *Sure.*

I didn't know if meeting at my apartment was a good idea, but I wanted to be as agreeable as possible. Having him involved was the most important thing to me, and whatever I had to do to make things easier on him I was going to do it. I was determined that my child would have a father. I was fine with him only wanting a relationship with our child, but if he wanted us to have a relationship I wouldn't rule that out either. Maybe that seemed foolish to some, but having grown up the way I did, the dream of having a stable home life, with a complete family, was too good to pass up. I knew how the real world worked and I had no illusions about Brad being in love with me. Hell, he could still be with his fiancée for all I knew. But if he wanted to work things out with me, I'd be willing to try. Because knowing my daughter and I weren't alone in this... would mean everything.

The next day when my doorbell rang, I felt as though I might vomit. For the first time in months it wasn't due to the pregnancy but rather because of the massive amount of nervous energy that was spinning in my stomach. I tried to calm down and not fidget.

I opened the door and was immediately met by a pair of steely blue eyes set in a handsome face. Brad was an extremely good-looking man with his blond hair and toned body. His looks were what drew me in the night I met him. Now those eyes weren't staring at me in lust like they had that night, instead they flicked to my pregnant belly. It seemed in that moment it finally hit Brad that he was going to become a father. The quick intake of breath and widening eyes were a dead giveaway that reality was setting in.

Brad was just under six feet, but next to my five-foot-two-inch frame, he could be very intimidating. I had seen his anger often when we'd gone out, and even though it had never been directed at me, it was scary nonetheless. At the moment, he didn't look happy to be here, but I was relieved that he didn't appear angry.

"Hi," I said, quietly.

His eyes shot back up to meet mine again and he took a deep breath before speaking. "Hey. Can I come in?" he asked, equally quiet.

I pushed the door open and moved aside as an unspoken invitation for him to enter. He had been in my apartment many times. Most of our hookups happened here. It wasn't 'til recently that I understood why he never invited me to his place. I could feel the bitterness seeping in so I quickly pushed that thought away. I wanted today to be about making amends and starting fresh, no matter what had happened in the past.

As he walked by me, I couldn't help but notice that he moved stiffly and had a few bruises on his face, like he'd gotten into a fight. I swallowed hard, wondering if he had — with the green-eyed man. That man had looked fit enough to take on Brad, who was definitely not out of shape. While I didn't condone violence of any kind, to have someone defend your honor... it was a nice idea. Granted, he would have been defending the honor of Brad's fiancée, but one could dream. Knowing Brad's quick temper, I wasn't going to ask what happened. I needed him calm and focused.

He took a seat at one end of the couch, which was the only option in my tiny living room. I sat on the other end putting as much space as possible between us. I turned, propping my knee up on the cushion, and waited silently for him to start.

"So," he said, slowly. He appeared to be choosing his words carefully so I gave him a moment. "I'm going to want proof that the baby is mine."

My jaw went slack with surprise. I was slightly taken aback that that was the first thing he'd say after days of silence. In my mind, I wanted to throw back at him that I wasn't the one with a fiancée that I had been cheating on, but I refrained. Lashing out wasn't going to solve anything or make him want to be involved.

And even though his assumption offended me, I couldn't deny that he had the right to ask. "Okay, I understand wanting to know for sure. I have no doubt that you're *her*

15

father but I'm happy to have the test done," I said, emphasizing the gender of our child.

"Her?" he questioned, his eyes growing wide again.

"Yes, we're having a daughter." I smiled, hoping to see some kind of excitement from him.

For some reason, my answer seemed to displease him. His expression turned grim. "Oh, well, I've done some research and I found out you can do a paternity test while still pregnant. I would prefer that so we could know sooner rather than later. If it's" — he paused when I eyed him questioningly — "I mean, if *she's* mine, I'm prepared to do the right thing," he said with zero enthusiasm.

"And… what do you think the right thing would be?" I inquired timidly, almost afraid to ask, but I had to know what he was thinking.

He looked away, resignation in his voice. "We'll get married and raise the child together."

Chapter 1

Simone

Present Day

My shift at the Ocean View restaurant didn't start for another fifteen minutes so I had time to call Brad. I wanted to let him know that his mom had kindly offered to keep our daughter, Stella, overnight so he didn't have to rush to their house after work to pick her up.

Brad worked at Erik's Auto Performance, which was owned by one of his brother's best friends. While he worked an 8-to-5 job five days a week, I worked four nights a week as a waitress. It didn't allow us a lot of time together, but it did help us figure out childcare for our young daughter. When our schedules overlapped, Brad's mother, Marla, would watch Stella. It was a perfect setup.

I took a moment and leaned against the side of my car, enjoying the early March breeze. Two things I loved about living in San Diego were the smell of the ocean and the year-round mild weather. I didn't get to enjoy the beach as much as I used to, but it was nice to be near it while I worked. I dug out my cell phone from my purse, squinting against the afternoon sun bouncing off the waves of the Pacific.

I called Brad's number and it rang four times and then went to voicemail. Thinking he may have left his phone in his work locker, I decided to call the shop.

"Erik's Auto Performance, how can I help you?" Tiffany, the receptionist, answered.

I had met Tiffany a couple times and each interaction left me unimpressed. If you were a woman, she would do the bare minimum necessary to help you. If you were a man, you would get her undivided attention and usually a flash of her cleavage when she purposely leaned over the counter.

"Hi, Tiffany, it's Simone. I was wondering if Brad was available?" I asked, trying to sound as friendly as possible.

"Oh, he left a little while ago," she answered, and I could hear the smacking of her gum in my ear.

"Um... Okay, thanks," I responded, somewhat confused.

"Yep," she said, and then hung up.

Brad wasn't supposed to get off work for another hour, but I wondered if he had plans that I may have forgotten about. I decided to try his cell phone again, and this time, he picked up after two rings.

"What?" he greeted in a flat tone. Brad had never been overly affectionate; in fact, most would probably call him uncaring. I wasn't dumb enough to believe that Brad was with me for any other reason than he had knocked me up. I had accepted the fact that our marriage would never be filled with love like you'd find in romance novels. However, his previous indifference toward me had recently started to shift toward irritable and angry. I could live in a loveless marriage, but I wouldn't stay in an abusive one, and I was starting to fear Brad's recent mood swings. His anger made me feel helpless and I had no defense against it. My childhood had been filled with the same fear, and it was still difficult for me to deal with it. My instinct was to pacify and get out of the situation as quickly as possible, usually by apologizing or remaining silent. During the first few months after we'd gotten married, Brad had almost seemed… okay with the idea and it'd been nice. Recently, though, it was like a switch had flipped. The charming man who had attracted me in the first place was long gone. Instead, I only saw the side of him that made no effort to hide just how unhappy he was.

"Hey," I said cautiously, trying to keep my tone neutral. "I was just calling to let you know that your mom and dad are keeping Stella overnight so you don't have to go pick her up tonight."

"Okay," he said, and that was it.

I tried not to read into his one-word answers. He never seemed to want to have a conversation unless it interested him. After two years of marriage, I was used to it, but it disappointed me at the same time. I didn't know what he wanted or how to please him.

"I called the shop a few minutes ago and Tiffany said you had already left. Do you have something going on tonight?" I asked, hoping he would at least be home when I got off of work. We hadn't spent any time together, just the two of us, in at least three months.

"It's Friday and I finished my work early tonight. Damn it, do you have to question everything I do?" he asked, irritated.

Another thing I had learned early on was that Brad hated answering to anyone. Even if the question was an innocent one, he immediately became defensive. Not only did his behavior negatively affect my attempts at communicating with him, it also caused strain in his relationships with his brother, Trent, and his parents.

I closed my eyes briefly, trying to be patient. Sometimes I wanted to snap back with a retort that would shock him. I was tired of walking on eggshells around him all the time, but I also worried about pushing him too far. Between my own parents and a couple of my foster families, I knew how ugly things could get. Instead of focusing on how Brad treated me, I focused on Stella, reminding myself that everything I did was for her, so I sucked it up and tried for civility.

"I wasn't questioning you, Brad. I was just curious if you had plans," I answered, trying to be even-tempered. I didn't want an argument right before I started my shift and then end up taking it out on customers. I needed the money from tips. "I was thinking I could bring dinner home from the restaurant tonight and maybe we could watch a movie together. I just thought it might be nice."

He pondered that for a moment. "I guess we can do that. What time do you get off?" he asked.

"I'm actually getting off early, around eight," I answered, surprised he was taking me up on the offer, "they over-scheduled the staff tonight."

"Fine, I guess I'll see you then," he said and then hung up.

He didn't sound too excited, but at least he agreed to a date of sorts. Maybe we could try to kindle some sort of spark in our marriage. Maybe that's what Brad felt he was missing. If I showed him some affection, focused on us, perhaps he wouldn't be so angry. Even with his lack of enthusiasm, I had a good feeling when I headed in through the back door of the restaurant to put my stuff in my locker.

About halfway through my shift, I saw the hostess seating a couple in my section. I couldn't see them clearly, but I watched with envy as the man guided the woman through the restaurant with his hand on her lower back. At their table, he pulled the chair out for his date to sit down. It was a simple gesture, one I had never been on the receiving end of. Brad had never taken me out on a proper date. In the beginning, I was blinded by his charisma and good looks so I accepted whatever time he was willing to spend with me. Once I was pregnant, he knew he didn't have to put forth any effort. But how nice would it be to feel cherished and like I was worth the effort?

After giving the couple another minute to get settled, I approached the table to take their drink order. The man's back was to me as I walked over to them, but I could see how absolutely gorgeous his date was. Sure, we lived in Southern California, where it almost seemed like a prerequisite to be beautiful. This woman, though, was definitely a 'ten' on the hotness scale. Her blonde hair cascaded past her slender shoulders in large curls and her makeup was perfectly applied, highlighting her bright blue eyes. As I took the last step toward their table I saw her flash her date a seductive smile.

"Welcome to the Ocean View. My name's…" I started but was interrupted by the man I had yet to fully see.

"Simone?" the man next to me questioned.

Recognizing the voice, I looked over, and was immediately met by a familiar pair of green eyes. Kyle O'Neill was here, sitting in my section with a model-perfect date.

I smiled at him briefly, almost forgetting I was there to take their order. "Hi, Kyle," I said, trying to go for casual, but my voice caught in my throat and it came out breathy and shaky. His date gave me a quick up and down look, then seemed to dismiss my very existence.

I had seen Kyle a few times over the last couple years. He

and my brother-in-law, Trent, spent a lot of time together so I would occasionally run into him, usually at my in-law's house. He knew I worked here, but this was the first time I'd ever seen him come to this restaurant. I suddenly felt nervous and could feel my face get a little warm.

Every time I saw him, I was in awe of his good looks. Tonight wasn't any different. He wore a pair of black slacks with a crisp, burgundy button-down shirt. The sleeves were rolled up to his elbows, giving him a somewhat casual look. His hair was gelled and styled perfectly.

"Courtney, this is my friend's sister-in-law, Simone. Simone, this is Courtney," Kyle said. "She's a lawyer, too."

"Oh, how nice," I acknowledged, and mentally kicked myself for the lame response. The fact that Kyle took the time to introduce me to his date was a surprise. It also warmed something inside of me. The two of us had never talked about the night we unofficially met but he never seemed to hold a grudge. Everything I knew about him led me to believe he was a really nice guy. It also wasn't lost on me that he hadn't introduced Courtney as his girlfriend, but something more platonic, and Kyle's date hadn't missed it either. She had given me a haughty look and promptly picked up her menu without saying anything to me.

"How've you been?" he asked.

My attention veered back to Kyle. He was smiling warmly up at me and his gaze was direct. Like I wasn't some no-nothing waitress or the woman who had ruined his sister's life—but instead, someone who deserved as much attention as his date. He treated me like we were equals when we really weren't. It was flattering, if not a little disarming. I'm sure he was like that with everyone, especially toward his dates. And I bet he had plenty of dates. He was probably like Trent, who dated a lot but didn't have a steady woman in

22

his life.

"Good," I finally answered, realizing I needed to stop thinking about Kyle's relationship status and focus on my job instead. I turned toward Courtney and smiled politely at her. "It's nice to meet you," I offered, but moved on quickly so I could leave. I focused on my duties as their waitress and it helped with my nerves. I gave them my spiel about the specials and took out my pen and notepad. "Can I take your drink order?"

I spent the next bit of my shift glancing at Kyle and Courtney in between serving my other customers. I didn't know why I was so interested in what was happening at their table, but my focus was glued to the both of them, at their interaction and expressions. Kyle was attractive, but that wasn't all that had captured my attention. I couldn't help but notice the small things like the flirty way Courtney placed her hand on Kyle's arm or the smile he would throw at her in the middle of their conversation. It made me long for something I didn't have.

A couple hours later, once I was done with my shift, I grabbed the meal I had ordered from the kitchen and headed out the back exit. I was a little less excited now about heading home to see Brad. I knew it was because I was jealous of the date I had spent an hour and a half observing. I had fantasies years ago that I would be with a man who was attentive like the way Kyle had been with Courtney. But I had come to terms with knowing that wasn't ever going to be my reality.

I placed the food in the backseat of my Honda Civic, next to Stella's car seat, and got into the driver's seat. The drive home only took about fifteen minutes and I spent that time making an effort to change my attitude. By the time I pulled into our designated parking space at our apartment complex, I'd convinced myself that I was looking forward to my impromptu date night with my husband. I noticed Brad's truck parked in our other space and I felt a sense of relief that he was actually home. There had been a part of me that thought he was going to bail on our night together. I wouldn't have been surprised. He'd done it before, and me pointing that out only caused him to get mad at me.

I climbed the two flights of stairs to our apartment, which we had moved into a couple months before Stella was born. It was a two bedroom in a nice part of San Diego. I unlocked the door and immediately saw Brad sitting in the living room playing some video game. He was quite animated, yelling at the screen and moving around with the controller. He didn't acknowledge me as I closed the door and set my purse on the counter. Since I was hungry and Brad likely was too, I wanted to eat dinner before getting comfy. I moved to the kitchen to prepare our plates. I grabbed a beer for him and a water bottle for me then carried everything over to the couch, knowing Brad wouldn't want to move over to our small dining room table to eat.

"Hey, can you take a break from that for a minute?" I asked, setting his plate on the coffee table.

"Yeah." Brad tossed his controller down and switched the mode to regular TV where some sort of car show was playing. "This actually looks pretty good," he said and then dug into the pot roast and vegetables. It was probably my favorite thing on the menu at the restaurant. He gave me a look of appreciation and it made me happy that he was enjoying it as well.

Kind words from him, a cordial moment like this, were few and far between so I remained silent as to not break the spell. For a brief second, the illusion that we were a happily married couple almost felt possible.

I couldn't remember a time growing up where someone spoke kindly to me. In my childhood I had seen more than my fair share of physical and emotional abuse. As I got older and moved around in foster care, I was mostly ignored. I knew that witnessing beatings and being neglected had a profound effect on me and was the reason why I tolerated Brad's behavior. Did that make it worse, knowing his treatment of me was poor but accepting it anyway? Lately, I was starting to wonder if I was repeating the patterns of my childhood. Of keeping silent, enduring the problems, and just trying to get by.

In truth, I was all grown up, but very little had actually changed. Brad and I had both settled for this life and sometimes I thought it was enough. But I was learning that *having* a family and *being* a family were two very different things. In many ways, my casual relationship with Brad hadn't changed since we'd first met. We still didn't know the little things about each other, like what made us happy or what our goals in life were. Brad had felt obligated to do the right thing, and acted on that. But he wasn't invested in our relationship, just physically here, and every day, that became more apparent. I hadn't known what to expect when we married, I'd just hoped for the best. But hoping didn't make things happen or our lives better.

I thought back to a specific couple as I ate, blindly watching the TV show and not really tasting the food. However long they'd known each other, be that just recently or not, Courtney and Kyle had clearly been into each other. Kyle was not shy about showing his interest. He was engaging and attentive, talking to her and listening, but he was respectful at the same time. I couldn't recall a time when Brad had doted on me, or even smiled warmly at me, just because, or wanted to hold my hand. When we were out and about—and that too was a rare event—he always acted like he didn't really know me, or Stella, for that matter. I looked at Brad, who kept his own eyes on the TV and didn't attempt any conversation with me at all.

For the next half hour, we continued to eat, but Brad seemed to be filled with anxious energy. His leg never stopped bouncing up and down and he kept fidgeting with his utensils. I knew something was up when he literally jumped up off the couch to take his plate, and mine when I was finished, to the kitchen.

"Is everything okay?" I asked, eyeing him suspiciously.

"Uh, yeah." He wouldn't look at me as he set our plates in the sink. "I had an energy drink right before you came home. Guess the caffeine is getting to me," he explained.

I got up to help him in the kitchen and as soon as I walked in, Brad grabbed me and pushed me up against the wall and then his lips were crashing down hard on mine. I gasped at the suddenness of his movements and he took advantage of that and shoved his tongue into my mouth. Confused by his abruptness but also slightly turned on, I started to kiss him back. Our relationship was far from perfect, but that didn't mean I didn't have needs that I turned to my husband to fulfill. Sex had been the one way I would allow myself to feel close to someone and I wanted to feel close to my husband.

When he finally broke the kiss, he turned away from me. It took me a moment to catch my breath. "What was that?" I asked, a little dazed by what had happened.

He must have mistaken my question because he started shouting. "What? I can't kiss my wife? Jesus Christ, Simone! What the fuck is your problem?"

Whatever arousal I had been feeling was quickly dissipating due to his outburst. "I don't have a problem. You caught me off guard, that's all. I'm sorry," I apologized quickly in an effort to calm him down.

He turned back around and his eyes had taken on a dark quality. I wasn't sure if it was lust or anger, but both possibilities made me nervous. I was suddenly five years old again watching my parents fight in the kitchen. I was too young at the time to comprehend what was happening. All I knew was they would fight and things would either end with them suddenly kissing and leaving me alone as they went to their room, or my father beating the crap out of my mother. I would often run to my room not wanting to see how things would end.

"We haven't fucked in a month, Simone. I thought that's what you had in mind for tonight," Brad finally said, bringing me out of my memories.

"Well, yeah, I did," I responded, and that was the truth. I was hoping we would spend some time talking and then *eventually* end up in bed together. I just wasn't expecting it to happen like this.

"Well then, what are we waiting for?" he asked while grabbing my hand and pulling me to our bedroom.

Once we were through the door, he pushed me up against the wall again and started pulling up my shirt. He was kissing me roughly and sucking on my neck hard. While it felt rushed, I tried to go along with it. I wasn't sure if not having sex for a while was making him impatient, but I tried to relax and be in the moment.

He ripped the shirt over my head and immediately his lips moved down to my breasts. I was trying to focus on the sensations but he was all over the place. He pulled the cups of my bra down and drew one nipple into his mouth while pinching the other one between his fingers. He was not being gentle with me and I yelped when he bit down firmly on the nipple between his teeth.

"What?" Brad said mockingly, moving up to my neck. "You used to like it rough."

I pushed gently on his chest. "Can you just slow down a little bit?" I asked.

"Fine," he huffed, using the wall to push away from me. "You want to be in control then why don't you go ahead and undress me?"

That wasn't exactly what I had meant, but I did as he instructed, hoping to change the pace a bit. I moved toward him and reached for the button of his jeans. I leaned up to kiss him softly, slowly moving my tongue against his lips. I continued to kiss him deeply while undoing his jeans. I pushed the denim down taking his boxers with them.

"Get on your knees," he demanded, catching me off guard again, but I did as he requested. "I need you to suck my cock, now."

I looked up at him hoping to make a connection since he sounded distant. Instead, his eyes were screwed closed and his hands were fisted at his sides. The deep crimson color on his face made him look angry. Not wanting to upset him more, I moved my lips to the head of his dick and kissed the tip. I took him in my mouth going as far as I could before engaging my gag reflex. When he hit the back of my throat, he fisted my hair in both hands and started pumping into my mouth at a furious pace. I tried to slow him down by putting pressure on his hips with both my hands, but he ignored me. I no longer wanted to prolong this and instead started praying he would finish quickly.

He abruptly pulled free of my mouth and I gasped for breath. He yanked me up off the floor and pushed me onto the bed. I tried to flip over onto my back but he was already on the bed between my legs. He pushed my pants and panties down, and then grabbed my hips roughly, pulling them up so he could enter me from behind.

He thrusted into me violently, not caring if I was ready or not. I buried my face into the comforter to keep him from hearing me yell out. I'm not sure why I muffled my scream. He needed to know that he was hurting me. Instead, I cried into the bed while he continued to take me roughly. In that moment, I was becoming someone I never wanted to be. Even the desire to provide Stella with an intact family wasn't a good enough reason to tolerate this behavior.

His movements became more frantic and he grabbed my hair to pull my body up off the bed. This time I couldn't keep quiet and I shouted out in pain. For some reason that seemed to spur him on and he shot forward even harder. A few agonizing minutes later, I felt his release inside of me.

He pulled out of me and immediately put his boxers back on. "Thanks. I needed that," he said casually as he walked out of our bedroom and back to play his video games.

I lay motionless on the bed, completely stunned by what had transpired, and knowing I couldn't live like this. Brad wasn't known for being a gentle lover or really caring about my needs, but this went far beyond that. He was completely detached from what was happening and there was absolutely no care for my well-being. I felt used and degraded. Needing to wash Brad off of me, I stumbled to the bathroom to clean up. The pain I felt while walking fueled my outrage. I decided I didn't want to see him any more that night so I put on my pajamas after my shower, and climbed back into bed. As I lay in bed, I tried to figure out why Brad acted that way tonight and I couldn't come up with anything. Instead, I fell asleep crying into my pillow.

*****

The sunlight shining in through my bedroom window woke me up and I could hear someone rummaging around in the bathroom. Figuring it was Brad getting ready for whatever he had planned today, I decided to stay in bed and pretend to still be asleep. He'd stayed in the living room last night, which wasn't unusual, but I was grateful for it. I had enough trouble sleeping as it was, but knowing he was next to me would have made it even harder to get some rest.

While my intention was to ignore him, Brad had other ideas. "Hey, are you awake?" he asked somewhat gruffly when he walked back into our bedroom.

I sighed, and slowly pushed myself up onto my elbows. He was standing by the door in tan cargo shorts and a white T-shirt. His blonde hair was still damp from his shower and he looked handsome, but his good looks no longer gave me butterflies. "Yes," I said, only feeling capable of one-word answers.

"What's your problem?" he asked, not looking me in the eye. "Are you mad about last night?"

I glared at him. "Mad?" I asked, incredulously. "Of course, I'm mad. You hurt me!"

"Whatever," he responded agitatedly. "I don't want to argue with you. Just wanted to let you know that I'm going out with some buddies today. I don't know when I'll be home."

With that, he walked out of our bedroom. As I lay back down in bed, I could hear him grab something from the kitchen and then I heard the click of our front door. My mind was racing. I knew I needed to make some changes and decide whether my future included Brad or not, because this wasn't working for me.

I heard my text notification go off when I finally got out of bed. I grabbed my phone from the side table next to me and checked the display. I was happy to see that it was from my coworker Kayla.

Kayla: *Do you have time for coffee this morning?*

I didn't have to pick up Stella from Brad's mom until lunchtime. So some time out with a friend definitely sounded like a good thing.

Me: *I do. When and where do you want to meet?*

Kayla: *How about Starbucks on Mission at 10?*

Me: *Perfect! I'll see you then.*

I looked at the clock and realized I only had an hour to get ready and make the ten-minute drive to the coffee shop.

I opened the drawer in my bedside table and searched for ibuprofen, hoping for some relief since I was sore all over. Then I hopped into the shower and started to wash my hair. My scalp was still tender after the way Brad had pulled my hair. Taking care to be gentle with those spots, I rinsed the shampoo out and then found my favorite citrus body wash and lathered up.

After drying off, I decided to choose an outfit that would help elevate my mood. I settled on a black maxi skirt with a white chevron pattern. I selected my favorite pair of black strappy sandals and a white cardigan over my black tank top to complete the outfit.

Since my long, thick hair took too long to dry, I decided to pull it up into a bun on the top of my head. I added a little mascara and lip-gloss to complete my ensemble, and was out the door.

I pulled up to the coffee shop right at ten and saw my friend sitting at a table inside by the window. Kayla and I met a couple years ago when she started waitressing at the Ocean View. We were the two youngest servers, about the same age, and had hit it off right away. She was tall and thin with typical California looks of lightly tanned skin, blonde hair, and blue eyes. She was the perfect contrast to my darker features. Her shoulder-length hair was half up and made her heart-shaped face look even younger. In addition to working at the restaurant, she was also going to school to get her nursing degree.

When I'd needed a girls' night out, she'd been there for me and, in a pinch, she had babysat for me as well. Stella absolutely loved her, and for someone like me who didn't have very many friends, she had been a godsend.

"Hi, girlie! I already ordered you a chai tea latte so come sit your butt down," Kayla said as soon as I walked through the door. Her friendly face made me feel so much better, like someone actually cared about me.

"Thank you for the drink and for asking me to come out this morning," I said, sitting down and then wincing a little. I'd have to be a little more careful until I didn't feel so achy.

"Well," she drawled out, wrapping her hands around her cup, "we haven't hung out for a few weeks—and being at work together does not count—so I thought it was time for a catch-up session."

I smiled a little, taking a long sip of my latte. I instantly felt less stressed, and more like a normal twenty-one-year-old. Kayla was my closest friend and she knew many details of my marriage that I didn't share with others. Like the fact that Brad had been engaged to another woman when I found out I was pregnant with Stella. More importantly, she always listened without judgment and would offer advice if I asked.

"Looks like date night went well," she remarked, grinning. She leaned forward, eyeing the dark mark on my neck that I'd completely forgotten to cover up. "I want all the details!" Since she was at work last night, Kayla knew of my plans for my 'date' with Brad.

Five little words and last night flashed in my mind. At how horrible it'd been. Every feeling flooded my senses. And that simple request had me bursting into tears.

"Oh, my God," Kayla said lowly. She moved closer and rubbed my back gently. I tensed a little then relaxed. When I got emotional and someone touched me, I would sometimes flinch. It was a subconscious reflex left over from my childhood, but right now I felt comforted since I trusted Kayla. "Simone... are you okay?"

The concern in her voice was reassuring and I didn't feel as alone in this. It hit me that I'd held back what I'd felt last night and this morning from Brad, but I couldn't now, not with Kayla. I was shaking, my hands trembling, and I felt so cold inside. It took me a full ten seconds to stop crying and take a few calming breaths. A couple people nearby gave us funny looks, but I didn't care. I looked down into my latte, trying to find the words. "Date night didn't go exactly how I planned," I finally answered in a hushed whisper. I sounded nasally, but at least I'd stopped sobbing. I sniffed, wiping my nose on a napkin and dabbing at my eyes.

"What does that mean, exactly?" Kayla asked, giving me an encouraging smile to continue.

I was too ashamed to tell her much else.

"What happened?" she asked again, not letting it go, not because she was nosy, but because she was actually concerned about me.

"When I got home, Brad seemed a bit out of sorts. He blamed it on the energy drink he had before I got there. We ate dinner and he barely said two words to me..." I continued to tell her how the rest of the night went, I just couldn't look her in the eyes until I was done speaking.

When I glanced up, the look of horror on Kayla's face confirmed that my anger was justified. While I knew in my heart what Brad had done was not okay, knowing my best friend was just as upset by it comforted me a bit.

Kayla grabbed my hand, and squeezed it briefly. "Simone, you can't stay with him if he is going to act like that." She paused until I numbly nodded in agreement. "You don't deserve that kind of treatment."

I knew she was right, and I had thought the same thing all morning. But things weren't so simple. First off, I wasn't sure I was ready to break up Stella's family. When I found out I was pregnant with Stella, I'd promised her and myself that I would give her the family I never had, making sure she felt that she had a stable family life. My in-laws were wonderful people and I knew they'd be there for her, but that wasn't the same as Stella having her own immediate family. Second, I didn't have anywhere else to go. I had no family and my only friend still lived at home. My income from waitressing wasn't enough to pay for my own place, even with any child support I would be entitled to. Third, while Brad's parents adored Stella, I was just the woman who had gotten pregnant by their son. What if they decided they didn't want anything to do with me if Brad and I divorced? I didn't want to force them to take sides, mostly because I was afraid they would automatically take the side of their son and I would lose them as well. I'd seen that happen while growing up. It's why I kept defending Brad even when I knew it was useless.

"He apologized this morning. I don't think he'll try that again," I said, though not really sure if I was trying to reassure Kayla or myself. I knew I didn't sound confident, and when I picked up my cup, my hands shook. Kayla's lips thinned into a straight line. Yeah, neither one of us was reassured. I set the cup back down without taking a sip and sat there, not sure what to do but knowing I might have to figure it out soon.

We didn't speak for a long minute and I could tell Kayla was trying to figure out what to say to me about my situation. She'd never had anything nice to say about Brad, but she also kept her negative comments to herself because she knew that I'd just sweep her observations aside. It was so automatic for me to do that after all this time.

"Look, I understand you needing to do what you feel is best. I just don't want you to get hurt, like *really* hurt," she finally said, genuine worry on her face. "Just promise me you will leave if he tries that again…"

I nodded firmly. "I promise." I added nothing further, but gave her my best easygoing smile. Truthfully, I rarely smiled unless I was with my daughter. She was the only thing that made me happy these days.

After that, Kayla decided to lighten the mood and we spent the rest of the morning sharing the latest gossip from work. I knew she didn't want to ignore what was going on, but she respected me enough to know I didn't want to talk about it anymore. We said goodbye when it was time for me to head over to my in-laws to pick up Stella. I left feeling a little lighter and ready to face the day. Since Stella was going to be home, I hoped that would keep Brad calm enough so we could have a mature conversation about what happened. I wasn't ready to let it go. I wanted to address him in a civil manner, and not cause a huge blowout.

Unfortunately, we didn't get to have a conversation that night since Brad didn't come home until early the next morning. For the next few weeks, he did his best to avoid me.

Chapter 2

Kyle

 $\mathcal{S}$ tanding in front of the grill with a beer in my hand, I turned toward my buddies, Erik and Trent, who were busy leaning over the deck railing to check out the women passing below. We tried to get together at least once a month, usually on the weekend, and we started out at my house since I lived by the beach. Today was perfect: the early April weather, the mid-spring sun, sand, and calm waves were the reasons the beach was packed this Saturday. The only thing missing was Ian, but that would be changing soon since he was getting out of the service later this year.

"So are you guys coming to dad's birthday party next weekend?" Trent asked us, taking a swig of his beer. "It's just going to be a small family get-together."

When I was younger, I'd spent most of my time at Trent's house. His parents, Jim and Marla, had always made an effort to make both Addie and myself feel like we were part of their family. The fact that we were almost family by law had seemed like fate, then Brad had ruined it. Despite that, I continued to spend a lot of time with them. My grandmother took excellent care of my sister and me, but it was still nice to spend time at a house with a *family*, one with parents and children who loved each other and liked to spend time together.

Although, I thought, briefly checking on the burgers and steaks under the grill hood, *Brad oftentimes dampened the mood at their family get-togethers*. I hadn't liked him before I knew

37

he was a cheater and I liked him even less now that he'd hurt my sister. However, he had married Simone, appearing to have done the *right* thing. Still, I couldn't stand the guy.

"Of course, I'm going. Did your mom tell you she invited Addie?" I paused, glancing over at Trent again. "Do you think your brother and Simone will be okay being in the same room with her?" I asked.

Not that I really cared about Brad's feelings if Addie did go. But I didn't want Simone to feel uncomfortable. It was maddening how Brad lucked out with a woman like Simone. He sure didn't deserve to have such a loving, not to mention gorgeous, young wife.

Motherhood had somehow made her even more stunning, and whenever I saw her, like at the restaurant a few weeks ago, I'd find myself staring at her for too long. Even Erik looked, though neither of us would ever do more than that—and not openly, that's for sure. Trent would kill us if he caught us checking her out. He saw Simone as a little sister and was highly protective of her.

She didn't smile often, but when she did, even a little, it lit up her brown eyes and made you want to return it. Made you want to keep that smile in place for as long as possible. There was a sadness behind her eyes that I found compelling and I wished I knew more about her to understand why; however, we'd likely never get close enough to really know each other. Me being Addie's brother, she shied away from me.

I looked out toward the ocean, thinking back... I still remember the look of complete shock on Simone's face two years ago that matched my sister's. But at least Addie had gotten out of a crappy relationship. Simone had stepped right into one and she was paying the price. She seemed pretty miserable whenever I saw her, which wasn't often, and I knew from Trent that she could be a little guarded toward the rest of the family. No one could really blame her for that. It's why we all tried to be extra nice to her and Stella. Brad, well, he could go to hell and stay there.

I shook my head, focusing on not burning anything on the grill, when another thought entered my mind. The idea of my sister and Brad seeing each other for the first time since they broke up was unsettling. I loathed the fact that Brad had damaged Addie's relationship with his parents, which had waned significantly. She needed that sense of family, especially a motherly bond that only Marla could give since Grandma was gone. I was hoping that the relationship between all of us could be patched up a bit since Addie had moved back home a few weeks ago.

She'd tried to make a new life for herself in San Francisco after her breakup, but she never sounded truly happy when we would talk on the phone. After some discussion, Trent and I offered her a position at our law firm, acting as a legal secretary. It wasn't what she went to school for, but she'd felt lost at the time, and I figured doing something out of her comfort zone might help her make a decision about what she wanted to do with her future. It had taken a lot of begging on our part and I understood her resistance. However, with more begging, groveling, promises, and a little guilt tripping from me about us being our only family now, she finally agreed.

God knew there were a lot of bad memories for her here, and seeing Simone and Brad wasn't going to make her feel better. She had confided in me shortly after her breakup that she had worried that things were not going to work out with Brad. Even with those suspicions, it hurt like hell knowing he had cheated on her.

If Addie did attend this party, I hoped it wouldn't

convince her she'd made a mistake moving back here. And if Brad said or did anything... I'd beat the shit out of him *again*. He might act tough, but he knew to stay in line when I was around. That thought made me smile a little.

"I'm sure Simone will be fine," Trent answered, then continued with a slight grimace, "but Brad will probably act like a douchebag."

"You know, Brad's actually a talented mechanic, but if he wasn't your brother or had a family to support, I would've fired his ass by now," Erik said with a snort. He shook his head, eyes scanning a small group of women playing beach volleyball. "Dude's been acting strange lately; showing up to work late, making stupid mistakes. Always on his phone, openly flirty with female employees and clients, and being ruder than usual. Hopefully he'll be on his best behavior since it's your dad's birthday."

Erik owned his own auto shop where they made modifications on cars to enhance their performance, specifically for street racing. When Brad decided to marry Simone, Erik had done him a huge favor by offering Brad a full-time position with benefits. We all knew how lazy he was, spending more time on his video games than looking for a job and taking care of his young family. Out of friendship and loyalty, Erik had gone out on a limb for him. And did Brad act like he appreciated it? Nope. Granted, Brad did have some talent with cars, but how Erik put up with him on a daily basis I would never understand. We were all hopeful that the punk kid we'd barely tolerated growing up had finally changed his ways for the better. Unfortunately, spending any time with him only proved that he hadn't. If anything, he seemed to move further into the asshole category—especially recently.

"I wouldn't hold your breath," Trent added, dryly. "If not

for Simone and Stella, I'd say, go for it. Fire his ass."

Erik and Trent had a laugh, but I think Trent meant every word—especially the 'fire his ass' part. I couldn't help but agree with him. I pulled the meat off the grill and the three of us moved over to the table to eat. The pub-styled table allowed us to continue looking over the railing toward the beach below.

I would never get tired of this view. My house was pretty badass, especially the rooftop deck where we were currently relaxing with panoramic views of the beach and pier. I'd found this three-story gem within a month of house hunting and couldn't pass it up. It had four bedrooms and three baths. That might be considered overkill for a bachelor like myself, but I figured one day, in the very distant future, I would have a family and this house would be perfect for that. Although, the cynical part of me wondered if that was really in the cards for me. My own father surely hadn't been a great role model on how to be a husband or father. After my parents divorced, their combined actions had destroyed our family with little thought to the consequences— including how it'd affect Addie and me. I often wondered if I would ever feel confident in taking on a parenting role myself. Would I be a better man than the one I shared DNA with?

Being able to afford this house so early on in my career was a little bittersweet. Sadly, my grandmother passed away a year ago, and she'd left a large inheritance for Addie and me. While I made a great living practicing law with Trent and his father, I would never have been able to afford this place without the money from my grandmother.

"Dude, check out the view over there," Trent said as another group of bikini-clad women walked by. "Buying this house was the smartest decision you ever made."

41

I laughed. Trent sounded like an excited kid who just saw a shiny new toy.

"There are a couple of girls over there I wouldn't mind getting to know a little bit better," Erik added, still gazing at the volleyball girls. He'd hardly touched his steak. Trent, too.

I smirked at Erik's wistful tone. I think all the jumping and sand all over their sweaty bodies was really what was on his mind. We were all in swim trunks and T-shirts, and had plans to use my beach access later. The whole point of today was about relaxing, in whatever form that came.

Plus, none of us had a girlfriend, and were in no hurry to change that, so we could look all we wanted. We all had our fair share of casual hookups, but none of us were ready to settle down just yet.

Erik had been pretty serious with his high school sweetheart, Willow, back in the day. They continued to date for a year after we graduated but when Erik started focusing on street racing, she was out. She said it was too dangerous and that he had no time left for her after spending all day at the shop and the evenings at the races. She probably had a point, but racing was his passion. She moved out of state shortly after they broke up and he hadn't heard from her since.

I thought about Ian as Erik and Trent continued to eat while discussing how to approach the women playing volleyball. Ian had an off and on relationship with his high school girlfriend, Jenny. They finally called it quits for the last time about three years ago. Since then, he'd been fairly quiet about who he was dating. The fact that he lived across the country made it harder to razz him about any of his hookups.

Trent checked his phone when it wouldn't stop pinging. Erik deftly plucked it out of Trent's hand and held it back. "Seriously, man? What did we all agree on when it came to our guys' weekend?" he asked, disgruntled. He chucked the phone back—at Trent's head. "No work, all play, remember?"

"It's not like I was going to answer!" Trent shot back, glaring. Having caught it before it hit him between the eyes, he smartly put his phone away. "It was just an update on a case of mine that I've been keeping close tabs on."

Like me, Trent was an admitted workaholic and, also like me, we loved the single, bachelor life. He liked dating a new girl every couple weeks. He didn't seem to have a problem finding women who agreed to his no-strings-attached dating, much to the disappointment of his mom, who would love to have more grandchildren. We were both twenty-six and having slaved through four years of college plus three years of law school, it was time to have some fun and recharge. Not take our personal lives too seriously. That's why weekends like this were perfect.

I laughed at their bantering as I grabbed all the empty plates, dishes, and bottles and stepped inside to put them in the kitchen sink to take care of later.

When I walked back out, Trent glanced over at me as he headed down the back steps right behind Erik. "So, Erik and I came up with a game plan on how to start mingling with those volleyball babes over there," he said, glancing back at them briefly. "Time to officially jumpstart this weekend... You ready, bro?"

I smiled, grabbing my sunglasses and followed suit. "Hell, yeah I am."

*****

The following week in the office had flown by. Addie knocked quietly on the doorframe then entered my office. "Morning, Kyle. I have the Wilson files you wanted." She hefted up the files in the crook of her arm. "What do you want me to do with them?"

It was early Friday morning and things were already busy. It was always like that right before the weekend. Addie had only recently started working with us, but she was already proving to be a great addition to the office. It made me extremely happy to have my sister back home and I loved being able to spend time with her at the office as well.

"I need you to search the court records from last month. I want to make sure they are in compliance with the ruling made," I told her.

She gave a nod. "Sure thing. Anything else?" she asked.

"I could really use some coffee," I said. When I looked up she had her eyebrow raised in question. Knowing she had a smartass response ready, I quickly added, "Please."

"Just this once." She laughed as she exited my office.

I rubbed my eyes behind the glasses that I wore while working, then went back to staring at my computer and finished up the last of this morning's slew of emails before getting to my paperwork. Filings, court appearances, meetings with judges, other lawyers, research... it was endless, but I loved it.

Jim had started the law firm twenty years ago when he got tired of working for other people. Now he was ready to retire and was prepping Trent and me to take over. We provided and specialized in many legal services, but our bread and butter was family law and mediation. However, Trent and I kept up-to-date in other areas of practice to give us a broader appeal.

Jim only worked on special cases now and pretty much let Trent and me run things as we saw fit while he played endless rounds of golf or played grandpa whenever he could. He was counting down the days to when he could fully retire. Right now, we had one junior associate, a paralegal, a receptionist, and Addie, our legal secretary. The operational work was done between me and Trent, but with our increasing caseload, we'd have to hire someone for that soon. I was proud of the work we did and that our firm was growing. I just wished my grandmother could see how successful I was. It was because of her that I had my strong work ethic. She was the first person to encourage me to go into law, turning elements of a bad childhood into something positive and helping others.

As well as we were doing, Trent and I were more ambitious. We planned on expanding the firm in the next five to ten years, and eventually move our offices to a more modern and bigger space. We also wanted to move closer to downtown San Diego rather than staying near the airport, which wasn't an ideal spot with the loud planes taking off and flying overhead. Currently, our office was small, but everyone had their own space to work in. There was also a basic break room, and a small conference room for meetings. It wasn't glamorous like those law firms you see on television dramas, but it served its purpose and kept our overhead low.

"Hey, Addie, do you want to do lunch today?" I shouted from my office, knowing she could hear me since her workspace was only a few feet away.

"Yeah, that sounds good," she shouted back.

"Hey, assholes, you going to invite me?" Trent yelled from his office, which was across the hall from mine.

"Well… I guess, if we have to," Addie answered, sighing loudly. Those two had teased each other since childhood and could go back and forth all day. I shook my head at their relentless banter, but mostly, I was glad Addie had settled in without any issues.

Once lunch rolled around, the three of us walked a couple blocks over to our favorite Mexican restaurant since the weather was perfect for a quick stroll. Living in Southern California provided us with many options, but Anita's was definitely a favorite of ours. With the spring tourist season in full bloom, we had made a reservation in hopes of not getting caught up in a crowd of clueless visitors.

We were seated in the back corner of the restaurant, which suited me just fine. I enjoyed watching people come and go.

"Hi there, can I get you all something to drink?" our server asked. He was a young guy, and once he spotted Addie, he couldn't keep his eyes off her.

"Yeah, I'll have an iced tea," Trent answered, looking the menu over.

I glared at the waiter. "I'll have the same, and I would appreciate it if you stopped checking out my sister," I added. I heard Trent chuckle next to me.

Addie glared at me then turned to our waiter with a sweet smile on her face. "Ignore him, he's just a big jerk. I'll take a Diet Pepsi." As soon as the waiter left, she asked, "Was that really necessary?"

I just shrugged my shoulders. I didn't step in when she

dated Brad, even though I knew he wasn't good enough for her. I should have protected her and not let her get tangled up with him. Instead, I'd let her do what she wanted — and look how that turned out. I would never fail in my brotherly duties again.

After we got our drinks and ordered, Trent cleared his throat. "So, what time are you guys coming over for the party tomorrow?" he asked in an effort to stop an argument from starting. It worked like a charm.

"Do you think Mom needs any help getting things ready?" Addie asked. We'd been referring to Jim and Marla as Dad and Mom since we were kids. It felt natural at this point, even if Addie hadn't talked to them much in the last two years.

"Probably," Trent said, after some consideration. "We plan on eating at one so why don't you guys get there around eleven. Mom would never ask for help, but I know she would appreciate it."

Marla loved to cook. I couldn't remember any get-together at their house where she hadn't cooked the meal herself. She reminded me a little bit of a 1950s housewife you would see on TV; the main difference was how Jim treated her. He viewed her as an equal and was always appreciative of all the effort she made to create a comfortable home for them. He never acted like it was expected. The love they had for each was evident to all those around them.

"We'll be there," I responded. Addie nodded in agreement, but quickly looked away, keeping her eyes on the pedestrian traffic. I knew what she was thinking.

While I was excited to share in Jim's special day, I was also expecting Brad to find some way to ruin it. And I wasn't sure how Addie and Simone would deal with seeing each other. I took a sip of my tea, hoping Jim's celebration didn't end up being a complete disaster.

Chapter 3

Simone

$\mathcal{T}$he bed dipped down as Brad climbed in, rousing me from my sleep. I glanced briefly at the clock where the huge red numbers informed me that it was two in the morning. Since that night a couple weeks ago, Brad had been spending even less time at home, often not coming home at all. The first few times, I'd texted him, worried that something bad had happened to him. He took that opportunity to accuse me of trying to control him. He reminded me that he was an adult and didn't answer to anyone. So even though I had been genuinely concerned, I stopped texting him after that. I really didn't mind when he wasn't home because it meant I was able to relax and not worry that I would inadvertently piss him off.

"Hey, are you just getting in?" I asked sleepily.

Brad huffed in irritation. "Yeah, I went out with some friends after work. Is there a problem?" he asked, while arranging his pillows.

Why he continually sounded angry when I asked him anything had always been baffling but now it was starting to grate on me. I constantly felt on edge around him and I was wondering why I even bothered anymore. A thought I had been having a lot lately.

A couple weeks ago, he'd told me that I had no right asking him where he was or who he was hanging out with. When I'd reminded him that I was his wife and that most married couples shared basic information with each other, he'd laughed and then left the apartment and didn't come back for two days.

Brad treated his parents the same way. If they said anything to him that he perceived as negative he would stop talking to them. Even though he treated them poorly, they continued to do everything in their power to help us out. And while I didn't know for sure, I suspected they had recently started giving Brad money since ours seemed to never last as long as it should. I hoped he wasn't wasting his paycheck on going out with the boys instead of paying for his part of the bills.

I rolled away from him, wanting to go back to sleep. "I don't have a problem, I was just asking," I said, tiredly. It was obvious he was wound up and I didn't have the energy or desire to engage with him.

"Well, why don't you come over here and put your mouth to better use instead of asking me questions," he taunted.

The idea of sex with him held no appeal whatsoever. The thought of Brad ever touching me again made me want to run away from this room, from him.

I thought about the two reasons Brad had stayed in this marriage. First, he didn't want to look like a deadbeat dad, even though he wasn't very involved with Stella. And second, he had easy access to sex. Not that we had sex often anymore, not like before when we both got something out of it and it'd been fun. After having Stella, my body had changed and I was curvier than I used to be when we'd first met. Brad commented on those changes often and could be rather critical of my appearance. I couldn't deny it'd slowly eaten away at my self-confidence. I tried to ignore his negative comments and I did my best to look good for him, but my priority was our daughter, not making sure I looked like a model at all times.

All pretenses of being romantic had disappeared even before we'd gotten married. For the past year or so, he would simply tell me what he expected, and he was either happy when I complied or angry if I wasn't in the mood.

"Not tonight, Brad," I said when he prompted me again. I was already worn out by this conversation. "Stella had a rough day and I'm exhausted. I had just fallen asleep when you came in here."

"Why do you always have to be such a bitch, Simone? When I first met you, we had sex all the time. You were a lot more fun and adventurous. Now it's a huge production just to get a fucking blowjob," he accused, the agitation in his voice clear.

I was ready to bring up the last time we had sex and remind him how he had treated me, but honestly, I was tired. Not just in a physical sense, but mentally as well. I didn't know how much longer I could pretend to be okay with our relationship. Not that I could even call it a relationship. "I'm sorry you're not happy," I said instead.

"Yeah, well, you're always sorry. Don't know why I bother to come home some nights," he responded missing the hint of sarcasm in my voice.

I didn't want to continue this conversation with him. Especially since I knew it would just lead to a fight and nothing would be resolved.

"Hey, let's both get some sleep, we have your dad's birthday party tomorrow," I said, hoping to end on that.

"I'm not going tomorrow," he stated flatly.

I rolled back over and looked at him with surprise, now

wide-awake. "Why not?"

"Because Trent's going to be there," he answered, rolling his eyes as though I should have already known that.

"But… it's your dad's birthday," I said slowly, not hiding the disapproval from my voice or face. I wanted to add that tomorrow wasn't about him and his issues with anybody, but I knew that would piss him off. "Don't you think you can make peace with your brother for one day?"

"Fuck, Simone!" he shouted. "Just leave it alone, okay? I don't want to go, end of story."

I rolled back over, facing the wall, hoping his shouting hadn't woken up our daughter.

I really wanted to go to Jim's party as a family, for Jim and Marla's sake, but I knew it wasn't likely I'd be able to convince Brad once his mind was set on something. I was going with Stella, no matter what his final decision was because unlike him, I cared about his — my — family.

*****

I spent Saturday morning getting Stella and myself ready for the party while Brad slept in. It had taken a while for him to settle down and finally fall asleep. But all of his tossing and turning had kept me awake.

After I put Stella in a cute pink jumpsuit, I set her up with a few toys in the living room so I could check on the brownies that my father-in-law had requested I bring to the party. Most people wanted to have a cake on their birthday, but Jim loved my homemade brownies and requested that I bake them for every family get-together. I think he was just being nice, but it always lifted my spirits a little.

52

"When are you leaving?" Brad asked, causing me to jump at his sudden appearance. His hair was sticking up at odd angles and he was still in his flannel pajama bottoms and a T-shirt. The scruff on his jaw was getting darker and thicker. His bloodshot eyes scanned the kitchen until they landed on the coffee pot. I hadn't noticed his eyes last night, and he hadn't appeared drunk when he came home. He looked awful now, like he'd partied all night.

When he gave me a bleary-eyed look, I realized I'd been staring. "In about thirty minutes. Are you sure you don't want to go?" I finally asked, hoping he had changed his mind since last night. Although, if he didn't go, I might actually get to enjoy myself instead of waiting for Brad to start an argument with every member of his family.

But, Jim was turning the big 5-0 and I was worried Brad would eventually regret missing his father's birthday party. It was inconceivable to me that he could so easily pass up spending time with his family, who were nothing short of amazing.

"I told you last night I wasn't going, so just drop it already," he snapped, pouring himself a cup of coffee.

"Well, what should I tell your parents? They know you have the day off." I was worried I was going to be forced to lie to them and I really didn't want to do that. Not only did it make me feel bad, but I was also a terrible liar.

"Just tell them I'm not feeling well," he muttered.

He moved into the living room, plopped down on the couch, and turned on the television. He set his mug down on the coffee table so he could dig into his pocket and pull out his cell phone. For the last month, he was on that damn thing all the time. He gave it more attention than he gave to me and Stella combined. It was just one more thing that was making me revaluate my life—but then I thought about Stella and how our situation could turn bad in an instant. I hated how I talked myself off the ledge, but this wasn't just about me. It never had been, which is how I got into this mess.

"Fine," I agreed, even though I hated the idea of being dishonest with his family. I also didn't need us to get into another fight before I left. When the timer went off, I put on my oven mitts and took the brownies out to cool. I glanced over at Brad. "Can you keep an eye on Stella for a couple minutes while I finish getting ready?"

"I guess," he responded without moving his eyes away from the TV.

I moved Stella to her playpen so at least she wouldn't be able to leave the living room. I wasn't convinced Brad would actually pay attention to her. I desperately wanted him to be an involved father, but she was one-and-a-half years old now and he still didn't seem interested in taking his fatherly responsibilities seriously. I had thought throughout the pregnancy and birth that he'd bond with her, but he never had. He'd also never really put in any effort. I'd tried to get him to interact with her more, but that seemed to push him further away. I didn't want to nag so I stopped and hoped he'd come around on his own. But that hadn't happened yet either. He remained distant and aloof with her, like she wasn't even there. It hurt that he had no interest in his own daughter. The family I'd wanted—that I had—was in appearance only, and finally accepting that was painful. With Brad mostly gone these last couple weeks, my old fears and insecurities had begun to haunt me. Having seen this same sort of dysfunction all throughout my childhood, I felt that my future and my daughter's future was barely hanging on by a thread.

I pushed those thoughts to the back of my mind and focused on getting ready. Seeing my in-laws always made me happy and I was looking forward to getting over there. I rushed to our bedroom to grab my sandals, made sure my dress wasn't too wrinkled from holding Stella, and touched up my makeup. I tried to finish quickly, not wanting to upset Brad any more by taking too long. I put up my long hair since the weather forecast for today said it could get a little warm.

I went to the kitchen, put a lid on the brownies, then set all the stuff I'd need to take with me on the kitchen counter. I moved to the living room to pick Stella up, who made it very clear she didn't want to leave her toys, but I got her to cooperate eventually. I tried to balance a grumpy toddler, a container of brownies, and a diaper bag while Brad continued to sit on the couch flipping through the channels with one hand and texting on his phone with the other. I attempted to open the front door, but it was proving to be impossible since my hands were already full.

"Brad, can you come help me get everything out to the car?" I asked.

I was only a few feet away since our apartment wasn't very big, but Brad continued on like I hadn't said anything. Realizing he had no intention of helping me, I sighed loudly, and transferred the diaper bag to the same hand that was already balancing the brownies and turned the knob.

Somehow, we made it out to the car in one trip and I was able to get everything loaded in the trunk, then I buckled up Stella in her car seat.

"Go bye bye?" Stella asked as I started to back out.

"We're going to Grandma and Grandpa's house; it's Grandpa's birthday today," I explained, while looking at her in the rearview mirror.

Stella absolutely adored her grandparents and the feeling was definitely mutual. Where Brad was often absent, Jim and Marla Thompson made their granddaughter a priority in their life. To be honest, I don't know how I would have made it through the first few months of Stella's life if it hadn't been for my in-laws. They were such kind people and I thanked my lucky stars every day that they were there for the two of us.

"Unky Twent?" Stella asked, in her cute baby talk.

Trent was another person that I was thankful for. He would often take his niece out for his famous "Trent and Stella Dates," giving me an occasional break. He was the complete opposite of his brother. He never acted like Stella was an inconvenience or burden and seemed truly happy to spend time with her. The thought of them playing together made me smile.

"Yes, Uncle Trent will be there too, baby," I told her.

For the rest of the car ride she chattered on and on about all the things she was going to do with Trent. Even though I couldn't make out everything she said, it sounded like he was going to have a busy day keeping up with his niece.

I arrived at the house about an hour early since I'd promised Marla I would help set everything up for the party. I noticed that Trent's truck was already parked in the driveway along with a fancy BMW that looked vaguely familiar. The Thompsons' ranch-style house was more inland but still a short drive to the ocean. I wondered if we'd spend some time in their backyard pool, which Stella loved to play in. I had packed our suits in her diaper bag, just in case.

I walked in through the front door, having been told early

on in my relationship with my in-laws that family and friends don't have to knock at the Thompsons' door. From stories I'd heard, all of their sons' friends treated their home as their own. Kids had been constantly been coming and going and Marla had absolutely loved it. Many of their friends still called Marla and Jim 'mom' and 'dad'. I had a hard time calling them that and usually used their first names. I could tell that they wished I would call them mom and dad, but they never pushed.

"Hello?" I called out as I entered the house with Stella on my hip.

The living room was large and inviting but currently empty. There were leather couches in a U-shape around a square glass coffee table, pictures on the wall, and knickknacks from their travels lined the built-in shelves. Walking in I could feel my whole being just... relax. This was how a home was supposed to feel. Stella's eyes took in everything, even though she knew this place well.

A gust of wind blew the door shut behind me. The loud bang caused me to jump a little.

"Is that my favorite daughter-in-law and granddaughter I hear?" Marla's sweet voice called as I walked toward the kitchen.

As soon as Stella heard her grandmother she wiggled to free herself from my arms. I set her down and she started running toward her Grandma the moment her feet touched the ground.

"Gramma!" I heard her shout as she went.

As I rounded the corner to the large, open kitchen, I saw Marla, in a navy blue A-line skirt and off-white blouse. Her short, blonde hair framed her pretty and still youthful face. She always looked put together yet still approachable. Her eyes lit up when she spotted me. She had Stella in her arms giving her a giant hug while Jim leaned over and peppered the side of Stella's face with kisses. Jim was in tan slacks, and a golf shirt, his robust, tall frame almost overpowering Marla's more petite stature. I took a second, enjoying the three of them together.

"The only birthday gift I need," Jim stated, grinning at me. "And my brownies, of course." He winked, and then gave both Stella and Marla a bear hug. I smiled fondly at Stella, who was grinning from ear to ear, and I was really glad I'd decided to come. Even though they babysat Stella several days a week they always acted like the last time they saw her had been ages ago. I loved that about them. They were the image of happiness as they held Stella, who was giggling and happy with all attention. Then my eyes took in the rest of the kitchen and my stomach dropped.

Sitting at the island was Trent, his friends Kyle and Erik, and someone I hadn't seen in two years—Kyle's younger sister, Addison. There were a lot of windows, all of them open, but all the light from the late morning sun seemed to shine directly on her.

The only interaction I'd ever had with her was when I had showed up at her house looking for Brad so I could inform him that I was pregnant. Seeing her staring back at me with her own frozen, tense expression made me re-live that day. And I knew she was going through the same thing. I felt clammy all over, my stomach rolled with tension, and I felt a little nauseous. I figured, at some point, our paths would cross. How could they not, considering the complicated relationships of everyone involved? And if anyone had told me she'd be here, I probably would have used Brad's excuse and avoided this moment. But we were both here now and I reminded myself that Addison had a longer history with this

58

family than I did and she'd been the one hurt. If she had things to say to me, I'd take it, but I hoped it wouldn't turn ugly.

"Hi there," I managed to squeak out at all four of them. I stood by the doorway, not willing to venture in any further.

"Hey," Trent answered, getting up to give me a hug. I returned it hesitantly while stepping back a little. Marla and Jim usually let me initiate physical contact. They figured out early on that it made me uncomfortable at times. Especially during tense or stressful moments, which was pretty much all the time being married to Brad. Trent had never really noticed or he figured I would say something if it bothered me. With an encouraging smile, he moved over to grab his niece out of his mother's arms. Jim had his arm casually around his wife; their need to always be close was evident. He gave me a fatherly smile while Marla looked between everyone.

Erik gave a small wave and a close-lipped smile and then retreated toward the back of the kitchen in an attempt to avoid getting caught in the middle of a potential showdown.

"Hi, Simone," Kyle said, his deep voice was kind... and sexy.

His voice drew my gaze to his and his stare made me feel like he was *looking* at me, like he really saw me—it always did. I wasn't used to that from a man, especially one as attractive as Kyle. I'd only been in the same room as him a few times over the past two years, and we rarely talked to each other. The longest conversation we'd had was when he had been seated in my section at the restaurant, and that was only because I had a job to do. It was the only reason I hadn't been as rattled since I knew I couldn't screw up at work. But here, without my job as my shield, I felt a little exposed.

"Um… hi there," I muttered, my throat dry. God, I was an idiot, I'd already said hi. I clammed up, not sure what else to say since every single person was watching me. It made me feel a little vulnerable, like it was me versus all these other people. I was nervous all over again but for different reasons this time. The heaviness in my stomach was gone, but the kitchen suddenly felt a little too warm.

"Did you have a nice drive here?" Kyle continued. It was obvious he was trying to lessen the tension in the room and I was grateful for that.

"Yeah… it was nice," I said, slowly. I felt my cheeks burn, wishing I wasn't so nervous.

Seeing Kyle though always reminded me of the day he'd opened the door. So tall and lean, his eyes peering down at me curiously and his light brown hair a bit tousled. He'd looked handsome in his gray slacks and an aqua-blue shirt. The entirety of his focus had been on me, and I'd almost forgotten why I was there. Or that maybe I'd rung the wrong house, but glad if I had. I'd always thought Brad was the best looking guy in San Diego, but the minute my eyes had landed on Kyle… it'd all gone to hell.

Today, he was in a plain green shirt; the color nearly matched his eyes, and dark fitted jeans. He looked like someone who had his act together and there was a quiet confidence to him that was almost intimidating. I was always tongue-tied around him and didn't know how to be easy-going when he talked to me, or any of Trent's friends, really. I was the 'other woman'. They never made me feel like that, but I had a difficult time not feeling it when other people were around that knew all the sordid details.

I licked my lips and darted my eyes away, looking around the kitchen, taking a moment to collect myself. I concentrated on not saying something stupid or making a fool out of myself. Without Brad here I couldn't just fade into the background. Brad usually made a scene right away so I was used to not being the center of attention. Not today, though. I felt everyone's eyes on me.

Hi," Addison finally said, somewhat forcefully. She sounded just as nervous as I was feeling and it was almost a relief since she didn't look angry or like she was about to yell at me.

"Where's my other son?" Jim asked, breaking the silence after our awkward hellos. Another uncomfortable silence fell as everyone turned toward me. Jim even looked behind me, as though Brad would walk in any minute.

Flustered, I tried to come up with an excuse more plausible than the one Brad had given, but I couldn't. "Brad isn't feeling well," I lied, feeling absolutely terrible for doing so. Everyone just stared at me for a moment and I knew that none of them believed me.

"That's bullshit!" I heard Trent mumble from beside me. "What's the real reason he isn't here?"

"Watch your language in front of Stella," Marla reprimanded, glaring at Trent.

Trent looked appropriately chastised, giving his mother an apologetic look. I glanced over at my brother-in-law mutely. He and Brad had similar facial features but their looks were otherwise very different. So were their manners. But I could feel Trent's anger radiating off of him, which felt the same as when Brad was mad at me. I almost shrank back from it. I knew he wasn't mad at me, but his fury still made me uncomfortable. I just stood there frozen in place, not knowing what to say. I didn't want to hurt his parents' feelings or make things worse.

Trent then turned back to me calmer than a moment

before. "It's because I'm here, isn't it?" he asked, still angry but keeping his voice milder.

They all knew that was part of it. Still, I wanted to somehow give a better explanation, one that would not make Brad look like a terrible person. I looked to my daughter making sure the tense conversation wasn't having an effect on her, but Stella was none the wiser. I felt a slight pang at the way Trent held my daughter close to his chest — the way a dotting, loving uncle would. Even Trent's friends showered Stella with attention when they were around her. It was a stark contrast to the fact that Brad rarely held Stella, or played with her, or even looked at her. I'd been ignoring that glaring fact but I couldn't anymore. She was currently playing with the buttons of his light blue, button-down shirt with a content expression on her chubby, cute little face. Here, surrounded by her family, Stella was genuinely happy.

"I don't know, Trent..." I said, quietly, staring at my daughter, "all he told me was he wasn't coming."

"Don't worry about it, sweetie," Jim said as he wrapped an arm around my shoulders. His fatherly hug felt like he was on my side, but he didn't hold on for long, much to my relief. At this point, I really just needed some space. "More importantly, where are my brownies?" He winked, trying to lighten the mood. It didn't really work, but I pretended it did.

I smiled back, tightly. "Oh. They're in the car along with Stella's things. I'll be right back." I quickly exited the kitchen, the smile falling right off my face as soon as I was out of view. I took several deep breaths. I needed a few minutes to myself before I had to face everyone again — for the rest of the day. Not only was I upset with Brad for choosing to not be here, I was still a little shaken from coming face to face with Addison.

"Simone, wait up," I heard a voice say, just as I reached the door.

I paused with my hand on the knob and waited for Addison to catch up. Panic had me freezing in place and wondering if now was the time she was going to unleash her anger on me. I gulped, terrified but also wanting the confrontation that I had been anticipating to be done already. It was unnerving, knowing that I was going to be alone with the woman my husband betrayed in such a horrible way. I had no idea what she thought of me. Did she know that I was in the dark about their relationship or did she think I was some slut who hooked up with him not caring that he had a fiancée?

I'd heard that she had gone back to San Francisco a couple days after I had interrupted their holiday meal. I had no idea if she was just visiting or was back in town for good now. The various times I'd known she was in San Diego for a visit, I'd always thought about this moment, and apologizing, but now that it was here, I was dreading it.

I turned around when Addison entered the living room. Like her brother, she was tall, lean and the all gray maxi-dress she was wearing made her seem even taller. She was stunning with her green eyes that seemed to pop against her lightly tanned skin; they were slightly lighter in color than her brother's and I was a little shocked to realize that I could tell the difference. Her light brown hair had streaks of blonde throughout and was up in a chic ponytail that accented her angular cheekbones and oval face. I could see why Brad fell for her.

"You mind if I help?" she asked, grabbing the knob and opening the door for me. "Gotta make sure your famous brownies stay safe from the boys. I hear they're pretty great."

I blinked at her slowly. I hadn't expected this from her. Instead of saying anything, I nodded and we walked silently down the driveway, side by side. The silence, the weight of our history, made us both uneasy. Neither of us uttering another word until we reached the trunk of my car.

She put a hand on my arm. I tensed, but then looked up at her. "Simone, I know we haven't ever had the chance to talk..." she started, then trailed off and appeared to be thinking of what to say next. "I've never blamed you for what happened between Brad and me. Even Brad more or less admitted that you'd had no clue he was engaged..." She paused, swallowing hard. "I thought it was important for you to know that I don't have any bad feelings toward you. And I'm sorry if you felt like what Brad did to me, to you, was in any way remotely your fault. It wasn't."

"Uh... ah, um, well, th-thank you," I stuttered. Her statement caught me completely off guard. I never expected her to be so nice to me. "That means a lot, Addison. I want you to know that—"

"You don't have to explain yourself," she said, gently cutting me off with a kind smile. "Truthfully, I knew things were off with Brad. Once I had time to really reflect on our relationship, I wasn't that surprised to find out he had been cheating on me. It hurt but all the anger I had was directed at him not you." She grabbed the brownies from the trunk while I threw the diaper bag over one shoulder. "And please call me Addie. Only Kyle calls me Addison and that's just when he wants to annoy me." She rolled her eyes, and then gestured with her head for us to go back inside.

I looked at her for a moment as she walked back to the house. Having this conversation with her had suddenly relieved a burden I'd been carrying around for two years. To have her understanding, as much as her forgiveness was more than I'd ever expected or even deserved. I decided at that moment that Addie had given me the opportunity to let go of my guilt and I needed to take it. I was not responsible for Brad's behavior. That was something I was reminding myself of more and more each day.

Chapter 4

Kyle

*E*rik and I watched Trent chase his niece around the backyard while we waited for Addie and Simone to return from the car. Addie had confided in me on the way over here that she was feeling nervous about the prospect of seeing Brad again. She hadn't seen or spoken to the asshole since the day Simone announced she was pregnant. I knew she was relieved that Brad wasn't here and I was happy to see her reaching out to Simone.

The thought of them clearing the air had me reflecting back to that night two years ago.

My sister had been heartbroken and I was so enraged I was seeing red. Brad had left pretty quickly once he realized he wasn't going to be able to talk his way out of his latest fuck up. I had only managed to get one shot in before Jim stepped between us. I respected the man enough to stop then but Brad still deserved an ass-kicking. It took a couple of hours, but I was finally able to get Addie calmed down. Once I knew she was asleep, I called Trent and told him I needed to pay his little brother a visit. He could either go with me or stay home, but he wasn't going to be able to stop what I had planned. Truthfully, I wasn't surprised when he said he would pick me up in thirty minutes and drive me to the apartment where Brad was staying.

Knocking on the door we could hear Brad shouting on the other side. I knocked a little harder, my knuckles turning red quickly. After a few moments, Brad opened the door with his cell phone to his ear. He was furious, his face was red, teeth grinding together, and his hand was clenching the phone so hard I thought for sure it would break.

"See if you can score..." He paused, looking at his brother and me. "I'll have to call you back," he said to the person on the other line, and disconnected the call. He glared at both of us, like we had no right to interrupt his precious phone call. "What the fuck do – "

My fist crashed into his jaw before he was able to finish the question.

"How could you do that to my sister, asshole?" I yelled as I grabbed his shirt in my hands and yanked him back up to his feet.

This time I punched him in the stomach and let him fall back to the ground. With a final kick to his ribs I turned around to walk back down the steps. My job was done.

However, Trent wasn't. When I turned back to see if Trent was following me, I saw him pick Brad back up off the ground and then shove him up against the wall. Getting in Brad's face, Trent spoke in a voice that was so quiet and menacing that it actually scared me.

"You need to do the right thing and make sure the mother of your child is taken care of!" Trent growled.

"We don't even know if that bitch is pregnant with my kid! Why should I do anything until we know for sure?" Brad continued to speak defiantly as though he wasn't in the middle of a shit storm. He would probably have blamed Simone for it all if he could.

"Seriously?!" Trent shouted in Brad's face. He shoved his younger brother back into the wall every time Brad tried to dodge free. "Stop being a punk ass bitch and think of someone other than yourself for once. Mom and Dad are so disappointed in you. The only hope you have to redeem yourself is if you tell them you're taking responsibility for your actions. And if you don't, Mom and Dad will cut you off. How do you feel about that? No more *sponging off them. You'll actually have to figure shit out for yourself without their help."*

With that, Trent shoved away from Brad and joined me on the landing where we started down the stairs together. Even though I doubted Trent's parents would ever cut Brad off, the look on the asshole's face made me think he believed it.

"Do you think he's going to step up?" I asked, knowing that Brad had always been irresponsible, reckless, and completely selfish.

Trent's jaw ticked, not cooling down yet. He looked over at me, his eyes hard. "He won't do it on his own, that's for sure. My parents will have to convince him to make the right choice. But he'll listen," Trent said grimly. "I'll make him…"

"Ky play?" the sweetest little voice asked me, bringing me back to the present.

I looked down at the cutest toddler I'd ever seen. She had big chocolate brown eyes and soft, wavy black hair that barely touched her shoulders. She was a mini version of her mother. On occasion, I would hang out with Trent when he would take Stella for a couple hours. While I didn't have much experience with kids I'd always been good with them.

"Sure, I'll play," I answered and turned to Erik, my eyebrow arched in question to see if he was going to join us.

He chuckled and shook his head. "I'm going to see if they need help inside." I smiled at his back. Erik had made it clear that kids made him nervous. He was an only child and his experience with small children was extremely limited.

"Hide Unky Twent!" Stella exclaimed as she grabbed my hand and started running toward the large oak tree at the back of the Thompson property. She wasn't a master at speaking yet but I could understand her enough to know we were playing hide-and-seek.

She raised her finger to her lips. "Quiet!" she shouted which made me laugh out loud. When those brown eyes glared at me I quickly quieted down. She was obviously taking the game very seriously.

"Ready or not, here I come," I heard Trent announce when he finished counting.

I watched Trent wandering around the backyard pretending like he had no idea where we were hiding. Then suddenly I heard Stella shout, "Daddy!"

When I turned around I saw the one person I didn't care to spend any time around. He was coming in through the side gate; he must have had some reason for avoiding the house. I only felt disgust when I looked at him.

I watched Stella run across the large yard directly to her father. I was expecting him to wrap his arms around her and lift her up. Instead he let her grab onto his leg. He barely glanced her way when he firmly nudged her off him and away. That infuriated me beyond belief. Stella was still young enough to not understand rejection but that would soon fade. Her innocence wouldn't last forever. When Stella tried to latch back on to her father, Brad snapped at her to knock it off. Stella pouted, but like all little kids, she got over it quickly. However, it wouldn't be long before her little mind would start asking: how could her own father not want her? I knew, because I had asked myself that same question when my own father had rejected me. The very thought that Stella would go through that was disheartening and it pissed me off.

The guy was such a douchebag. Here he was, lucky enough to be blessed with both a beautiful wife and daughter, yet, he couldn't be bothered to acknowledge his baby girl.

"So you finally decided to show up, huh?" I heard Trent scoff as he walked toward his brother on the deck. I wasn't far behind him, just in case.

"Mom called me, pissed that I wasn't here," Brad answered but he wasn't looking at his brother. Instead he was scowling at me. There was definitely no love lost between the two of us.

"It was pretty shitty that you asked Simone to lie for you," Trent seethed getting right in Brad's face. "What was so important that you were going to miss Dad's birthday?"

"None of your business, and I didn't come here for you to start interrogating me," he responded, not backing down.

"Daddy play?" Stella interrupted, not sensing the thick tension between her father and uncle.

"Not now, Stella. I'm going inside," Brad said and then turned around without another look at his daughter or brother.

I clapped Trent on the shoulder. "Not much has changed with your brother, has it?" I asked quietly, so Stella, who was staring at the sliding door her father just passed through, wouldn't hear me.

"Nope," he said grabbing a beer from the cooler set up on the deck.

I knew Trent was upset. We all tolerated Brad's behavior because we didn't want to upset his parents. Jim and Marla had a hard time acknowledging that Brad wasn't the sweet son they wanted him to be. They had always tried to see the good in him and had probably babied him too much when he was younger. But, Brad's downward spiral over the last few months was making it difficult for even his parents to ignore.

70

"Hey, baby girl, let's go find your mama," Trent suggested, leading Stella by the hand into the house.

When we entered, it was obvious Brad's sudden appearance had put everyone on edge. Brad was sitting at the island completely engrossed in something on his phone. Addie was helping Marla grab plates of food and Simone was helping Jim and Erik set the table. No one was speaking to anybody.

I noticed the occasional glances Simone shot toward her husband. A couple times it appeared as though she wanted to say something but then she would slightly shake her head and not say a word.

"Time to eat," Marla called out from the dining room.

Everyone made their way to the table and took a seat. Addie and I had shared many meals at the Thompson household, but it had been years since all of us were here together and we had never shared a meal with Simone and Stella.

Jim took his spot at the head of the table with Brad and Trent on each side of him. There was a highchair next to the seat Brad occupied and Simone took the seat on the other side of it. I sat next to Trent with Addie on the other side of me and Erik next to her. Marla took the seat at the other end of the table.

There continued to be a lack of conversation as the dishes were passed around. I noticed that Brad served himself but made no attempt to fill Stella's plate while Simone silently took care of their daughter.

"I just want to say how happy I am to have all of you here today," Jim said, again breaking the silence that had started to feel overwhelming.

"It's wonderful having all our kids under one roof. We just wish Ian was here," Marla added.

Brad muttered something rude under his breath at his mother's statement about "her kids" but we all chose to ignore him.

"Mama, water please," Stella asked, making the word 'please' sound like 'peas'. She was too cute.

"Brad, can you please pass the pitcher?" Simone asked meekly.

I watched Brad grab the pitcher and pass it over without even looking at his wife.

"Thank you," Simone said, while being ignored by Brad.

Trent dropped his fork on his plate, the clanging drawing everyone's attention. "Seriously? You can't even acknowledge your wife?" he asked, fuming.

"Stay out of it, dick!" Brad yelled back.

"Boys! We are not doing this. It's your father's birthday, let's just enjoy the day, okay?" Marla pleaded, hoping to put a stop to the fight that was brewing.

A soft whimper across the table caught my attention. Stella's eyes were watery, fat tears threatening to spill over, and her lip was quivering. It was a heartbreaking sight.

"Uncle Trent's sorry for yelling, baby girl." Trent tried his best to comfort his niece. "Everything's fine." He smiled at her and everyone went back to eating quietly.

After lunch, everyone except Brad helped clear the table. Trent suggested going out to the pool, so most of us changed into our swimsuits so we could continue the party outside.

Addie, Trent, Erik, and I were already in the pool when the sliding glass door opened up and Stella came running out to the edge of the water, with her floaties on her arms, asking her uncle to catch her. I, however, couldn't tear my eyes away from the beautiful woman still in the doorway. Simone wasn't very tall, maybe a couple inches over five feet, but somehow her legs managed to look long in the light pink bikini she had chosen to wear. The color of the suit contrasted perfectly with her olive skin and dark hair. She had gorgeous curves most likely enhanced from carrying a child not too long ago.

I realized I was staring so I quickly averted my gaze and turned my attention to Stella. I couldn't believe I had been checking out Simone. Forget that she was married. And not just married, but married to my best friend's brother and had a baby with him. She was also five years younger than me. That might not seem like a huge difference, but she was only twenty-one. College-aged and I was done with that scene. Looking at her with lust in my eyes was something I should not be doing. But... *damn.*

The last time I'd seen her was at her work. It'd been Courtney's idea to go there even though I'd wavered about it. Simone was always so tense around me and I didn't want to add to her discomfort. But, as luck would have it, we'd been seated in her section. Then I was distracted the whole time, trying to focus on Courtney and not constantly trying to catch a glimpse of Simone. I knew Courtney had caught me noticing another woman, which meant I'd had to lay on the charm real thick to compensate. Even in her all-black work uniform and fully covered, she was a stunner. But now, seeing her scantily clad, it was starting to turn me on at the most inappropriate time. I felt a little guilty at my physical reaction to someone completely off limits.

And even though I tried to stop myself from looking back at her once she started walking toward us, I was mesmerized once again. I watched as she walked over to the steps to make her way into the pool. I swear it was like she was walking in slow motion, all the while torturing me with her smoking hot body.

I felt someone staring at me and caught Erik watching me with an unreadable expression from the far side of the pool. I looked away, but in the next moment, something else caught our attention.

"Simone, couldn't you find anything to cover your ass better than that? Maybe you need to buy something that actually fits," Brad said from where he was lying on one of the lounge chairs on the deck.

A fiery blush crept up her neck and cheeks, showing just how much Brad's words embarrassed her. Her shoulders slumped and I could see her cringing. Instead of stepping into the pool she changed direction, grabbed a towel and wrapped it around her body before sitting on one of the chairs. I couldn't believe he was making such a beautiful woman feel ashamed of her body.

"Hey! Stop being a dick," Trent yelled back at his brother.

"Fuck off!" Brad returned, seething.

"Boys! Let's not do this in front of Stella again," Marla scolded, reprimanding both of her sons once more. Jim had been inside, getting some water toys for Stella, and came back out just as Marla had finished her scolding. He raised his brows when he noticed all our unhappy faces. Marla got up to deflect, grabbing some toys from his arms, and leading him to their chairs.

Brad opened his can of beer and had his phone in his face. It was like the guy was glued to it, as if whatever he was doing on it was more important than anything else. I hoped he didn't plan on drinking much. I didn't think any of us could stomach a drunk Brad. I continued to think Addie had dodged a bullet; but, regrettably, Simone had taken a direct hit. I'd always hoped Simone would have been the female version of Brad—in which case, they'd have been perfect for each other. But Simone wasn't. And that made me feel for her situation, and for her daughter even more. I believed there was nothing but bad things to come if Simone stayed with him. I could guess she was staying with him for some concept of stability. My assessment wasn't just based on personal experience of having absent and uncaring parents, but also from my work as a lawyer. But fate didn't care about good intentions or decent people getting saddled with shitty luck, and I was afraid fate was going to hit her hard in the near future.

Erik had brought a portable speaker and started playing some music from his phone. Everyone pretty much broke into groups at that point. Trent and I spent the next hour swimming and playing with Stella, while Erik and Addie talked at the other end of the pool. Jim and Marla were on the other side, talking quietly to each other. Brad didn't move other than to use his thumb to swipe at his touchscreen or sip from his beer can. Simone sat on her chair, towel still wrapped around her protectively, and merely waved at Stella whenever her daughter called out to her. She at least seemed to enjoy *watching* us play with Stella even though she didn't join us. In hindsight, that was probably for the best because seeing a wet Simone might have had my brain going to places it had no right to.

It didn't take long before we exhausted the little one so Simone came to the edge of the pool to grab her. I watched as she dried her off and told her it was time to go lay down for a nap.

"I want Daddy," Stella cried.

I looked over at Brad, who didn't look up from his phone at his daughter's request.

"Brad," Simone called over to him while cradling her daughter. Her tone was weary as she addressed her husband, who didn't look up at all. "Stella wants you to put her down for her nap."

I could hear his sigh even though I was a good twenty feet away from him. He threw his phone down on the lounge chair and got up.

"Fine, let's go," he huffed as he led his wife and daughter into the house.

I looked at Trent, who appeared just as flabbergasted as I felt. Erik seemed slightly uncomfortable, eyeing everyone else while Addie had turned around and was hanging off the side of the pool. She faced the fence so I couldn't see her reaction.

"Mom, you have to see that he's getting worse with Simone and he barely speaks to Stella. What the hell is going on with him?" Trent asked, hoping his mother would have the answer. "I'm trying to understand how you and Dad can accept this because I can't!"

Marla hung her head. "I honestly don't know," she said with tears in her eyes.

Trent and I exchanged another quick look. His was one of complete shock. For the first time, Marla wasn't going to put on a happy face and try to explain Brad's awful behavior away. Jim sat next to her, holding her hand and his expression was also one of sad disappointment.

I knew Jim and Marla loved their daughter-in-law and granddaughter just as much as they loved their boys. It had to hurt them to see Brad as a poor excuse of a husband and father. I knew he hadn't been raised that way. On the other hand, it wasn't like Brad was any different today than any other time. But I think, Brad not even trying to be tolerable on his own dad's birthday was the final straw.

My mood had soured a bit and I decided to get out of the pool. I dried off and headed to the bathroom to just get a few minutes to myself. Making my way down the hall, I could hear muted arguing.

As I got closer, I could hear Brad questioning his wife. "What the fuck did you say to my parents? My mom called me in tears, upset that I wasn't coming over."

"I told them you were sick, but no one believed me. I'm sorry," Simone said, apologizing. Again. She was so quiet I could barely make out what she was saying.

"Whatever. At least coming here gave me the opportunity to check Addie out. Damn, she's looking good. I can't believe I left that for you. I doubt she would have let herself go after having a baby," he mocked.

For a second time, Brad had me seeing red. That was it. I'd heard enough. First of all, he'd lost all right to look at my sister that way when he broke her heart. Second, he was a complete dick to treat his wife that way. Simone was gorgeous, and there was nothing wrong with her body. The guy was blind on top of being the biggest asshole in San Diego.

I rounded the corner and cleared my throat. Seeing Brad's tight grip on Simone's arm pissed me off even more. Brad turned around and his eyes widened at the pure rage I knew was showing on my face.

"Is there a problem in here?" I growled. My fists clenched at my sides just waiting for him to say something stupid.

"Nothing that concerns you, O'Neill," Brad said as he walked out of the hallway, giving a wide berth as he passed me.

It was mildly satisfying that he still feared me. I wasn't a violent or aggressive person, but Brad brought out my protective side. I turned toward Simone, who now had a stream of tears running down her face. As soon as she met my gaze she turned away from me and walked toward the bathroom. I reached out and touched her shoulder. She flinched away from my touch, which raised my suspicion immediately.

"Simone," I said, trying to temper my tone but it came out in a pained whisper instead. I could see her shoulders shaking, crying softly. How often had she cried over something her asshole husband said? Because I knew she had. Probably too many times to count.

"I'm sorry you saw that," she said, her back still to me.

"Don't apologize," I told her gently, using my hand on her shoulder to spin her around and pull her into a hug. Sometimes, something as simple as a hug could do wonders. For a brief second she tensed and I thought she would pull away. Instead, she wrapped her arms tightly around my waist, melding her front into mine, and started sobbing, her face buried in my chest.

I wrapped my arms around her back trying to provide her comfort. It touched something inside of me to see her so broken. In that moment I wanted to do anything I could to help her. I felt her shiver as my hand caressed her bare skin. I used one hand to massage the back of her neck and up into her hair, which seemed to help calm her.

"That feels good," she murmured so quietly that I don't think she meant for me to hear her. She rested her cheek over my heart, breathing slowly, breathing with me.

"Oh, shit… sorry…" a familiar voice interrupted from the other end of the hallway. I immediately felt Simone tense up again. Looking over Simone's shoulder I met Erik's ice-blue eyes that were looking at me questioningly. "I was just heading to the bathroom. Everything good here?" he asked gesturing between Simone and me.

I reluctantly pulled away from Simone. She stepped back but kept her eyes on the ground, still sniffling. I immediately felt the loss of her warmth and wished our—whatever this was—hadn't been broken. "Yeah, Brad was just being Brad." I hoped that explanation would be enough to keep Erik from asking any further questions, at least for now.

Erik nodded and entered the bathroom but not without a long, pointed look directed at me before he closed the door.

I ran my hands through my damp hair as Simone moved away. I knew Erik would ask me about this later, but privately. Thankfully, he wasn't one to make a scene. Not that I had anything to hide or had any reason to feel guilty. I was just comforting a… friend? While Simone and I hadn't really established a friendship before this, I couldn't leave a woman, who was that upset, all alone. I was just being a nice guy.

Who liked the way her body fit into yours. That thought had me hyperaware of her body, and how I still felt the imprint of her on my skin.

Simone was now looking at her reflection in the mirror on the wall in the hallway, swiping under her eyes in an attempt to remove the evidence of her small breakdown. And probably forgetting all about our little moment a few seconds ago, which was for the best.

"Are you going to be okay?" I asked. It was a stupid

question. I knew she wasn't going to be okay. How many times had I seen my own mother in tears over the hurtful things her latest boyfriend had said? I also knew Simone was the only one who could decide when she would have enough of Brad's behavior.

"Please don't worry about me," she said, her mask firmly back in place.

"Well, if you need a friend, I'm here." I was surprised by my words, but I knew I wanted to help her. Just as a friend.

But if that was the case, I thought as we headed back toward the pool, why couldn't I forget how wonderful it'd felt to hold her in my arms?

Chapter 5

Simone

*I*t had been a week since Jim's birthday party and I was still confused and embarrassed by what had transpired between Kyle and me. I hadn't meant to break down in his arms and I was surprised that I'd let him hold me for those few minutes. Even more surprising was how good his embrace had felt. Normally, I would have pulled back right away, but I'd felt safe in his arms. And I believed him when he said if I needed a friend he'd be there because that's who Kyle was—a great guy who was there for those he cared about. But I knew he didn't care about me in that way or in any way, really. He was a guy who saw someone in pain and wanted to do something about it.

Brad had left shortly after we'd returned to the backyard, and I think everyone was relieved. Even Marla and Jim hadn't seen him off like they usually did, and had ignored him when he said he was leaving. I wasn't surprised that he didn't say goodbye to me or ask about Stella, who'd still been napping in her room upstairs.

As the evening continued, Kyle kept looking at me. He must have thought I was pathetic. He didn't reveal anything on his face or in his attitude toward me, but I could see something in his eyes—pity. That was a worse feeling than being ignored your whole life. I could handle neglect but I wasn't some wounded animal licking her wounds. I could own up to my mistakes, like my marriage, and while I'd been blind about a lot of things, I was starting to see things with Brad as they were. I didn't need anyone feeling sorry for me.

Other than Brad's drama, it'd turned out to be a great day. Addie and I talked a little more, and I'd felt the most relaxed I'd ever felt around the Thompsons and their friends. Stella had fun and that'd brought me more joy than anything.

But since that day, things between Brad and I had become even more strained. We only talked when it came to things dealing with Stella. Even then he wasn't all that interested. He would leave for work just as Stella and I were waking up. I would then take Stella to his parents' house before he got off work. Often when I got home from a long shift, he would already be asleep, or we would just ignore each other and go about our own activities. On my days off, he almost always had plans with friends in an attempt to stay away from home.

Tonight, my restaurant manager had once again scheduled too many servers for the Sunday night shift so I'd only had a couple tables all night. I needed to start looking for another waitressing job because I couldn't afford to continue losing out on tips. Even so, once my shift was over I was extremely happy to be headed home. I was exhausted and a quiet night at home sounded good.

I pulled into my parking space and saw Brad's truck in his spot. I was a little shocked to see it there. I sort of thought he would have taken Stella to his parents' house and gone out for the evening. I had been anticipating a text while still at work telling me to pick her up over there.

It was a little after nine so I expected Stella to be in bed. While my world revolved around my little girl and I loved everything about being a mom, I wasn't going to be upset if I didn't have to deal with the bedtime routine tonight.

When I walked into the apartment, the living room was completely dark. Brad wasn't sitting on the couch playing video games like usual. Assuming he was still putting Stella down, I slipped past her closed door as quietly as I could so I wouldn't disturb them or risk waking her up.

As I reached out to turn the knob on my bedroom door, I heard an odd sound coming from the other side. Maybe Stella was already asleep and Brad was getting ready to settle in for the night? Suddenly a hot shower and my pajamas sounded like a wonderful idea.

I pushed the door open, still being quiet so I wouldn't wake our daughter. I saw Brad sitting on the edge of our bed facing away from me. I was just about to call out to him when I was stopped dead in my tracks.

"Oh, yeah, baby, keep going just like that," Brad moaned.

It took a second for those words to register in my brain. They made no sense; Brad was just sitting there. It wasn't until I took a couple steps in his direction that I saw a woman kneeling between his legs.

I was frozen to the spot right there on the carpet. Brad still had no idea I was in the room.

"What the fuck?" I asked so quietly I wasn't sure anyone could hear me. As everything started to sink in I yelled, "Seriously! What. The. Fuck?"

Both Brad and the woman on the floor turned to look at me. It was then that I recognized the other woman as Tiffany, the auto shop's receptionist.

Suddenly, the loud crying of a toddler took my attention away from the humiliating scene in front of me. I rushed out of my bedroom and into Stella's. She was standing in her crib and crying at the top of her lungs, no doubt, angry over being woken up by my yelling.

"It's okay, baby girl, mama's here," I said, picking her up and snuggling her against my chest. I stayed in her room gently rocking her back and forth. I wasn't sure who was comforting whom in that moment.

As I sat in the rocking chair with my daughter, it hit me that Brad may have actually planned this. He knew my schedule at work, and there was a routine set in place for when he went out. He'd wanted me to see them... to see it all. For him to be that cruel, to purposefully hurt me, shocked me. Brad had gone to a level that surpassed even his usual standards of reprehensible behavior. I felt dizzy, trying to process everything. It was all so overwhelming. Stella fussed a little at my tight hold on her but almost seemed to understand I needed her and she settled into me. I was drawing strength from my daughter to do what I needed to, what had been a long time coming.

I could hear voices moving down the hall, but I didn't care what they were saying to each other or what they were doing. Part of me wanted Brad to leave while I was distracted with our daughter, but another part of me wanted him to stay so he could hear everything I had to say, once and for all.

After another fifteen minutes of rocking Stella, she had calmed down and fallen back asleep. I made sure to give her the stuffed animal she had been sleeping with since birth and tucked her in with her favorite purple, fuzzy blanket. I turned off the light and moved through the door, shutting it quietly behind me.

Inhaling deeply through my nose and exhaling through my mouth, I took several more deep breaths in an effort to calm myself down. I don't know what possessed me to, but instead of going directly to the living room where I assumed

Brad was waiting for me, I walked into my bedroom. I knew there might be things I didn't want to see in there but I still felt an uncontrollable urge to look. I looked at his side of the bed and could see the indent of where he had been sitting in the blankets. It acted as proof that he had actually been there. I was about to turn around when something on the nightstand caught my eye. I walked over to get a closer look and was completely shocked by what I saw. Lying on top of the dark wood was a small mirror with two lines of coke on it and a rolled bill that looked like it had already been used. Of course, right next to the drugs was a strip of condoms.

So that's where all our money had been going. *On fucking drugs?!* And he was probably spending money on his sidepiece, too. It explained why he was always on his phone; he could have been arranging to meet his drug dealer or Tiffany. Memories of dealing with my drug addicted parents and the night Brad and I met floated to the surface.

The first night Brad and I hooked up, both of us had experimented with cocaine. At the time, I was an impulsive nineteen-year-old who saw sex as a way to form the connections I was so desperately craving. When Brad showed the slightest bit of interest I felt like the luckiest girl in the world. I'd let him charm me into trying coke. It was the stupidest thing I'd ever done considering I knew the kind of damage drugs could do. I had absolutely no desire to ever do it again. Brad had told me at the time that he didn't use it very often, but now I had to wonder if that was the truth. Drug use could explain some of the recent changes in his behavior. And I couldn't believe that he had been doing drugs while he was responsible for our daughter! That was what had my jaw clenched, hands balled into fists and ready to hit something — or someone. I could hear the blood rushing in my ears with how fast my heart was beating.

I felt my eyes sting but I wasn't going to cry. I was tired of crying. Not too long ago, I had feared that I was repeating my childhood. Turned out, I was, and that's what made this even more devastating and infuriating. I hadn't learned from my past but now, I had a choice, a chance to correct things before it went too far.

Before I walked out to the living room, I looked dispassionately around my bedroom that no longer felt like my space anymore. I shouldn't have been as surprised as I was. Brad and I didn't really share a life together. We were nothing more than acquaintances thrown together by circumstance.

Walking out to Brad, the only thing I knew for sure was this night was definitely the end of my marriage. I had desperately wanted to provide Stella with the family I never had, so desperate, in fact, I had ignored the lack of love and affection in our relationship. I never wanted Stella to feel unwanted, but even I couldn't pretend any longer that this was a healthy environment for her. By protecting myself, I was, in essence, protecting her as well. I needed to teach her that accepting this sort of treatment was not an option for her. I wouldn't want her to be in a relationship like this, which in turn meant I shouldn't be in one like it, either.

I had no idea what to expect but I knew it wasn't going to be pretty. I had never felt this much anger before, not even with my parents and growing up in the system. I was so furious that every part of my body was shaking. I looked around, making sure Tiffany was actually gone.

"Simone," Brad started the moment I walked into the living room.

He was fully dressed and seated but ceased speaking when I put my hand up to stop him from saying anything else. "No, don't even start. You don't get to say anything right now. It's my turn to talk," I said, livid.

He must have realized how serious and enraged I was, or I had shocked him by shutting him down, because he didn't continue. Whatever he had to say, I didn't want to hear it unless he was answering my questions.

"How long have you been using drugs?" That was the first question I needed an answer to. It made me sick to my stomach thinking of all the times he had been alone with Stella and could have potentially been high.

"Huh? What are you talking about?" he asked, trying to sound confused but I could tell he was just playing games.

I threw both my hands in the air, exasperated by his answer. "We are not doing this! You aren't going to sit there and treat me like I'm an idiot. I want real answers."

"It was just this one time, I swear," he answered. I didn't know if he was telling the truth, but I sure as hell hoped he was.

"How long have you been having sex with other people?" As soon as I looked into his eyes I knew it wasn't the first time.

"Do you really need an answer to that?" he scoffed.

"Of course I need an answer!" I hissed. My nails dug into my palms as my hands fisted tighter. "I'm your wife. I deserve to know."

He jumped up and started pacing the living room when he finally said, "Damn it, Simone, I never wanted this!"

I stood there waiting for him to elaborate. My anger had cooled but not my decision. This was me seeking closure.

"C'mon, it's not like we got married because we wanted to. I felt pressured to do right by you and you were so preoccupied with your ridiculous idea of a perfect family," he exclaimed. I could tell it was the drugs making him high-strung and, surprisingly, truthful. Any other time he would have deemed it beneath him to explain himself. "If you'd never gotten pregnant our relationship wouldn't have gone past the occasional hookup. We definitely didn't get married because we were in love and wanted to spend the rest of our lives together. Did you really think this was going to be some sort of happily ever after?"

"Get out," I seethed. I wanted to yell at him but I didn't want to wake Stella.

"Fine! I'll leave tonight but you and Stella are going to need to find another place soon because this is my apartment," he informed me callously. He headed to our bedroom without a backward glance. A few moments later, he came back out with a bag and left without a word or a look my way.

I sunk down onto the couch replaying what Brad had said. There was no denying the truth he'd spoken because he'd finally said the words I'd been thinking for weeks, and for once, we actually agreed on something. Two years ago, when he said we should get married, I knew it was because I was pregnant, not because he loved me. I wouldn't be lying, though, if I said a part of me back then had hoped our marriage could grow into love and that we could be happy together. I had also naïvely thought that he'd honor our vows, but once a cheater, always a cheater. Lesson learned, and one I'd never forget.

The way he treated me proved what I had always known, that he didn't care for or respect me — and never had. And while I was extremely angry with him, I was also angry with myself for tolerating his behavior for so long. I'd been living in a dream while Brad had always been living in reality.

I knew I needed a divorce; but I would need help navigating the process. And thankfully, I knew who to turn to for help.

*****

The next morning, I was barely functional having tossed and turned on the couch after Brad had left. I had no desire to sleep in our bed given what I had seen. I only slept about 2 hours total but Stella was ready to start her day so I was up.

I didn't have to work today, which was good because I had a lot to figure out and only today to do it. I had no doubt Brad would make good on his word and force me and Stella to find another place to live soon.

After fixing a breakfast of scrambled eggs and toast, I decided a walk to the park would do both Stella and me some good. I had been so happy to move into this apartment when Brad and I decided to get married. It was in a nice neighborhood where I felt safe taking Stella outside. I was worried I was going to have to move back to a place like I had before.

I pushed those depressing thoughts aside and tried to be happy for Stella's sake. She had no idea her life was about to be turned upside down. It was a beautiful spring day and I was going to enjoy the calm before the storm hit. There was a cool breeze and the trees and flowers were in full bloom. The sunshine and fresh air helped clear my head a little bit. I knew I had a lot of things to do and decisions to make, but I wanted to enjoy this small bit of time where I could play with my daughter and not think of anything else.

As soon as we returned to the apartment my anxiety

levels shot back up. I didn't know how long Brad was going to stay away and I wasn't ready to face him. I started to think of the logistics of splitting our household. We each had our own bank accounts. He took care of the rent and utilities from his paycheck while I took care of anything Stella needed and groceries from mine. There was rarely anything left over so I didn't have the funds to get my own place yet and I knew I'd get no help from Brad.

It was about ten when I put Stella down for a nap. I knew her days of taking two naps were coming to an end but I was grateful today for the chance to make a phone call I had never planned on making.

"Thompson Law Firm. This is Linda. How may I help you?" a sweet voice on the other end answered.

Trying to gather strength, I took a deep breath. "Um, yes, I was hoping to speak with Kyle O'Neill," I replied.

"May I ask who is calling?"

I dreaded this question. I was taking a huge risk by calling my father-in-law's law firm, but I was hopeful Kyle could help me. I wasn't ready to tell any of Brad's family that I was planning on divorcing him quite yet. I didn't want to lose the only family I'd ever had, however, after last night it had become evident divorce was my only option. I could only cross my fingers that Kyle would be willing to keep my secret for now.

As a family law attorney, I knew he had experience in handling divorce cases. I'd heard Jim and Trent chat about the law firm enough times to know that Kyle was more than capable of handling this.

"Um, my name is Simone." I paused. If I told her my last name she might have been able to connect the dots. Simone wasn't a very common name and sharing a last name with two of the attorneys might be a dead giveaway. "He'll know who I am," I explained.

"Okay," the woman said, a little uncertain, "hold please."

I held the phone to my ear for what felt like a long time but was probably only a minute.

"Simone?" I heard the deep baritone of Kyle's voice come across the line.

Just hearing him say my name was enough to set off my tears. I was really doing this. I was going to divorce Brad.

"Simone, are you okay?" Kyle asked, his tone laced with concern. He must have been able to hear my sobs through the phone.

I cleared my throat, trying to control myself. I wasn't the hysterical type, I just felt all over the place and scatterbrained. "Not really. I was hoping to talk to you about what it would take to get a..." I couldn't force the word 'divorce' out of my mouth.

Kyle sensing my hesitancy, gently prodded, "Simone, what do you need help with?" He was speaking to me in a quiet, gentle voice that immediately made me feel calmer.

"I need a divorce," I finally blurted out.

There was no response for so long that I thought I might have lost our connection.

"Okay..." I heard him exhale loudly. "Are you sure I'm the one you want to get advice from?" he asked, carefully.

"If you aren't comfortable talking to me... I'll understand. I just didn't know where to start and honestly you were the first person that came to mind. Could you please do me a favor and not tell anyone that I called you?" I asked hastily, ready to hang up.

"Simone, wait," he implored. "Simone?"

Slowly, I brought the phone back to my ear. "Yes?" I whispered, my nerves getting to me. I was hot all over and sweating. How could a phone call freak me out that bad?

"I'm more than happy to talk to you; I just wanted to warn you that there could be a perceived conflict of interest," he explained, his voice smooth and businesslike. Somehow his tone calmed me and I eased my grip on my cell phone. "Do you want to come down to the office today so we can talk?"

That spooked me and I shook my head vigorously a few times but realized he couldn't see me. "I'm not really comfortable coming into the office. Could we meet somewhere else? Please?" I asked, almost begging. I hated how I sounded, but Kyle really was my only hope.

"How about if we meet for lunch," he suggested, "around one. Would that work for you?"

"Yes that will work," I said, not hiding the relief in my voice.

"Let's meet at the diner down on Aspen Street."

"Sounds good. Thanks, Kyle... Bye."

"Bye, Simone," he said. Even if Kyle wasn't comfortable being my lawyer, I was hoping he could point me in the right direction so I could do this on my own. How I would pay for lawyer fees, on top of finding a new place to live, had me nearly in tears but I held them back. Stella needed me to be stronger than ever before. I had no time to break down.

I took advantage of Stella napping and grabbed a quick shower. Looking at myself in the mirror, I gasped at the dark circles under my red, puffy eyes. I decided I definitely needed a little makeup help before I left the house. After some concealer, I added some mascara and lip-gloss to complete my simple look that slightly reduced my zombie-like appearance. I pulled my hair into a low ponytail and went to the bedroom to pick out my clothes. Being in that room caused a strong wave of nausea to roll over me. When I looked at the bed, all I could see was Brad's betrayal. If I could burn the bed, I would have, but that probably wouldn't look good if I wanted sole custody of Stella and child support from my soon-to-be ex-husband.

Once I was dressed I moved quietly into Stella's room and packed a bag for her day at the beach with her grandparents. I didn't have to take much over there since they had almost anything she could possibly need. Today was going to work out perfectly because I had a babysitter for Stella yet I wouldn't have to explain to them where I was going since their trip had been planned for a few days.

I wasn't sure if Brad had talked to his parents so I made sure to act as though all was normal when I dropped Stella off and was relieved when Marla and Jim didn't mention anything. As I drove my car to my meeting with Kyle, I thought about what I was doing. I knew I was making the right decision but it wasn't going to be easy. The anxiety of the unknown was starting to get to me. My only wish was that Stella and I would make it through this okay.

Chapter 6

Kyle

To say that the phone call from Simone had surprised me would be an understatement. Trent, Addie, and I usually had lunch together, so leaving the office without a bunch of questions from the two of them hadn't been easy. During the drive to the diner, all kinds of thoughts ran through my head. The scene I'd witnessed on Jim's birthday was still weighing heavily on my mind. I tried to focus on the seriousness of Brad's hostility toward Simone, but images of her curvy body in her tiny, pink bikini kept creeping in.

"Kyle, focus. She needs your help, not a lechery lawyer," I muttered to myself. It wasn't very professional of me to have these sorts of thoughts about a potential client. Especially one who was married. It didn't matter that she was seeking a divorce.

I'd spent a lot of time during the last week thinking about Simone and how she was doing. I worried about her and Stella in a way that I hadn't expected since we weren't much more than acquaintances. But something about her drew my attention. Simone was naturally quiet for someone her age, but I didn't mind that. She was poised, and clearly took her responsibilities as Stella's mom very seriously. She probably thought more about her daughter's own happiness than she did her own and that had been more than evident last weekend.

My grip on the wheel tightened as I thought about how

shitty Brad had treated everyone, especially his own family. I'd had awful parents and knew firsthand the sort of pain that caused a child. It pissed me off on a whole other level to see him treat Stella poorly. He had done everyone a favor by leaving early, as the rest of the day had gone smoothly.

Jim didn't believe in birthday gifts and the only request he'd made was for all of us to show up, and for Simone to bring her famous brownies. However, none of us ever listened to him so me, Addie, Trent, Erik, and even Ian, all the way from South Carolina, had pitched in to give him a year's worth of weekend golf at Torrey Pines — with Marla, of course. Those two did everything together. Trent added professional lessons for both of them as well. After he'd opened his other gifts and cards, we'd spent the rest of the evening hanging out outside around the fire pit and shooting the shit. Without Brad there to destroy the good mood, we'd all had a great time — even Simone, once she had finally relaxed and let her guard down a bit.

Now, I was going to spend more time with her if I took her on as my client, and help her with her divorce.

When the guys and I were younger, we had barely tolerated Brad since we'd all seen right through his games, and we would do everything in our power to ditch him. Marla had never seen how manipulative Brad could be until recently, and would occasionally bribe us to spend time with him. Jim had decreed that we had to include him when Brad complained about how we were mistreating him. Playing the victim card he had cultivated to perfection as an adult. That's what I had to watch out for during this entire ordeal if I represented Simone. I could see Brad totally throwing her under the bus to protect his fragile ego.

I pulled into the parking lot of the small diner, grabbed my leather messenger bag just in case I needed to take notes, and headed in. The place was always packed on the weekends but on weekdays it was usually pretty quiet.

I walked through the door, the bell alerting the wait staff that a customer had entered. My eyes started searching the restaurant to see if Simone had already arrived. There, in the back corner booth, I found her. She was hunched over the table picking apart the paper napkin in front of her. As though she could feel my stare on her, she lifted her head and our gazes locked.

I smiled at her and started to make my way across the restaurant. I took a seat on the bench across from her, setting my bag down next to me.

"Hi," I said, greeting her. That's when I saw her red-rimmed eyes up close and the dark circles underneath. It was obvious she was exhausted and emotionally drained.

Before Simone could respond, our waitress—CeeCee, an older woman with white fluffy hair, blue eye shadow, and a nice smile, interrupted us. She took our drink order and gave us each a laminated menu and rattled off the day's specials. After I ordered water and Simone ordered lemonade, we made a show of perusing our menus for about a minute before setting them down at the end of our table.

"Thank you for meeting with me," she whispered, after another full minute had passed.

I watched her tear another napkin apart, piece-by-piece. "Of course. Anything for a friend," I said, echoing my sentiments from last weekend. Briefly, I placed a hand on hers in an attempt to still her fidgeting. She stopped and looked at me. "Hey, things will be okay. I'm here to help you. Want to tell me what happened?"

I hadn't planned on jumping right into discussing what was going on. I had wanted her to lead the conversation, but

I'd sensed that she needed to talk to somebody and that it'd be easier for her if I initiated it. She removed her hands from under mine and hid them under the table. I drew my hand back as well, still wishing I could comfort her in some way.

"Um... I decided to end things with Brad last night," she started, her voice hoarse. She sniffed, eyes downcast. "He was cheating on me." Her words broke at the end. She was trying to hold back her tears.

It was clear she was embarrassed by Brad's cheating although she had no reason to be. This didn't make her look bad, it only reflected negatively on him. He'd cheated on Addie. Cheating on Simone, unfortunately, wasn't surprising. In fact, thinking about it, he'd probably been cheating on Simone from the start of their marriage. The reason they got married was so fucked up, all of us should have seen this coming. From what Jim and Marla had said back then, Brad had 'appeared' to get his act together. Clearly, he'd always been good about concealing his true intentions.

CeeCee returned with our drinks and we both ended up getting the half sandwich and salad special. After she left, I switched into lawyer mode. I needed to remove the personal element and try to get answers. It was the only way I was going to be able to help her.

"Are you sure he was cheating on you?" I asked, opening my bag and taking out a legal pad, pen, and my glasses. Treating this like any other meeting would help both of us. I put my glasses on and gestured at her to continue.

"Well, considering I walked into my bedroom and he had his dick halfway down Tiffany's throat, I would say I'm sure," she said bluntly.

Well, fuck. I wasn't expecting that. There was no

expression on her face but I saw her eyes flash with anger and her jaw tighten. I'd never seen that side of Simone before. When Brad was around, she was meek and quiet, carefully treading in dangerous waters.

I wrote down Tiffany's name, and I knew exactly who she was. Erik was going to flip out once he learned of this, but it wouldn't be from me even though I felt an obligation to inform him.

"And he planned it so I would walk in on it," she added. "He wanted me to catch them in the act."

I looked up at her. The cheating didn't come as a huge surprise but the fact that he'd done that in their bedroom with the intent to hurt Simone was inexplicable.

"I should have known he was messing around with her. She always gave me an attitude any time I called or visited the shop," she continued, sighing. "I should have known better. He had a history of it…"

We were both quiet for a second, both of us looking at each other and thinking about Addie. I moved on quickly. "Simone, are you positive you want to file for divorce?" I asked. She wouldn't be the first person I met with who decided cheating wasn't enough of a reason to go through the painful and time-consuming process. But because I was so familiar with her situation, and I doubted anyone would want to stay married to a guy like Brad, I knew she had more than enough cause.

She looked directly at me and I could feel the daggers she was shooting at me.

I held up my hands in surrender. "I agree with your decision," I admitted, "but I just want to confirm that you're ready to move forward."

Her eyes softened a bit but they were absolutely determined. No doubt at all, and I would never question that again. "Yes, I'm sure I want to file for divorce. I should have done it a while ago." She said that last sentence under her breath but I was still able to hear her.

I paused for a second, wording my next question carefully. "Simone... has Brad ever hurt you?" I asked quietly, watching her body language as much as listening to her words. "Physically, I mean?"

Her eyes widened a bit, and had a lost, faraway look as she recalled something, but then she slowly shook her head negatively. I moved on from that question since it appeared I wasn't going to get any more of an answer from her on that topic, but I knew I'd have to revisit it.

"What about Stella?" I asked, watching her closely.

I didn't like what was registering on her face but again; she shook her head in the negative. I swear to God, if I found out that Brad had ever harmed Stella, I'd crucify him.

As a lawyer, a family law lawyer at that, learning to read people was essential. And Simone was an open book. It didn't take much to see it on her face or in her body language. She had no idea what I was gleaning from her silences alone. It's why I knew there was a history of some sort of abuse, never mind the emotional and psychological abuse Brad inflicted upon her and I'd witnessed myself. I still remembered the way Brad had gripped her arm back at the Thompson house and the way she always flinched whenever anyone but her daughter touched her. I did have a basic understanding of her past from what Trent had relayed to me a long time ago. I knew she never talked about it in depth and I wasn't sure if anyone had really pressed for that info. Whether she liked it or not, that too would be a topic we'd be discussing at length.

99

"Has he cheated on you before?" We lived in California, which was a no-fault state, so it didn't really matter for filing purposes if he had cheated multiple times. I was just curious if she was aware of any other indiscretions.

"I suspect he has, but I never really thought about it before nor did I go out looking for evidence of it. You know how our marriage started, and he was never completely on board with it. He told me as much last night when he said he was basically forced into marrying me."

I winced a little at that. My own involvement lingered in my mind even though I'd had nothing to do with forcing Brad to marry Simone, I still *knew*. "I have to ask, and this is as a friend, not as an attorney, why did you stay with him so long?" This was something I had wanted an answer to but I wasn't sure she would open up to me.

She was quiet for a moment and I figured she wasn't going to answer. "It sounds so stupid now that I know he never cared about me or Stella. But I really wanted Stella to grow up in a loving, stable family. My parents were horrible, so bad, in fact, that I was removed from their home and placed in foster care. I wanted better for my daughter."

So maybe that was the reason for her silence when I asked about abuse. "It doesn't sound stupid at all; it makes perfect sense," I stated firmly. I leaned over, making sure she was looking me in the eyes. "You probably don't know this but… Addie and I had pretty shitty parents, too. Our father left early on and our mother was in and out of our lives before she died. I understand the desire to have a perfect family. That doesn't mean you should feel bad for picking the wrong person, and you shouldn't feel bad for getting yourself out of that situation. The fact that you realize you deserve better, that you and Stella deserve so much more, is a brave step. I hope you realize that."

I could see the tears welling up in her eyes again and it broke my heart. I'm not sure what possessed me but I got up and moved over to her side of the table. I sat down next to her and wrapped my arm around her shoulders and just let her cry. It wasn't a professional move, but I felt an overwhelming desire to comfort her. I knew she didn't have very many people to support her but if I could help her in any way, I was going to.

Again, she surprised me when she returned my gesture and wrapped her arms around my middle. She let me hold her as she cried softly in to my shoulder. I propped my chin on the top of her head, and rubbed her back, letting her cry it out. It was odd how natural my actions came, but Simone felt oddly familiar in this position, like holding her was something I did often. It reminded me of our moment during Jim's birthday.

After a few minutes she was able to pull herself together. She disengaged, almost reluctantly, and looked up at me. "Thank you," she whispered, eyes still tearing up but not as much. "You're really sweet, Kyle…"

I didn't know what to say because I couldn't stop staring at her. Our faces were so close that I could feel her breath against my lips and I could see my reflection in her dark brown eyes. The expression on my own face unnerved me. I smelled the scent of her shampoo or whatever she was wearing, and breathed it in. When she licked her lips, which seemed to be another nervous tic of hers, my eyes darted to the curve of her mouth. For a split second, I swear she moved closer to me. Or maybe it was the other way around. I swallowed hard, looked away, and pulled back.

"Better?" I asked, but my voice was a little hoarse and I could feel the pulse at my temples thudding against my skull. What the hell? Back at Jim's birthday party, I'd felt drawn to her and her sadness, but at that time, my intentions had been... mostly... innocent. But here, this was something different, a little bit dangerous. I felt it in my body, the way I reacted to her, the turn of my thoughts from friendly to something akin to lust. When I looked back at her, I wasn't sure if she'd felt what I'd felt. Probably not. She had bigger problems to deal with than me being irresponsible.

I handed her the napkin from my side of the table so she could wipe her eyes although she was no longer crying. I had to force myself to move back to my seat, needing the distance to compose myself and get back into my lawyer mode. The worst possible thing I could do was to start thinking about Simone in any way other than a client. No more touching, even though it felt instinctual for me when it came to her. She was vulnerable, afraid, and probably felt all alone. She had come to me for help, to find a safe haven from the shit storm she was about to go through. I wanted — no, needed — to be that stable force for her in a way that wasn't just about being a damn good lawyer, but something else I couldn't quite put my finger on. Something I didn't want to focus on right now. So I forced myself to think about the next steps she would need to take.

"So I can get the paperwork started as soon as you're ready," I informed her, clearing my throat and taking a long drink of my water to cool off. I still felt overheated and my heart was still doing jumping jacks in my chest. Jesus, what the hell was wrong with me? "You said Jim and Marla don't know you are doing this, correct?"

She shook her head. "I doubt it. I kicked Brad out last night but I don't think he went over there. They're watching Stella right now and they didn't say anything to me when I dropped her off."

"You should consider telling them," I advised. "They're

going to find out eventually and they love you. I'm sure they would want to hear it from you first, and I wouldn't trust Brad to come clean with them any time soon."

She didn't respond, just began fidgeting again, but this time with her glass of lemonade. She had long, slender fingers, and short nails. I glanced at the simple gold band on her left ring finger and noticed that it was a size too big. Either Brad hadn't made an effort when buying it or she'd lost some weight from all the stress she was under. Both were possible.

"I'm scared," she said quietly.

Nodding, I could see it on her face, too. I considered my next words thoughtfully. "About what, exactly, Simone?"

She took a deep breath. "Jim and Marla have been so accepting of me even though I came into their life unexpectedly. Brad is their son; it's only natural that they'll continue to support and even side with him," she said, her voice wavering again. "I refuse to put them in the middle of our mess, and if they end up in that position I'm afraid I'm going to lose the only people I ever thought of as family."

I felt bad that she believed she'd actually lose Marla and Jim. That her only connection to them was through Brad, or her daughter. She had no idea how much they adored her. "Simone, I have known the Thompsons for twenty years. Trust me when I say they're coming to terms with the fact that they have to let Brad stand on his own instead always fighting his battles. You and Stella mean so much to them, don't ever doubt that," I told her, trying to allay her fears. "Things may be a little uncomfortable, but they won't abandon you. In fact, I think they might help you more than you expect."

For the next half hour, we ate our lunch while we

continued to talk about the process of filing for divorce. Simone had asked for a piece of paper to write some of the details down for her own notes while I continued to take mine. I explained to her that I was willing to take her case pro bono. She tried to argue but I absolutely refused. Then she broke out in tears again. She explained that Brad told her she was going to need to move out of their apartment since he was the one on the lease. She wasn't sure how she was going to afford rent, lawyer fees, and any other expenses that would probably come up, especially for Stella.

I was surprised by Brad's statement since I was pretty sure Jim and Marla were on the lease for the apartment — not Brad. It was another reason for her to speak with them. I didn't believe they would make their only grandchild and her mother move out. Especially since they had a room at their house for Brad if he needed a place to live.

We were just finishing up when I heard a voice behind me say, "Uh, hey, Kyle."

Shit. I turned around and saw my sister. Her gaze flicked between Simone and me with a raised brow. "Hi, Addie…" I said, smiling wanly at her. I wasn't sure what else to say because my brain was still trying to figure out how to explain the two of us together, and Simone's miserable expression and puffy eyes.

Addie and Simone had talked at Jim's party, and as far as I knew, there weren't any hard feelings between them. It didn't make this moment any less awkward, though.

"Hi, Simone," Addie greeted politely, and walked closer to our booth. She was giving me a 'you'd better explain this to me later' look that I knew too well.

"Hi," Simone returned, her face nearly bloodless. She looked toward me but like her, I was still at a loss for words, which was not only usual for a lawyer, but for me personally, as well.

"Well, I guess I'll see you back at the office," Addie said, once she realized we weren't going to explain why we were having lunch together. She gave me another speculative look then turned back around to grab her to-go box at the register and left the restaurant.

"I'm so sorry, Kyle. I hope you helping me out won't cause any problems between you and your sister," Simone started, unsettled. Like we'd been caught doing something illicit.

I shook my head, knowing Addie would keep things to herself until she got the details out of me. "Don't worry about it and I won't tell Addie anything about you filing for divorce yet. She's my assistant but I'll keep your files in my office and type up all your documents myself. Please don't worry about anything except taking care of yourself and that beautiful little girl of yours."

She smiled at the mention of her daughter. Her smile was beautiful, and I wanted her do it more often. Living with Brad probably didn't give her many reasons to. Simone may have made an awful choice when picking Brad, but she came out with an amazing child from that union. I knew she was determined to be the best mom ever, and from everything I had seen, she was doing a great job.

"You don't need to keep this a secret, especially since you work with Jim, Trent, and Addie," she said, biting on her lower lip for a second but she seemed less uncertain now. Maybe she was already beginning to accept that her divorce was going to happen. I admired her ability to roll with the punches. Sometimes life took a very wrong turn to let you know when to stand up and fight. "I'm going to talk to Brad and then his parents this afternoon so you don't have to hide any paperwork. You've convinced me that it's probably a good idea."

We talked a bit more and then it was time for me to head back to the office. I picked up the check the waitress had dropped off at our table and we moved to the register so I could pay for our lunch. I saw Simone digging around in her purse for her wallet. No way was I was going to let her give me money.

"I've got this covered," I told her.

After I paid the bill, I placed my hand on her lower back and led her out of the restaurant. I had managed to not think about pink bikinis all through lunch; however, as soon as I placed my hand on her, it was all I could think about. I really needed to stop touching her, but it felt too good and it was like my hand had a mind of its own. At her car, I said, "I'm going to need you to come into the office in order to draft the divorce filing. I'll also need you to sign a disclosure agreement acknowledging my connection to Brad."

I pulled my phone out of my pocket and handed it to her. "Here, program your number then I can text you so we have each other's numbers," I said. "You can text or call me when you want to take care of the paperwork."

I didn't give my personal cell phone number to my clients, but I felt better knowing that she would be able to get ahold of me if she needed anything.

I texted her number to test it, and heard her notification alert go off. "You can call me, for anything, day or night," I offered, the words out before I could stop them. She stared up at me, and then she hugged me again. She squeezed me tight around the middle, hard. I wanted to return it, let this moment linger, but she pulled back and got her keys out of her purse.

"You're wonderful," she said, eyes tearing up. "I feel so much better knowing you're on my side. *Thank you.*"

Her emotions got to me; a simple 'thank you' was never more powerful to me than hers. I opened the car door for her and then watched her drive away, disappearing into the busy afternoon traffic.

While driving back to the office, I thought of all she had shared with me and I hoped she would be okay. I knew she was worried and scared about a lot of things. It was obvious to me she didn't know she had people in her corner. I'd do what I could to prove that to her, and I would protect her, like I should have done for Addie. Brad still needed to learn a lesson, and I had no problem teaching it to him.

*****

I had just sat down at my desk when Addie came in and closed the door behind her.

She crossed her arms over her chest and leaned back against the door. "So what in the world did I walk in on back at the diner?" she asked, sounding genuinely curious.

There was no point in keeping this from her since it would come out soon enough. Plus, I trusted Addie explicitly. "Simone called me this morning, asking to meet so we could discuss her filing for divorce," I answered, matter of fact.

Addie just stood there silently contemplating. I could see the wheels spinning in her head. She was probably thinking some not so nice things and a lot of 'could have seen that coming' comments, too. I also saw sympathy in her expression. Addie wasn't heartless, and while she was probably still bitter about Brad, she knew she'd come out of that deal rather well. And Simone did not deserve what she got; we both knew that without question.

"What happened?" she finally asked.

"She caught him cheating on her," I stated, shrugging.

Addie could have taken some joy in the fact that Brad had cheated on the woman that he had cheated on her with, but she wasn't that kind of person. Instead, I saw the frown form on her face as she nodded her head, showing she wasn't surprised by his actions.

"You and I know he's a total douche. I had really hoped he'd changed his ways for Simone and Stella." Addie sighed, shaking her head. "She must be heartbroken."

"Honestly, I don't think Simone is upset about her relationship with Brad not working out. She is, however, worried about of losing Jim and Marla, and possibly the relationship they have with Stella. She shared with me some things from her past—like the fact that she had it rough like we did except she wasn't lucky to have people like the Thompsons or Grandma stepping in to help her out when she was younger. She wanted better for her daughter and now she feels like a failure."

"She's not a failure," Addie said adamantly. Her expression went a little hard. "That title belongs to Brad."

"And I wish I had done better by you in making you realize that before he hurt you," I said softly.

She smiled a little, but it was slightly strained. "Brad could charm a nun out of her habit," she said grimly. "I fell for it, and so did Simone. Regardless of what she thought or was hoping for when she married Brad, her reasons were genuine. Brad's weren't." She paused, narrowing her gaze me. "You are going to help her, right?" she asked, although her tone made it clear she expected me to.

"That's the plan," I informed her. "Pro bono."

She visibly relaxed. "Good. I'd be mad at you if you didn't. And if you need help, of any kind, count me in."

I smiled at that, glad my sister was on board. Then I frowned somewhat, thinking about how the rest of this day might unfold. "I'm just hoping it won't make things awkward with Trent," I said, meeting Addie's gaze. "Simone is telling Brad that she's filing for divorce and then she plans on talking to Jim and Marla afterwards. I'm going to need to sit down with Trent this afternoon before we leave for the day."

"Hopefully, there won't be any problems there. And, again, please let me know if you need me for anything. I'm serious, Kyle," Addie repeated, pointing a finger at me. "Don't leave me out. Even if it's to babysit Stella or hold Simone's hand or buy Kleenex, I'll do it."

I grinned. "Okay, I get it, now go file some papers already," I teased.

She stuck her tongue out at me but then opened the door and went back to her workspace. I scrubbed my face hard, wanting to get things squared away quickly. I didn't want to give Brad too much time to weasel his way out of this if he felt that staying married to Simone would benefit him in the long run.

In regards to Trent, I didn't think I'd get much resistance from him. Since he wasn't a fan of his brother, I knew he wouldn't harbor any ill will toward Simone. But I also wasn't sure how he would feel about me representing her, or our law firm getting involved in something this close to home. She didn't have the resources to pay for an attorney and I didn't want her to risk missing out on anything she was entitled to by filing for divorce on her own or getting preyed upon by some sham lawyer. I knew I couldn't leave her to deal with this alone, and I wasn't going to walk away from Simone until I saw her smile again. And damn it, some selfish part of my brain wanted *me* to be the reason she never stopped smiling.

Chapter 7

Simone

*H*aving lunch with Kyle had been extremely confusing. I wasn't confused about my decision to divorce Brad; that was a long time coming. The confusion came when Kyle wrapped me in his arms when I was upset… again.

And, I didn't pull away. That was twice now that Kyle had made me feel safe. His body had felt warm and solid, and fit with mine like a puzzle; it'd been comforting. The impulse to keep feeling that way was why I'd given him another hug before I'd left. It was foolish of me and he'd probably thought it was strange, but I didn't care. Even though I knew he was just a nice guy and doing his job, I'd liked the way his hand felt on my back, how firmly he'd held me against his body, and the way he looked at me. If he hadn't released me—I blushed again at what I might have done. I'd wanted to burrow in further, and never let go. And *that*, I knew, was crazy thinking.

I knew he watched me leave the lot and pull into traffic. He even wanted to make sure I got on the road safely. I mean, was that something most men did? Or just Kyle? He was so thoughtful, and despite having awful parents, he was the epitome of a gentleman. He was caring and he listened, never mocking me or making me feel stupid for anything I said. He believed me, and vowed to help in any way he could. And I knew I could trust him.

I'd never had that before. Trusting someone and knowing

they would stand by their word. Again, it reminded me of what Brad wasn't and never would be.

I wasn't blind. I had always noticed how good-looking Kyle was. His short, brown hair was cut to maintain an air of professionalism but didn't look pretentious. He had beautiful green eyes that were bright and when he looked at you, there was a kindness in them. Today, those eyes had been hidden behind thin, metal-framed glasses. I hadn't ever seen him wear glasses before, but they made him that much more handsome.

And while I had always noticed him before, I had never allowed myself to focus on how attractive he was. First, I was married. Second, his sister had been engaged to my husband and the only reason they broke up was because of me. And last, he was best friends with my brother-in-law.

But now, I was having a very hard time focusing on anything other than how hot he was. It was completely wrong for me to have thoughts like that about Kyle and I really needed to get my shit together.

As I drove away from the diner, I decided to go home first. I wanted to speak with Brad before going over to Jim and Marla's. I had no idea how Brad would react to my news, but I had a feeling he'd welcome it. You don't stage what I'd walked in on without the intention of ending something. I was hoping he would go with me to his parents' house so we could break the news to them together. I felt like it'd be less of a blow for them that way and also prove that Brad and I could handle this like adults, and that the divorce could be a clean break. I wanted this process to be as pain-free for everyone as possible. At the next red light, I decided to text him and make sure he was going to be home.

Me: *I'm on my way to the apartment. Can you meet me there so we can talk?*

Brad: *Already here.*

Me: *Ok. Be there soon.*

I tried to plan how I'd word everything during the rest of my drive home. Once I parked and headed up the stairs, I still wasn't sure exactly what to say. I could hear the video game playing on the television as I slipped my key in the door to unlock it. When I walked through the door and closed it behind me I saw Brad on the couch with the controller in his hands. It was the same spot I usually found him any time we were home together.

I didn't say hello and neither did he. Not acknowledging my presence was also quite normal for him. I placed my purse and keys on the small table next to the door and made my way to the couch. Getting comfortable, I sunk down onto the soft cushion, kicked off my shoes so I could put my feet up, and faced Brad.

"So what did you want to talk about?" he asked, without taking his eyes of the screen where he was currently shooting up some building.

"Do you think you could stop playing for a minute and actually listen to what I have to say?" I asked. I didn't hide the annoyance in my voice, though he didn't seem to notice. He never noticed anything that mattered.

"Simone, I'm fucking listening to you, just say whatever you need to say," he demanded.

The fact that something monumental had happened in our relationship last night and he couldn't even spare me a few minutes of his undivided attention pissed me off. I wanted to handle our divorce in a mature manner. It was now clear that would not happen.

Realizing he was going to continue to ignore me, I grabbed the remote control from the cushion next to me and turned the television off. "Maybe now you'll actually listen to me," I said as I tossed the remote back on the couch.

"Seriously?" he asked, laughing at me. But it wasn't a humorous laugh. No, Brad was completely furious with me. And that scared me a little bit, but I wasn't going to back down, not now. I needed to have this conversation with him so I could move on.

"I met with an attorney today," I informed him, of course not disclosing that it was Kyle. That was a discussion we could save for later, if needed. "I'll be filing for divorce as soon as possible. It will take about six months for everything to be finalized if we can agree on custody of Stella and the division of the few assets we have."

I stopped, waiting for any sort of response from him. Instead he picked up his phone and started typing on the screen.

"Really? You have nothing to say? You're just going to start texting?" I snapped, my hands fisting in my lap. I could hear the anger in my voice and I'm sure my face was red at this point.

He stood up and started to move into the kitchen. "What do you want me to say? When you caught Tiffany giving me a blowjob, I kind of figured that was the end of things," he retorted over his shoulder. I swear I saw a smirk on his face when he said that.

"I know you aren't upset about our marriage ending, but we will have to eventually talk about custody of Stella..." I let those words hang out there, expecting some sort of acknowledgment from Brad. Instead, he took a drink of water and shrugged his shoulders.

His lack of response broke my heart. Not for me, but for my daughter. She deserved to have a father who would do anything in his power to spend time with her. Someone who would be upset at the thought of not seeing her every day.

I looked at the clock and noticed it was time for me to go pick her up. "I'm heading over to your parents' to get our daughter. Do you want to come with me so we can tell them together about the divorce?" I asked, hopeful he wouldn't make me do this on my own.

"Nope. If you want to tell them that's your business. I have no desire to have a conversation with them about this," he replied. Of course, his answer didn't surprise me.

"Fine," I said, getting more frustrated with him by the minute. I got up to gather my things so I could leave. "I guess I will see you when I get back."

"Wait a minute!" he said, stopping me in my tracks. "You aren't planning on coming back here tonight, are you?" he asked.

"What?" I stared at him, jaw dropping. Did he really think I would have another place to live lined up already? "Where would you expect me and Stella to go?" I fired back.

"I don't give a fuck where you two go, but you aren't coming back here. I told you last night you needed to find a new place to live. This is my apartment," he sneered.

I couldn't stop the tears from falling down my cheeks. Was he really kicking his daughter and me out of the apartment? It hadn't even been twenty-four hours yet. While I didn't want to share a bed with him ever again, I thought I would be able to stay on the couch until I could come up with a plan for Stella and me.

"Besides, Tiffany is coming over tonight. I'm guessing you don't want to be here for that. Things might get a little awkward if I'm fucking her and you're hanging out in the living room," he said with an evil grin.

The visual Brad just provided had my stomach churning. Not wanting to risk losing my lunch, I grabbed my purse and flung the door open. "You're such a fucking asshole!" I shouted back toward him before slamming the door behind me.

I stood on our third floor landing, leaning on the railing for a couple minutes, trying to collect myself. I was shaking so hard and breathing so fast I thought I might pass out. Brad had always been careless and selfish, but this crossed over to cruel and heartless. I was so mad at myself for letting my silly childhood fantasies convince me to enter into a marriage where love wasn't the foundation. This was going to be a painful lesson for me to learn, but I was determined to be strong for my daughter. I pushed off the railing and numbly made my way back to my car. I'd do the best I could for Stella all on my own, which I finally understood had always been the only option.

*****

It was almost four when I knocked on my in-laws' door and waited, unsure how I was going to break the news to them about Brad and me. Marla opened the door with her usual bright smile but the moment she saw me, I could see the lines of worry etched on her face.

116

"Oh, sweetie! What's wrong?" she asked, placing her arm around my shoulder and directing me into the house.

I immediately turned in her arms and started sobbing into her shoulder. She hugged me as tightly as she could and this time, I didn't pull back right away. Like with Kyle, I held on because I needed her strength right now. I had always longed for someone to care for me like this. Now I worried this might be the last time she'd embrace me. I wished I had shown her more often that I appreciated her and Jim; that I truly cared about them. But trusting anyone with those emotions was hard for me and Brad had eroded my faith in others even more.

She pulled away slightly and wiped the tears off my cheeks with her thumbs. "Come sit down and tell me what's going on," she coaxed gently.

"Where's Stella?" I asked, sitting down next to Marla. I looked around the living room, not wanting to talk about this in front of her. Even though she was still young, I knew she picked up on nonverbal clues and I didn't want her to have any negative impressions about this moment in her life.

"Jim is putting her down for a nap upstairs. The beach wore her out today—I'm so sorry, I hope it doesn't completely ruin bedtime for her tonight. Do you want me to have him wake her up?" she asked, starting to get up to go call them.

I placed my hand on her arm gently. "Oh no, I actually wanted to speak to the two of you so it's fine."

Marla patted my hand and gave me a reassuring smile. "Sure, whatever you want dear. Can I get you something to drink while we wait?"

"I would love some water. Thanks."

Marla got up and left, heading toward the kitchen just as Jim made his way down the stairs. "Simone!" he said, his face lighting up. "I didn't even hear you come in. I just got Stella tucked in. Do you need to leave already?"

"I've only been here a few minutes," I said, suddenly nervous. I tried not to fidget and kept my hands, folded, in my lap. "I don't have to leave right away; I was actually hoping to talk to you both."

Jim took a seat on the loveseat that was perpendicular to the couch I was sitting on. As he sat down, Marla came back in with my glass of water and a plate of cookies. She was the perfect hostess, always providing some sort of baked good and drinks for her guests. Today's cookie was my favorite, peanut butter. I took a moment to savor the comfort only something as simple as peanut butter cookies could provide.

"So what did you want to talk about?" Marla asked, placing her hand on my knee as a sign of support.

I closed my eyes briefly and took a breath. "This is so hard to tell you guys, but Brad and I are getting a divorce." I rushed the words out and held my breath, waiting for their reaction.

Marla's eyes widened slightly and her mouth parted in an 'O' of bewildered surprise. Jim continued to watch me in silent contemplation. Neither of them said anything for a few seconds.

"Oh, dear. Can I ask what happened?" Marla asked, blinking a few times. Her brows furrowed as she looked at me. She didn't sound angry with me, which was a relief, but I was hesitant to tell her and Jim what exactly happened last night. I knew the ugly details would eventually come out, so I took a big, calming breath, and with my heart in my throat and my fears on my sleeve, I explained.

"Well, you know why we got married in the first place," I said, starting off slow. I definitely did not want give anyone a huge shock, but I was done protecting Brad and making excuses for him. They had to know what kind of man their son was, and I had to have faith that they'd at least hear me out. If not for me, for the sake of their granddaughter. "In the last few weeks, I realized I married him for the wrong reasons and that Brad had never wanted to get married either. I wanted to make sure Stella had a family, so I didn't think about the fact that Brad and I really weren't meant to be together. I think this was a long time coming. Better now than another year of misery." I paused, looking at both of them before continuing. "And last night, I walked in on him with another woman in our apartment. He didn't care how that looked..." I stopped, swallowing hard. I decided to leave out the drug part because from Marla's gasp and her falling back on the couch, she wouldn't be able to take much more. "That's why I decided to file. I told him before I came over here and he's definitely on board with the divorce."

Marla said nothing, staring off with a stunned expression on her face. Jim didn't seem all that surprised. Even though I was terrified they'd throw me and Stella out, I felt a huge burden lift off me. I was finally able to breathe for the first time in two years.

"I'm guessing there's more to the story than you are sharing, and I can respect that, Simone," Jim said gravely, finally breaking his silence. He scrubbed his face with one hand and sighed. He looked ten years older in just a fraction of second, and I felt bad about that, but I wasn't sorry I had said something. "Simone, I have my own confession to make—I feel like this is partly my fault as well."

Marla sat up, and looked over at her husband. "Jim," she said, her voice tense. "What did you do?"

Jim didn't flinch as he looked at his wife, however, when he looked at me, he seemed almost ashamed, like he'd done something wrong. "When you announced you were pregnant, that night... I made it clear to Brad that he had to do the right thing or Marla and I would cut him off."

Marla sagged back into the couch again, bringing her hands to her flushed cheeks. She shook her head. "Oh, Jim..."

"I'm sorry, Simone," he said, his voice hitching. "I should have never interfered. A part of me thought I was helping him realize what he *should* do, not what he *had* to do. I'd hoped he'd grow into being a responsible husband and father." He looked at Marla then glanced back at me. "I was wrong, and your unhappiness... I'm partly to blame for that and I own up to it. But clearly, my son has failed you and his daughter and that's on him."

I broke down. So that's what Brad had meant when he said he felt pressured to marry me. Was I really that stupid to have believed he came to that decision on his own? Just when I thought I couldn't shed another tear, another round overtook me. Marla gathered me up in her arms, patting my back until I regained control over my emotions.

"Can I ask why Brad isn't here with you telling us what's going on?" Jim asked, but from the look on his face, he already knew the answer. Marla handed me a tissue and I wiped at my eyes.

"I asked him to come with me but he had other plans." I left my answer purposely vague for Marla's sake. She was finally coming around, but the sadness in her eyes made my chest feel tight.

"I... can't say I'm surprised by this, not really," Marla said, subdued. She kept a motherly arm around me. "I've been blind to his faults for too long, and like Jim, I prayed he'd turn himself around. Him marrying you gave me false hope that he could change and be the man I thought he could be." She paused, and took one of my hands in her free hand. "You need to know that we will be here for you and Stella while you navigate through this. You're not alone."

I nodded. I wasn't able to respond with words because the tears had started flowing again. My biggest fear was losing them and Marla was telling me I didn't need to worry about that.

"Sweetie, please don't cry," Marla cooed, squeezing me into her side.

"I was so worried I was going to lose the two of you. You're the only family I have," I sniffed, voicing my fears out loud.

"That will never happen," Marla said firmly. "You'll always be our daughter. You and Stella are a part of our lives, and nothing will ever change that. I won't allow it, and Jim won't either."

After I calmed down a bit and swallowed down some water, Jim resumed his questions. He scooted forward, elbows on his knees and fingers laced loosely together. "So, where is Brad right now?" he asked.

"He's at the apartment," I answered, nasally from all the crying.

"Is that where you're going when you leave here?" he continued, frowning.

I had to remember that Jim was an attorney and firing off questions rapidly was just his way of learning the details he deemed important. It also helped me focus and rein in any more emotions floating through me. His pointed questions were cutting right to the heart of the matter.

"Um... Brad said I needed to find somewhere else to live as of tonight since the apartment is in his name," I answered, not able to meet Jim's eyes.

"Bullshit!" Jim boomed. That made me and Marla both jump. His mouth was in a thin line, his brows snapped together, and his nostrils flared. The man seldom cursed or raised his voice so I knew he was furious. "Simone, you obviously don't know this, but that apartment is in our name not Brad's. We signed the lease two years ago as a favor to him—as a *reward*." He shook his head, almost to himself. The angry expression dissipated to one of disappointment, at himself, at the situation, or maybe at whatever else that was going through his mind. "Since you moved in, we've helped pay the rent several times because we didn't want you and Stella to be evicted. I'm going to call Brad right now, and let him know that he'll be the one vacating the apartment, and that he'd better be gone by tomorrow morning."

My first instinct was to not allow Jim to do anything that would upset Brad, and I almost pleaded with him to not say anything, but I realized, for the first time, Brad's feelings were no longer my concern. He was on his own. At the same time, I didn't want to create a divide in which Marla or Jim had to pick sides. Brad was their son, their flesh and blood, and I couldn't blame them if *their* instinct was to protect him, no matter what. "If you're sure..." I said, taking a deep, unsteady breath. "You don't have to do that, Jim. I appreciate the gesture, though."

"I won't have my granddaughter uprooted from her home like this. He can move out. I'm sure he has *somewhere* to go," Jim said, grimly. "For tonight, you'll stay here."

I closed my eyes briefly. "Thank you..." I whispered, on the verge of tears again. There was nothing else I could say.

Once again Jim and Marla proved just how wonderful they were.

"Have you talked to an attorney yet?" Marla asked, tentatively.

This was the question I was worried about. I didn't want them to think Kyle was betraying them by helping me. I also didn't want to cause problems between Trent and Kyle. But this too wasn't something that I could keep secret forever.

"Yeah, I spoke with Kyle this morning, and he offered to help prepare the paperwork. I didn't know who else to ask," I said, still fretting about going to Kyle. "If it makes any of you uncomfortable I can find someone else —"

"I don't see a problem with that. Kyle is an excellent lawyer," Jim said, adamant. He stood up and walked over to me. He leaned over and kissed me on the top of my head, just like a loving father would do. It made me smile and he returned a gentle smile of his own. But then he grew serious. "I'm going to call Brad now. And by tomorrow, the apartment is yours and Stella's, okay? I'll even go over there before to make sure he's gone."

With that, Jim went back upstairs, probably to his study. I had no desire to hear any part of that conversation or whatever excuses Brad would make.

"Since you're staying here, why don't you head upstairs and take a bath or a nap?" Marla suggested. "Dinner will be ready in a couple hours so you should rest until then, or just have a moment to yourself. If Stella wakes up we'll take care of her."

We both got up and hugged once more at the bottom of the stairs before I walked up to the spare bedroom. I was extremely grateful that Stella and I both had a place to stay tonight. I set my purse at the end of the bed in the guestroom. A bath sounded heavenly. Before I could enter the attached bathroom, though, I heard a light knock on the door and welcomed whoever it was to come in.

"Here's a pair of pajamas," Marla said. "There are some spare toiletries in the bathroom. If you need anything else just holler."

I took the pajamas with a grateful smile. "Thanks again. And Marla, I'm really am sorry."

"You don't have anything to be sorry for, Simone, so please don't apologize," she returned. I could tell she was sad about the whole thing but understanding, too. She reached out and gave my hand a squeeze. "We love you very much and just want things to work out for you and Stella."

I'd really hit the jackpot in the in-law department.

As I was getting ready to enter the bathroom I heard my phone chime with a notification. I went back to my purse and dug out my phone, wondering who it could be now. I prayed it wasn't Brad messaging me about the apartment. The very thought of dealing with him right now made me positively ill. However, I was a little surprised when I saw who the message was from. I opened the text and read the message.

Kyle: *Just wanted to check on you.*

I sat down on the bed, warmed by his thoughtfulness. I got real lucky in the lawyer department, too. I texted him back immediately.

Me: *Thanks. I'm at Jim and Marla's. Just told them.*

Kyle: *How did that go?*

Me: *Well they aren't mad at me and they're letting me stay here tonight with Stella.*

Kyle: *I had no doubt they would be supportive. I'll have some documents ready tomorrow afternoon if you want to come by the office and review them.*

Me: *Sure, I can be there at 2. Will that work?*

Kyle: *See you then.*

After a long soak in the tub, I put on the pajamas, which didn't fit too badly considering I was curvier than Marla. I was about to put on the gold wedding band that I had set on the bathroom sink but ended up putting it in my purse. The band had never fit and I wasn't even sure it was real gold. I hadn't had a traditional engagement or wedding. We got married at City Hall with just Marla, Jim, and Trent there. I almost laughed when I remembered how no one had smiled or seemed happy during the brief ceremony or when Jim had taken everyone to a fancy restaurant downtown as an impromptu reception. It'd been the most anticlimactic event ever.

I made my way downstairs for dinner. Stella noticed me as soon as my feet hit the last step.

"Mama!" she shrieked and ran to me. Watching a toddler run was pretty comical, her arms and legs seemed to be completely out of sync.

"Hi, baby girl," I said as I scooped her up in my arms and kissed the side of her face. I carried her into the kitchen but stopped short when I saw Trent sitting at the island talking to his mother. Marla was at the stove, pulling a glass casserole dish of lasagna out of the oven. I knew Trent would find out about the divorce sooner rather than later. I certainly hadn't planned on seeing him tonight, though.

"Hey, Trent," I said, setting Stella on the counter but keeping my arms wrapped around her. I eyed him, wondering if Marla or Kyle had told him yet.

"Hi, Simone," Trent said, eyeing me back.

And I knew he knew. "Who told you?" I asked but I wasn't mad. Maybe I should have been, but I was actually okay with not having to break the news to anyone else.

"Mom was just filling me in on what was going on with that douchebag brother of mine," Trent said with a snort.

"Language!" Marla warned him.

"Sorry, Mom," Trent said in a tone that didn't sound the least bit contrite. He looked over at me. "I kind of found out on my own this afternoon when Kyle was filling out some documents… It's a small firm and both Addie and Kyle were acting odd, so I already knew something was up." He gave me a sheepish smile. "Kyle gave me a brief explanation before I headed over here." He paused, drumming his fingers against the countertop as he made faces at Stella, who found it hysterical. "You know, you could've asked me…"

I walked over to Trent and gave him a hug. I think I surprised him but he returned the gesture with a hug of his own. If I could describe the perfect big brother, Trent would be it. I let him go and shook my head. "This is already super awkward," I said to him, "there was no way I was putting you in the middle. It's nice to know you were willing to help, but I couldn't ask that of you."

"All right enough talk about this for now, let's eat," Jim

suggested, walking into the kitchen.

I didn't ask how his conversation with Brad went as we walked into the dining room. Instead, I took my seat next to Stella and we talked about everything other than the divorce for the remainder of dinner. I enjoyed sharing a meal with the people I'd considered family. I hoped that things would remain this comfortable between all of us.

*****

The next morning the smell of bacon and coffee woke me up. I picked up my phone to check the time and panicked a little when I saw that it was just past eight. Stella must have been up already and I was relieved when I saw Jim at the table eating breakfast with her.

After breakfast, Jim informed me that he was going to meet with Brad later to continue their 'discussion' from last night. I just nodded and didn't inquire further.

Even though I didn't want to, I called up Kayla after I'd gotten dressed, and asked to swap shifts since I knew she didn't usually work Tuesday nights. I'd given her a brief rundown of the past couple of days, and her response, like Jim's and Marla's, was nothing but supportive. Another wave of relief washed over me and I felt even stronger about my decision. After breakfast, Stella and I ran a few errands, picking up a few things for myself, and then we had a quick lunch with Marla. I had bought some slacks and a nice businesslike top while we were out and put them on. I wanted to look professional for my meeting with Kyle. I left Stella with Marla, since Jim had not yet returned. Once I arrived at the office, I greeted Linda, who called Kyle to let him know I was here. I was terrified and yet, calm because I knew without a doubt that this was the right thing for Stella and me.

While I was waiting for Kyle, I saw Addie walk through the office. She stopped when she saw me and abandoned whatever she had been doing and headed my way.

"Hi, Simone," she said with a smile on her face.

I smiled in return. "Hey…"

"I hope you don't mind but Kyle told me why the two of you met for lunch yesterday. I'm really sorry you are going through this," Addie said, heartfelt.

When we had talked a week and a half ago, I'd believed her when she said she didn't have any bad feelings toward me. Seeing her today just reinforced that she meant every word. I didn't know how she managed to be so nice, but she was. I'm not sure I would be so kind to the woman that my fiancé had cheated on me with.

"It's fine," I told her, squeezing her hand. She squeezed back. "And thank you, for your words…"

"Simone?" I heard Kyle call from next to the reception desk.

I stood up, Addie taking her leave as I stared at my lawyer. Kyle had been in nice slacks and a plain white button-down shirt when we'd met at the diner yesterday; but today, he was in a suit, with a tie, the shirt underneath was light blue with thin, white pinstripes. He looked like a powerful and well-to-do businessman—or something out of a fashion magazine. His bright green eyes, his captivating smile, and focused gaze had me a little flustered. I hated that I couldn't get my mouth to work and say something as basic as 'hello' but I couldn't. I about died when Linda smiled, eyeing her boss then me.

Linda covered for me and cleared her throat, drawing Kyle's intense gaze away from me so I could actually breathe. "I'll be sure to hold all calls until further notice," she said, smiling at me, "or direct them to Trent."

Kyle nodded, then looked back at me. "Why don't you come on back so we can get started."

I nodded, gave him a brief smile, and silently followed him into his office. Those dreaded butterflies fluttered in my stomach and I tried to ease my anxieties by smoothing out the non-existent wrinkles from my blouse.

For the next hour he explained the whole divorce process for California residents in detail. Brad and I didn't have much in the way of assets so division of property wasn't going to be difficult. He told me that based on the length of our marriage and our income, I probably wouldn't receive spousal support.

"We need to figure out what you want to ask for in relation to custody of Stella. Is there any reason you and Brad might not have joint custody?" Kyle asked. He had his glasses on, and was writing things down on his legal pad. His professional demeanor helped set the tone of the meeting and aided in me focusing on the discussion and not the man sitting in front of me.

I had to think of what I wanted to say before I could answer him. Honestly, Brad was not a very hands-on father. He didn't spend much time with our daughter unless I nagged him about it. Sure, he was with her while I was at work on occasion, but that's all he did. He didn't interact with her. If those had been my only complaints I may have been open to the idea of joint custody. However, the events from two nights ago kept playing through my mind. There had been cocaine on my nightstand. If Brad was using drugs there was no way I was okay with sharing custody with him.

And since he never seemed to have money, despite learning that Marla and Jim assisted him with the rent, God only knew how much he spent on drugs or other vices I didn't know about. I didn't even want to think about the possibility of him wasting money on his girlfriends.

"Um…" I started, biting my lip. "The other night when I caught Brad with Tiffany, there was something I didn't tell you." I was hesitant to voice these details out loud, even though I knew it was the right thing to do. I hadn't shared this with anyone yet. "They had been using cocaine together. He said it was a one-time thing, but I'm not sure he was telling the truth. Stella was there in the apartment with him."

The fact that Brad and I had experimented together one night a couple years ago made me feel hypocritical using this against him. At the same time, Stella had not been in the picture and I couldn't get past the fact that he had been using while he was responsible for our daughter.

"What?" Kyle asked, exasperated and his face getting red with anger. I was a bit surprised to see his intense reaction.

"I'm not sure how long he's being doing drugs, or if it's a recent thing…" I trailed off, trying to be as fair as I could. Brad didn't deserve my consideration but I was, however, trying to avoid any prolonged battle and I knew Brad well enough that not upsetting him was key to getting his cooperation. I knew I'd have to concede some things, even if my lawyer said otherwise. I had never been this decisive in my life, but for once, I knew what I wanted and how to do it. I only thought of Stella and that gave me a lot of strength.

I heard Kyle mutter something under his breath that sounded a lot like "motherfucker." He leaned back and ran a hand through his hair, musing it up. "We can ask that he submit to a drug test before determining custody. He could also agree to supervised visits, which could mean Jim or Marla being with him when he has Stella. Do you think he will fight you on full custody?" he asked.

"Honestly, I don't know," I said, shifting in my seat. "He isn't an active father, but I could see him doing something just to be vindictive. He isn't the nicest person to deal with when he feels attacked."

Kyle placed his glasses on the desk and rubbed his temples with his fingers. "Simone, has he ever been abusive towards you, or Stella?" he asked again, bluntly. "I know I asked you yesterday if he's ever hurt you, but that isn't the only way someone can be abusive. I heard the way he was talking to you at Jim's birthday party. Does he do that a lot?"

Not able to answer him with words, I looked down and just nodded my head. I was embarrassed that a man who seemed to have his shit together saw me in such a vulnerable position. That he might think I was weak, that he might really believe I was to blame for this whole mess but was too kind to say otherwise. If I entertained thoughts like that, I knew others had too.

"I don't want to overstep, but talking with someone, a professional, might be beneficial. You've been through a lot. I could give you a recommendation."

Kyle was right. Talking to someone probably wasn't a bad idea. "I think I'd like that," I responded, grateful for his continued concern.

He reached over and handed me a business card. "Well, I believe we have enough to get started," Kyle said, smiling encouragingly at me. "Based on what we've discussed, I don't think the judge is going to have a problem with requesting a drug test and he'll probably require some parenting classes for Brad."

"Thank you again for all your help," I said, knowing I sounded like a broken record at this point. It was all so overwhelming and I was still waiting for something to go screwy. I got up and gathered my purse. Kyle got up as well and walked around his desk. Before he opened the door for me, I looked up at him, placing a hand on his chest. "There is no way I could've figured this all out on my own, Kyle. You have no idea just how grateful I am that you're on my side."

He smiled, placing his hand over mine and pressing it into his chest. "It's no trouble at all." He paused, his eyes searching my face. "I'm going to be with you every step of the way," Kyle promised. "You can count on me, I swear it."

I nodded, slowly removing my hand. His fingers flexed around mine before he dropped his hand and opened the door. When I walked to my car my step was a little lighter, less burdened. I knew Kyle would keep his promises, and that, too, gave me strength.

Chapter 8

Kyle

May flew by. Simone had served Brad with the divorce papers without incident and things seemed to be moving forward quickly.

From what we could tell, Brad had moved in with Tiffany, who Erik had fired immediately when he found out about the affair. Erik had kept Brad on at his shop, knowing that he would be forced to pay child support. Erik didn't want to hurt Simone by firing him but it was clear that it was not going to last. Erik no longer hid his contempt for the bastard and Brad rarely even showed up for his shifts.

Simone and I had spent a majority of the last month focusing on what she wanted to ask for in regards to custody. We usually met in my office, or her apartment if she couldn't get away because of Stella.

So far, Brad wasn't asking for anything. Maybe he'd felt relieved that he no longer needed to go through the motions of pretending to be a husband and father. He probably thought he had held up his end of the bargain, and if Simone wanted a divorce, that was on her. For Simone's sake, I hoped that things would continue to remain peaceful. However, knowing Brad the way I did, I wasn't holding my breath.

By mid-June, Simone seemed more than comfortable with the idea of no longer being married to Brad. In fact, I could see she walked a little lighter and smiled more. Not to say it was smooth sailing or going to be. She still worried about Stella's adjustment, but there seemed to be no obvious or outward damage done. Stella was perfectly content and never asked for Brad. That would change, as she got older, but we were all glad she was coping.

The true test would come when we all met next Monday to discuss the Marital Settlement Agreement. Brad was representing himself instead of hiring a lawyer. While I preferred to discuss this matter with another attorney and a mediator present, Brad had indicated he just wanted to get it done. I'd asked Jim to sit in on the meeting as a witness to the discussion and to act as a buffer in case things got heated.

As I was going over my calendar for the next few weeks, my eyes landed on tomorrow's date. I had spent the entire week throwing myself into my work so it'd snuck up on me. While I normally took my work seriously and did a damn good job, I also knew how to balance it with other aspects of my life. I made time for the things that I enjoyed: working out, spending time with friends and family, and doing small things that helped me unwind and relax. But tomorrow was a day I dreaded every year.

June seventeenth always brought up horrible memories, things I would rather shove to the dark corners of my mind where I didn't have to think about it or deal with them. Unfortunately, I wasn't the only one with those memories and I knew Addie would want to talk about it. It was easy to ignore the day while she had been living in San Francisco. Sure, she called me and tried to talk, but I was able to distract myself with other things. I just needed to throw a couple "yeahs" and "okays" into the conversation till she was done. But now that she was here it was going to be harder to avoid.

But what was there really to say on the anniversary of your mother's fatal overdose? I had been there. Hell, I was the one who had found her. Why did we need to talk about it? It was the final way for her to show us that she chose drugs over her own children. I stared out my office window reliving that moment...

We were staying with our mom for a couple days in the small, one-bedroom apartment she had recently moved into. Being a typical sixteen-year-old boy, I got bored quickly. That morning, I begged her to let Addie and me go to Trent's house so we could go swimming. It was an unusually hot summer and a morning spent swimming in the Thompsons' pool sounded like a lot of fun.

On our way home, Addie and I had decided to race each other for the last few blocks and I was a bit ahead of her. I pushed the door open and slammed it closed behind me.

"Hey, mom, we're home," I yelled in the direction of her bedroom. I was met with silence, which I thought was odd since I'd passed her car on the way in. "Mom?" I called out again as I walked down the small hallway toward her bedroom. I could hear a soap opera playing on the television in her room and I almost turned back around to go to the kitchen, but something on the floor caught my eye. My mom's foot was poking out from beside her bed.

I heard the front door open, Addie finally making her way in. "One day, I'm going to beat you," she shouted from the living room.

Her words didn't register with me as I walked slowly to the other side of my mom's bed. My legs felt like lead and I could hardly get one foot in front of the other. I knew what I was going to find but my body was rebelling against me, hindering my attempt to reach her. When I finally rounded the corner of her bed, I saw my mother, lying face down on the floor.

"Kyle? Where are you?" Addie shouted, still in the living room.

"Addie, call 9-1-1!" I instructed. I sounded totally calm but I

was freaking out on the inside.

"What?! Why?!" she screamed and I could hear her footsteps coming down the hall.

"Don't come in here! Just go call. Tell them Mom's unconscious."

"Oh, my God," she whimpered.

"Do it now!" I had never yelled at Addie before, but I needed her to listen to me. I reached out to roll my mom onto her back but when my hands touched her body, she felt ice-cold. I knew in that moment we had lost her. She had promised me just the night before that she was clean and I'd believed her wholeheartedly. I was so stupid to have trusted her.

The next couple of hours were filled with law enforcement and the coroner coming and going from the apartment. Our grandmother had rushed right over to get us.

Grandma and Addie spent the rest of the night comforting each other. One having lost a mother, the other having lost a daughter. They were both so distraught. Me? I was pissed. How many times had we asked Mom to get some help? Every time we found her with drugs she would always have an excuse; they weren't hers, it was just a one-time thing, she would get help. It went on and on. And now she was gone —

Unlike Addie, who wanted to reflect on the day, every year, by talking about it, I preferred to ignore it.

I turned back around and saw Addie standing in my office doorway, staring at me. It was like she knew what I had been thinking about. Her eyes looked sad. I didn't want her pity. She could spend tomorrow doing whatever she wanted to memorialize our mom, but I was over it.

"What do you want, Addie?" I huffed not making any attempt to disguise my irritation. Not one to ever be deterred by my bad mood, she walked around my desk and planted herself on the corner, crossing her legs and arms.

"Hey, no need to be testy with me. I just wanted to invite you out for lunch tomorrow." She tried to make her invitation sound innocent. I knew what she was up to, though.

"I have plans," I stated dryly, and turned my attention back to my computer. I was determined to treat tomorrow like any other day.

"You know, pretending that Mom's death didn't have an impact on you doesn't mean that it didn't. You tell everyone you're fine, but every year at this time you act like a surly asshole," she stated.

"Stop!" I said, putting my hand up. "I act like an asshole because everyone expects me to be sad or talk about what happened. If it makes you or other people feel better — great. Really. But it doesn't help me. The facts remain the same." I paused, taking a breath. I wasn't mad at Addie, I just didn't want to do this anymore. "She died, it sucked. It sucked even more that I was the one who found her, but it's done. I don't need to talk about it or deal with it every year. Nothing I do now will ever change what happened back then," I groaned. Rubbing my temples, I finally looked up and met my sister's gaze. She looked pissed.

"You may think it's done but it's not and it won't be until you finally deal with it. You don't come out of a childhood like ours completely unscathed," she said, placing her hand on my shoulder. "Mom and Dad were poor examples of a healthy relationship, and the way they forgot about us has closed you off to certain things. We've both worked hard at not being anything like either one of our parents. I think we've done a great job, but that doesn't mean it doesn't affect how we see and interact with other people. I know how you are, and you can't live a life where Trent, Erik, Ian, and I are the only people you trust."

"I trust Jim and Marla, too," I joked, hoping to distract myself from the truth my baby sister was throwing at me.

"You know what I mean," she said, not letting it go. "I just want you to live life happily, without worrying about when things will go wrong."

I sighed, throwing my glasses on my desk. "What's that supposed to mean?" I asked, trying to not sound annoyed but Addie was making that tough. "Live life happily? Who says I'm unhappy?" I didn't feel like I was at all. I had a great life. Wonderful friends, a great sister —most of the time, and a job I loved. What more could I ask for? I was getting more irritated by the second. "And I don't 'worry about when things will go wrong', or whatever you meant by that."

It was Addie's turn to sigh loudly. "Outside of your small circle of trust, you've kept yourself insolated. You don't attempt to make new relationships," she said, almost accusingly.

"And your point?" I drawled, bemused.

"When's the last time you had an actual relationship with a woman?"

I rolled my eyes. "You, Marla, and now Simone and Stella."

"I mean, romantically, smartass," she interrupted and poked me in the arm. "Before anything meaningful can develop, you bail."

"Are you dating?" I asked, turning the tables on her.

She wagged a finger at me. "Nice try, but my situation is different from yours. My trust issues aren't rooted in my childhood, or even Brad's betrayal —"

"What if I want to be a bachelor for the rest of my life?" I scoffed, shaking my head.

"Why'd you buy that huge four-bedroom house?" she shot back, then smiled gleefully when I had no answer.

Gah! My sister was infuriating sometimes. "Look, it's not that I don't want a relationship that eventually turns into something more — "

"Exactly! Subconsciously, you do want to have a family, but you can't commit and you don't allow yourself to even try."

"Maybe I haven't met the woman worth trying for?" I piped up, exasperated.

She gave a soft snort. "When have you ever taken a risk on anyone or anything...?"

I wanted to ignore everything she had said but, of course, she had a point when it came to my past. I hadn't really dealt with our dad leaving and our mom dying. It was easier to just live in the present. Maybe Addie was right. I knew deep down that my issues with my parents kept me from pursuing meaningful relationships.

Truthfully, if what had happened to Addie in her relationship with Brad had happened to me, I know for a fact my reaction would have been a lot worse than hers. I would have let that betrayal in and allowed it consume me, and eventually destroy me. Addie had been devastated but she'd weathered that moment and chose to not let it rule her life. I knew that her concept and understanding about relationships, in general, was likely a lot more realistic and open than my idea of it. I just had a very difficult time seeing things her way.

What if I wasn't as different from my dad as I wanted to

believe? What if I put my trust in someone and they lied to me repeatedly like my mom had? Or left me when I thought I could rely on them, and had truly believed they'd be there for me, no matter what? Addie was right. Our parents' actions had done a number on me and they'd shaped who I was now. I was afraid to let anyone in and give them the chance to damage me even more. I wasn't sure I'd be able to go through that again, and survive.

*****

After the intense conversation with Addie, I needed to get out of the office. Luckily I had told Simone that I would stop by her apartment to discuss the Marital Settlement Agreement. The informal meeting hadn't taken long, just an hour. I had planned on leaving after we'd gone over the details, but Simone wanted to take Stella out to play. It was sunny, hardly a breeze, and the best weather we'd had in days. She'd invited me to join them and I couldn't say no. So I didn't.

I walked the few blocks with the girls to the park and found a bench by the large playground area. It was a popular spot and pretty busy. Parents drank from coffee mugs and idly watched over their kids while chatting it up with the neighbors.

I watched Stella for a few minutes. "She seems happy," I noted and glanced over at Simone, sitting on my right.

"She is, she really is..." Simone smiled softly toward her daughter, who was playing in the sandbox with a couple other toddlers.

I dug into my messenger bag and took out my phone to

take a few pictures of her playing. I wasn't one to take constant photos of myself or document everything I did on social media. In fact, I barely had a footprint on the Internet, but I couldn't deny myself a selfie of Simone and me, which she agreed to with a charming laugh. I had an urge to analyze the picture of us but refrained, just barely. I leaned back and just enjoyed the morning and the lovely company.

She turned slightly toward me after a couple seconds, a hand on my arm. "Kyle, I wanted to thank you for recommending Dr. Hamilton. I don't think I've told you how much I appreciate you suggesting therapy. She's been really great and has helped me a lot this past month. I knew I had issues about my past and my childhood but... she's been amazing."

I wrapped my free hand over hers and smiled. "Of course. Stephanie works with the courts quite often and she's an excellent therapist."

Some flicker of emotion crossed Simone's face before she looked down then back at me. "Stephanie...?" She paused. "*Oh.* Dr. Hamilton's name... You two are... close?" she asked, her voice guarded.

"We're friends," I told her, glancing around the playground.

"You two dated, huh?"

That question threw me. Since I took Simone on as my client, we've had face-to-face visits on an almost weekly basis and had each other's full contact info. We'd texted quite often—not all business-related, sure, but we've kept our conversations... safe. What details we'd learned about each other was volunteered, not asked.

She's never really asked anything *personal* directly. Until now. We were still at that awkward phase of getting to know one another on a more intimate level so there was a lot of hesitation that we both felt and hadn't fully discussed head-on. I didn't want to push her by being too invasive and I think she felt the same, though I hoped that wouldn't always be the case. The complications of our pasts certainly didn't help, but I genuinely liked Simone and admired her inner strength. And I liked the fact she felt comfortable enough to ask me anything that was on her mind, personal or not.

"A little," I admitted, "but we were better suited as colleagues."

"Oh."

That one little word made me frown. What did that mean? And her expression and tone of voice alerted me that something was off. That I'd said the wrong thing. When she removed her hand and sat back, I immediately felt a distance from her that I didn't like at all. "Is something—"

"Well, thank you for the recommendation," she interrupted softly. Her hands were in her lap, fingers fidgeting with the soft-looking fabric of her dress.

I stared at her profile, my eyes traveling to her mouth, the curve of her cheek and jaw, then lower, down her throat, the rise and fall of her chest... She was wearing a low-cut spring dress that hugged her body, and since I first saw her at the apartment two hours ago, it had left my mind racing with inappropriate thoughts. I forced my gaze off her entirely and shifted uneasily in my seat. I was in a plain white tee and jeans, but I felt like I was wearing more based on how I was starting to sweat.

"Sure, no problem. So, ah... did you have any other questions about the MSA?" I started, clearing my throat. Talking about work helped me keep my thoughts clean.

Just then, an older couple approached our bench. "You mind?" the older man asked, a little red in the face. "Wifey's a little winded from the grandkids and this bench is closest for us to keep an eye on 'em."

"Oh! Yes, please, sit," Simone urged. She scooted toward me. I lifted my right arm and settled it along the back of the bench. I'd already been sitting near the edge but the other couple took up a lot of space. Simone was pressed into my body like she'd been glued there.

I wasn't complaining that her hand was now on my thigh to help her balance, and it was damn near killing me. I settled my messenger bag in my lap so I didn't have someone calling the cops on me.

"I'm Kurt and this is Cindy." The gentleman introduced himself and his wife as we did the same.

"Which ones are yours?" Simone asked.

Kurt pointed to three boys, the oldest not looking more than ten years old. "Got the grandbabies for the weekend," he said with pride, using his pageboy hat to fan himself.

His wife smiled on. She didn't look remotely winded but glanced at the two of us with a twinkle in her eyes. "Which one is yours?" she repeated back.

Simone tensed slightly but I answered first. I pointed to the sandbox. "Stella. She's in the white hat and blue dress."

Kurt and Cindy 'oohed and awed' appropriately and it made me chuckle a little. Just then Stella had joined in a game of tag and appeared to be having a blast. We all laughed when the other toddlers started chasing her while giggling and shrieking.

"So precious..." Cindy said on a sigh and looked between Simone and me. "Your daughter is beautiful."

"Thank you," Simone murmured.

"Wish I could say I had something to do with that, but it was all Simone here," I told the older couple.

Simone looked up at me, a questioning expression on her face as I looked down at her.

"You okay, sweetheart?" I asked, winking at her. My fingers played with the ends of her long hair.

"Uh-huh," she said, sounding a little winded herself. "You?"

I smiled. "Couldn't be better…"

*****

On our way back to Simone's apartment, Stella asleep in her stroller, we were both quiet, contemplative, and in our own heads. I was looking at my phone, reviewing the pictures of me and Simone, Simone and Stella, me and Stella—all of which made me grin like an idiot.

When she bumped her shoulder into my left arm, I looked over and smiled. "What's got you smiling like that?" she asked lightly. "A hot date or something?"

I laughed and reached out, placing my hand on the back of her neck and squeezing it gently. I liked how she relaxed into my touch now and no longer tensed. I didn't keep my hand there too long, though. "Dating… not really. At least, not lately," I started, dropping my hand but letting my fingertips trail the spot between her shoulder blades.

She shivered. "No?" she asked, sounding confused.

"Yeah, I know," I said dryly. "I date a lot but not as much

as Trent."

She snickered. "Uh-huh." She bumped into me again. "So what's got you hiding out from the female population?"

Again, I had to laugh at her teasing and how comfortable I felt around her. "I don't know… a lot of things, I guess." I paused. I couldn't tell her that lately she was the only woman I seemed to notice. Instead, I blurted out the other thought that was weighing heavily on my mind. "Tomorrow is the anniversary of my mom's death…" I said to her, rather bluntly surprising myself that I was sharing this information with her.

Simone gasped, stopping the stroller and facing me. "Kyle—I'm… so sorry," she whispered.

I shrugged. "It was a long time ago, Simone, but Addie said something earlier today… it made me think, reassess."

She gave me a hug, one that I savored and one that I missed when she let go. It was never long enough. She held my hand and looked up at me with sympathy in her pretty brown eyes. "Losing a parent is never easy. I know, believe me. If you ever need to talk about it, I'm here for you, okay?"

I didn't know why, but those words, from her hit me square in the chest. The look in her eyes, the sadness in her voice, her sympathy for what happened to me long ago… it tugged at me hard. I pulled her back in for another hug; emotional in ways I hadn't been since finding my mom's body. I swallowed the lump in my throat, and held Simone to me like she could somehow save me from my own demons. Demons I'd never acknowledged before and tried to sweep aside—and I was good at it. Her arms were around me, holding on just as firmly, and it was everything I needed in that moment.

145

Addie had asked what I'd ever risked?

The answer was 'nothing'.

Simone let me hold on, much longer than necessary, but it felt good and her presence was comforting. I really needed to stop touching her, I just couldn't help it. When I released her, some deep, dark part of me knew I'd risk anything when it came to her and Stella. I pushed that thought away as soon as it'd entered my mind because Simone saw me as a friend, her lawyer. After things were finalized, she wouldn't have any reason to need me. Knowing that kind of hurt.

"Thank you," I finally said at last, "I appreciate it, and I might take you up on that someday."

"Good," she said, sounding pleased. When Stella made a slight noise in her stroller, it broke the moment. It was a good kind of a break.

It allowed me to compose myself. "So, have you thought much of the future?" I asked, as we resumed our slow walk toward her apartment. "What you want to do?"

"I want to finish college," she said with certainty. "I'm trying to save up enough money so I can take a couple courses this fall." She frowned, and I could tell she was a little apprehensive about that plan. "I'm trying to get an online class and Marla offered to watch Stella a couple times a week if I have a regular class."

She hated to ask for help so I knew that's where her hesitancy stemmed from.

"That would be great. Have you decided what you want to major in?"

She nodded. "Yeah, early childhood education. I would love to teach kindergarten someday," she answered.

I loved learning new things about her. Simone was really

an exceptional woman and I was happy to see her working toward her dreams.

"What made you want to be a teacher?" I asked, wanting to know even more.

"Well, growing up the way I did, I never had much stability, but my teachers were the one constant in my life. A couple did the bare minimum to get through the day, but a majority of them truly cared about their students." She paused, the memories bringing a smile to her face. "The ones that took an interest in me made me feel like I could do anything I wanted, like I was worthy of something better. I want to be able to make the same kind of difference in the lives of other kids who might be struggling like I was."

"That's really amazing. I know any student of yours would be lucky to have a teacher like you," I said, hoping she heard the sincerity in my words.

She gave me a big smile then a sly look in my direction. "So. Why did you become a lawyer?" she asked, turning the tables on me.

I took a deep breath. I didn't often share personal things about myself but I liked that Simone was curious. "Honestly, I like being able to help people when they feel they're most vulnerable. A lot of my clients need to feel like someone is in their corner and I like to be that person for them. My mom went through a lot when my dad left. She started using drugs around that time. My grandmother told me she blamed the stress of the divorce for her turning to heroin. I never want anyone to feel that lost, that desperate. That's also why I volunteer at the recovery center on Second Street."

"I didn't know you volunteered there," she said with a look of surprise on her face. "I think that's a really great thing."

"When you mentioned Brad's possible substance abuse, it made me see red. I wanted to make sure you and Stella were protected," I said, choosing my words carefully. "I grew up with a drug addict. The damage that comes from that never completely goes away. I wouldn't want Stella to go through what I did."

When I looked back over to her I could see her eyes glassy with emotion. "Wow," I heard her mutter under her breath as she looked back down at the stroller.

I reached over to move the lock of hair that had fallen in her face behind her ear. "Are you okay?" I asked.

"I am. It's crazy that we had such similar upbringings. I'm lucky to have somebody in my life who can understand some of what I've been through," she said quietly but with feeling. "Makes me feel less alone."

"Yeah." It was all I could say since the emotion of our conversation was getting to me.

Before any more could be said, Stella started fussing again. By then, we were at her apartment. I followed them up the stairs, carrying the stroller, but I hung back at the door when we reached the top.

"Are you leaving?" Simone asked, holding Stella, who was rubbing her eyes still trying to wake up.

"Yeah, I've got a few more things to work on back at the office before I can start my weekend."

I couldn't help but notice the look of disappointment on her face. Was she upset that I was leaving? Did she enjoy spending time with me as much as I enjoyed spending time with her? I shook my head to get rid of those thoughts.

"I guess I'll see you Monday at our meeting," she said,

standing on her toes to plant a kiss on my cheek.

At least I think that was the spot she'd been aiming for, but I turned my head at the same time, and her lips landed on the corner of my mouth instead. Because I was still turning my head, my lips brushed against hers. She jerked back, startling Stella, her face turning pink in an instant. Lips tingling, I stared at her mouth then away and when I looked back, Simone's eyes had lowered, staring at the ground.

"Thank you for this morning," she said, her voice shaky, and she wouldn't look at me, "for everything you're doing for Stella and me."

"Um, I... yeah... I-I'll see you next week," I stuttered like an idiot, still feeling her lips on my skin, everywhere. "Call or text if anything... for anything..."

"Okay, bye, Kyle. Thanks again for going over the settlement with me," she said, finally lifting her eyes and meeting mine. There was always a moment when we were together that I felt a deep connection with Simone, and it appeared to be getting stronger the more we saw each other. Did she sense that connection, too, or was it all in my head? And why did my thoughts keep going to places that I had no right to think about?

"Bye, Simone. Bye, Stella," I said, receiving a smile from the little one.

When I got into my car, I tried to focus on anything other than the way I felt when I was alone with Simone. How could two hours feel so good, so right? I rested my head back, heart beating fast and hard in my chest. We still had a couple more months before all this was over and done with. I had a feeling they were going to be a longest months of my life.

*****

Surf, pizza, beer, and the San Diego Padres' game were on today's agenda, but my thoughts kept going back to Simone. Always back to her. This entire weekend, I'd been wrestling with something I could no longer deny.

I had it pretty bad for Simone.

Since Friday, all I could think about was her; our time at the playground, her mouth, pretty much everything about her. I couldn't lie to myself about what I was feeling anymore. It was a fact, and the sooner I realized that, the easier I could deal with it without causing any damage. How I could reconcile that fact and still act as her lawyer was going to be torture. I also wasn't entirely sure about Simone's feelings. She was going through a lot and relying on me. I didn't want to mistake her behavior for something it wasn't and ruin a real friendship with her, if that was still in the cards.

"Checked out the waves on the drive over here. They look freakin' awesome, should be a good day," Erik stated as we walked down to the water, his surfboard under his arm.

Erik was right. The waves were perfect. Trent and I were on either side of him as we assessed the packed beach, ocean, and ideal weather.

"I checked out the chicks; they looked awesome, too," Trent added with a smirk.

I had to laugh. His carefree attitude and running commentary pulled me out of my head and into the present. As much as Trent didn't want a relationship, he sure couldn't go long without the company of a woman.

"Dude, we're surfing today, not looking to score with

random women." I didn't know why I said that. I was usually right there with Trent, but I hadn't felt the desire for a random hookup in weeks. Longer than that, actually, going on several months. I didn't dwell on that particular thought.

"Can't we do both?" Trent teased back, but thankfully, he let the subject drop.

Erik shot me a sidelong glance, which I easily ignored. To avoid any more discussion, I took off toward the waves, Trent shouting his surprise and Erik's laughter at my back.

We spent the next couple hours in the water. There was nothing like a little ocean therapy to put things in perspective. Once we were finished, we headed back to my house and ordered some pizzas. I turned on the big screen TV while we ate.

"Nervous about tomorrow's meeting with Brad?" Trent asked around a bite of his pizza.

"Not really," I said, opening a round of beers for the three of us and placing them on the coffee table.

"I saw Simone at my parents' house yesterday," Trent added. "She seemed pretty stressed."

That comment bummed me out. I didn't want Simone to feel stressed. I wanted her to feel confident that I would get her through this process. I hadn't exchanged any words with her since Friday, which felt like an eternity. I'd stopped myself a dozen times from just sending an innocuous message. "Huh, I'll text her later to make sure she's good for tomorrow," I said, the words just slipping out. I paused, throwing a look Trent's way, but he was engrossed in the game.

Erik, however, was eyeing me suspiciously again. We'd

never discussed what he saw at Jim's birthday party—not that it was necessary since nothing happened that day. Besides, Simone and I had become friends—of sorts.

"That's probably a good idea. She might have some last minute questions about what to expect tomorrow," Trent finally said at a commercial break and nodded at me approvingly. Thankfully, he saw my comment exactly as it was, a lawyer helping out their client. "Be right back, I gotta pee," he announced, hopping off the couch and disappearing into the bathroom down the hallway.

As soon as the door closed behind him, Erik turned toward me and quietly asked, "What the hell is going on with you and Simone?"

While I had been expecting this question, I still didn't know what to say. I took a sip of my beer, giving myself a couple seconds before I answered him. "I don't know what you're talking about. In case you've forgotten, I'm her attorney and helping her with her divorce."

"Oh, so you hug all your clients like that?" he asked. His stupid, cheeky grin was pissing me off.

"At the time, she wasn't my client, and if you had heard the way Brad was talking to her, you would have done the same thing," I said, gritting my teeth. But as soon as I said it, the visual of Erik holding Simone entered my mind, and suddenly, I wanted to punch my friend in his face. He must have seen my balled fists resting on my thighs and decided not to push any further.

"Hmm, you're probably right," he said, although the look he gave me told me he wasn't buying my story. He then changed the subject to some race he had coming up.

The rest of the evening was spent talking shit and watching the game. The guys left my place around seven and I headed to the kitchen to clean up. I saw my phone lying on the counter and decided to text Simone before it got too late.

Me: *Hi there. Just checking in and hoping you're not too stressed about tomorrow.*

I continued to tidy up around the house, waiting for a response. I'd be lying if I said I didn't check my phone a couple times to make sure I hadn't missed her response.

Around nine, I headed upstairs to my room, grabbing my laptop from my bag that I kept next to the staircase. I usually checked my emails each night before I went to bed and I wanted to review the MSA I had prepared to ensure I had covered everything. I wasn't going to give Brad any room to get out of his responsibilities.

I was just about to close my laptop and turn off my bedside lamp when I heard my phone chime. I grabbed it off my nightstand, feeling relieved that she had finally texted me back.

Simone: *Sorry for texting so late. I just got home from picking up Stella. I worked until nine.*

Me: *How was work?*

Simone: *It was fine but slow.*

Me: *Are you feeling okay about tomorrow? I don't want you to worry. I have everything under control.*

Simone: *I'm nervous about sitting in the same room with Brad, but I have this awesome lawyer that I know will take care of everything. :)*

Her confidence in me was definitely an ego boost, and was there a flirtatious tone in her text? Or was that just Simone being Simone and I was finally seeing that side of her? Or... Shit, I never got all worked up over a damn text.

Me: *He sounds pretty great. LOL*

Simone: *He is...*

Great, now I was trying to text-flirt but I couldn't wipe the grin from my face. I'm sure I looked like an idiot staring at my phone but I didn't care. Alone in my house, and no one to judge me, I could indulge in a little fantasy—I just had to be careful, and not get caught up in something that would likely never be...

*****

The next morning in the office was tense. Jim and Brad were already seated and it was just Simone and me standing outside the conference room. I looked at Simone. Her eyes were wide as she stared at the closed door, and I could see her hands trembling.

"Hey, look at me?" I instructed softly while lifting her chin with my finger. "The worst thing that can happen today is we walk out of that room without an agreement. He's in no position to fight you on anything." I started to open the door. "Okay?"

"Okay," she repeated softly, and followed me into the conference room.

When we walked in, we saw Brad sitting on the far side of the long oak table, while Jim was seated at the head of the table. I pulled out a chair for Simone to sit to Jim's right and then I sat down on the other side of her.

"Hello, Brad," I greeted as professionally as possible. I couldn't let my emotions get the best of me in this situation. But frankly, I was disgusted by the fact that he hadn't even tried to look presentable and I could see the anger and disappointment on Jim's face. Brad looked like he'd just rolled out of bed and was on his phone, not acknowledging anyone. "Thank you for meeting with us. We're hoping we can sign this agreement today to help avoid any court battles—"

"Whatever," he interrupted, leaning back in his chair. His arms were folded across his chest and he looked bored and annoyed, like this meeting was beneath him and a complete waste of his time. "Can we just sign it and be done already?"

Needless to say, from his sneering and contemptuous expression and snarky commentary throughout the meeting, I could feel Simone's stress like it was a SOS beacon. Brad signed the papers without even looking at them and barely allowed me to go over some of the more important details, constantly telling me to hurry up. At the end, when Simone asked Brad about seeing Stella, things really blew up.

"I have plans this weekend," he stated emphatically, getting up from his seat and taking a step toward the door.

"Unbelievable!" she shouted, throwing her hands up in the air. Her outburst surprised both Jim and me, but I couldn't blame Simone for her reaction. "What could possibly be more important than seeing your daughter? How can you just abandon her?" I could hear her voice breaking. She had come to terms with Brad never fulfilling the role of husband, but she desperately wanted him to be a father to his little girl.

"Fuck you, Simone! The great thing about getting divorced is I don't have to answer to you." And with that, he left the room, slamming the door behind him.

"Excuse me, I just need a moment," she said and I could see the tears falling down her face. She left the room and turned down the hall toward the restroom.

I glanced at Jim. He had his hands clasped on the table in front of him and was staring down at his shoes. I couldn't imagine what he was feeling. As Brad's father, he probably wanted to believe his youngest son was a better person than that, but as Stella's grandfather, he must have been extremely disappointed.

Knowing there wasn't much to say, I exited the room quietly, gently clasping his shoulder as I passed by. I was approaching my office when I heard quiet voices and soft sobs coming from the break room. Curiosity getting the better of me, I walked over to the doorway. Inside, I saw Simone and Addie sitting close together trying to keep their voices low.

"My marriage was complete bullshit, but I tried to stick it out for Stella. Now he can't even make time for her. He's a total asshole," Simone said, between deep breaths.

"You won't get an argument from me on that one," Addie quipped. "You know, if you need anyone to talk to you can come to me..."

I decided to give the two of them some privacy and went back to my office before either noticed me. It pleased me to see Addie continually reaching out to Simone. I knew she had a close work friend, but Simone could definitely use a friend who understood the whole history of the situation, Addie was great at being there when you needed her.

And while their budding friendship was a good thing, I couldn't help but want Simone to confide in me. For me to be the one she turned to.

Chapter 9

Simone

*I*t was a warm August morning and I was driving home from registering for two courses at Beachside Community College. Talking about it with Kyle had stuck with me since he was so encouraging of me pursing my degree. One of the classes I registered for was online. The other required me to be in class a couple times a week, but Marla had agreed to watch Stella for me. I was extremely grateful for the continued help. However, I didn't want to take advantage of their kindness.

In fact, in an effort to prove to myself I could do this without being a burden on anyone, I had taken Stella with me to the counseling office. She had been so well behaved, I promised her a surprise on the way home, which was why we were now pulling into the parking lot of the ice cream parlor.

"Ice cream!" she exclaimed from the backseat. "I want chocolate." Stella was turning two years old in ten days, and I was constantly amazed by how quickly her vocabulary was growing.

"What do we say?" I asked, gently reminding her to use her manners.

"I want chocolate, pleeeease," she said.

We went inside, and once Stella saw all the choices, she decided chocolate wasn't for her and chose rainbow sherbet instead. Knowing how slow she ate and how messy she could be, I asked the teenager working behind the counter to put hers in a cup and I ordered a scoop of cookie dough, also in a cup, for myself.

We sat down inside and dug in to our treat. "Is your ice cream good?" I asked, and laughed at the fact that she had the same amount of ice cream around her mouth as she had managed to get in it.

"Yes, thank you, mama," she replied and flashed me a huge cheesy grin. Man, I loved this little girl more than I ever thought it was possible to love another person. She was my entire world and small moments like this brought me unexplainable joy.

We finished eating and I dug out a baby wipe from my bag so I could clean her up. Once she was no longer a sticky mess, we walked out to my car. I got her buckled in and sat in the driver's seat. Placing the key in the ignition, I turned it only to hear a clicking noise instead of the engine turning on. I tried it again with the same result.

"Crap," I muttered under my breath, not wanting Stella to repeat the word. I had just spent all the money I had managed to save on college courses and knew I wouldn't be able to afford costly car repairs right now.

I pulled my phone out of my purse to call Trent. I hated to bother him, but Jim and Marla were out of town for a couple days and I really didn't have anyone else to call. Brad would know how to fix whatever was wrong, but I knew he wouldn't bother to come help. I probably couldn't get ahold of him if I tried.

"Hey, Simone, how's it going?" Trent answered on the second ring.

"Hi, Trent," I started. "I really hate to bother you, but I'm stuck at Harry's Ice Cream shop on Bay Street and my car won't start. I wouldn't have called, but I have Stella with me."

"Oh man, I'm getting ready to head over to the courthouse. Ya know, Kyle's here and I think he's free. I'll send him over to help you out," he said.

I knew he was trying to be helpful, but calling Trent for help had been difficult enough. There was no way I could ask Kyle to leave work to come all the way out here.

"No, don't worry about it. I'll call a tow truck," I said, even though I really couldn't afford it.

"Don't be silly. Hold on. Hey, Kyle!" I could hear Trent shout, even though it seemed like he tried to cover the receiver. "Can you go help Simone? She's having some car trouble." A few moments passed and I could hear muffled voices before Trent came back on the line. "Kyle says he'll be there in twenty minutes. Will you be okay 'til then?" he asked.

"Uh, yeah. We're fine but you really didn't need to ask Kyle. I could have figured something out," I said. Trent wasn't having any of it.

"I'm not going to let my sister-in-law spend money on a tow truck when you might just need a jump-start. Kyle will be able to help you out."

"Well, thanks, I really appreciate it. I'll talk to you later," I said.

"Bye, Simone," Trent said and then disconnected the call.

It was sunny, hot, and there was no breeze, so waiting in the car for Kyle was out of the

question. Instead, we sat on the bench in front of the ice cream shop and played I-Spy to pass the time, but all I kept thinking about was what I'd say to Kyle once he got here.

Whenever we were together he made me feel like I could be myself. But I was also attracted to him and I wondered if I was interpreting his kindness for something that wasn't there.

Since the meeting in June, I hadn't seen much of him, but he would call at least every other week with updates on the divorce proceedings, although there wasn't much else to do but wait. I kept finding myself looking at my phone, wondering if he was going to stop by, but of course, there was no point. He was a great guy, but just my lawyer. I was an obligation only, and I needed to remember that. It wasn't easy, though. I could still recall the day at the playground, and the older couple inferring Kyle and me as Stella's parents. He hadn't even realized it. Then afterwards at my apartment, there was the near-kiss. Once again, I felt my face get hot with embarrassment at how uncomfortable he'd been by that accident. At the meeting with Brad the following Monday, Kyle was back to normal, like that day had never happened. For him, it had been just another day. For me, I relished it. Every moment, all the details.

About fifteen minutes later, I saw a familiar sleek, black BMW pull into the parking lot. The windows were tinted so I couldn't see in, but I knew it was him. The parking lot was pretty empty so he was able to park right next to my car. My old Civic looked even worse next to his beautiful car. It was a reminder of how different we were.

I heard a small gasp when he stepped out of his car and quickly realized it came from me. He was wearing gray slacks that were tailored perfectly, highlighting his strong thighs and perfect ass, and a black button-down shirt. He looked incredible. Every time I saw him, he looked better than the time before.

"Having car trouble, ladies?" he asked, grinning. Just

looking at his smile made me blush like a silly girl with a crush.

"Hi, Ky!" Stella exclaimed, her eyes lighting up. "I got a treat, I was a good girl."

He laughed at her enthusiastic explanation of what we had been up to.

It was a gut-punch, to see how great Kyle was with her — a complete contrast to how disinterested Brad continued to be. He'd hardly seen her since he moved out and only came around when his parents nagged him about it. When he did show up, he never played with her or paid any attention to her. However, Stella was learning quickly that there were others who would always be there for her to turn to. Like Kyle. He picked her up and gave Stella a kiss on the top of her head, making her giggle. I felt a pang deep inside at this vision before me. Handsome, successful Kyle holding my precious daughter, both of them happy and smiling, while she played with the sunglasses he'd hooked in the collar of his shirt.

My daughter had, in the past, spent more time with Kyle than I had. Her outings with her Uncle Trent occasionally included his best friend. I knew Stella liked Kyle a lot, and the way he was looking at my daughter showed that the feeling was mutual. He was so natural with her and I knew he'd make a great father one day.

I shook my head, and knew I needed to come back to reality. "Hi there..." I stood up from the bench and moved next to him. He looked over at me, studying my face, then looked away when I met his gaze. "I'm sorry you had to come all the way out here to help us. I told Trent I would call a tow truck," I explained, feeling nervous.

"It's not a problem at all," he said, moving closer and

putting an arm around me. I immediately relaxed at his touch, his hand at my lower back and pressing me into his body. God, I loved the feeling of his arm around me. "No sense in calling for a tow unless you need it. Trent said you might just need a jump."

Why did that comment sound so dirty? I needed to get my mind out of the gutter. "Yeah," I started, not moving back. Instead, I slipped my left arm around his waist while I plucked his expensive sunglasses from my daughter's crafty fingers. "I tried to start it, but it's making a clicking sound."

"Okay, can I have your key?" he asked, handing Stella to me as I gave him my keys. "Go ahead and sit back down over there, and I'll see if I can get this started for you." He turned from me and started walking to the trunk of his car.

"Kyle, I can help," I huffed. I was a little annoyed that he was acting like I was helpless.

He stopped and turned to look at me, gently placing his hand on my shoulder. "I know you can, but you don't need to. Letting me do this for you doesn't make you less capable. It just means you are accepting help. That isn't a bad thing." Then he turned and opened his trunk.

Wow, I thought, humbled. I often felt inadequate because it seemed like I was always turning to others for help. Kyle's words made me feel a little less guilty for accepting what others offered.

I sat back down with Stella and we watched Kyle work. He took a moment to roll his sleeves up, revealing his muscular forearms, before pulling the jumper cables out. What was it about a man's forearms that could drive a girl crazy? He opened his driver's side door and pulled the latch to pop open his hood, and then did the same on my car. My eyes followed every movement as he attached the cables to both batteries and then started his car. He waited a few minutes and then attempted to start my car. It sounded like it wanted to turn over but still wouldn't start. He waited a couple more minutes, tried again, and this time it started without a problem. He got out of my car and removed the cables. Once they were put back in his trunk and both hoods were closed, he walked over to us.

"Any idea when the battery was last replaced?"

I shook my head. "I sorta left the car stuff to Brad since he was a mechanic. I don't know if he ever did anything to my car," I replied.

I saw him roll his eyes and it made me chuckle. His dislike for my ex was not something he was able to conceal. "Well, I think you need to get a new one. I'd be happy to switch it out for you." His offer was very sweet, but I couldn't accept, despite his little lecture earlier. He was already handling my divorce pro bono.

"I'll take care of it. Thanks though for helping me today," I said, standing up with Stella in my arms. "Can you tell Kyle thank you for helping us?" I gently encouraged my daughter.

"Thanks, Ky," she said with her head lying on my shoulder. It was past her naptime and I knew I needed to get her home before we had to deal with a toddler tantrum.

"No problem, sweetie," he answered her. He touched her face then squeezed her shoulder softly.

I walked to my car and placed Stella in her car seat and buckled her up again. As soon as the car had started the AC came on so it was already cooling off inside. I closed her door and faced Kyle, who was standing right behind me. "So what have the two of you been up to today?" he asked. "Stella mentioned being a good girl."

"I registered for two college courses today," I answered, grinning up at him. "One's online so I can do that when I'm home with Stella. The other is two days a week. I'm hoping to arrange my schedule so I can go to school then directly to work. That should help with Marla watching Stella." I was rambling, but I was anxious to share the news with someone.

"Wow, that's fantastic, Simone," he said with a smile. He held my car door open for me. "I think it's great you were able to make that work."

"I'm really excited. It's going to take me a long time to finish, but I need to start somewhere," I said. "When we talked about my future I realized just how much I wanted to go back to school. I guess I have you to thank for reminding me that I can do what I want now," I said sincerely.

"You are going to do great, Simone. If I can help in any way, let me know. I mean it," he said firmly. He reached out, tucking a flyaway strand of hair behind my left ear. His fingertips grazed along my jaw, making me shiver. It was something he did often, although I didn't think he was aware of it.

I was holding my breath and couldn't exhale until he wasn't touching me anymore. "Um, thanks again, Kyle," I said, my voice a little husky. "Once again, saving the day for me and Stella."

He nodded, his expression soft, quiet. "Text me when you get home so I know you didn't have any more car troubles," he ordered gently, pulling me in for another hug. It was almost torturous, this constant contact. I tried not to read into any of it because Kyle was a friendly guy. It was just his way of showing kindness, and I loved that about him. He wasn't afraid to show his emotions or affections.

"I will, I promise," I said, reluctantly pulling myself out of his arms. He really did give amazing hugs.

He continued to hold my door open and waited 'til I was settled into the front seat before he closed it. I rolled down my window and said, "Bye."

"Bye, Simone," he said, and walked over to get into his car.

I pulled out of my space and he pulled out right behind me. I drove out of the parking lot with a huge smile on my face. What was this man doing to me?

*****

It was Stella's second birthday and we were at Jim and Marla's house getting ready to drive up to Anaheim so we could take Stella to Disneyland for the first time. I was just as excited for the trip as my daughter was. It was about a two-hour drive, so I had spent the night at their house so we could get up early and get on the road. Since we were going to be out late tonight we had done the whole cake and gift thing last night. That's when we surprised Stella with the trip.

Everyone had such a nice time celebrating that I was almost able to ignore the fact that her father had decided not to show up. I hadn't seen or heard from Brad since our meeting two months ago. I had come to accept the fact that he wasn't going to have a relationship with his daughter. While it infuriated me that he would toss her aside so easily, I made sure she spent plenty of time with Jim and Trent, the two men in her life who loved her unconditionally. I wasn't sure if his parents were in contact with him, but from the sound of it, Brad had cut off all ties with his entire family. I felt especially bad for Marla and Jim. Trent, I knew, was fine with it, since he didn't get along with his younger brother.

Marla told me last night that she invited Trent to join us today and that Kyle and Addie were coming as well. I knew Stella would be happy to have her Uncle Trent there and I was excited Addie was going. I really liked Addie and was so happy we had developed a friendship. In fact, I would say she was quickly becoming my closest friend besides Kayla. It may have been an unlikely friendship, but I was so grateful to have her as part of my life.

My anxiety came from knowing Kyle was coming with us. I knew Stella would love it, but I wasn't sure I could spend an entire day hanging out with him casually without thinking of the way he made me feel. I knew it would never be reciprocated so it was silly of me to even entertain the lustful thoughts I'd been having of him.

Changing my focus to the fun day ahead, I finished packing my backpack with some snacks, sunscreen, diapers, wipes, and a change of clothes for Stella. It was the middle of August so I'd put Stella in a pair of red shorts and a white shirt with red polka dots. I was wearing a pair of dark denim shorts and an olive green tank top.

I brought our bag down and placed it by the front door. I could hear my little one chattering with her grandparents in the kitchen. Knowing they were ready to go, I put on my shoes and joined them at the counter.

"Good morning," I said as I poured myself a cup of coffee. I wasn't much of a breakfast eater, but I needed my coffee in the morning to feel human.

"Morning," they all said in return. I took a few more sips of my coffee, already feeling more awake.

"Trent texted a couple minutes ago, Kyle and Addie just picked him up. They should be here in about ten minutes," Jim informed us.

I tried to ignore the butterflies in my stomach at the mention of Kyle. I really needed to stop with this infatuation. All I was going to do was embarrass myself. A few minutes later we heard the front door open.

"Where's the birthday girl?" I heard Trent shout from the entryway. Stella immediately hopped off the chair and went running to the living room.

"I'm here, Unky Trent!" she yelled, and giggled all the way to him. She was capable of saying the word 'uncle' just fine now, but she refused to call Trent anything except Unky. It was pretty cute and I had a feeling it would always be her thing with him.

I walked around the corner just in time to see him scoop her up in his arms and twirl her around twice. "Hey there, Simone," he said as he set Stella down.

"Hi, guys," I responded as we all moved around to greet each other with hugs. When Kyle hugged me, my imagination must have been playing tricks on me because it felt a little tighter and lasted a little bit longer than the others.

"Are we ready to go?" Marla asked, coming back into the room with her own backpack ready.

"Yes," we all answered as I pulled away from Kyle. It appeared everyone was looking forward to the day at the amusement park.

Jim and Marla were taking their minivan and Stella and I were going to ride with them. I assumed the others would ride together in Kyle's car.

"Can I ride with you guys?" Addie asked while looping her arm through mine as we walked out the front door. "I would much rather talk to you than listen to the two of them talk about baseball and chicks the whole way there," she teased while eyeing her brother.

The thought of Kyle talking to Trent about other women had me feeling a pang of jealousy deep inside my chest. That was a new feeling for me. I had never felt that way about a man before. Not even Brad. I didn't have time to analyze that thought, so I answered, "Sounds good to me." It would be nice to have another person to chat with on the way up.

We loaded everything up into the two vehicles and headed out on the freeway for the drive there. I chatted with Addie about the classes I was enrolled in and she responded the same way her brother had—full of pride and encouragement. I felt lucky to have all these people who actually cared about me in my life. It wasn't something I was used to, and it felt good.

The drive went by quickly, and before I knew it we were pulling into the parking garage. We had timed our trip well and it looked like we would be at the gates when they opened. We walked out of the parking structure to the trams that would drop us off at the front of the park.

"I want to sit by Unky Trent," Stella called out as we walked off the escalator.

I had a feeling Stella would be making a lot of demands of who she would be sitting next to throughout the day.

We walked up to the entrance just as they started letting the guests in. As soon as we passed through the turnstile, Stella spotted her favorite princess. Of course, we had to stand in line to make sure she was able to meet her, and each of us must have taken a dozen pictures. I had to chuckle when I saw six cell phones all snapping photos of one little girl. Seeing the pure happiness on my daughter's face filled my heart.

As we walked further into the park, Stella grabbed both Trent and Kyle's hands while walking between them so they could lift her up and swing her. She was giggling and having the time of her life. Watching Kyle with her made me yearn to find a man that would love my daughter like that. In my dreams Kyle would be that man, but I knew that would never be a reality. He seemed quite content with his bachelor lifestyle and I was nothing like the women he dated.

The rest of the day was filled with rides, pictures with characters, lots of junk food, and endless smiles for all of us. I couldn't remember a time when I'd had more fun. This was exactly the type of childhood I wanted to provide Stella with. Memories filled with people who loved her more than anything.

After dinner, we sat on Main Street and watched a parade. The park was open until midnight, but it became clear that Stella wasn't going to be able to stay awake much longer. By the end of the parade she had fallen asleep in Trent's lap. That was our signal to call it a night.

"Obviously, Stella is done for the night," Jim said as he hefted her up on his shoulder. "We're going to head home, but why don't all of you stay?" he suggested.

I started to hug everyone goodbye when Jim interrupted me. "I meant you as well, Simone. We can take Stella home and you can pick her up in the morning."

"I can't leave her on her birthday," I argued.

"She's asleep and I don't think she's going to wake up 'til tomorrow. You should definitely stay with us," I heard Kyle say from behind me. "We'll have a good time."

"We've still got five hours before the park closes," Addie chimed in.

After a couple more minutes of debate, I relented. It really did sound like fun and I enjoyed spending time with the three of them. It felt nice that they wanted to include me.

We had skipped some rides earlier because Stella wasn't tall enough or they were a little too scary for her so those were the ones we hit up first. My first choice was Space Mountain; I had always wanted to ride it. As we approached the front of the line, Trent started complaining to Kyle about the two of them not having enough legroom if they rode next to each other.

"Simone, care to join me in my row?" Trent asked formally, with a smile on his lips. I had to laugh.

"I would love to," I answered with the same level of formality.

When I looked back at Kyle he was glaring at his best friend. When I looked at Addie she looked away from her brother and winked at me. I didn't know what was going on, so instead, I focused on enjoying my evening.

After a couple more rides, we decided to catch the fireworks show. It was extremely crowded so Kyle standing right up against my back didn't surprise me. He placed his hands on my hips and I shivered.

"Are you cold?" he asked.

I shook my head even as I shivered again, feeling his breath against my cheek. "I forgot to bring a sweatshirt, but I'm good," I answered, trying to keep my voice even. The warmth of his hands on me was distracting.

"You have goosebumps, Simone. Here, you can wear

mine," he said as he pulled it off.

I immediately felt the loss of his hands on me but then he placed his sweatshirt over my head. Once I had it on, he put his hands back where they had been. I couldn't help it; I leaned back and rested my head against his chest. We watched the entire show like that, neither of us moving away from each other.

I felt a huge pang of disappointment when the show was over, but it quickly went away when Kyle grabbed my hand as we tried to move through the crowd. Of course, once we were clear of others he let my hand go. While all these little gestures had made me feel warm and fuzzy inside, I had to remind myself that he was only acting as a friend. We were just comfortable with each other and it was nothing more than that. However, I wasn't sure how to deal with my feelings for Kyle, which continued to intensify whenever he was around. It was both confusing and exciting.

The rest of the night was spent full of laughs, the four of us running around the park like a bunch of overgrown kids. We had a blast. When it was finally time for us to leave, we were all a little bummed. We spent the drive home talking about all sorts of things; the fun we'd had, how work at the law firm was going, baseball, and anything else we could think of. When we hit the San Diego city limits it was decided that we would drop off Trent first, then Addie, and I would be last. My apartment was the furthest away from the freeway so it made the most sense.

Once it was just Kyle and me in the car, I felt the atmosphere turn a little awkward again. I was so attracted to him and it made me nervous.

"I hope you had a good time tonight," he said as he turned into my apartment complex.

"It was the most fun I can remember ever having," I told him truthfully. My answer seemed to make him happy if I was judging by the huge smile on his face.

I expected him to pull up behind my car to let me out. Instead, he parked in one of the visitor spots. Once he put the car in park, he hopped out before I could say anything. He walked over to my door and opened it for me. It was a gesture I had been on the receiving end from him before and each time it warmed my heart a little bit. I never had anyone do that for me before.

"Such the gentleman," I teased. "Always opening the door."

He smiled. "Yeah, you can blame Jim for that one," he explained. "When Trent and I were teenagers, he constantly lectured us on the proper way to treat a lady."

"Well, it's very sweet. Thank you," I said as I went in for a hug.

Kyle put his hands out in front of him to stop me. I was confused for a moment because we always hugged goodbye. Then he said, "He also taught me to walk a lady to her door to make sure she made it home safely, especially at night."

"All right then, let's head up," I suggested and started to lead the way to my apartment.

I unlocked my door and opened it. Once Kyle was convinced everything was safe, he leaned in and hugged me. When he started to pull away, he didn't remove his arms from my body. Instead, he moved his hand up and gently cupped my cheek. I stared into his eyes and for the first time I saw the same attraction I felt reflected back at me.

Just a second later I felt his lips come down on mine. I was so caught off guard it took me a minute to realize what was happening. His kiss was soft at first, but as soon as I kissed him back, he pushed against me harder. He traced my lips with the tip of his tongue and when I opened for him, it was like he couldn't contain himself.

I had never been kissed like this before. It was filled with lust and passion and I couldn't get enough. But then he pulled away.

When I finally opened my eyes, I looked up at him only to find him staring at me in disbelief.

"Oh, my God, Simone, I'm so sorry," he said as he reached up ran his fingers through his hair. "I don't know why I did that."

Well, that wasn't what a girl wanted to hear after the best kiss of her life. I was still feeling the moment and my mind still in a fog, saying nothing in response. I wasn't sorry. Not at all.

"That was totally inappropriate. I just got caught up in the moment, in you..." He swore under his breath, looking like he made the biggest mistake of his life by kissing me. "It won't happen again," he continued, not giving me a chance to say anything. Then he turned and sprinted down the stairs.

I walked into my apartment feeling horrible. I knew I wasn't the type of girl he went for, but was kissing me really that bad?

I don't know how long I stood there in my empty living room, staring out at nothing, still seeing him in front of me and feeling his mouth on mine. I finally forced myself out of my stupor and closed the door. A little numbed by his... rejection... I went through the motions of getting ready for bed. I thought about the day and all the fun I'd had. I couldn't believe it had ended this way. After tonight, how was I ever going to face Kyle again?

Chapter 10

Kyle

*S*imone was sitting in my office having just received the dissolution papers for her marriage.

I watched her as she reviewed the documents carefully. Ever since the night of Stella's birthday, I had kept my distance. I clearly could not control myself around her and I was lucky she hadn't told Trent or Jim about my out-of-line behavior. I could just see Trent now, thinking I was taking advantage of her. Simone, thankfully, hadn't mentioned it again. Her bewildered, silent response had told me enough about what I'd done. The fact that she'd kissed me back was likely reactionary since I'd taken her by surprise, but I'd had spent plenty of time thinking otherwise and wondering 'what if'. I was worried about upsetting how things were, the way they had been for me. She deserved so much more, and since I didn't know what I had to offer her and Stella, I'd stayed away.

It appeared she had forgiven me, and I appreciated that, but I missed seeing her and talking to her. The past six months had been a rollercoaster for me, on many levels. Things we talked about in those months, I'd find myself dialing her number or starting a text, only to remind myself that I couldn't—shouldn't—do that until I was in the right headspace, and knew the full repercussions of my decisions. I would not hurt Simone. She'd had a lifetime of hurt and I wouldn't bring more to her doorstep.

When I did text her with updates on her case and to check in occasionally, I tried to keep everything professional.

But now that the judgment was in I couldn't put off seeing her. She had been through a lot these past six months, but it was finally over. Brad's mandated drug test had come back negative, which, honestly, was more than a little surprising. Not that he needed drugs to continue acting like an ass. Thankfully, his behavior didn't deter Simone from making a better future for herself and Stella.

Once Brad realized that the MSA required him to pay child support, he'd quit his job at Erik's auto shop. We tried to keep tabs on where he was working so Simone could get the money she was entitled to, but if he was working, it appeared he was getting paid under the table.

Simone was granted full custody and Brad had supervised visitation every Saturday. The judge agreed it was best for all visitations to take place at his parents' home since he didn't have a permanent residence. Truthfully, if the past few months were any indication, he probably wouldn't make these visitations a priority. He'd even missed her birthday two months ago. While Brad was missing out on time with his daughter, it appeared Stella wasn't suffering too much. She had a wonderful mother; doting grandparents, and Trent couldn't go more than a week without spending time with his niece. All things considered, they were all doing well.

"I can't believe it's actually done," she whispered. She exhaled loudly and leaned back in her chair. "I'm no longer Mrs. Bradley Thompson..."

"You plan on changing your name?" I asked. She hadn't made a decision on this when we first filed her petition so I was curious.

177

She thought about it. "Yeah, I think I'll go back to my maiden name—Clark. Really make it official that Brad and I are over." I smiled at her when she looked up at me, her gorgeous eyes brimming with happy tears. "I can't thank you enough for everything you've done. I wish I could repay you somehow."

For a moment, very lewd thoughts of exactly how she could pay me back rushed through my mind. I was such an asshole! I didn't want her gratitude. I wanted... hell, I didn't know what I wanted from her. That was why I really needed to stay away until I could get my head straight and feelings sorted out about Simone. I gathered up the papers and placed them in a folder for her. "You don't owe me anything, Simone. I'm just happy you can move forward," I said politely.

Simone stood up to leave and I walked over to open my office door for her. Automatically, I reached out and gave her a hug before she could leave. I knew I was probably sending her mixed signals because I was sending them to myself. But what my body wanted and what my mind thought was best were at war with each other. I couldn't control my desire to reach for her when she was this close and so touchable. I sighed when she instantly wrapped her slender arms around my waist and the feel of her body against mine again felt so right.

"I'll see you around, Kyle," she said with a bright smile and pulled back. She went up on her tiptoes and gave me a quick peck on my cheek. My heart rate sped up at the unexpected gesture and she smiled again before walking out. She wore tight jeans that hugged her lower body and a teal-colored tank top. Even though it was October, the weather was still warm. Another perk to living in San Diego. I tried real hard to not stare at her ass as she left since Linda was eyeing me suspiciously with a smile on her lips.

I gave her a quick smile and ducked back into my office. I still felt the pressure of Simone's lips on my cheek and I was slightly dumbfounded by my horny teenaged boy response. I'd felt that way after our kiss a couple months ago, which was understandable. But this... this was just a chaste kiss, and it was affecting me just as much as that other one. Once I sat back down behind my desk, I stared at my computer screen still thinking about Simone's jean-clad ass. If she had known even one of the thoughts I'd had about her in the past six months, she probably would have fired me. Never mind I was doing this pro bono. At least now, I felt less guilty considering she was a single woman. Still, I needed to stop.

A very random thought about asking her out startled me out of my daydream because that was completely out of the question.

Or was it?

I rubbed my eyes, constantly going back and forth about the pros and cons of pursuing Simone. Was it just an attraction due to the situation? No, I decided instantly. I was physically attracted to her, had been for a while, but I knew that once Brad had faded out of the picture, feelings and thoughts had started to creep in, and I had started to see her in a different way. Was this just about sex? Yes, and no. I wanted more than just a few nights and some dates with Simone. That's where I got stuck. I wasn't a long-term type of guy. And Stella came with the package, and I knew how protective everyone was of her well-being and happiness because I felt the same exact way.

Other than her now being divorced, nothing had changed.

My conversation with Addie back in June came back to

haunt me again. What the hell did I want? I had no clue, and that was the problem. What I needed to do was stop thinking about it or I'd lose my mind. I shook my head; I needed to focus on work.

I eyed the small pile of folders Linda and Addie had dropped off this morning and after lunch. It was Friday afternoon and I wanted to wrap up some paperwork so I could get out of here at a decent time. The guys and I were meeting up tonight. After eight years in the military, Ian was finally home so we had plans to go out and celebrate. The four of us had spent most of our lives together so his absence had been hard on all of us, as we hadn't been able to see him nearly as much as we wanted. Having him home was going to be a great thing.

"Hey, are you heading out?" Addie asked, popping her head in through my door.

"Yeah, as soon as I finish a few things, I'm out," I said, a little distracted. "Are you going to join us in welcoming Ian home tonight?"

At the mention of Ian's name, something passed over Addie's face. Something had happened between them but I'd never figured out what, exactly. Over the years, I had attempted to ask both of them what caused their apparent falling out, but they both acted like they had no idea what I was talking about. After a while I let the subject drop, but now I was wondering how they'd act around each other since they were living in the same town again.

"Well?" I prompted when she continued standing there, zoned out. "You coming, or not?"

Her expression was shuttered and she shrugged. "It really should be a boys' night out," she said too casually. She was also looking down at her nails like they were the most interesting things in the world. Addie dressed well and took care of herself, but she was no fashionista and could not care less about how pretty her nails looked.

I narrowed my gaze at her, suspicious. "What happened between you and Ian?" Now she looked nervous. I took my glasses off, glad to have my mind off a certain curvy woman with brown eyes and black hair. "You've always told me it was nothing, but you and he used to be so close and then all of a sudden you both stopped talking." Saying it out loud made me pause. "Wait! Did he do something to you? You better tell me right now because I will give him a totally different welcome home if he hurt you."

"What? No!" Her eyes bugged out a little. "It was nothing like that. He and Brad just didn't get along. Once I started dating Brad I sort of stopped talking to Ian..." she said, trailing off and back to acting casual. She gave a one-shouldered shrug for emphasis. "And we never got back to that level of friendship even after I broke things off with Brad."

Fucking Brad Thompson. That guy could ruin anything just by existing. I was so glad he was no longer Simone's problem, and that he was barely around at all. Marla and Jim seemed okay without seeing their youngest son as often, which had to be hard for Marla, especially, but everyone's lives were much better without the negative energy that seemed to follow him.

"You're not lying to me, are you?" I asked.

She rolled her eyes at me. "Stop being the overprotective big brother. It's annoying," she said, crossing her arms across her chest, even though she was smirking.

Okay, so she was probably telling the truth. Mostly. There was something else, I could sense it, but she was keeping it to herself and that was her right. I knew I could only push so far before Addie dug her heels in and shut me out. We were alike that way.

Hopefully, she and Ian could rekindle their friendship now that he was home permanently. I really liked the idea of all five us back together, like it was when we were growing up. I wanted *all* of us to hang out, not just a portion of the group.

"So, you want to come out with us tonight?" I asked her, one more time.

"Actually," she drawled out, "I'm going out with Simone and a couple of her other friends tonight. It's Simone's birthday today, plus we're celebrating her divorce."

Addie and Simone had been spending a lot of time together, which was good for both of them. At least there was one positive that came out of the mess Brad had caused. But then my brain caught onto the other bit of information I'd hadn't paid attention to.

"Crap, I didn't realize it was her birthday," I groaned, leaning back in my seat, "she was just here and I didn't say anything."

"I'm sure she'll forgive you," she said with a wink. "Anyway, I'm outta here. Have fun tonight with the boys."

"You too," I said, distracted once again.

*****

The guys met at my house around nine so we could pregame before we hit up the club. Not only were we all together for the first time in years, but we were all single as well. It was going to make for an interesting night out for sure.

I didn't know what I was looking for tonight. On one hand, a simple hookup sounded like fun. On the other hand, I couldn't stop thinking about Simone and the possibility of something more with her. Unfortunately, trust in romantic relationships didn't come easy for me, as Addie had clearly overstated back in June. I wondered if that was because my father left one day and never looked back or because my mom continually chose drugs over her children. It was probably a combination of both. My conversation with my sister kept playing in the back of my mind. When I did think about my future—family, wife, kids—my next thought went to Simone and Stella. But taking that risk didn't just affect me.

"Hey, assholes, drink up! I want to get to the club," Ian yelled from the living room. He was always ready for a party. It looked like things hadn't changed much.

We called an Uber to take us to Euphoria, one of the newer nightclubs in the downtown area. We all knew we would be drinking so none of us wanted to drive. We were dropped off in front of a three-story building with a brick façade. There weren't any signs on the outside so the only hint that we were in the right place was the thumping bass coming from inside.

There was a small line at the entrance but it only took about fifteen minutes to get in. Once inside, the flashing lights and loud music instantly put me in the mood to dance. I looked around trying to see if anyone caught my attention.

"Hey, let's grab some shots and then scope out the dance floor," Trent yelled over the music.

We made our way to the bar where Erik ordered us each a shot of tequila. Shooting mine back I turned my attention back to the dance floor. After a couple quick scans, my eyes landed on a woman, and I was unable to look away from her. She was facing away from me but the sway of her hips had me hypnotized. She wore a tight, short black dress that showed a lot of leg. It was dark so I couldn't make out all her features, but from what I could tell she had dark hair. Though I couldn't tell how long it was because it was pulled up. She was on the small side and I was worried if I took my eyes off her I would lose her in the crowd.

I felt someone elbow me in the side. "Hey, look, Addie and Simone are here," Trent said in my ear. He was standing next to me and I realized he was looking in the same direction I'd been staring.

"Fuck," I muttered under my breath. I had been so focused on Simone that I hadn't even noticed Addie dancing next to her.

Now knowing it was Simone, I couldn't pull my eyes away from her even if I tried. She always looked amazing, whether she dressed up or down, makeup or none at all, but right now, she was unbelievably gorgeous. I couldn't help but smile at how carefree she looked out there dancing.

"Who are the other two girls with them?" Trent asked.

"I think one is Simone's friend Kayla but I don't know who the other one is," I answered.

"Damn," Ian said, staring. "Addie and Simone look really hot."

Trent reached behind me and punched Ian in the arm hard enough to make him flinch.

"What the fuck, man?" he asked, rubbing his bicep.

"You kidding me?" Trent snapped, glaring. "Dude, that's my sister-in-law and Kyle's sister. Have some respect."

"Seriously? I didn't mean it like that," he muttered, but stepped back toward the bar, shaking his head.

I stared at Trent, feeling his words and actions were rather harsh, so I tried to defend Ian. "He was just saying—"

"I know what he meant," Trent said, still pissed. "Addie and Simone are off limits to that kind of talk."

Trent had always been protective of Addie when we were growing up, but I realized that fierceness had long since extended to Simone. That not only included saying they looked hot, but there has always been this unspoken rule that sisters were just that, off limits. You don't have dirty thoughts about them, kiss them, or fuck them.

Shit. I looked away, feeling the guilt burn through me. I'd broken two of those rules already.

At the end of the song, we watched the girls leave the dance floor and start walking toward the bar. They were giggling together and totally unaware of our presence.

"We should probably go say hi," Erik suggested, looking at me when he said it.

I rolled my eyes at him. As we moved into their path, I noticed Simone walking backward, sharing something with Addie, when her back slammed into my chest. I placed my hands at her waist to steady her—and it was a good enough excuse for me to keep them there and not feel like a creep or like I was doing something wrong. It wasn't like I was her lawyer anymore. I was her friend, too. And according to Trent, I could only be that. But at the moment, all I could think about was how good it felt to be near her and touch her.

"Oh, excuse me," she said as she turned around to face me.

I smiled down at her. "Hey," I greeted. I wasn't sure she heard me, but she returned my smile.

"Kyle!" she yelled a little louder than necessary. "What are you guys doing here?"

"We're out celebrating the return of this guy," Trent said, thumbing toward Ian, who waved and smiled. Trent hugged Simone to his side. "By the way, happy birthday, sis."

"Happy birthday," we all chimed in.

"Thank you!" she exclaimed, clearly excited and in a great mood. She hugged Trent back like he was her favorite teddy bear. I frowned and looked away, annoyed. I felt possessive of her, even though she wasn't mine to possess.

Simone wasn't technically part of the Thompson family anymore, at least not on paper, but you couldn't tell that to Trent or his parents. Trent gave her a brotherly enough kiss on her right temple, but damn if I felt a little irritated at how touchy feely they were. They were close, I knew that, but I rarely saw it. Whenever Simone and I were together at the office, the Thompsons' house, or her apartment, it was about the job, and advising her through the proceedings — well, most of the time. Now that I didn't have that shackle of duty and obligation, I rubbed the back of my neck, still conflicted about my role now and how to act around her. Not to mention, jealous as hell that Trent had his hands all over her. If Trent viewed her like a sister and still got to hug her like that, I could definitely get the same privileges, right?

I was so screwed.

"Come have a shot with us," she said, grabbing Trent by the hand and leading him to the bar. Erik followed, wasting no time seeing that Kayla and the other girl were all by themselves.

I hung back, still sorting through some weird thoughts and uncomfortable feelings, when I watched Ian walk over to my sister. For just a moment Addie looked panicked. Then she turned on her smile and hugged him. It was a little awkward. Like two strangers instead of longtime friends.

Ian and Addie started their own conversation while Trent and Erik started talking to Simone and her friends.

I made my way over to Simone, placing my hands on her waist again, and spoke into her ear. "Happy birthday, Simone. I'm sorry I didn't realize earlier."

"Thank you, Kyle," she said, spinning around to face me. She placed her hand on my chest, and leaned in for a hug.

Her touch felt amazing, and like many times before, I felt my heart speed up and I could feel every contact point her body made with mine. I had to be honest, hearing her say my name in that moment was a huge turn-on. When she pulled away, we stared at each other for a few moments before I removed my hands from her waist. She eventually slid her hand off my body as well, and goosebumps broke along my skin. Shit, I needed to control my reactions to her touch or I was going to give myself away soon.

"You want to sit down?" she inquired, climbing up on a stool and pointing to the empty one next to her.

I was in jeans and a plain black T-shirt, but I felt like I was wearing a damn parka. Didn't the club have the air conditioning on to counter all the people inside? Knowing I needed a little breathing room before I did anything stupid, I mumbled something that she couldn't possibly understand, let alone hear, and walked over to Trent and Erik.

"I'll be right back," I told them. They barely registered what I'd said, too engrossed in Kayla and the other woman. When I glanced over at Simone, she had a quiet expression on her face as her gaze met mine. She wore the same expression from when I'd kissed her, except this time, I saw disappointment. Could that be right? She gave me a small smile and turned around to face the bar. I knew my hasty departure was odd and might have hurt her feelings when she'd been so happy just a few minutes ago, but I had to take a break from standing next to her. I headed toward the back of the club where the restrooms were. My mind couldn't focus on anything except how beautiful she looked and the thoughts running through my head were not appropriate at all.

After I returned a few minutes later, I watched the guys put away another round of drinks. If we were going to continue to hang out with the girls, I decided to stay away from the alcohol. I was already having a difficult time controlling myself; I didn't need to add any liquor to the mix. We all decided to move to the dance floor where Erik immediately pulled Addie to dance with him, and I was glad to see her laughing and not so tense. After her talk with Ian, they'd both migrated to opposite ends of our merged groups at the bar, like they'd had their obligatory 'talk' and now it was time to keeping avoiding each other. I didn't get it, but I had my own problems to deal with. Ian and Kayla started dancing together and then Trent went over to Ashley, the other girl in their group. That left Simone and me dancing together.

For the first couple of songs we kept a respectable distance between us, barely touching at all. Soon, Addie, Erik, Kayla and Ian left us to go get more drinks at the bar. Trent appeared to be interested in a hook up with Ashley. They had moved off to a dark corner of the dance floor. And I was perfectly happy to see him go off with her.

Simone seemed to be enjoying the dancing and I didn't

want to make her stop so I chose to stay out here with her. There was no way I was going to allow any other guy in the club to dance with her. She looked way too hot to be left unattended.

The next song that came on had a slower beat, and without a second thought, I moved closer to her, slipping my arms around her from behind. For just a moment I felt her stiffen in my hold, but then she relaxed. I looked over her shoulder in the direction I had seen Trent go and saw he was in full make-out mode with Ashley so I didn't have to worry about him seeing us. The bar was on the other side of the club and I was sure the rest of our friends couldn't see us, either.

We started to move together to the beat, her ass slightly grinding against my groin, giving me an instant hard-on. If she kept doing what she was doing, she was going to know right away what was on my mind. I leaned my head forward and whispered in her ear, "Is this okay?" I didn't want her to feel uncomfortable. As far as I knew, she hadn't so much as gone on a single date since leaving Brad.

"It's totally okay," she answered out of breath, and I wasn't sure if that was because of the dancing or because of how I was affecting her. I hoped it was the latter.

We continued to move and she snaked her right arm up around the back of my neck, pulling me even closer to her. I started trailing my hand up and down her side. She was playing with the hair on the back of my head while continuing to grind on me. I could tell she was feeling something between us as well. Unable to resist any longer, I placed my lips on the side of her neck.

I could feel the small vibrations of her moans as I continued to assault her with kisses. Suddenly, she turned in my arms wrapping both arms around my neck.

189

"Please don't stop," she pleaded while looking up at me. Before I knew what possessed me, I slammed my lips over hers and started kissing her deeply. It took just a moment for her to start returning the kiss, her tongue meeting mine stroke for stroke. As soon as we took a breath, the song stopped and a much faster one came one. We broke apart and stared at each other. The beat of the music made the tension between us that much more palpable. She also didn't look like she hated me kissing her; in fact, she was moving toward me again, her eyes on my mouth like she wanted more.

I'd spent weeks — months — debating with myself about my feelings for Simone and how to deal with them. I could choose to not see her at all, but that wasn't really an option. I couldn't abandon her and Stella like that, just because I couldn't control myself. So instead, this was me, taking a risk, a chance, and hoping it didn't blow up in my face.

"I need some fresh air, you want to come out back with me?" I asked, feeling overwhelmingly hot now. I needed a moment to think, and give Simone a chance to think, too.

"Sure," she said, sounding a little flustered from our short make-out session.

I knew I was probably confusing her, having left abruptly at the bar earlier, and stopping us now, but Simone made me feel like I had no game whatsoever. I grabbed her hand and led her through the crowd and out the back of the club. As soon as we opened the door, a blast of ocean air hit us slightly cooling the heat we had been feeling. I looked at Simone closely and saw red tinting her cheeks.

"Look, I'm sorry if I pushed you too far in there. You look beautiful and your dancing is extremely sexy..." I trailed off. I knew she was in a vulnerable place, and I didn't want to make her feel pressured into anything.

"You think I look beautiful?" she asked, beaming up at me like that was the first time she'd ever heard it. I still remembered Jim's birthday party and Brad's ridiculous comment about her body.

"You're gorgeous," I told her, meaning every word. I couldn't believe this woman in front of me could ever doubt her beauty. Then I remembered whom she had been married to. I'm sure he never made an effort to give her any sort of compliment. Knowing how her childhood had been, it was very likely she rarely heard any form of praise.

I bent down slightly to meet her eyes. "You are the most beautiful woman here tonight. It took everything in my power to not get carried away back there," I told her honestly.

She glanced up at me again, moving closer to my body. "I think I might have enjoyed you getting carried away, Mr. O'Neill," she whispered, and damn if that didn't make me harder.

"Oh really?" I asked right before meeting her lips with mine yet again. I had her pinned against the building, my hands traveling up her sides before brushing over her breasts.

She started moaning against my mouth just like she had been moaning on the dance floor. She had my self-control hanging on by a thread. Kissing her wasn't going to be enough.

"I really want to take you home with me tonight," I told her, taking a break, both of us panting.

"I really want to go home with you," she said, making me smile.

I grabbed her hand and led her back inside. "We should

see what everyone else is doing," I said, moving us quickly through the club.

I dropped her hand as we approached our group. Ian informed me that Trent had already left with Ashley. Everyone else looked ready to leave so we all headed toward the door. Addie and Kayla were both pretty drunk, and being the responsible brother I was, I offered to let everyone stay at my house. I may have had an ulterior motive for the offer. I hadn't been able to think of any other way to get Simone back to my house without raising suspicions. Erik was going to head home since he had to be at the racetrack in the morning, but Ian was coming back to my place since he was crashing there until he got settled into his own place.

We managed to snag a cab with enough room for all five of us. It was a fairly quiet ride. In the back, Ian, Kayla, and Addie were half asleep already. With Simone next to me for the twenty-minute ride, I had to remind myself to not lean over and touch her or keep staring at her legs.

Once we pulled up to my house, I had Ian help me get both Kayla and Addie inside. I had three extra bedrooms, but Ian was already occupying one. All the bedrooms were on the second floor, mine at the front of the house facing the ocean. Ian had decided he wanted the one at the far end of the house since we both appreciated our privacy. I put Kayla and Addie in the room next to Ian's, and Simone in the one next to mine.

Addie and Kayla were passed out the minute their heads hit the pillows. I made sure they were comfortable before closing the door behind me. Ian immediately retreated to his bedroom, leaving Simone and me alone. Finally.

"Do you want some water?" I asked, leading her back down the stairs to my kitchen.

"Yes, please," she answered behind me.

We sat at my kitchen island making small talk, the heat between us having cooled down a bit after driving home and getting everyone settled.

"I love the sound of the ocean, you're so lucky to hear it from here," she said softly, her eyes never leaving mine.

"It sounds even better up on the roof. Come on, let me show you," I said, grabbing her hand and pulling her up both flights of stairs. I directed her to the half wall that was at the edge of the deck.

As she stood there, I moved in behind her, caging her in with my arms resting on the railing. I knew she could feel me directly behind her by the way her body tensed for just a moment. I wondered if I made her nervous or if it was something else. There was so much about Simone I still didn't know. She was reserved with most people, but not as much if she felt comfortable around them—like Marla, Jim, and Trent. I knew with a childhood like hers, without having any stable figures in her life, that some part of you never really outgrew the damage done when you were younger. I was glad that she was seeing Stephanie, and working out some of those issues, and I had seen a huge improvement over the past few months. She was more open and confident, and coming out of her shy, quiet shell.

"Oh, this is beautiful," she said on a long sigh. She swiveled her head around, staring in the direction of the pier that was lit up. Against the dark sky it shined brilliantly.

"Absolutely beautiful," I said, not taking my eyes off of her.

She turned to face me when she felt my breath on her neck. Even though our faces were only a couple inches apart I couldn't move away. I knew moving things this fast was risky. She was Trent's sister-in-law, well, ex sister-in-law, and he was extremely protective of her. She also had a child, and while I adored Stella, I wasn't sure I was ready for that kind of responsibility. But at the same time, I couldn't seem to make myself pull away from her.

The lust in her eyes wasn't helping my resolve either. She looked at my mouth, licking her own lips, giving me all the signals that she wanted more as well. She had totally been into it when we had been kissing on the dance floor and she apparently wanted a repeat. Feeling a bit more daring now that we were alone, I leaned down so our lips could meet. I was planning on taking it slow and kissing her gently, but then she grabbed my hair and pulled me closer, thrusting her tongue in my mouth. She tasted so good, and I loved how confident she was in this moment. She knew what she wanted and right now she wanted me.

Even so, I was reminded of the fact that she had been drinking earlier. I didn't want this night to turn into a huge regret for her. I broke our kiss and she looked at me in confusion.

I almost laughed at her huffy frown. "Why do you keep stopping, Kyle?"

"How much did you have to drink tonight?" I asked.

"Only two the whole night. I really don't like to drink," she answered, arching her body again. I believed her. She had definitely not shown any signs of being intoxicated.

"I want to make sure you aren't drunk," I explained to her, being the good, honorable lawyer that I was. "I want this, but I don't want to take advantage of you."

"Kyle, I want this just as badly as you do. Please don't stop again," she whispered.

With that, all of my resolve was gone and I pulled her over to one of the lounge chairs. Sitting down, I directed her to straddle me, which caused her dress to ride up a bit on her hips. I could feel the heat between her legs, which just spurred me on.

We continued to kiss with my hands roving up and down her back, sides, and smooth legs. When she started unbuttoning my shirt I knew she was ready to move this forward. Following her lead, I pushed the shoulder straps of her dress down her arms revealing her black, lacy bra. It was strapless and presented her large breasts right in front of my face. I bent my head down and placed gentle kisses along the top of her amazing tits.

Her soft moans continued to turn me on so I unhooked her bra, throwing it aside so that she was exposed to me. Her nipples were a dark rose color and hard. Taking one in my mouth I sucked on it roughly, making her throw her head back in ecstasy.

While I was focused on her breasts, she started grinding down on my cock that was trying to make his presence known. I brought one hand down to reach between her legs, trying to supply the friction she was desperately seeking. As soon as my fingers touched her silk panties I could tell she how aroused she was. Moving them to the side, I started rubbing my fingers through her wetness.

"Oh, Kyle, that feels so good, but I need more," she said breathlessly.

Listening to her command, I gently pushed two fingers inside her, using my thumb to rub her clit. Balancing herself with her hands behind my head, and her feet on the ground, she started riding my fingers. Watching her use my hand to bring her to orgasm was making me hard as granite. I just wanted to see her come before sinking myself inside her. I could feel her pussy grip my fingers as her body started to convulse. She nearly collapsed onto me, but caught herself with her hands on my shoulders, and our gazes locked. Every time we looked into each other's eyes, I felt a connection to her that took my breath away. The first time we'd ever met, our gazes had met like this. Back then, she'd been off limits, but she'd always stayed on my mind.

"That was amazing," she said, her voice hoarse and her breathing still fast. She closed her eyes, coming off the euphoric high she had just been on.

When she came back down, she moved her hands to my pants and started to unbuckle them. Slowly pulling the zipper down, I didn't know how much more of her teasing I could take.

"You're killing me here, babe," I said as I lifted my hips so she could push both my pants and boxers down. I heard her gasp when she first caught sight of my dick... and what an ego boost that was.

Her small fingers reached out and wrapped around my hard length. She shuffled backwards and placed her knees between my thighs. With a one last quick glance up at my face she lowered her head and licked the drop of pre-come off my tip. That earned her a deep groan as I tried to keep my hands fisted at my side. I wanted her to lead this, take things at her own pace. After a couple more strokes with her hand, she placed her lips around my cock and went all the way down 'til I felt myself hit the back of her throat.

"Holy shit, Simone!" I exclaimed as she came back up off me. She seemed pleased with the torture she was putting me through, and she went back down my length and then started sucking me off with just the right pressure and rhythm. It only took a couple minutes before I felt like I was going to shoot my load. Not wanting to finish in her mouth,

I pulled her up off of me.

"If you don't stop, I'm going to come," I gritted out, my whole body tight.

"Isn't that the point?" she asked with a chuckle.

"Tonight, I don't want to do that until I'm deep inside you," I told her, making her blush a deep crimson. But I could see the eagerness in her eyes, her need obvious as she pulled her dress off, along with her panties.

Kicking off my pants the rest of the way, along with my shoes, I gently flipped her over so she was lying on her back on the chair. Right now, I was grateful I had spent the money to buy the most comfortable loungers I could find. Lifting up my pants, I rummaged in the pocket so I could grab my wallet. It had been awhile since I'd hooked up with anyone — not since Simone asked for help with her divorce — but I always made sure to have a condom with me. I never fucked anyone without one.

I placed the wrapper between my teeth and maneuvered so I was kneeling between her spread legs. That gave me a clear view of her pussy. Even though it was dark out I could see her glistening in the moonlight. I ripped the wrapper open and rolled the latex down my shaft.

Lining my cock up with her entrance I bent down and kissed her as I pushed my way deep inside her, touching as much of her body as I could. I had to pause for a moment though. She was so tight that I was worried about embarrassing myself and coming instantly. Swallowing her screams of pleasure, I kept kissing her as I thrust in and out. I moved my hand down so I could press on that special spot again to make sure she came a second time.

"I'm going to need you to come for me, Simone," I whispered in her ear, and I felt her detonate instantly.

I pumped into her a couple more times and then my release overwhelmed all my senses. I lay on top of her for a few moments, just trying to catch my breath. Once I felt like I could move without passing out, I pushed up and looked down to see a contented smile plastered across her face.

"Babe, that was the hottest thing ever," I told her, not able to remember a time sex ever came close to feeling this good.

"I'd have to agree," she told me, just as out of breath as I was.

"We should probably get cleaned up. Want to join me in my shower?" I asked. Hoping I could convince her to continue this party for two in my bed later on.

We both got up to retrieve our clothes and put them back on. "I'm not sure that's a good idea," she said, adjusting her dress, "anyone in the house could see us together. I think I'm going to head to my room."

Of course she was right; however, it stung a little bit that she was willing to part ways so quickly.

"Ok, sounds good," I said, bending down to place one more kiss on her lips. "I'll see you in the morning."

We both made our way back downstairs and into our separate rooms. She seemed to have no problem treating this as a one-time deal. Wasn't that... a good thing? It's what I used to like about the women I dated—a few good days and nights and then no hard feelings.

As I got into bed, alone, I had this heavy feeling sitting right in the middle of my chest. Truth was, I didn't like that my time with Simone had been so brief, and that by tomorrow, she might not think twice about our night together. I knew it was all I'd be thinking about. I'd had just a taste and I wanted more.

But what if once was enough for her?

Where the hell did that leave us now?

Chapter 11

Simone

I stood under the showerhead letting the hot water pound on my back. What had I done? I let my silly schoolgirl crush on Kyle get way out of hand, that's what. I had done a lot of stupid, impulsive things in my past when it came to sex, but this had to be close to the top of the list.

Sex was always the way I tried to find acceptance. Now that I knew better, it sounded stupid, but growing up feeling like I didn't belong to anybody really did a number on me. Then being married to Brad didn't help matters; instead, he'd made me feel even worse about my past.

I hadn't had sex with anyone since the last time with my ex. He'd turned me off it and I hadn't had much of a desire until Kyle waltzed into my life. Six months of meetings and phone calls, giving so much of his time to help me with my divorce had meant so much to me. He'd shown his attentiveness and kindness toward me and Stella, but had always maintained a level of professionalism so I never thought he saw me in that way. Sure, he kissed me a couple months ago, and then he had pulled away quickly and we never talked about it again.

For all I knew, he still didn't see me as anything more than a one-night stand, which was why I wanted to savor that perfect moment and not spoil it by wanting more than he was willing to give. I knew enough to know Kyle got any girl he wanted, but he wasn't a relationship kind of guy. It wasn't like I was looking for anything serious either, but I *liked* him. A lot, too much. Even though I didn't want to ruin things with him on a friendship level, I wondered what dating someone like Kyle would be like. He was so different from other guys I'd known.

But I finally had perspective, and I felt a little wiser coming out of this process. That was partly due to seeing my therapist. A therapist Kyle had dated and probably slept with. Man, I was an idiot. Still, she made me realize I was strong and resilient. I wouldn't always get it right, and I'd screw up but I'd learn, and keep growing. I also had a great support system to catch my fall.

It was why I felt that being with Kyle tonight was like taking ten steps backwards. Resorting to old behaviors in an effort to feel wanted. I hadn't realized that I'd been lonely, missing having a man in my life. And once again, I'd slept with somebody who didn't have any real feelings for me. I was just a hookup, someone convenient. It wasn't that Kyle was a bad guy; in fact, everything I knew of him proved he was actually pretty great, but I just couldn't imagine for a second he'd want to be in a relationship with someone like me. I was a twenty-two-year-old divorcée with a child, and if that wasn't enough of a reason, he was an educated, successful lawyer and I was just a waitress with only a high school diploma. We really had nothing in common.

When he'd kissed me on the dance floor, I knew what I was getting myself into, but I didn't want to stop it. Even knowing it was going to be a one-night stand, I felt an inexplicable need to keep going. And he definitely didn't disappoint.

I had been with my fair share of guys, but none of them had ever made me feel the way Kyle had tonight. Sex with Brad had never seemed so intimate. On his best nights, Brad preferred to get off as quickly as possible and never showed much concern for my needs. On his worst nights, he seemed to enjoy degrading me with his words and not caring if he caused me physical pain.

Kyle was so different. He kissed me passionately; he looked into my eyes, said kind words to me, and most importantly, made me come. Twice! I had been so tempted to take him up on his offer to continue things, but figured it would be even harder for me to leave his room afterward. This way, it was a clean break and we could both move on with a great memory.

*****

The next morning I woke up a little after nine feeling refreshed. I was a little leery of making my way downstairs, but told myself that I wasn't going to make this awkward. I was an adult and I was going to approach the situation like one.

I stepped into the kitchen, stifling back a laugh at the three zombies barely sitting upright in their seats. The kitchen had windows all around, so there was no way for them to hide from the bright morning sun. Seeing how miserable they all looked, I was glad that I hadn't had much to drink.

"Good morning," I said in a sing-song voice.

I was met with three groans coming from my fellow partiers as they passed around a bottle of aspirin and guzzled down water.

"Morning," Kyle said. He was the only other person who appeared to be fully functional this morning. The fact that he didn't seem hung-over made me feel better about last night. At least he couldn't write me off as a drunken mistake.

"I'm making eggs and bacon for breakfast. Hopefully the grease will help these three," he said with a grin, while pointing at the others with his spatula. Ian was still in his pajamas, and Addie and Kayla were in same outfits they wore last night. Same as me. Kyle was in athletic shorts and a thin white T-shit. I looked at him for a second too long, remembering his body above mine. I felt my whole body flush, every sensory memory flaring, and I had this sudden urge to touch him, to remind myself of how his skin felt against mine. I hadn't gotten to look at his body as much as I'd wanted. I remembered that he had a tattoo on his chest from when we had been swimming at Jim and Marla's. That had been an unexpected surprise and I was disappointed I'd missed my chance to check it out a little closer last night. Everything happened so fast, the urgency and frantic pace. It was like two colliding stars going supernova. Seeing Kyle now, looking as sexy as ever, just reminded me that I'd never had a sexual experience like what we'd shared — and I likely wouldn't again.

"Can I help with anything?" I asked, trying to distract myself.

"Sure, you want to make some toast?" He pointed around his state-of-the-art kitchen. "The bread is in the pantry and the toaster is over there."

Kyle was talking to me as though nothing had happened between us, and while a part of me was grateful for that, another part wondered if last night had meant anything to him at all.

Ugh! I was sounding like a foolish little girl and it was making me mad. I should have been relieved that he wasn't making things weird. It was exactly what I wanted. Or was it?

Truthfully, I'd always wanted to have a man desire me and want a relationship with me. The idea that someone would actually pick me for who I was... it was something I never thought would happen for me. It didn't need to be Kyle, but I wanted somebody to want me like he had last night. I wanted that every night, for the rest of my life. In the past, guys wanted me for sex, and once they got it they were gone. Brad was only with me because of Stella. I longed for a man to choose me because he wanted me, to be friends as well as lovers, one who cared about me and could come to love Stella.

Deep down, however, I feared making the same bad mistakes. Another thing Dr. Hamilton had taught me was that I needed to stop thinking that I didn't deserve things. That underlying belief that I had no right to a good and decent life had fueled my early behaviors, and what had convinced me to marry Brad despite my misgivings. Brad had been a huge mistake—but he'd given me Stella, Trent and his parents, as my new family. And indirectly, Addie and Kyle. He was still a jerk, but I couldn't say I got totally screwed over.

I was feeling all these emotions from my one night with Kyle so I concentrated way more than I needed to on the task at hand. I placed the bread in the toaster and went to grab the butter and jelly. As I passed him, he looked up at me and smiled. The look he gave me was sweet with a hint of concern. I wasn't entirely sure what that look meant so I smiled back at him, hoping to convey that I was okay even though I wasn't.

We continued to move around each other, getting breakfast ready for everyone. Then I heard a text notification from Kyle's phone go off. He picked his phone up off the counter and read the message.

"Looks like we need to make another plate. Trent will be here in five minutes," he noted, setting his phone back down.

I had forgotten that Trent had gone home with Ashley. She was one of Kayla's friends from college, studying to be a nurse as well. To cheer me up one night, Kayla had organized a painting and wine event with a bunch of her school friends. Ashley and I had hit it off and she was now a regular participant in our girls' nights out.

On schedule, the doorbell rang five minutes later. Not waiting for anyone to answer, Trent walked into the house. Our three semi-conscious friends were finally waking up but still complaining about headaches and the bright sun. Trent didn't look worse for wear as he took a seat next to Ian. He must have stopped by his apartment, because he looked freshly showered and ready to start the day. He was also in cargo shorts and a red T-shirt, which he had not worn last night. His hair was still wet and he clearly wasn't suffering from a hangover.

"So this is where everyone ended up," Trent said with a smile. He nudged Ian with his elbow to which Ian scowled and pushed Trent back, harder than necessary, nearly unseating his friend. Kyle laughed. I shook my head. Boys. "Guess I'm the only one who got lucky last night."

I hoped no one could see the blush that crept up along my cheeks when I made eye contact with Kyle. He smirked at me. In turn, I giggled and then quickly covered it up with a cough while getting plates and silverware out.

"Are you going to be seeing this one again?" Kyle asked Trent. The way he asked that question was another reminder of how casual the two of them treated their hookups.

"Nah, man, not looking for anything serious, and the way she kicked me out this morning, Ashley isn't either," Trent said, good-naturedly.

"So what are we doing today?" Ian asked, finally able to speak in more than just grunts since we got some coffee in him.

"We should try to catch some waves, the surf is supposed to be pretty good today," Trent commented, looking behind him and eyeing the horizon.

"Sounds good to me," Kyle said. "What are you girls up to?"

Kayla and Addie had finally woken up as well, but that was probably because of the loaded plates of food being passed around. "What time do you need to pick up Stella today?" Addie asked me.

"Not until this evening," I said, standing across from the rest of them. "Jim and Marla are taking her to the zoo and then I'm supposed to have dinner with them."

"Let's have a girls' day then," Addie suggested, brightening.

I grinned, liking that idea a lot. "Sure."

"Pedicures and shopping it is," Kayla added.

I smiled and nodded, jabbing at my eggs. In my peripheral, I watched Kyle. I could feel him even before he walked toward me. He was the last to plate his food and he went to move in right next to me. So close that there was barely even an inch of space between us. Too close for it to not be on purpose. His closeness made it difficult to finish my breakfast. I just hoped no one could tell how much I enjoyed having his body next to mine.

*****

Trent was nice enough to drop all of us off at home since none of us had driven last night. Once I was ready, I picked up Addie and Kayla and we headed downtown. We spent a couple hours at the salon, walking out with fresh manicures and pedicures. After that we headed to the Gaslamp Quarter for some shopping. There was a distinct chill coming off the water, but walking around and the sun overhead helped keep us warm. Since it was Saturday, it was a little crowded but not as bad as it was in the summer. During tourist season, this area of San Diego felt like an international city, with visitors coming from all over the world.

I very rarely treated myself, usually spending what little extra money I had on Stella and the necessities. And with Brad not disclosing where he was working, I didn't get anything from him in the way of child support, but his parents, once again, came to my rescue. I truly appreciated their help, but at some point, I wanted to be able to pay for the rent and other things, and just be more independent. Most of my clothes were years old, but I took care of the things I had. Being that it was my birthday weekend, I treated myself to a matching bra and panty set. It was an impulse buy and I had a particular guy in mind when I'd bought it, which I knew was silly. Dating was still a scary thought since I had a daughter to think about. I couldn't date just any guy.

Just before one, we headed to Seaport Village for lunch. The restaurant we chose was right on the water and provided a beautiful view of the harbor. It didn't take us long after placing our order to get our food.

"So that Ian guy is pretty hot, huh?" Kayla asked, between bites of her turkey club.

Addie started choking on her water, causing us both to whip our heads around in her direction. She cleared her throat. "Sorry, wrong pipe," she said catching her breath.

Kayla arched an eyebrow. "Sounds like there's a story there," she pushed.

"No story," Addie said, shaking her head. "We've known each other a long time, haven't seen him in a while, that's all. So, Simone, did you have fun last night?"

I felt my cheeks blush and for a moment I thought she was talking about me hooking up with her brother. I then quickly realized she was simply asking about our time at the club and trying to get the attention off of Kayla's question about Ian.

"Last night was great," I answered, keeping it general and focusing on my pasta. "Thank you so much for planning a night out."

"Too bad the boys had to show up," Addie returned dryly. "Trying to find a guy with all of them sticking to us like glue was useless. They wouldn't have let anyone get within ten feet of us."

"Yeah but you're Kyle's sister and his friends have known you forever," Kayla pointed out. "I'm sure Simone or I could have hooked up with someone last night if the opportunity arose."

Addie poked at her salad, mulling something over before speaking. "I don't know. Trent sees Simone as a sister and would protect her probably more fiercely than he would protect me," she said. "That means Kyle would do the same. Whomever is important to one of them becomes important to all of them."

I didn't know how that made me feel. On one hand, I felt

honored knowing that Trent felt so strongly about me. On the other hand, I didn't want Kyle seeing me as someone who needed protecting. And while I was sure our night together was a one-time thing, I didn't want him to think I was too fragile to pursue.

We continued to make small talk throughout the rest of our lunch. Once we were done, I dropped Addie off at her apartment, and then drove to Kayla's place.

"Thanks again for last night, I really had a great time," I told her as she exited my car.

"It was good to see you letting loose. You should do it more often," she said with a smile as she closed the door.

It did feel good to let go last night. I felt free and at peace for the first time in a while. Until Kyle, that is. Now that my divorce was finalized, we'd have no reason to purposely see each other at all. Right? The thought of that saddened me a little. He'd sort of become a staple in my life and he got along with Stella well. In some ways, our night together signaled an end. I didn't like that thought at all, though.

I tried not to dwell on it and instead thought about positive things on the rest of the drive to my apartment. I'd just turned twenty-two. My daughter was healthy and happy. I had wonderful friends and a family that had stuck by my side. I was free of all kinds of baggage and I could do whatever I wanted. My life was pretty great and I had to remember that.

My phone beeped just as I'd entered my apartment and locked the door behind me. I'd managed to not think about Kyle for a whole fifteen minutes and now he was texting me. But I was smiling. I dropped my purse on the side table and read his message.

Kyle: *Hi. I wanted to make sure you were good.*

I read the text a couple times trying to figure out exactly what Kyle meant. Was he concerned that I was freaking out about what happened? Was he worried I was upset with him for some reason? I didn't want him to worry so I sent a reply.

Me: *I'm good. Thanks for checking. And thanks for letting us all stay at your place last night.*

I spent entirely too much time second-guessing and over analyzing what I had just sent. His text had been vague and so had mine. Finally, he texted a reply, which I had to read a few times.

Kyle: *Any time. :)*

Any time?

What in the world did he mean by that? Was that an invitation to spend more time with him? Did he want that?

Confused, I set my phone down and headed to my bathroom, deciding a nice soak in the tub would help me relax before I headed over to Marla and Jim's for dinner. I couldn't spend any more time thinking about Kyle. All it was going to do was cause me to start fantasizing about things that could never be. Instead, I sank down into my tub, closed my eyes, and tried to think of anything other than the tall, handsome man who had rocked my world last night.

*****

Around six, I knocked on the front door and Jim answered, greeting me warmly with a hug. "Hey, kiddo," he said with affection in his voice.

I hugged him back without hesitation, feeling like he was the dad I'd always wanted. "Hi, Jim," I replied, smiling big. As I walked into their home, I could immediately smell the fried chicken and mashed potatoes we were having for dinner. "How was Stella today?" I looked around but didn't see her in the living room. But I followed Jim toward the kitchen.

"She was wonderful as always," he said over his left shoulder. The twinkle in his eyes made me happy, because he truly loved his role as grandpa. "She seemed to enjoy the zoo, especially the monkeys."

When I walked into the kitchen, I laughed. Stella was sitting on the island watching Marla put together a salad while holding a brand new stuffed monkey.

Jim and I shared a grin.

"Okay, she really, *really* liked the monkeys," he said, and chuckled. Jim and Marla didn't go overboard spoiling Stella. They were already helping me out enough as it was, but I did appreciate that they could give her things that would be difficult for me to do.

"That's an awfully big salad," I commented, looking at the bowl in front of Marla. "Is Brad joining us?"

Technically it was his visitation day but I couldn't remember the last time he saw Stella. I had no desire to see him, but I would deal with it if he showed up.

"No, honey, he's not coming," she answered with a sad

look in her eyes. I knew how disappointed she was in Brad. I did think she continued to hold out hope that he would eventually change his ways. "But Trent and Kyle are coming over for dinner."

"Oh, really?" I said, trying to sound nonchalant. I wasn't ready to come face to face with Kyle. My thoughts had been all over the place since I left his house this morning. Now I was going to have to pretend that he didn't affect me and I was going to have to do it with the Thompsons in the same room.

As if on cue, the front door burst open and in walked the two guys I had just seen a few hours ago.

"Where's my favorite niece?" I heard Trent yell from the doorway. When Stella was around, no one else existed in Trent's mind. In every way that mattered, Jim and Trent completely filled the father role in Stella's life. For me, it made the sting of Brad's continued apathy toward his daughter just barely tolerable.

"Unky Trent!" Stella squealed.

"There she is," he said as he rounded the corner, scooping her off the island and moving over to kiss his mother on the cheek. Then he moved to me and repeated the gesture.

Kyle greeted Trent's parents and then turned his gaze on me. "Hello, Simone," he said, a bit formally. He didn't give me a hug or a kiss like Trent had but the look he gave me was smoldering.

I quickly averted my gaze. Last night was all that had been playing in my head. I had to stop those thoughts, though, or I'd be blushing all through dinner. "How was surfing?" I asked, focusing on generic conversation.

"Cold," Trent said, giving a mock shiver. We all smiled

when it made Stella giggle. "I was thinking of doing a bonfire out on the beach, but Kyle wanted to come over and crash your little party here instead."

"Just to deliver something," Kyle said quickly. From behind me, he placed two envelopes on the island right next to me. "Since we didn't know we would end up seeing you last night."

I stared at the envelopes in surprise and turned, looking at him. "You didn't need to get me anything, but that was very sweet," I said, ridiculously pleased at the gesture.

"Well, one of the cards is from me, y'know," Trent said teasingly.

I grinned at him. "You're the best," I proclaimed, which seemed to appease his ego.

"You all ended up at the same place last night?" Jim asked, overhearing my conversation with Kyle.

"Yeah, at a club," Trent explained.

"I hope you boys didn't keep the girls from having a good time," Marla admonished lightly.

"I'm pretty sure they had a good time. Didn't you, Simone?" Kyle asked, smirking at me.

I blushed furiously and said, "Um yeah, I had a good time." I couldn't even look over at him afraid that I would give everything away with just one look.

"Okay, kids, the food is ready," Marla announced as she and Jim headed to the dining room.

Trent, still holding Stella, eyed the two of us a little too long before leaving the kitchen.

Kyle looked at me and smiled, and then he held his hand out in front of him and said, "After you."

As I passed in front of him, he placed his hand on the small of my back gently guiding me out of the kitchen. As we came into view of everyone, he removed his hand from me.

Trent had taken the seat next to Stella and was already dishing up food on her plate. That left the two seats that were next to each other for Kyle and me. He pulled out my chair for me and once I was settled, he again placed himself just inches from my left.

Dinner was quite enjoyable with everyone chatting with each other but Kyle constantly distracted me. Every time he shifted in his seat, or his leg bumped into mine, or his elbow brushed against my arm, it sent little sparks along my skin. After a few 'accidental' touches I looked over at him, but he never looked back at me. Instead, he stayed engaged in the conversation. I knew it was just in my head. I was putting myself on edge over nothing. Just my imagination in overdrive and it was annoying.

"Stella and I have a surprise for you," Marla announced when we were all done eating. I was actually relieved that dinner was coming to an end. Sitting next to Kyle was becoming torturous.

"Cake!" Stella exclaimed, moving her chubby legs and arms in the air and causing all of us to laugh.

Marla stood up. "Stella helped me make a cake for your birthday. I'll go get it."

When Marla returned, she was carrying a double layer chocolate cake that had twenty-two candles on it. Jim quickly got up to turn off the lights and then Marla led the guys in singing to me.

"Make a wish," Marla said.

I took a moment to look around the room before making my wish. Seeing everyone's smiling faces made it easy for me to decide what to wish for. I wished that I would never lose this family I had come to love with every part of my heart. I smiled and then blew out my candles.

After indulging in a very large piece of chocolate goodness, I started to pack up so Stella and I could go. Leaving everyone in the living room, I ran up to the guestroom to get her favorite blanket. I found it in the crib that Jim and Marla had set up when Stella was just a newborn. When I turned to head back downstairs, I ran right into a solid brick wall. Kyle's hands reached out and gently grasped my shoulders to steady my balance and my hands landed on his torso, gripping his shirt. It took my brain a moment to realize it was actually a person and I looked up and met his darkening gaze.

"You startled me... I-I didn't know you were there," I stuttered.

"I'm sorry, I just needed to have a minute with you..." he said, his voice low and urgent. His expression was intense and the same single-minded focus I'd seen last night echoed in his eyes right now. All he saw was me.

You're gorgeous.

He'd said that. To me! And he had meant it. Two words that had made me feel like I was the most desirable woman in the world. And while I didn't see myself that way, I trusted Kyle to tell me the truth, a trait he practiced in his business and personal life. He'd proved that to me over the past six months.

I almost took a step back, but I was rooted to the spot. I let my hands drift off his body. He released me too, excruciatingly slow, to the point where just his fingertips danced across my skin until he was no longer touching me. I exhaled the air I'd been holding, caught up in the moment. I was anticipating his next move, wanting that light touch again. It was confusing — he was confusing — but it was also exhilarating. I'd never had this kind of attraction to someone before. Kyle's very presence was heady.

"I needed to talk to you before you left," he said, looking over his shoulder briefly before resuming. "I was going to try and pretend like nothing happened between us since it appeared that was what you wanted — but I can't do that. I can't stop thinking about last night. About you."

I took a moment to process what he was saying. At the real possibility that Kyle wanted me, wanted to be with me and something more.

"I can't stop thinking about it, either," I finally said. I needed to be honest, though. "This is... complicated. I have Stella and she thinks the world of you and... it could be really confusing for her."

He nodded, sighing. "I know that, I do..." He paused, wearing a grim expression.

"What is it?" I asked.

"Trent."

I frowned, confused. "What?"

"Sisters are off limits. Kind of like a universal code."

"Oh..." I said slowly. Trent was super protective. "You've been friends with him for over twenty years." I bit my lower lip, all these complications multiplying. "Jim and Marla see you like another son, but I just divorced their actual son and... This could get really messy in an instant by moving too fast before everyone has gotten used to the new way of things."

"I just thought that same thing, too," he returned, brows furrowed.

I thought back to my conversation at lunch with Kayla and Addie. But I didn't voice the fear that they all might think Kyle was taking advantage of me. Even though he wouldn't be, I knew perception was just as dangerous as one's actions. I also had no idea how Brad would react. While his opinion didn't matter anymore, he knew how to hurt people, especially his family. And I knew he'd hate the idea of Kyle and me together. He'd lash out, just to spite us all. Why invite trouble when everything was calm and easy right now? Why risk rocking the boat, even if I wanted Kyle, and he wanted me?

Kyle was quiet for a minute and I think we were both second-guessing what he'd come in here to say. "You're right, there are some complications but none of them are making me want to stop pursuing whatever this is between us, and I know you feel it like I do. This back and forth has been going on for months, Simone. I back off, you back off, and we tell ourselves it's nothing or we let our fears get the better of us but last night proved our connection is real. It's special. And it's not going away," he paused, cupping my jaw with his hands. "We don't have to tell anyone right now. We could just explore things and see where they lead. I just know I want to spend more time with you *and* Stella. I'm hoping you want that, too."

He gave me a whisper-soft kiss on my lips and dropped his hands from my face, waiting for my response. Everything he'd said had caught me off guard. He was right. I had spent the entire day telling myself that what we shared had been nothing more than a one-night stand. That his interest in me was purely professional, and then just as a friend. Nothing romantic, no attraction, all those quiet looks and lingering touches, his hugs and his attention, that all those signs were innocuous. Innocent. I had enjoyed the time we had spent together these last few months, but I never thought he truly felt the same. Between seeing the kind of women he dated up close and the stories I'd heard, I knew I didn't quite meet the standards he was used to. What if I didn't measure up? But what if everything I was afraid of risking ended up being the best decision I could ever make?

"Simone?" Kyle gently prodded and I realized I hadn't responded to him yet.

I took a deep breath. Kyle was different from every man I'd been with, just as I was different from any woman he'd been with. "I would love that," I said honestly. "But are you really willing to take that sort of risk on me if people find out?" I had to ask it. I wanted no regrets and I wanted us to be on the same page.

"First of all, you don't give yourself enough credit. You are definitely worth the risk. But I think you're worrying about something that might not even be a big deal. Jim and Marla love you. Sure, it might be weird for them to see you with someone else, it's just because they had hoped that your relationship with Brad would have worked out. They aren't going to be mad at you for moving on."

He sounded so confident in the Thompsons' reaction that I had no choice but to believe him. I smile up at him. "Okay," I whispered, nervous and excited, so freaking happy, and really scared.

His smile lit up his whole face, like I just gave him the best present ever. "So how about having dinner with me this Wednesday?" he asked.

My mind immediately went to my daughter. "Uh, I don't have anyone to watch Stella," I stated, making it obvious this wasn't going to be easy. Even without the other complications I still had Stella to think about. My priority was always going to be my daughter. I hoped Kyle could handle that and not in a theoretical way.

"In case you haven't noticed, I like hanging out with that munchkin. She can go to dinner with us," he said.

The smile on my face couldn't have been any bigger. Here was a really amazing man who not only wanted to date me, but was willing to spend time with my daughter.

"That sounds great," I responded, beaming. "I better get back downstairs. Why don't you text me with the details?"

Just as I was about to move around him to leave, he reached out and grabbed my wrist lightly. "I can't wait for Wednesday," he said, his smile almost blinding me. Then he leaned down and placed a soft kiss on my lips.

He let me go and I went back to the living room so we could say our goodbyes. I drove home with the biggest grin on my face.

Chapter 12

Kyle

*M*ondays were usually busy for me in the office, but today was rather slow. That gave me plenty of time to think about my date with Simone that was coming up in two days.

I had spent the entire day on Saturday at war with myself over Simone. I didn't have much experience with the whole relationship thing. And while I didn't think she was looking for marriage right at this moment, I could guess that was her endgame. She wasn't going to be interested in the type of relationships I usually had, which were basically occasional dates, some sex, and nothing deeper than that. But there was something about her that made me willing to try to have an actual relationship. I could not screw this up.

When I thought about why I was willing to try this with Simone, I realized it was because I trusted her. That was a big deal for me and what had held me back from pursuing other relationships. I was so afraid of having a toxic relationship like my parents that I never completely opened myself up to another person when it came to dating. But I had seen how strong Simone had become, and I knew that we could communicate and work through things together.

I was definitely looking forward to spending some time with her, albeit a little apprehensive. Sure, I had seemed confident when I was trying to convince her to go out with me, but she was right when she said there would be complications regarding us seeing each other. However, unlike her, the Thompsons were the least of my worries. Simone was a mother and I knew stability for her and her daughter was of the upmost importance to her. I would be lying if I said dating a woman with a child didn't make me a little nervous. What if I wasn't so different from my own parents and didn't handle the responsibility of such an important role in a child's life very well?

But when I thought about Stella, I was excited to spend more time with her. That was a feeling I hadn't quite expected. I hadn't been around kids much until Trent became an uncle. He loved spending time with that little girl which resulted in me spending time with her. She was so easy-going and adorable. Keeping her entertained never felt like a chore; she was just fun.

As I sat staring out my office window, I heard a quiet knock on my door. I spun around in my chair to see Addie standing in the doorway.

I picked up my pen to give the impression that I was actually working. "Hey, sis, what's up?" I asked.

"I was going to ask you the same thing. I've walked by your door three times now and each time you were just staring out into space. Something on your mind?" she asked.

Addie knew how to read me. Trent, Ian, and Erik may have been my best friends, but she was the one person who knew me better than anybody. I don't think either of us would be the people we were today if it wasn't for the love and support of each other.

That was why Addie's reaction to what I was about to tell her mattered so much to me. I knew Simone and I had talked about keeping this to ourselves for now. I just couldn't hide anything from my sister.

"Yeah, I've got a bit on my mind," I said.

221

"Something you want to talk about?" she asked.

"Come on in and close the door," I said, leaning back in my chair.

She did as I asked and sat in the chair across from my desk. "This sounds serious, now I'm worried," she said.

"There's nothing to be worried about," I explained. "I asked Simone out on a date. I'm excited about it. I want to know what you think about it, though."

She looked at me, her mouth open in shock. "Oh, wow. Okay. Um..." She paused for a minute, probably trying to figure out what to say or at least how to say it. "The two of you have been dancing around each other for months now, but I'm not going to lie, I'm a little nervous about you pursuing something with her."

I wasn't expecting her to say that. I thought she had worked everything out with Simone. Now I was worried that things weren't as cool between them as it appeared. Although that didn't make sense since they spent a lot of time together and she had taken Simone out for her birthday.

"Stop," she said, shaking her head. "I can see the wheels turning in your head. I'm nervous, just not for the reason you're probably thinking. I really like Simone. She and I have become very close friends in the last couple months, even though that may be weird to some people." Addie paused. "I'm nervous for her. She isn't just some girl you can sleep with and then walk away from. She was married to an asshole. Someone who didn't treat her well at all. She's opened up to me a little bit, despite the fact that Brad really fucked with her head and did some horrible things. I know you would never intentionally set out to hurt her, but she *is* vulnerable. She needs to be handled with care even if she

222

doesn't think so."

I understood what Addie was saying. I knew how much damage Brad had done and I was also aware of how strong Simone had become. I could appreciate the fact that Addie wanted to protect Simone, but I was also a little disheartened she was unsure of whether I would be able to step into the role of boyfriend.

"Wait…" I said slowly. I stared hard at Addie. "What the hell did you mean by 'Brad really fucked with her head and did some horrible things'? I know he was verbally abusive and cheated on her—"

"There's more to it than that," Addie interrupted.

"What do you mean 'there's more to it'? What else did he do?" I asked, feeling my anger rising. I thought I knew all there was to know about their relationship. I found the idea that she may have hidden an important detail of her relationship from me slightly frustrating. On a professional level, it may have been something important to take into consideration for her filing, but more importantly, on a personal level, I wanted her to open up to me.

"Look, it's not my story to tell. I don't want to ever break the trust Simone had when she shared with me. Just know there will be some hurdles the two of you will need to climb over together if you pursue this."

"Okay, I get that. But I have to know… are you okay with me going out with her?"

She smiled. "I would love nothing more than to see both of you happy. If being together does that for you guys, then I'm totally fine with it."

"Thanks, Addie, that means a lot. I would appreciate it, though, if you didn't tell anybody about this. We've decided to keep it between us for now even though I just told you. I don't think I'm ready to tell Trent yet and I know she's not ready to tell anyone."

Addie laughed. "Yeah, I'm not sure he'll be as cool with it as I am. Ever since the divorce he has become super protective of both those girls. He would for sure kick your ass, especially if you hurt them."

"He wishes he could kick my ass," I said with a chuckle, even though her words made me consider his reaction to this possible news.

As my sister exited my office I realized how much her acceptance had meant to me.

*****

Two days had never moved so slowly, but it was finally Wednesday, which meant date night. I was able to leave the office at five, which was early for me. I went home to get ready, having told Simone I would pick her up at six-thirty. We had decided we would go out for dinner and then go to her apartment to watch a movie so she could put Stella to bed at eight.

It sounded like a perfect night, comfortable and relaxed. We were going to a family restaurant near her place since we had Stella with us. I dressed in a pair of dark-wash jeans and a black, long sleeve, button-down shirt. I rolled the sleeves up a little just to look a bit more casual. I grabbed the keys to my BMW and headed to Simone's apartment.

I knocked on the door and waited for a couple minutes before a flustered Simone answered the door.

"I'm so sorry, but we're running late. Stella took a late

nap, I just got her dressed and I haven't finished getting myself ready," she said without taking a breath. She ushered me in and closed the door behind me.

I looked her up and down as she ran her hands through her long, damp hair. She was in tight-fitting jeans and loose-fitted top. She looked damn good. "Why don't I watch Stella while you finish getting ready," I offered. "I don't mind."

She stared at me and then smiled. "Are you sure?"

"I've been around Stella often enough, Simone. I can handle her just fine," I returned, chuckling.

She grabbed my hand and dragged me into the living room. "Oh! I can put on a video for her," she said.

"Hey, it's all good," I said, squeezing her hand. "Stella and I will find something to keep us occupied. You just go do what you need to."

Stella was on the floor looking happy as she rolled around in her dress. Her dark hair was in a braid, which had a green bow at the end. When she looked up at me, she smiled big.

"Hi, baby girl," I said softly. "Let's go to find some toys while your mommy finishes getting dressed and then we can go get dinner. Does that sound good?"

Stella nodded her head affirmatively and grabbed ahold of my hand. I saw Simone just standing there, staring at us with a look of disbelief on her face. I smiled at her and she shook her head, coming out of whatever trance she was in, and headed toward her bedroom.

After about ten minutes, Simone came out in a simple, fitted cotton dress that showed off her curves. It was navy blue with a pattern of tiny, white anchors and she had a white sweater over it. Even though she was covered up, she was still sexy. She'd kept her hair down and her makeup was light so her features naturally came out. She caught me staring at her and I grinned when she started fidgeting by smoothing out her dress. "Do I... look okay?"

I took a minute to take her in, trying to remind myself to breathe in then out. Dinner at the Thompsons' last Saturday had been a trial, trying to not to be obvious in front of everyone. Sitting next to her for an hour and feeling her presence had made it difficult to keep up with the conversation. I wasn't even going to think about how she'd looked at the club and what followed afterwards. I did not want embarrass myself in front of both Simone and Stella.

"You look stunning, Simone," I said. She blushed, clearly liking my appraisal.

I got up from my spot next to Stella. I'd been reading her a Dr. Seuss book that she'd mostly poked at while telling me her own version of the story. I picked her up and we were all ready to go to dinner. Simone led us out of the apartment and I started to walk toward my car when she stopped me with a hand on my arm.

"We should probably take my car since Stella's car seat is already installed in it," she said, reminding me of the additional things kids needed.

"Ok," I responded. Having her drive wasn't my idea of taking her on a date, but it made sense. Truth be told, most of the girls I dated were excited to ride in my BMW. Simone was very different from those women.

We veered from my car and back to her parking space. Simone was much shorter than me and I had to remind myself to not take such long strides or she'd have to jog next to me. I didn't think she'd appreciate that in three-inch heels and carrying a diaper bag that was almost bigger than her. Meanwhile, Stella squirmed in my arms, her big brown eyes taking in the world around her. I think she liked seeing things from this vantage point.

We all piled into her late model Honda Civic and made our way to the restaurant. In the back, behind me, Stella chatted to both of us on the way. She seemed just as excited about this date as I was.

We were seated right away in a booth in the back of the dining room. Simone and I sat across from each other while Stella was in a high chair at the end of the table. After we ordered, and Stella was distracted by the crayons the hostess had given her, I asked Simone about work. I didn't know how she managed to work such late nights waitressing, keep up with classes, and still take care of Stella during the day. I knew Jim and Marla helped out a lot, along with her friend Kayla, but Simone did as much as humanly possible on her own. I knew being able to do for herself and Stella was really important to her. It made me respect her even more.

I think some of it was a pride thing for her. I also think she was worried she was inconveniencing those who helped her. I wish she could see herself the way I did. She was an incredible woman who was dealt a shit hand in life. That being said, she was making the best of what she had. And she was doing a damn good job, from everything I could see.

"Work is going okay, but balancing it with my school work is proving to be difficult," she shared with me.

"Have you thought about cutting back on your hours to focus on school?" I asked, knowing such a heavy workload had to be difficult.

She took a sip of her water. "I'm barely making ends meet as it is, and that's with help from Jim and Marla. I can't afford to lose any more hours."

It pissed me off knowing that if Brad would actually pay

his child support he would be able to lessen her burden.

"So how's work going for you?" she asked, effectively changing topics.

I wanted her to feel relaxed and enjoy herself, so for tonight, I moved along to safer topics. "I've been pretty busy lately with lots of late nights at the office. But I enjoy my work so it's not too bad."

We continued to talk about her plans once she finished school. She couldn't wait to be a teacher and I knew one day her dreams would come true. By the time we were leaving, I knew, without a doubt, I wanted to continue seeing Simone. She was beautiful, intelligent, ambitious, and more mature than most women her age. I was completely entranced by her.

We loaded up in Simone's car and made our way back to her apartment. Stella fell asleep on the way home so I got her out of her car seat and carried her into the apartment. Instead of going directly into Stella's room, Simone directed me to her room and told me to place Stella on her bed.

"It's easier to change her on my bed when she is asleep," she explained.

I sat next to the sleeping girl while Simone went to get a fresh diaper and pajamas. She came back and started to work on getting Stella ready for bed. As she did that, I took the time to glance around her small bedroom. The walls were freshly painted white. Her furniture was mismatched, probably pieces she found on sale somewhere, and her bedding was a very girly purple and pink flower pattern.

"I didn't take you for the super girly type," I teased, rubbing my hand across the top of the comforter.

She chuckled. "I'm usually not, but I needed a fresh start

in my new room."

"New room?" That had me confused. I knew this was the same apartment she'd lived in with Brad.

"Yeah, this is the second bedroom. The master is across the hall and is now Stella's room. I scrubbed that room clean but still couldn't stand to sleep in there knowing what had happened," she told me, matter-of-factly. "I figured changing the rooms around would help me deal with everything. Truthfully, I like this room a lot more than the other one and I feel better knowing my room is the first one that is accessible from the hallway rather than Stella's."

She really was a pro at this mom stuff.

I watched as Simone picked up the still-sleeping Stella and carried her across the hall. I stood by the doorway and watched as she kissed her daughter and placed her in her crib.

We walked back to the living room together and sat on the couch. It was obvious neither of us were quite ready for this evening to end.

Deciding I wanted to know where she stood with us continuing to see each other, I broached the subject gently. "So, I had a really great time tonight with you and Stella," I said, meaningfully. "I'm hoping we can go out again soon."

"I had a wonderful time, too," she said with a slight blush crawling up her cheeks. That blush was super cute.

My intention was to take this slow, but I still leaned in to brush a soft kiss on her lips. As soon as our mouths met, the kiss became much more passionate than I had anticipated. I wasn't complaining at all, Simone could kiss and I enjoyed the feel of her lips on mine.

I started to run my hands up her torso, and as soon as my

thumbs brushed under her breasts, she pulled away from me. That was a bit unexpected, so I wasn't going to push anything.

"I'm sorry," she said, breathing heavy. "It just feels weird to be making out with someone while Stella is here. That sounds stupid, I'm sure."

"Hey," I said, lifting her face to meet my eyes. "There is no need to rush here so please don't apologize. If you need to slow things down or set some boundaries, I'm totally fine with that. That's not to say that I'm not anxiously waiting to get you back in bed. Once you are up for it, I definitely want a repeat," I said, winking at her.

That made her laugh, which I was happy about. I didn't want her feeling bad about stopping, but I also wanted her to know how much I desired her. We spent two more hours just talking. That was definitely the most I had ever talked to a female in one night.

It was just after ten, so I got up to say goodbye. "Are you doing anything this Saturday? I really want to go out again," I told her.

"Saturday works for me. Trent actually asked if he could have Stella that day," she said, following me to the door. "I don't think he's planning on keeping her overnight, but he'll have her most of the day."

"Why don't you come over to my house and I can make you lunch?" I asked, thinking that was safe, and not too fast for her. Thank God Ian had found a place of his own and I had my house back to myself. "Then we could either take a walk along the beach or just hang out at the house."

"That sounds perfect," she said, sounding excited.

At the door I turned around and kissed her gently. As I

pulled away I noticed the slight smile playing across her lips. I was happy to be the person to put that smile there.

"I had a great time with the two of you tonight."

"Me too," she said. After another kiss, she gently closed the door behind me. I waited to hear her turn the deadbolt and then I walked down to my car. I didn't want to leave her tonight, but at least I had Saturday to look forward to.

Chapter 13

Simone

*W*hy did time move so slow when you were looking forward to something? At least I had Stella, school, and work to keep me busy while I anticipated my first date alone with Kyle.

My evening shifts at the restaurant were finally producing decent tips again. I was happy about that because I was tired of struggling for money at every turn, and taking handouts. When my car had broken down, Kyle had made a good point about accepting help, although this wasn't about me being ashamed that I needed help because I knew I did. It was about proving to myself that I had it in me to provide for my daughter. People treating me with kid gloves would only stop when I could show them that I wasn't broken — because I wasn't. I wasn't where I needed to be yet, but I would get there someday, and that was the point.

Kyle was also motivating me. He was successful, driven, and had an incredible life. He could have any woman, be with any woman, but for some reason, he saw something in me. Our long conversations made me feel like he really wanted to know me. No one had ever shown that kind of interest in the small details of my life. It was the difference in dating a man versus an immature boy. Like Brad, and all the other guys I'd dated in the past.

When Saturday finally rolled around, the anticipation I felt about a day alone with Kyle was both exciting and nerve-wracking. One would think the fact we'd already had sex would alleviate some of the butterflies I had swarming my stomach. Instead, the opposite was true. We could easily chalk that night up to getting wrapped up in the moment—a crazy night that became something that was never meant to be. Now that we had decided to start seeing each other, I felt like there was all sorts of pressure.

After Trent had picked up Stella, I spent the rest of the morning going through my closet, searching for just the perfect outfit. I wanted to look my best for Kyle since I felt like he was completely out of my league. I still didn't understand what a young, attractive, successful lawyer would want with an uneducated, average-looking, divorced mom.

I told myself I needed to let those insecurities go and instead focus on having a good time. I really wanted to give him a chance and see where things would lead. Seeing him interact with Stella the other night made him even more attractive. He paid more attention to her during our date than Brad ever had when we were together as a family. Kyle was making it too easy to fall for him.

I knew it was crazy, and moving fast, but I felt strongly for Kyle. It had only been six months since I filed for divorce, but I'd known for a long time things weren't right. A lot of good intentions had brought Brad and me together, but neither of us had brought any real emotion to our union. I didn't think I had ever felt this way about a man before.

Searching through my closet one more time, I settled on a pair of dark skinny jeans with a cream-colored sweater and brown boots. I figured that was casual enough if we went for a walk on the pier and would keep me warm since it was overcast today. I decided to wear my new bra and panty set I had purchased for my birthday. I wasn't necessarily planning on a repeat of last weekend, but it wouldn't hurt to be prepared. Besides, they made me feel pretty and I could use the self-esteem boost.

We had agreed that I would come over around noon. Seeing as it was twenty minutes 'til, I grabbed the cookies I had baked with Stella's "help" last night and went downstairs to my car. I was still slightly embarrassed that Kyle had been in my old vehicle the other night. He must have thought my car was just awful compared to his gorgeous BMW. He never said a word about it though, just rode around like it was the most natural thing in the world.

Once I reached Kyle's house, I parked in his driveway. I grabbed my purse, then the cookies off the passenger seat, and made my way to his front door.

As soon as I knocked, I felt the butterflies increase exponentially. When he opened the door I was overwhelmed, once again, by just how gorgeous this man was. I loved that his six-foot-two-inch frame towered over me. He made me feel safe and protected. His eyes shone like perfect emeralds and his smile lit up his entire face.

"Hi there," he said as he leaned in and gently kissed me on the lips. One thing was for sure, Kyle knew how to kiss. And he showed affection easily.

Breathlessly, I returned his greeting. His smile said he knew just how much he affected me. "This is a gift from Stella." I smiled as I handed him the plate of cookies.

"Oh wow, chocolate chip is my favorite. How did she know?" he asked with an endearing grin.

"Lucky guess," I replied as he led me into his house.

The night of my birthday, I hadn't really gotten a chance to truly appreciate the beauty of his home. The living room had large bay windows facing the ocean with a masculine black leather couch and large screen television. There was a dining room connected to the living room with the kitchen just past that. The kitchen had beautiful white cabinets and dark black granite countertops. All the appliances were stainless steel, and it was almost too beautiful to want to cook in. Just beyond the kitchen was another small seating area.

I followed Kyle into the kitchen where he placed the cookies on the counter. He pulled out a glass container filled with chicken that appeared to be marinating and then grabbed some utensils out of the drawers.

"I thought we could grill this chicken for tacos. How does that sound?" he asked.

"That sounds great," I answered. "What can I help you with?"

He pointed to the fridge with the tongs. "How about you grab a couple beers out of there and come keep me company upstairs."

I liked that he could cook; he even seemed to enjoy it. Cooking had never been enjoyable for me, but I did it because Stella and I needed to eat. I had a feeling cooking with Kyle could be something I could get used to. I followed him up to the rooftop deck where his grill was. As soon as I walked out I was flooded with memories of our night together. To say it was the best sex I ever had would be putting it mildly.

Kyle must have been able to read my thoughts because I looked up and found him staring at me with a knowing look on his face.

"This became my favorite part of the house last Friday," he said with a wink.

My smile grew wide from the simple comment. Knowing that it *had* meant something to him as well made me happy. I mostly watched Kyle as he grilled and I drank my beer, occasionally looking out at the ocean to watch the waves crash against the shore. The beach below wasn't busy at all since it was off-season, though I did see a few surfers.

After the chicken was done grilling, we went back down to the kitchen. He cut it up while I got out the toppings he'd prepped earlier. We made our tacos and sat at the dining table. Once again, conversation between the two of us flowed naturally. There weren't any awkward silences or small talk just for the sake of talking. Being with Kyle felt comfortable.

"Do you want to walk down to the pier?" he asked, after we had cleaned up.

"I'd love to!" I said.

The pier was just about half a mile down the street from his house so it was an easy walk. As soon as we were on the sidewalk he grabbed my hand, lacing his fingers with mine. It was a simple gesture that made me feel good. This was exactly how a date should be.

Once we got to the pier we decided to walk the quarter-mile down to the end. The sound of the waves was relaxing. At the end we stood together watching the sailboats out in the water and the birds flying around. Off in the distance we could see a pod of dolphins splashing around. The wind out here was a bit stronger and had brought quite a chill with it.

Noticing my shiver, Kyle moved behind me and wrapped his large arms around me. I leaned back in his embrace, and in that moment, I felt perfectly content.

"This feels nice, you in my arms," he said softly in my ear.

I nodded my head. "Yeah, it does," I agreed.

Kyle nuzzled into the side of my neck and placed a couple light kisses there. "You smell amazing and taste even better."

My knees went weak at that statement. I loved the way he spoke to me. Every word was genuine.

"How about we head back to my house," he suggested. "I'm not sure I can keep acting appropriately if we stay like this out here."

"Lead the way," I responded with a coy smile.

The walk home seemed to take twice as long as the walk there, even though it was obvious we were both speed-walking, anxious to get back.

As soon as we walked into the house, he spun me around and started kissing me passionately. His tongue was playing against mine. I returned his kisses just as roughly.

He pulled away, breathing heavily, and looked into my eyes. "Simone, if you want to slow down please let me know. I don't want you to feel like this is why I suggested getting together at my house, but—I'm not sure I can stop unless you tell me to."

"You'd better not stop," I said, surprising even myself with my demand.

"Thank God," I heard him mutter before slamming his lips back against mine.

I think I shocked him by pulling at his clothes. I wasn't normally this forward, but after so many months I was ready. The crazy thing was that I trusted him completely and felt like I could be honest about whatever I needed in the moment.

In one swift move I felt him lift me up so I wrapped my legs around his trim waist. He started to move and it took me a moment to realize we were headed for the stairs. I started to wiggle to get down so we could walk up.

"Keep your legs where they are, babe. I got you," he said.

Kyle was able to the climb the stairs effortlessly and walked us into his room before setting me down gently on his bed. I quickly looked around his bedroom admiring the way the light brightened up the space.

Kyle reached for the back of his shirt, grabbed it by the collar and lifted it up over his head. I stared at his toned chest and abs and I finally got a good look at the tattoo on the right side of his chest. He was the epitome of a professional attorney, but his tattoo was in complete contrast to that. Something about it made me hot. Maybe it was the bad boy vibe it gave off while still knowing I was safe with him. Realizing my mouth was hanging open, I quickly snapped it shut.

"See something you like?" he asked. The laughter was clear in his voice.

"Absolutely," I said. "Now get back over here so I can admire your body with my hands."

"That's the best offer I've ever had," he said and he climbed back on the bed, pushing me to my back.

Kneeling between my legs, he placed his hands on both sides of my face and kissed me deeply. All the while my hands roamed all over his back. A few moments later, he moved his hands down my sides so he could remove my sweater. As soon as it cleared my bra, he used his other hand to pull me up so he could pull the sweater off over my head.

"Do you know how beautiful you are, Simone?" he asked.

I never felt like anyone saw me that way so I had no idea what to say.

"You are the most beautiful woman I've ever laid eyes on," he said, not waiting for me to answer.

His hand snaked up to my breast where he pinched my nipple through the lacy fabric. Seeming irritated to not be touching my skin, he yanked down the cup exposing the nipple that had been hidden. He trailed kisses down my chest and then took the hardened point into his mouth. He sucked hard, making me moan loudly. My moans spurred him on so he quickly pulled down the other cup so he could lavish my other breast with the same attention.

The stimulation on my breasts was increasing my arousal, and before I realized what I was doing, I had my legs hooked together behind his back while I rocked my hips up against him.

"I could stay here playing with your tits all day, but the way you're grinding on me tells me you want a bit more," he said playfully. His hands descended toward the button of my jeans. He was able to pull them down quickly somehow getting my boots off too in the process.

His hand moved into my panties and I was slightly embarrassed by how wet I was. His fingers slid around, occasionally rubbing my clit. It was just enough to drive me wild, but not enough to allow me to orgasm.

"You're so wet, babe. I need to taste you," he said as he pulled my panties down.

Out of habit I closed my legs once I no longer had any fabric to cover me. I didn't have a lot of body confidence and was worried that once Kyle saw me completely naked in the light he wouldn't find me attractive. Brad had complained about my stretch marks and would tell me all the time how he had a hard time finding me attractive after watching me deliver a baby.

I shook my head to get rid of the old memories and be in the moment with the incredible man who was touching me in ways I had never experienced. But still, I placed my hands over my stomach to conceal the parts I wasn't comfortable with.

"Please don't hide from me. I want to see all of you," he said. His hands roamed over my entire body again. "You're perfect."

His words brought tears to my eyes. I had never had someone speak so lovingly to me. It allowed me to relax even more. Soon, his mouth had made its way to the apex of my thighs. He started with a couple long licks across my entire slit. The sounds of pleasure coming from him were a huge turn on. As he moved up to place quick flicks against my clit, he pushed two fingers inside of me.

Everything felt so good that I had moved my hands to the sides of his head in an effort to hold him in place. My hips started to buck and I was essentially grinding against his face. I quickly lost all control and felt my orgasm roll through me hard. Right then I was glad he had space between him and the neighbors, otherwise they would have been able to hear me yelling out my release.

As I came down from that earth-shattering orgasm, I realized Kyle still had on half his clothes. I pushed on his shoulders until he rolled onto his back and made quick work of his jeans.

"Condom," I demanded.

He reached into the drawer next to his bed and handed one to me with a smile, daring me to put it on him.

I grabbed it out of his hand, ripped open the packaging, and quickly rolled it down the generous length of him. Straddling his hips, I took him in one hand while I lowered myself down on him. When he was fully inside me, I took a moment to relish the feel of him. I felt completely full. Once my body had acclimated to his size, I began to move up and down his shaft. I maintained eye contact with him as I rode him hard. The look of pure pleasure on his face was a major confidence boost.

After a few minutes, he grabbed my hips and flipped us over so he was above me. He started pushing into me with a faster pace. He reached his hand between us and started to rub my clit with his thumb.

"Babe, I'm almost done, but I need you to come with me," he gritted out, strain on his face and in his voice.

"I'm right there," I told him, not wanting to take my eyes off him when he came.

A few more pumps of his hips, and some more pressure on my clit, I detonated around him for the second time. I could feel him find his release as well. He laid on me for a moment while I felt his final pulses before he got up to remove the condom.

He leaned down to kiss me again. "That was fucking incredible," he said as he got up and went to the bathroom. I could hear him rummaging around so I assumed he was cleaning up. When he returned he had a washcloth that he used to clean me up. I had never felt so taken care of.

Instead of getting back up, he threw the washcloth toward the bathroom door and scooted closer to me. When he reached the middle he pulled me to him so my back was against his chest and wrapped his arms around me. Being in his arms was quickly becoming my favorite place to be. We stayed like that for a while, completely content in the moment.

"Hey, babe, can I ask you a question?" Kyle asked quietly.

I loved when he called me babe. "Of course," I answered, although I was worried about what he wanted to say. I wasn't used to having conversations after sex.

"When you started to cover yourself and I told you not to, I saw the tears in your eyes. What was that about?" His words were gentle but firm. He wanted to know and wasn't going to let me brush it off.

I wanted to be honest with him, but the things I experienced with Brad were embarrassing. I didn't think Kyle would judge me. I also didn't want him to see me any differently.

"Honestly, I've never had someone look at me or treat me the way you do when we're together. No one has ever told me I was beautiful," I explained.

"That's crazy to me," he said. "Your ex-husband was an idiot," he added.

"I agree with you there, but it wasn't just Brad. Every guy I was with acted the same. Brad just happened to be the worst." As soon as the words left my mouth, I knew Kyle was going to pick up on that small detail.

"What do you mean he was the worst?" I could feel his body tense up behind me.

"It doesn't matter," I said, trying to end the conversation.

Kyle wasn't having it. "It matters to me," he said.

I took a deep breath; maybe it was better to just get this out now. I had obvious hang-ups when it came to sex so he might as well know why. "Brad never cared about me or my

242

feelings and when it came to sex..." I heard Kyle growl behind me, but I continued anyway, "he would often say horrible things to me, degrading things, reminding me how slutty I had acted in my past, how horrible I looked since having a baby, things like that. He also never took into consideration my physical needs and would occasionally get too rough. The last time we were together he actually hurt me." I could feel myself getting upset recalling that night and I didn't see a need to give Kyle any more details.

Kyle was quiet for a while so I finally turned around to look at him. His eyes were glassy, and I could also see his anger radiating from them.

"I swear to God, Simone, I'm going to kill that motherfucker the next time I see him." From the rage in his face, to the stiff muscles in his body, I knew it wasn't an empty threat. He meant it every word.

"Hey," I said softly, placing my hand on his cheek. "It's over, he can't hurt me that way anymore."

My touch must have calmed him down a little because I felt his body relax. "You deserve to be treated so much better than that and I'm going to make sure you always feel beautiful and cared for when we're together," he promised.

I rested my head on his chest, listening to his heartbeat, and I closed my eyes. I let my mind drift; the echo of his promise was everything I could hope for. We must have dozed off because the next thing I knew, a text alert woke me up and I noticed the sun was just starting to set, which meant we had been asleep for at least an hour. Unfortunately, it also meant I was going to have to leave soon so I could pick up Stella from Trent's house.

I felt Kyle stir next to me when the text alert went off again. He reached over to his phone on the nightstand and swiped to read the text message. An inexplicable jolt of jealousy hit me at the thought of another woman possibly texting him. Just more baggage from my marriage.

"It's Trent. He wants to get together later tonight after you pick up Stella," Kyle said, frowning. His openness about his message was a refreshing change from being in a relationship filled with dishonesty.

I started to sit up. "Yeah, I need to get going. I'm supposed to pick her up in an hour," I said, ignoring the fact that he and Trent were making plans for tonight. Kyle was Trent's main wingman, and I was guessing Trent wanted to hit up the clubs again.

"I need to come up with an excuse to not go tonight," he said, tossing his phone aside and falling back against the pillows.

"Why?" I asked as casual as I could. I threw the covers off, looking around for my clothes.

"Well, Trent is going to want to go out to meet women." He paused and propped himself on his right elbow, stopping me from slipping off the bed. I turned and glanced back at him. I almost smiled at how nervous he looked. "I know we haven't really talked about us being exclusive, but I hope that's what you want because I know I don't want to see anyone else. However, we agreed to keep this quiet for the time being so I can't exactly tell him the truth about why I don't want to go out," he explained.

Now I felt horrible. I didn't want to be the reason he was lying to his best friend.

"I'm sorry. And I definitely don't want to see other people," I told him honestly.

"Hey, don't apologize. I know you have your own

worries so I get not telling anyone this minute; however, we can't keep this a secret forever. Maybe we need to decide on a time when we should tell other people."

His suggestion sounded reasonable.

"How about if we're still together at Thanksgiving we can announce it then," I suggested.

"Thanksgiving is less than a month away, I think that sounds good. But, Simone?"

"Yeah"

"There is no question in my mind that we'll still be together," he said with a huge smile on his face.

His confidence in us as a couple was making me think things I shouldn't this early on in a relationship. I was starting to imagine a future with him. Not wanting to say anything stupid that would send him running, I leaned over and kissed him instead.

Chapter 14

Kyle

*T*he rest of October and early November was spent trying to find a balance between work and spending time with Simone and Stella. Those two girls had quickly cemented their place in my life, and surprisingly, I was okay with that. Since our date at my house, Simone and I had only managed to be alone a couple other times. Otherwise, our dates consisted of us spending time as a trio, which required a lot of creativity and speed if we wanted to be intimate. Thank goodness Simone had overcome her discomfort at being together when Stella was in the house.

I had to admit that I didn't mind spending most of our time together with her daughter. Maybe that was odd, but somehow, having Stella play such a large role in our relationship made me feel even more invested. Even though our relationship was very new, there was absolutely no doubt that I had extremely strong feelings for Simone, and by extension, Stella as well.

Tonight, I was reluctantly going out with Trent, Ian, and Erik. The three of us hadn't gone out together since Simone's birthday weekend and I knew I couldn't put it off any longer since I'd bailed on him a few weeks ago. Trent liked to start the fun on Friday and continue through the weekend. Erik was always game, but I was not feeling it.

Simone had made plans with Addie. They hung out at least once a week, usually with Stella. It made me happy that my sister and my girlfriend got along so well. The phrase, "my girlfriend," still felt strange when thinking about Simone, but I loved it at the same time. Knowing our relationship had Addie's stamp of approval definitely made things easier.

I also appreciated her efforts in distracting Simone. Tomorrow was Brad's visitation day and he'd probably be a no-show again. Hence, girls' nights on Fridays or something on Saturday morning. While expectations were quite low, visitation days still tended to be stressful for Simone as well as for Marla and Jim, and I liked that my sister was trying to help ease some of Simone's nerves.

According to the text from Ian, we were going to meet up at Dixie's, a small bar that had live music. While I was looking forward to spending some time with my three best friends, I knew they would notice I wasn't trying to flirt or hit on anyone. Truth be told, when we used to go out, we usually each went home with a woman. I wasn't exactly proud of my casual dating history, but things had definitely changed for me.

I put on a pair of black jeans and layered a T-shirt with a gray sweater and then headed out. The weather was getting colder at night as we approached the holidays. While we didn't get freezing cold temperatures here, the evening breeze off the ocean could get downright chilly. I didn't want to drive since we would probably be drinking, so I chose to walk the ten blocks to the bar. I could always Uber back home if I needed to.

I decided to text Simone while I walked since I knew I wouldn't be able to be on my phone all night without drawing unwanted attention.

Me: *On my way to meet the guys. Hope you have a fun night with Addie.*

Simone: *We've decided on movie and pizza night. Enjoy your time with the boys.*

Me: *I would rather be with you.*

I knew I sounded completely whipped. But it was true. I would rather be with Simone. I loved the feel of her in my arms, just being around her and doing nothing at all. She brought a sense of calmness and meaning to my life that I hadn't experienced before. Work had always been my main source of feeling like I was contributing and doing something meaningful, but now, with my two girls, I felt like I had that in my personal life as well. And it felt amazing.

Simone: *Me too. :)*

I put my phone back in my pocket when I reached the bar. My three friends were already there, outside, watching me.

"Why the fuck do you look so happy? You already lining up something for tonight?" Ian asked, slapping my back.

"Shut up. I was just checking messages for work," I lied.

"Nothing at work ever makes me smile like that," Trent quipped dryly. "Someone send you a naked selfie?"

Great, now Trent had inadvertently put the idea of a naked Simone in my head. Not what I needed to be thinking about at the moment. Especially because it had been four days since we'd had sex.

We made our way into the bar just as the band was starting their set. We had seen this group before and they did some pretty good covers of classic rock songs. The four of us headed to the bar where we each ordered a beer on tap and managed to find a table off to the side of the makeshift dance floor.

We took some time to really catch up with each other, something we hadn't done since Ian had returned home. He told us how things were going with the contracting business he was taking over from his father. Unlike Trent and me, Ian had never planned to work in the family business. Unfortunately, his father had started to have some health problems so Ian agreed to move back home and take over.

Erik shared with us how his business was going. He was making a name for himself in the racing circuits and his auto shop was taking off. So much so that he had to hire two additional mechanics, bringing his staff up to six.

"So, Mom wanted me to ask all of you what you were doing for Thanksgiving. She said you're all welcome to come over for dinner," Trent said, addressing all of us.

"That sounds good to me. My folks are heading back to Florida to visit my sister since my dad doesn't need to stick around for the business," Ian said.

"I can probably stop by," Erik added.

"What about you, Kyle?" Trent asked. "We invited Brad, but once he found out Simone was also invited, he told us he had other plans. Mom called Addie and she said she was coming."

"I'll be there," I stated. There was no way I was going to miss spending the holiday with my girls. Besides, Simone and I had agreed to let people know we were together at Thanksgiving and I was more than ready to take our relationship public.

We continued making small talk, scanning the crowd, and listening to music. A couple girls approached our table, striking up conversations with whichever guy interested them. Trent and Erik were all over that while Ian and I were mere observers. Even though I knew why I wasn't joining in, I was a bit surprised that Ian wasn't showing any interest. I looked over at him with a raised brow, questioning his intentions. He just shrugged his shoulders and went back to drinking his beer and avoiding further eye contact. I wasn't going to push him if he didn't push me.

After a few minutes of conversation, Trent and Erik headed out to the dance floor with two of the girls, leaving their other friends with Ian and me.

"So you guys don't dance?" the blonde asked me, while the brunette tried to stand as close to Ian as she could without making it obvious.

"Not really my thing," I answered quickly. Now it was Ian's turn to raise his eyebrow at me. I was usually the first one out on the dance floor. I gave him an answering shrug like he had given me. A knowing smirk played across his face.

"Well then, maybe we can just hang out here," the blonde one said, scooting her chair closer to me. I was trying to ignore her attempts to gain my attention when she placed her hand on my leg and started rubbing it up and down. Just as I was planning my exit, a text alert came through on my phone.

"Sorry, I need to check this," I said, jumping up quickly. Honestly, I didn't care who it was since it provided the perfect escape plan. I wasn't trying to be an ass, but with some women, the harder I tried to politely act uninterested, the stronger they came on to me, thinking I was playing hard to get or something.

Once outside, I pulled up my text messages. I saw I had a couple missed ones from Simone, the most recent having just come through. The first was a picture of my girls and Addie sitting on the couch watching a movie. The next was a picture of Stella curled up next to my sister fast asleep. The last one, though, almost made me drop my phone.

Simone: *Addie left, Stella is asleep. I'm just lying in bed wishing you were here with me.*

Attached was a picture of her in a tank top and the tiniest pair of black panties. I was instantly hard. I was having a good time hanging with the boys, but I seriously needed to cut this night short and get over to her apartment.

I was about to turn and let the guys know I was leaving when I almost slammed into Ian. After we recovered from our near head-on collision, I quickly hit the home button on my phone to clear out of my text app. I didn't need anybody seeing the picture of Simone.

"Hey, I can't believe you left me alone in there with those two. What's so important you had to walk out here?" he asked, glaring at me.

I looked back down at my phone when another notification came through, completely ignoring Ian.

"Dude, seriously. What's going on?" he continued. "It's not like you to be so secretive and it's especially not normal for you to pass up a chance with a couple girls that seemed like a sure thing."

"I didn't see you jumping at the chance to hook up with
251

them, either," I said, deflecting his inquisition.

Ian glared at me again. "Really? That's all you're gonna give me?"

I hated lying to my friends. The four of us shared everything. I had to give him something. "Well... I'm sort of seeing someone, but it's not something I really want to talk about right now," I said, hoping the small sliver of information would satisfy his curiosity.

"Picked an ugly one, did ya?" he joked.

I punched him in the arm. "Shut the fuck up. I'll kick your ass if you keep talking shit." It didn't matter how old we were. We quickly slipped right back into teenage boy mode when we were together.

He shook his head. "Fine, I'll let you keep your little secret. Seriously, though, you know we all have your back. There's no reason you need to hide anything from us."

I appreciated that, and it wasn't so much Ian or Erik that Simone and I were both concerned about. Nonetheless, it was nice to hear. "I know that, and you all will know about this soon enough. We just need a little more time. On that note, I'm outta here. Can you tell the guys I took off?" I asked, getting antsy. Ian was keeping me from getting to Simone. Who was waiting for me... hopefully naked.

"Sure. Be safe," Ian said with a smile.

He headed back inside and I wasted no time. Since I only drank one beer I was able to walk to my house and hop in my car so I could drive over to Simone's. I'll admit that I looked at her picture more than once during my walk-jog home. Keeping my dirty thoughts under control on the drive over to her apartment was not easy. Or sticking to the speed limit. No way was I going to be delayed by getting pulled over. But I felt on edge the whole drive to her place. It was like my body was craving its favorite meal and knew it was finally dinnertime.

I knocked on her door, anxious to get my hands on the woman who was driving me crazy. She must have been in bed because it took a few minutes for her to answer the door.

When the door swung open, I rushed her and crashed my lips on hers, making her lose her balance. I wrapped my arms around her back to keep her upright. When I broke away from the kiss I saw her smile.

"You must have gotten my picture," she said, batting her eyes at me and trying to look innocent.

"That was the hottest thing I've ever seen," I told her honestly. "I couldn't get here fast enough."

My statement made her blush, and damn if that didn't make me want her more. Channeling my inner caveman, I scooped her up and threw her over my shoulder. I gave her ass a light smack and her responding shriek made me laugh.

When we reached her room, I tossed her onto the bed. The sex was fast-paced but still mind-blowing. I would never get tired of being with her. Once we were done, we settled in the middle of the bed and cuddled.

"Mmm," I heard her softly moan. "This is exactly where I want to be."

"Me too, babe," I replied, kissing her lightly. Then we both feel asleep.

After what only felt like fifteen minutes, I heard Stella start to fuss. I must have worn Simone out because she didn't even stir. I gently pulled my arm out from under her and climbed out of bed. I grabbed my pants off the floor and headed toward Stella's bedroom. When I walked through the door, I saw her standing in her crib, holding onto the rail with tears streaming down her cheeks.

"Hey, beautiful. What's wrong?" I asked, not expecting an answer from her. However, she did reach her little arms out for me to pick her up, melting my heart a little. She had been having a rough time with her molars coming in so I assumed that's what was wrong. Never thought I would know about things like teething, but being here taking care of her felt right.

I went over to the rocking recliner in the corner and sat with her in my arms. I rocked her while gently rubbing her back. After a little while she settled down and seemed to fall back asleep. Not wanting to risk waking her up, I quietly lifted the leg of the chair and reclined so I could close my eyes while still holding her to my chest. Before long, we were both asleep.

At some point, I felt someone lifting Stella out of my arms and my reflexes pulled her back toward me.

"It's just me," Simone said quietly. "She's starting to wake up."

"Oh... Okay, what time is it?" I yawned and allowed Simone to take Stella from me.

"Just a little after seven," she answered, her voice soft and her expression unreadable.

I was surprised Stella and I had managed to sleep in the recliner most of the night.

"What time did you come in here?" Simone asked, holding her daughter. She'd put her hair up in a messy bun and was wearing my T-shirt from last night. She had never looked more beautiful.

I stretched, stiff as a board. "I think around one," I answered, standing up from the chair.

"Thank you for taking care of her. It's been rough going since she started teething again," she said, putting a hand to my chest and raising herself up to give me a quick peck on the lips.

That quick kiss had me thinking of a quickie in the shower, but Stella started to get a little fussy, which immediately put an end to my dirty thoughts. The two of them headed into the kitchen and I walked to the bathroom. Guess a solo shower would have to do. While cleaning up, I thought about how much I truly enjoyed being the person to help Simone with Stella. While I wished Stella wasn't in pain, I was happy to be the one to provide them both with some comfort. It was at that moment that I realized I was falling in love with both of those girls—and there wasn't anywhere else I wanted to be.

Now that I knew I loved Simone, I needed to decide when to tell her. I had never said those three words to anyone in a romantic sense before. And I wasn't sure Simone was ready to hear that type of sentiment from me yet. We had only been dating a few weeks. But we'd known each other for a while now, and if I was honest with myself, my feelings had started to develop the minute I offered to help her through her divorce.

I got dressed in my same clothes from yesterday, sans T-shirt, swished around some mouthwash, and headed into the kitchen. Stella was in her highchair, eating some cut-up banana and a piece of toast, and Simone was pouring each of us a cup of coffee.

I walked up behind her and wrapped my arms around her waist, kissing her cheek gently.

"How are you this morning?" I asked.

"I was able to get some sleep, so I'm good," she answered while turning around to kiss me again. "Thank you for your help last night."

"I didn't do much. She fell back asleep right away," I said, releasing her when the toast popped up in the toaster. She moved away and buttered them for us then we moved over to the kitchen table. "After we're done eating," I added, halfway through our quick breakfast, "why don't you take a shower and I can get Stella ready to go to her grandparents."

"You don't mind?" she questioned, her voice sounding wary.

"Not at all."

We finished breakfast and Simone went to her room and I took Stella to hers. "We need to find something for you to wear, kiddo," I said as I looked through her closet for an outfit to change her into. I pulled out several options, all of which Stella frowned at. We finally settled on a pair of jeans and a purple and pink sweater.

I found her brush on top of the dresser and we sat in the middle of her room as I brushed her hair back into a ponytail. It brought back memories of me doing the same thing for Addie when we were young. For a while, our mother had decided she didn't need any help with Addie and me and had moved us out of our grandmother's home. Unfortunately, our mother was usually passed out when it came time for school so it often fell on me to help my sister get ready. That living arrangement was, thankfully, short-lived. I was now grateful for that skill so Simone wouldn't think I was completely helpless.

"Now we just need shoes," I stated.

She stood up and ran back to her closet. "Ky, I wanna wear these ones!" she exclaimed, grabbing the purple Converse her Uncle Trent had bought for her. I had her completely dressed and sitting on the couch watching a kids' program when Simone made her way out to the living room.

"Thanks for getting her ready. You're really good at taking care of her," she said, sounding genuinely surprised.

"Simone, you need to stop being shocked that I enjoy helping you out with Stella. There isn't anything I wouldn't do for the two of you. And I'm happy to be the one here to help," I said. Sure, I'd been thinking those thoughts in my head, but saying it — to Simone — added a level of intimacy to our relationship that took even me by surprise. And from her glowing smile, she understood.

"I'll get used to it, I promise," she said solemnly, even though her eyes were smiling. "So, what do you have planned for the day?"

"I have a few errands to run and a little bit of paperwork I brought home from the office. Call me as soon as you're done there?" I asked, hoping I didn't sound too pushy.

"Okay," she said without hesitation. She leaned down, kissing me deeply like it was the most natural thing in the world. She then picked up Stella while I got up to grab Stella's bag, and the three of us walked out to our cars together.

I helped her load up her car and opened her door for her. "Remember to call me as soon as you're done. If you need anything, I'll be here," I said, leaning down to kiss her one more time before she climbed in. I couldn't get enough of this woman's kisses. I had seen doting, head-over-heels couples before, but never understood the appeal. Now I did.

"Thank you," she said, a big smile on her face.

"Bye, Ky," Stella shouted from the backseat.

"Bye, baby girl. Be good for your mama," I told her.

Then I shut the door. I stood in the parking lot, watching them drive off. My life felt right, like I'd finally found the missing pieces, and they were Simone and Stella. I hadn't expected it or even asked for it, but here I was, lucky in love. I headed to my car, counting down the days 'til I could finally share my happiness with my family and friends.

Chapter 15

Simone

I watched Stella play with her grandparents. It was obvious Brad was going to miss another visitation. Everyone was having fun, but I was missing Kyle. He must have been missing me too because I heard a text come through on my phone.

Kyle: *Hey! How's everything?*

Me: *Everything's fine. Brad bailed on visitation.*

Kyle: *I'm sorry.*

Me: *I don't care but it makes me sad for Stella.*

Kyle: *How long are you going to stay?*

Me: *We're having lunch with them so probably till 1. Do you want to meet at the apartment?*

Kyle: *Sure!*

Me: *Ok I'll see you then.*

I ended that text with a kissing emoji and immediately questioned whether I should have done that. After watching him with Stella this morning and knowing how he always tried to take care of me, I knew without a doubt that I was falling in love with him. However, I had no idea where he was mentally with everything and I was afraid of pushing him too quickly when it'd been my idea to take things slow. We were definitely on the fast track in our relationship, but, somehow, it didn't feel like it was happening fast at all. It felt like a long time in the making.

I knew a relationship with me was a big undertaking, so he had to be into me at least a little to continue dating me with Stella as part of the deal. But I was all in and I wanted him to be as well.

Kyle: *Is that emoji a promise of things I have to look forward to tonight? I sure hope so.*

Well, thank goodness it didn't freak him out. I tried not to react and make Marla or Jim curious.

Me: *Maybe. :)*

We left Jim and Marla's after lunch. The plan was to put Stella down for a nap and then I could spend a few minutes getting ready before Kyle came over.

I got Stella out of the car and was climbing the steps to my apartment when I saw a man sitting next to my door. I stopped my ascent until I realized it was Brad sitting there. His clothes hung on him and it was evident he'd lost weight. Actually, he looked like he hadn't showered for a couple days, either, and he had dark circles under his eyes. For a split second, I felt sorry for him, but then I felt a burning rage start to build up inside of me.

"What the hell are you doing here?" I asked, the anger in my voice clear as day.

He jumped up and I realized he hadn't even noticed us coming up the stairs.

"Uh… hey." He stood there awkwardly, nervous. Brad was never nervous. He eyed Stella when I put her down and she just stared up at him with no recognition of her own father. She tucked in close, hugging my left leg. I put my hand on top of her head, smoothing down her hair and letting the motion calm her, and me.

"Well?" I demanded, hand on my hip.

"I wanted to come and talk to you and to see Stella," he said, quickly adding the part about Stella.

I glared at him, seething. "That's why I was at your parents' house earlier today. You aren't supposed to be here."

The Brad I knew emerged. He rolled his eyes. "C'mon, Simone, don't be a bitch."

"I'm being a bitch?" I yelled. I took a moment to calm down. This wasn't any way for me to act with Stella watching me. "I haven't heard from you in months and I'm just supposed to be nice to you when you decide to drop by?" I asked, quieter but no less angry.

"I'm sorry," he said, not sounding apologetic at all. "Can we just talk for a couple minutes? Please."

As infuriated as I was by his sudden appearance, I also needed to get Stella inside. I just wanted him gone. "Fine, I need to put Stella down for a nap. We can talk as soon as I'm done." I opened the door, walked through, and waited for him to close the door behind us.

I put the diaper bag down next to the door and then walked Stella into her room. As expected, Brad made no effort to interact with his daughter, which ticked me off even more. My girl deserved to have a father who loved her more than anything.

Someone like Kyle. A man who took time out to play with her, read her a story, or just talk to her even if her vocabulary wasn't stellar yet. A man who woke up in the middle of the night to calm her down when she was teething and then stayed with her so she felt safe and comforted. Why couldn't the man with a biological connection to her do the same?

"Time for a nap, sweetie," I said as I lifted her up and placed her in the crib. "I love you."

"Love you, Mama," she responded, her eyelids already growing heavy.

I closed her door gently behind me and walked back into the living room where Brad was sitting on the couch with his head rested on the back cushion and his eyes closed.

"Hey," I said while kicking his foot with my own to wake him. "What did you want to talk about?" I had absolutely no patience and I wasn't going to act like the old Simone and be passive in order to keep him calm.

"Can't you sit down?" he asked, but it sounded more like a demand.

"You don't get to tell me what to do, Brad." I crossed my arms and stared at him waiting for him to tell me why he was here. "Talk. Or get out."

He wasn't used to my sassy attitude. I wasn't either, but I was done being used and treated like crap and just taking it when I deserved better. This was about me finally standing up to this asshole. "So, how are things going?" he started, looking cagey and uncertain.

Seriously? He was attempting to make small talk? I had

262

no desire to engage with him.

"Brad, what do you want?" I asked again, my irritation with him growing even stronger.

"I want to come home," he said, matter-of-fact.

"*What?*" I couldn't believe what I was hearing.

"I miss you and I want to come home," he said, but he wasn't even looking at me.

"Bullshit!" I knew the bastard didn't want to come home. He made it obvious he could barely stand my presence when he was with me. There was absolutely no way he missed me.

"It's not bullshit, Simone! I've been thinking about things and I want us to be a family again." The jerk was totally trying to use my old insecurities in an effort to manipulate me.

"Okay, I'm going to stop you right there. In the seven months since we broke up, you have made no attempt to contact me, you've missed almost all of your visitation days, and you sure haven't paid any child support. *Now* I'm supposed to believe you want to play the family man?" I asked, the sarcasm dripping from my words. I rolled my eyes. "Forgive me, but I just don't buy it."

He looked shocked at my statement. Maybe because when we were together he never heard me stand up to him until the day I told him I wanted a divorce. I had always tried to keep the peace, to not make waves because I had wanted to make things work between us so desperately.

But now I knew how a real relationship was supposed to be, how it should feel. I never had to hide my feelings from Kyle. I was able to express my needs without worrying that he was going to verbally berate me. I could never go back to the kind of relationship I had with Brad. One where I had to hide my feelings. And knowing that my daughter was doing well despite an absent and uncaring father gave me courage to not fall back into the ridiculous notion that I needed to be with her father in order to provide stability or a happy home for her.

"What the fuck has gotten into you? I thought you would be happy I wanted to come back," he said, genuinely surprised I wasn't jumping up and down at his offer.

"Too much has happened," I stated. I shook my head. "I've changed. I'm not the same person you were married to."

"Is there someone else?" he asked, scowling at me.

"If there was, it wouldn't be any of your business," I shot back.

"Fuck that! Of course, it would be my business. Whoever you're seeing would be involved with my daughter. I should have a say in that."

That had my blood pressure spiking. "Like I had a say when you were fucking someone in our bed and doing drugs while our daughter was a room away?" I needed to take a breath. There was no point in arguing these details with him. I just needed him to leave.

I was about to tell him the conversation was over when I heard a knock at the door. I knew in my gut that Kyle was on the other side. Suddenly, I was filled with anxiety. There was so much bad blood between the two of them that I knew this could only end badly. It was one of the reasons why I'd wanted to keep our relationship quiet.

"Who the hell is that?" Brad asked, jumping up from the couch.

"None of your business," I replied as I got up to answer the door before he could.

I pulled the door open and Kyle must have seen the distress on my face.

"Hey, babe, what's wrong?" he asked, quietly.

"Is that the asshole you're seeing?!" Brad shouted, trying to catch a glimpse of who was at the door.

Kyle looked over my shoulder and then back to me again. His face was red and there was a look in his eye that I had never seen before. He looked like he wanted to murder someone.

"What the hell is he doing here?" Kyle asked through gritted teeth.

"He was here when I came home. He said he wanted to talk." I glared back at Brad. "I was just getting ready to ask him to leave," I answered.

Kyle pushed the door open and stomped over to the couch. "What the fuck are you doing here?" he asked, glowering at Brad.

Brad got right in Kyle's face. "I could ask you the same thing," he said. Then he turned toward me. "So this is the douchebag you're seeing?"

"You don't get to question her or her actions," Kyle growled, clearly pissed off and getting angrier. "You lost that right a long time ago. Now you get to deal with me."

I was worried this was going to get out of hand quickly.

Suddenly, Brad started laughing, like hysterically laughing. "I can't believe this," he managed to get out between laughing fits. "How in the world did this even happen? Wait, is this how you paid your legal fees. A fuck for every few billable hours?"

Brad couldn't spew another vicious word from his mouth before Kyle's fist was crashing into his jaw. Brad fell backwards onto the carpet but that didn't stop him from getting in one last jab, this one directed to Kyle. "How can you possibly want to be with the whore I cheated on your sister with?"

I saw Kyle start to charge so I jumped in front of him. "Stop!" I pleaded. "He's not worth it."

"He's not, but you are," Kyle declared, and lunged toward Brad again.

I placed my hands on his chest and gently pushed him back. I knew I wasn't strong enough to physically move him, but I hoped my touch would calm him a little. "Please, just let it go."

He finally made eye contact with me and relaxed a tiny bit. "You need to get the hell out of here," he said, looking around me at Brad.

"I'll talk to you later," Brad said to me as he pushed up off the ground and moved toward the door.

"No, you won't," Kyle sneered.

"Dude, you can't keep me from talking to *my* daughter's mother," he said, emphasizing that Stella was his, and then he slammed the door behind him as he left.

"Is your hand okay?" I asked, carefully grabbing hold of the hand he had used to knock Brad to the ground.

"It's fine," Kyle said, tension still radiating off him. "So what did he want to talk to you about?"

I walked to the kitchen and grabbed a bag of peas out of the freezer for his hand while he went to the sink to run water over his knuckles. "He said he wanted to get back together," I answered truthfully. I examined his knuckles but the skin hadn't split and it looked okay. I put the peas in a towel and placed it over his right hand, just in case.

"Are you serious?" he asked, incredulous and fuming. "The nerve..."

"Well, that's what he said, but I don't believe him for a second," I explained. Holding the frozen veggies on his hand, I looked back at Stella's quiet room, surprised she had slept through the chaos out here. I glanced back up at him. "There had to be more to it. There is no way he decided he wanted to suddenly play house. If I had to guess, Tiffany kicked him out *again* and he needed a place to crash."

He looked at me, then down at his feet. "What did you tell him... when he said he wanted to get back together?" he asked cautiously, but his face was tense, ready for bad news.

I didn't like his expression or the tone in his voice, like he knew what I'd say and it wouldn't be what he wanted to hear. In my heart, I knew I would never go back to the type of relationship I had with Brad. The feelings I had for Kyle went beyond anything I had ever felt before. Maybe he didn't feel as strongly about me and therefore didn't understand that I no longer wanted any part of that.

When I didn't say anything right away, he continued. "I know how much you wanted things to work out with him — for Stella's sake."

"Are you serious right now?" I asked with a hint of anger. How dare he doubt what I would do in this situation!

He hesitated and tossed the bag of peas aside. He ran a hand through his hair. I could see the doubt in his eyes as he faced me. "I'm just saying — "

"I know what you're saying. I just thought what we have together meant a lot to both of us. The fact that you think I would give that up to go back to him — well, it hurts." I was trying to keep the sadness out of my voice and tears out of my eyes.

I started to move away from him but he reached out and grabbed my hand.

"Hey, come here," Kyle said, pulling me into his arms. "You're right, I'm so sorry, babe. I shouldn't have doubted you for one second. Just seeing him here made me crazy. The thought of losing you freaked me out. Please forgive me."

"Kyle, of course, I forgive you," I said, sinking into his body. I looked up at him. "But I need you to trust that I'm not the same person I was when I came to you seven months ago."

"I won't ever question you on this again," he said. We stayed there in each other's arms in the middle of kitchen for a few minutes.

"Let me go get her," Kyle said when we heard Stella waking up.

The three of us spent the rest of the day together. I felt content hanging out at the house with Kyle and my daughter even after the crazy afternoon. I woke up Sunday morning in Kyle's arms. It was a perfect way to start my day. Then, my text alert went off, and with it, my bad mood started.

Brad: *So you and Kyle, huh? I wonder what he would think if he knew about the night we first got together.*

I swallowed hard, gripping my phone so tight I could hear it start to crack. Brad still knew how to hit me where it hurt. I hadn't told a soul about the night Brad and I met. I wasn't proud of my actions that night. I had done things I was ashamed of and had never done again. Kyle had told me about his mother's drug addiction and how she eventually died of a drug overdose. I also knew he was still angry with her even after all this time —

I felt it just then: fear, panic, and desperation, all at the same time and in equal measure. I never wanted him to view me in the same way he viewed his mother.

Me: *What do you want?*

Brad: *Well I wanted a place to stay but I guess that won't be happening.*

Me: *No it won't and that has nothing to do with Kyle.*

Brad: *Well I wouldn't get too attached.*

Me: *What is that supposed to mean?*

Brad never answered my last text and it left me feeling unsettled. I wanted to tell Kyle the truth, but I feared he wouldn't understand and eventually it would be a deal-breaker for him. I couldn't lose him over a one-time mistake three years ago.

*****

A week and a half later, it was Wednesday evening, the day before Thanksgiving.

Kyle was at my apartment where he spent a majority of his time now. He'd slowly brought a few things over, taking over a drawer in both my bedroom and bathroom. We hadn't really discussed it, but it felt natural and the three of us had fallen into a rather comfortable routine, our lives seamlessly blending together.

Tonight, like most nights, he'd come straight here after work, still in his suit. We had enjoyed a home-cooked dinner, and then I cleaned up the kitchen while Kyle had put Stella to bed. Now, we were relaxing on the couch, snuggled up and watching some crime drama Kyle liked and just enjoying each other's presence. This was how I'd always wanted my home and family life to be. I wasn't even watching the show. I stared at the screen but I was listening to beat of his heart. Right now, my life was better than I could have ever imagined it. Perfect, really.

But the past several days hadn't been all sunshine and roses. A couple things had been weighing on my mind, more and more. There was Brad's weird text that I was hoping was just him blowing hot air because he never followed through on anything. Add to that, I hadn't yet told Kyle about the threat. If Kyle's history with Brad wasn't so ugly, I may have shown him the texts. I hated not telling him the truth, but everything was going good and the old Simone kept whispering: *Don't ruin it*. It could all blow over, right? God, I hoped so. I really did…

"So are you ready to tell everyone about us tomorrow?" he asked during a commercial break. He looked down at me with a huge smile on his face.

It made me feel good to know he wasn't having doubts about announcing our relationship—but my doubts were still there. I reached up and tousled his hair, feeling the silkiness. I needed the comfort that I got from touching him.

"I'm ready as long as you aren't having second thoughts," I answered.

He gave me a look. "Are you kidding me? I've been dying to tell everyone for weeks now," he said, shaking his head. "I don't like sneaking around and it's not necessary —"

"Aren't you worried that someone might have a problem with it?" I interrupted.

I sat up and leaned back against the armrest, facing him. I knew Kyle was probably right and that everyone would be okay with us being together. I was just absolutely terrified of rocking the boat. I still felt this irrational fear like there was a chance I was jeopardizing Stella's happiness by doing something that might make the Thompsons reject me or view me in a different way. I knew I was taking that thought too far, but having been abandoned and ignored my whole life, I couldn't bear the thought that they might ever have a bad opinion of me and ultimately decide they didn't want me in their lives.

Kyle frowned at me. All I wanted was for him to take me seriously. He took my hands in his, squeezed lightly, and looked me straight in the eye. "No," he said bluntly. "If anyone can't accept it then that's *their* problem. I want to be with you and I don't want to hide it anymore."

My stomach tightened and my heart raced at his certainty. His confidence definitely made me feel better.

"So... are we showing up together?" I asked, cautiously.

"Of course we are," he said reassuringly. He leaned over and kissed me on the forehead then pulled back. "We'll be leaving there together so there is no reason for us to drive separate cars. I also have a surprise for you so pack a bag for you and Stella. You two are going to stay the night at my house tomorrow night."

As wonderful as that sounded, and as excited as that made me, I couldn't help but be cautious. "Um… okay," I started, trying to focus on the positives, like Kyle taking the next step and inviting the two of us to his house, "but I'm a little worried about where Stella will sleep."

"Just trust me," Kyle said, with a huge smile on his face. When he looked at me like that, I couldn't deny him anything.

"Ok," I said, smiling back. I burrowed back into his side, and when his arm came around me securely, I hoped things would always be like this.

*****

Kyle and I pulled up to Jim and Marla's house, and suddenly, I was hit with a bout of anxiety. I tried to discreetly wipe my sweaty palms on my pants, but Kyle noticed and gently grabbed my hand.

"Hey, everything is going to be fine." He lifted my hand to his lips and kissed it gently. "No worries, okay?"

I nodded my head. "Okay," I answered with a wavering voice.

If he heard my uncertainty, he didn't seem to mind. We both got out of the car. Kyle moved to the backseat to get Stella out while I got her stuff from the trunk. I walked next to him and knocked on the door. Trent answered and his eyes darted between the three of us, a look of confusion on his face.

"Did you two… come together?" he asked, brows furrowed as he looked between us then to Kyle's car in the driveway.

Kyle had recently purchased a car seat for Stella so we could take his car when we went out. It was another simple yet sweet gesture that showed just how much he cared about both of us.

"Yep," was all Kyle said, and then he shuffled past Trent and into the house.

Trent looked at me for more explanation. I didn't know what to say, so I shrugged my shoulders and followed Kyle into the kitchen. The entire house smelled incredible and the warmth from all the cooking took away the chill. Marla had decorated the entire house and it really did feel festive.

"Oh! There's my baby girl," Marla said as soon as Kyle rounded the corner and was quickly relieved of my daughter.

"Dude," Trent started, having followed us into the kitchen.

"Just chill, man," Kyle said, giving Trent a hard look. "I'll explain everything in a bit."

For some reason that seemed to appease Trent and he let the subject drop for the time being although he still looked confused.

Over the next twenty minutes the house quickly filled with the arrival of Addie, Ian, and Erik. Addie sidled over and gave me a hug. "You look hot," she said, giving a nod of approval to my attire.

I laughed but appreciated her comment. However, Addie was the one who looked like she'd just stepped out of the pages of a fashion magazine. She wore a tight-fitting dress with tights and knee-high boots. Her hair was in a loose braid that hung over one shoulder. I was just in black leggings and a red, cowl-necked, long-sleeved sweater. I had kept my hair up and out of the way. Definitely decent, but Addie was probably the best dressed here. As far as I could tell, Ian thought so, too. He kept glancing at us while he talked to the boys about some car stuff.

"So… what's really up with you and Ian?" I asked quietly, after catching him looking at Addie for the third time since I had started talking to her.

She shrugged casually. "I don't know what you mean…"

I rolled my eyes, but didn't needle her for more. I had no right to push for more information since my own relationship with her brother was on the down low — though not for long. And thinking that made me nervous all over again. For the next few minutes, Addie caught me up on her work, which she actually liked quite a bit. She was now working on completing a paralegal certification course. I was happy for my friend. Moving back here was working out well for her.

We made plans for another girls' night with Kayla and Ashley in the coming weeks then Addie got pulled away by Trent when the boys started to talk about law stuff. I looked over at Jim and Marla who were both lavishing attention on Stella as only grandparents can do.

I stood back a little just observing everyone together. This was truly a family. Not everyone was actually related but they all loved each other deeply. I was grateful that Stella and I got to be a part of this. I really hoped that would continue once Kyle and I came clean about our relationship.

"All right, kids, it's time to eat dinner," Jim announced ten minutes later.

Addie waited for me and looped an arm through mine as we headed to the dining room. Marla placed Stella in her high chair and I took the seat between the two of them at one end. Kyle immediately took the seat on the other side of Stella, adjacent to Jim. On the other side Trent sat directly across from Kyle. Ian and Addie did this odd little dance of not sitting next to each other and made Erik sit between them. I wasn't sure what was going on with them, but it definitely wasn't 'nothing' like Addie claimed. I was sort of glad for the distraction as we started passing bowls around and Jim carved the turkey.

Kyle helped me fill Stella's plate while food was passed around the table. Trent watched us like a hawk. The conversation flowed nicely, but I continued to feel uncomfortable under my ex-brother-in-law's scrutinizing stare. After a while, I could tell that Trent just couldn't take it anymore.

"Okay, I'm sorry to do this right now—but what in the world is going on?" he asked, pointing between us with his fork and interrupting all the other conversations going on at the table.

There was a range of expressions around the table. Addie, Erik, and Ian, continued to eat while looking around the table like the rest of us were entertainment. Marla and Jim shared the exact same confused expression as their son.

With all the attention now on us, I froze up like a deer in headlights and looked to Kyle, who placed his fork on his plate and wiped his mouth with his napkin before talking.

"Well, we were going to wait until after dinner but I guess now is as good a time as any," Kyle said, without any reservation or cold feet. He gave me a sideways glance and then looked around the table. "Simone and I are dating... and have been for a while."

I eyed everyone and saw a bunch of stunned faces. All except Addie, she was just sitting there with a huge smile on her face.

"We wanted to wait a little while before telling anyone," Kyle explained. He reached behind Stella's chair to gently rub my shoulder. The action made me feel a little better, though I was still tense, waiting for someone to say they objected. "I'm sure this is a surprise to most of you, but we hope you can all be supportive." He finished speaking and the room remained silent for what seemed like hours, even though I was sure it was only a few seconds. I looked to Kyle one more time and he smiled at me. He seemed so happy about claiming me as his girlfriend and it warmed my heart.

"Well, I think it's great," Marla said, her hands clasped in front of her and a huge grin on her face.

"Absolutely," Jim added. "There isn't anyone I would trust more with my daughter and granddaughter than you, Kyle." It wasn't lost on me that Jim referred to me as his daughter. That one statement made me tear up.

Erik and Ian took it in stride, not that I thought they'd really care either way, but at least they seemed accepting and went back to eating their meals, like Addie.

"Trent, you good?" I heard Kyle ask. It was then that I realized he hadn't said anything yet.

"I... honestly don't know," Trent answered. "She was married to my brother, that's my niece. Besides, there's a code about sisters."

"I get it," Kyle returned, solemn and adamant, "it's a bit unconventional but, I care deeply for both of them."

"I'm sure you do, it's just going to take me some time to get used to it," he said, clearly unsettled.

I had really wanted Trent's acceptance, but I would take this. At least he wasn't acting completely unreasonable.

"I can give you time. Just know this is serious. I'm not going anywhere," Kyle stated to Trent.

Trent nodded and went back to eating his dinner. The rest of the night went smoothly even if Trent was a bit distant. We had dessert and then Ian, Erik, and Addie all started to leave.

Addie gave me a huge hug on her way out and whispered in my ear how happy she was for her brother and me. The fact that she accepted our relationship meant the world to me. It was obvious she'd already known about us and it was nice to know she'd been in my corner all this time. If anyone had a right to be weird about it, it was her.

I was walking back to Kyle, who was sitting in the living room watching television with Jim, when I noticed Trent standing on the back porch alone, drinking a beer. I changed direction and decided to go to him.

"Hey, can I join you out here?" I asked, not sure if he wanted company.

"Sure," he answered, tipping his beer back to take another sip and staring out into the backyard.

"So I guess we gave you quite the shock at dinner, huh?" I chuckled, hoping to lighten the mood.

"You could say that," he responded dryly.

My attempt at some levity was failing. "I know Kyle is your best friend, but I just wanted to let you know that I really care about him. I'm sure you think he could do better than—"

"What?" His tone was sharp. "You think my problem is that I don't think you're good enough?"

"Well, yeah," I said, thinking it was obvious.

He stared at me. "Simone, you are *amazing*. Any man would be lucky to be with you. My brother was a complete idiot for letting you go." He sighed and shook his head. "I'm not worried about you being good enough for Kyle. I'm worried about Kyle being good enough for you and Stella."

That surprised me. Kyle and Trent were best friends. He should have known how wonderful his friend was.

"I don't get it…" I started, stumped.

"Kyle is a great guy, but he's never had a real relationship before. He had a pretty screwed up childhood, and even though their grandmother was great, he never really dealt with the loss of both his parents." He sighed and took another sip of his beer. "I just don't want him experimenting with you and my niece. He will make a great husband and father *someday*, but I'm not sure he's ready. I just don't want him to hurt you guys as he tries to figure out how to be what you both deserve."

"Oh…" That was all I could say. The fact that Trent was worried about us warmed my heart. However, I completely disagreed with his assessment of the situation.

I walked over to him and placed a sisterly kiss on his cheek. "Thank you. Thank you for wanting the best for me and Stella," I said, my breath catching. To have so many people care about us was the best possible feeling. I was still getting used to it, though it got easier every day. "And I truly believe Kyle is the best for us. Just watch him with Stella. They are crazy about each other and I'll let you in on a little secret"—I leaned in—"I'm crazy about him as well."

Trent assessed me, and while he still had some worry in his eyes, he smiled at me. "Well, if you're happy, then I'm happy for you," he said softly. He gave me a fierce hug. "And if Kyle gets out of line, I'll beat his ass," he added for good measure just like a proper big brother.

We both laughed and I knew that Trent would come around. Once he saw Kyle with Stella, he'd know everything was just how it should be.

A little while later, we were all saying our goodbyes. Marla pulled me aside, and at first I was a little worried about what she had to say. Jim had already made it clear that he was perfectly okay with the situation, even teasing Kyle about his duties with Stella. He was good-humored about it and laughed with Jim, holding Stella in his arms. It was obvious they had a bond. Even Trent seemed to realize it and was grinning.

"I just wanted to tell you that while I'll always be sad things didn't work out between you and Brad, I'm so happy for you and Kyle. You have both been through so much and deserve all the happiness in the world," she said, her voice full of emotion. She hugged me tightly.

I could feel the tears well up in my eyes as I hugged her back. This woman was exactly what I had always wanted in a mother and I could only hope I would be as wonderful of a mom to my daughter as she was to her children.

Kyle and I waved as we got into his car. We drove toward his house and I couldn't get the smile off my face. I was so relieved with how Thanksgiving dinner had gone that I had totally forgot Kyle had a surprise for me at his house until we pulled into his garage.

"Are you two ready to see your surprise?" he asked, waggling his brows.

"Yay! Prize!" Stella shrieked from the backseat.

I got out and took Stella from her car seat and followed Kyle into the house. I was still a little concerned about us

279

spending the night here since his house wasn't well suited for a toddler. It was the main reason we never spent much time here, especially overnight.

Kyle placed the leftovers Marla sent home with us in the fridge and then grabbed Stella out of my arms. "Follow me," he commanded and then started to climb the stairs. At the top of the stairs I noticed a baby gate. Had he childproofed his house for Stella? Before I could ask about the gate, he directed me to the closed door of the bedroom I had stayed in the night of my birthday.

Kyle had the most ridiculous smile on his face. "What's going on?" I asked, completely confused. I was nervous, but excited too because he looked absolutely ecstatic.

He took a deep breath. It was kind of cute how nervous he seemed to be suddenly. "This might seem a little fast, but I really wanted to have another option for us to spend our nights together. I don't mind going to your apartment. I just would like you to spend more time here." He was rambling a little bit, but continued before I could respond or even react. "I don't want you to only come over here when you don't have Stella. I want her to feel comfortable here as well so I turned this into a room for her."

Kyle then pushed the door open and I took in the sight before me. He had a crib that could convert into a toddler bed up against the shared wall with his bedroom. There was a toy box in the corner, a dresser against the opposite wall, a large rug in the middle of the hardwood floor, and in the closet were a few brand new outfits already hanging up.

I looked up at Kyle, speechless. I couldn't believe he would do this for us. It was overwhelming. This wasn't just a gesture — it was a promise. His to me and to Stella. That he was serious, that this wasn't some fling but something more permanent. His actions spoke volumes. And it filled my heart to the max.

"What do you think?" he asked quietly. I had been silent for so long he was probably starting to worry about my reaction. Or the lack of one. I was just stunned, utterly blown away. A million things were running through my head, and I felt even more emotions inside me about to explode.

Still speechless, I stared at him, the room, and then Stella — and promptly burst into tears. I immediately felt him wrap his free arm around me. Stella babbled on but I felt her little hand in my hair, as though stroking it in comfort. When I calmed down, I looked up at him, hiccupping out a response.

"Oh Kyle, i-it's p-perfect. I can't believe you did this for her. For us. Thank you!" I went up on my toes and kissed him soundly. This was the nicest thing anyone had ever done for me or for Stella.

"There's more," he said, breathless and, to my amusement, a little dazed by my kiss. "I wasn't sure about everything a toddler needed for the bathroom but I did purchase a couple things for her. I know, I went overboard but… it was important to me that you and Stella both feel at home here. Whenever you want to be here. If I'm missing anything we can go out shopping tomorrow."

Again, I had tears streaming down my face, just staring up at him for several long minutes. "Babe, what's wrong?" Kyle finally asked, sounding worried.

"Nothing's wrong," I assured him. He used a thumb to wipe the tears away. "It's just… you're so good to us. How did we get so lucky to have you in our lives?"

"I'm the lucky one," he said, wrapping his free arm around me once more, and placing a kiss on the top of my head.

We proceeded to get Stella ready for bed together. He had even bought her pajamas, in her correct size! Just before laying her down, Kyle grabbed a book off the tiny bookshelf I had missed earlier and sat on the floor so Stella could climb into his lap. He read her a bedtime story and then gave her a hug and kiss goodnight.

"Wuv you," I heard her say. I nearly lost it again.

I looked at Kyle and I could see her declaration had caught him off guard as well.

"I love you, too, Stella," he answered, and I swear I heard a slight crack in his voice.

We walked into his room together, and as soon as I turned around, he grabbed me and kissed me hard. Kissing Kyle was one of my favorite things to do so I took my time, enjoying the feel of his lips gently sucking on my bottom one, then his tongue exploring my mouth, my tongue joining his. After a few minutes he pulled away to just stare into my eyes.

"I think today was the absolute best Thanksgiving ever," he said.

I smiled. "Absolutely."

"And our announcement seemed to go over well," he added. "Even if Trent was a little weird about it."

"I got to talk to him for a bit outside. I think he's coming around to the idea already," I said.

Kyle sighed, somewhat relieved. "That's good because I'm not planning on letting you go anytime soon," he said before pulling me over to his bed. "Or Stella."

We both got ready for bed, me in one of Kyle's T-shirts

and him in his boxer briefs, and got under the covers. He wrapped his large arms around me and we just lay there in silence for a while. I was completely content in that moment which allowed the words I hadn't planned on saying tonight to flow freely.

"I love you," I said while he lay there silently. He was quiet for so long that I started to regret saying anything at all.

"Can you say that again?" he whispered, his voice wavering with emotion.

I turned my head so I could see him. It was dark but I could see his smile. It lit up the whole room — lit me up, too. "I love you, Kyle," I repeated.

"Oh, babe, I've been in love with you for a while now. I just didn't want to push you too quickly. I love you, too," he said so tenderly.

We started kissing and then Kyle rolled me onto my back. Hovering over me, he looked directly into my eyes. "I'm the luckiest man in the world," he said and then his lips found mine again. I was so consumed by his kiss that I gasped when I felt him nudge my entrance. We'd already had the birth control and testing conversation, but we hadn't made love without protection yet.

When he gently pushed inside of me, my whole body nearly convulsed. I wrapped my legs around his waist and he grabbed both my hands with his and laced our fingers together. He placed our hands on the bed above my head and continued to thrust into me. Each movement was slow and controlled, both of us focusing on every sensation. This was the most passionate and intense lovemaking I had ever experienced.

I could feel my orgasm building, and from the look on

Kyle's face, I knew he was right there with me. I allowed myself to fall over the edge and kissed him deeply. I felt his entire body shake with his release.

"I love you so much," he said and then kissed me again.

"I love you, too," I responded breathlessly. I knew right then I was with the man I was meant to love and be with forever.

Chapter 16

Kyle

*T*hings with Simone continued to be amazing. We had come out as a couple a week ago and had spent almost every night together since then, either at her apartment or my condo.

I decided that this afternoon, we were going to go out and find a Christmas tree for her apartment. I'd had a late client meeting last night so we had spent the night apart. I realized I no longer slept well if she wasn't in my arms.

I was considering asking her to move in with me even though we hadn't been together for that long. I knew it was a big step for both of us. I had never had a relationship where I had considered living together as an option. Simone had been married before, and still had scars that ran deep from that relationship. This wasn't a decision she would make lightly.

And it didn't just involve the two of us. She had to think about what was best for Stella as well. It would also be welcoming Brad back into my life. I had to accept the fact that while he may not have an interest in being a father right now... that could change. If it did, I would need to be prepared to deal with him.

All of those details didn't dissuade my decision, and I knew we had a lot to talk about before taking that step. I loved Simone with my entire being and I loved Stella, too. There was nothing I wanted more than to have them with

285

me every day. If things continued to move in the direction that they were, I was going to ask her after Christmas in hopes of starting the New Year together in *our* home.

I drove over to her house to pick her and Stella up. I ran up to her door feeling the excitement of doing something that felt like a real family outing. I missed out on so much of this growing up and I was happy to share it with these two. I knocked on the door with a big, cheesy grin on my face.

"Hey, babe," Simone greeted, after opening the door giving me a quick peck on the lips.

I walked into the apartment. "You ready to go?" I asked.

"We sure are!" She shut the door behind me. "Stella, Kyle's here," she called out, toward her daughter's room.

"Ky!" Stella shouted, running toward me with her arms in the air and waiting for me to pick her up.

Never wanting to disappoint the little bundle of energy, I picked her up and spun her around a couple times. Her squeals of delight made me laugh.

"Are you ready to go, sweetheart?" I asked her.

"Yes!" she exclaimed, sounding just as excited as I was.

Making sure Simone grabbed everything she needed for our outing, I led the way downstairs to my car. It still amazed me how long it took to get going with a toddler in tow. Who knew someone so little required so much extra stuff?

Once we were in the car, I turned on some Christmas music to help get us in the spirit for the day's activities. "I thought we could check out the tree lot down on Jefferson Street. Is that okay?" I asked.

Her eyes lit up. "I love that idea!" she exclaimed,

grinning.

"You seem happy this morning," I said, reaching across the center console to grab her hand. She immediately reciprocated and we continued to hold hands as I drove through the busy traffic.

"I *am* happy," she said without hesitation. "I've never gone shopping for a Christmas tree before and I'm excited to this year, especially for Stella."

It made me sad to think about the things she missed out on moving between foster homes for so long. In many ways, we had the same sort of baggage from our childhoods. I could only hope that we were helping each other heal from those times.

We arrived at the tree lot and started looking around for the perfect tree. According to Stella, they were all perfect. She pointed at every tree we passed and said, "This one."

After walking down each aisle we finally settled on a six-foot Douglas fir. It took some work getting it strapped down on my car, but the joy on both my girls' faces was well worth it. Once we were back at her apartment, I carried the tree upstairs while she followed behind with Stella.

It took some time to get the tree straight in the stand, but once we were happy with the placement, I ran down to my car to retrieve a surprise I had for Simone.

"What's in the boxes?" she asked when I returned.

"I wasn't sure if you had any ornaments for the tree so I brought over what I had. It's not much, but I thought it would get us started."

"Oh, that's perfect!" she said, taking the smaller box off the other one I was holding. "I have a few decorations but not much. It's really just some lights I want to put up later and a couple knick-knacks. All of that stuff's out in the storage closet on the balcony so I'll probably need your help getting them down."

We spent the next hour placing ornaments on the tree and spacing out the ones that Stella kept putting in the one spot she could reach. At one point I took a step back to just observe the two of them. Something so simple as decorating a tree made my heart full.

We took a break from decorating to have some lunch and then Simone put Stella down for a nap. Deciding the lights could wait a bit longer, we engaged in a pretty heavy make-out session on the couch.

"I should buy you a tree everyday if this is the kind of thanks I get," I said jokingly between kisses.

"You're a dork," she said, laughing at me. "But this has actually been a perfect day and I do want to give you something to thank you for that."

Suddenly she moved from straddling my lap down to the floor kneeling between my legs while I relaxed back into the couch. I looked directly into her eyes and could see the love radiating from them as she looked up at me.

Very slowly she slid her hands up my thighs finally reaching the button on my jeans. Continuing her slow seduction, she took her time undoing the button and then pulling my zipper down. She knew exactly what she did to me and was enjoying every minute of her teasing. I lifted my hips so she could pull my jeans and boxer briefs down. "Someone is a little impatient," she said with giggle.

"You have no idea, babe," I said agreeing with her assessment.

She moved back between legs after removing my pants all

the way. She had a firm grip on my cock and started to tease the tip with her thumb, spreading the pearly droplets that had appeared all around the head.

Bending down, she licked the underside of my dick from the base all the way to the tip where she swirled her tongue around. Unable to stop myself, I reached both hands out to tangle my fingers in her hair. I didn't want to control her movements, but I did want to move her hair out of the way so I didn't miss watching a single thing her mouth was doing to me.

"That feels incredible," I told her just as she started to suck on the head. After a few more playful sucks she took me as far as she could in her mouth. I felt the head of my dick hit the back of her throat. That didn't stop her, though. Instead, she swallowed around my cock providing the most exquisite sensation. She continued to suck me until I felt my balls tighten up in anticipation of an explosive release.

"Babe, I'm going to come," I warned. But her response was to suck me even harder. I couldn't hold out even if I wanted to. I felt myself explode in her mouth. She didn't falter at all, instead she swallowed everything down that I gave her.

After several pulses she pulled her mouth off me. I wasn't sure how long I sat there spent, with my whole body in recovery mode. I swear, I might have blacked out because my vision had gone blurry and I heard a ringing in my ears. When I was finally fully conscious, my eyes landed on her face with its pleased expression.

"Come here," I said, my voice hoarse. I pulled her back up into my lap where I kissed her hard. This woman was amazing. I pulled my boxers and pants back on, then we lounged around on the couch for a while longer. Eventually we decided we should try to finish decorating before Stella woke up.

"So, uh, where are these boxes of lights you have?" I asked, trying to focus.

She smirked at me since I was still a little out of it. "In the storage closet out there," she said, pointing to the door off the tiny balcony. "Let me get you the key."

The cold air woke me up when I stepped outside. I opened the door and found the chain to turn on the overhead light. The space was small, just enough room for a couple shelves. I barely fit in there. I looked to the shelving on my right and found two boxes of Christmas lights all the way at the top. When I reached up to grab them my hand knocked something off the shelf.

I bent down to pick it up and saw that it was a small mirror. Underneath it was a small baggie. Not quite believing my own eyes, I picked up the baggie. Upon closer inspection, I could see the remnants of white powder at the bottom.

My mind immediately went back to my childhood when I couldn't walk anywhere in my mother's house without seeing drug paraphernalia lying around. I must have been standing out there for a while, staring at the offending baggie, because I heard Simone call out for me from the living room.

"Babe, are the lights not out there?" she asked.

I was still in shock and unable to answer her. I heard the screen door slide open. "Hey, what's going on out here?"

I turned around to face her. "Um…" I didn't know what to say. A huge part of me didn't believe she was capable of using drugs, but then I remembered that at one time my mother had been the epitome of the sweet girl next door.

Unfortunately, that didn't stop her from falling down a drug spiral.

I still hadn't answered Simone so she looked down at my hands. "What is that?" she asked.

"I could ask you the same thing," I said, hating the way my voice sounded accusatory.

I heard her gasp when she got a better look at what I was holding. "You don't think that's mine, do you?"

I heard the hurt clearly in her voice, but I was so lost in my own feelings that I couldn't push past it. All I saw were the drugs, and that they were in Simone's closet.

"It's in your storage closet, Simone," I pointed out.

"Oh, my God, Kyle! I don't do drugs. You should know that!" she said, her face getting flushed with anger. "You're with me almost all the time. That has to be Brad's. I told you when I filed for divorce that I was worried he might be doing drugs."

She sounded heartbroken that I hadn't immediately come to that conclusion myself. And truthfully, I was a little ashamed I hadn't thought that first either. Unfortunately, the ghosts from my past were taking over, so I continued.

"Yeah but his drug test came back negative," I reminded her.

She stared at me her mouth open in disbelief. I knew my words had hurt her. I saw her pick up her phone and start typing a message.

"What are you doing?" I asked.

"I'm texting Brad to tell him we found his drugs," she said, furious.

A few minutes later her phone buzzed with an incoming

message.

"Ugh! Of course, he is denying it's his. I fucking hate him," she said, throwing her phone down on the couch. She seldom said "fuck" so I knew she was truly pissed.

Seeing her on the verge of losing it hurt me. I felt like an ass for doubting her. Of course she would never do drugs. I knew her, knew the kind of woman and mother she was.

Realizing my own baggage was hurting her I reached out for her. "Babe, come here. I'm sorry I accused you. Finding that crap just brought back some really bad memories for me. I have no reason to believe any of that was yours," I said, gently kissing her.

I sat down on the couch and pulled her down next to me. We sat there just holding each other for a bit. Anger at myself was seeping in. This was exactly what Addie had meant months ago when she said I didn't trust easily. I loved Simone too much to let my issues come between us. Just as I was about to open up and explain my irrational response I heard my text alert go off.

Brad: *Dude, she's not as innocent as you think.*

I read the message a couple times. What the fuck was Brad talking about? I was just about to text him back when a picture from his number came through. The image on the screen caused me to gasp out loud. There was a girl on her hands and knees in a black lacy bra and matching thong. On her right ass cheek was a line of what I assumed was coke. But the part that caused my heart to break was when I recognized the woman looking over her shoulder. It was my Simone with a look of seduction on her face that I hadn't seen before. She wasn't looking directly at the camera, and it was a little grainy, but I knew it was her.

While I was still trying to wrap my brain around what I had just seen, another picture came through. This was obviously from the same night but this one showed Simone leaning over a table with a straw to her nose while snorting a line.

All the air left my body as a hundred thoughts and scenarios crossed my mind. I tried to think back to our entire time together, wondering if I'd been so infatuated with Simone that I'd ignored the reality before me.

My mother had constantly told me she wasn't using. And for a while, that seemed to be the case, but she always chose drugs over her own children. Had I missed the signs? Had I been blind to it? Being duped again… I felt sick.

Once again, I felt like my world had just ended. It was like I was a kid again. My head was swimming, and my heart felt like it might literally burst out of my chest. It hit me that I might be having a panic attack. I leaned over and rubbed my temples, hard.

"Kyle?" she said, slowly. "What is it? You look like someone died…"

Suddenly the guilt I had been feeling earlier quickly turned to anger. I lowered my hands and met her gaze; this entire thing was surreal, like a horrible dream. "So you don't do drugs, huh?" I asked, lashing out. I tossed my phone in her direction, feeling old angers and new ones mingling and focused solely on Simone.

She picked it up and looked down at the pictures Brad sent. Her face turned pale and I saw tears form in her eyes. "Kyle, this isn't what it looks like," she said quietly.

"Oh, really?" I scoffed. "It looks like you doing coke while acting like a whore." My voice was cold and harsh, but I didn't care, not right now.

Her head snapped up to look at me. She couldn't have looked more pained than if I had actually reached out slapped her. At the moment, I didn't care. She'd lied. How many times was I going to allow a woman to lie to me before I learned my lesson? This was why I didn't do relationships, didn't do long-term. I always got burned in the end. When she tried to reach out to me, and scoot closer to me, I flinched. She jerked back.

"This is from the first night I met Brad," she explained, her voice panicky.

"So you aren't going to deny using cocaine?" I couldn't move past that detail.

"I tried it once. I hated the way it made me feel and told myself I would never touch drugs again. That was more than three years ago. You have to believe me," she pleaded, the tears running down her face.

I wanted to believe her. I wanted to believe her more than anything, but my whole childhood had been ruined by drug use. My mother was a master manipulator and could get anyone to believe she really didn't have a problem. I couldn't fall into that same routine with Simone. I couldn't let her convince me she didn't have a problem just because I never saw her use. "I can't do this," I said, not able to look at her.

"What do you mean?" she asked, the fear evident in her voice.

"I can't be with someone I can't trust."

"Kyle, I swear to you, I don't use drugs," she said,

grabbing hold of my arm.

I needed to get out of this apartment so I could think. I didn't want to see her in pain, but this was too much for me. I pulled my arm away and got up, grabbing my phone. "I need to go," I said, moving toward the door.

"Please don't go," she whispered. "Stay and talk to me about this."

"I can't. I need some time to think," I said and then I walked out of her apartment and away from the first woman I ever loved.

Chapter 17

Simone

My heart was broken. Completely broken. The moment the door closed behind Kyle I fell to the floor, a total sobbing mess. I hadn't stopped crying for the last thirty minutes. I heard Stella start to stir in her room. I was grateful she had slept as long as she had. I needed to pull myself together and take care of my daughter. No matter what other crap was going on in my life, I would not ignore Stella when she needed me.

I pushed myself up off the floor then shuffled to her room. Picking my daughter up out of her crib, she looked at my face and her mouth turned down at the corners. "Mama sad?" she asked.

"Mama's okay, baby girl," I told her, trying to sound cheerful.

My heart may have been crushed, but I was determined to make this the best Christmas for my daughter.

Her eyes darted around when we entered the living room. "Where's Ky?" she asked, looking for the man who had just walked out on us.

I understood he needed some time to think things through, but to walk away without letting me explain? That wasn't fair and that wasn't the Kyle I had come to love. He knew how upset I had been about Brad walking out of Stella's life and I couldn't believe he was going to do the same thing.

296

Speaking of Brad—I was furious with him. First, I had no idea he had taken any pictures that first night we were together. Second, why was he determined to hurt me so bad? He had to have suspected Kyle would react horribly based on his childhood and dealing with his mother's drug use. I still didn't believe he wanted to be with me, despite him coming over a few weeks ago, so that wasn't his motivation. If anything, I had been more than fair during our divorce. Why was he punishing me?

My curiosity got the better of me and I decided to send a text him. I went back to the couch and sat down with Stella then grabbed my cell phone I'd thrown there earlier

Me: *Why?*

He would know exactly what I was asking and I didn't want to say much more than that to him. Knowing him, if I started to rant he would just ignore me.

I heard my phone buzz and I dreaded what I was about to read. When I picked it up to look at the screen I was surprised to see a text from Marla.

Marla: *This is last minute but I was wondering if Stella could come spend the night? We're getting a tree tomorrow and thought it would be fun to take her.*

Knowing how much fun Stella had today shopping for the tree and then decorating, I knew she would enjoy another round with her grandparents. I had talked with Jim and Marla about not scheduling Saturday visitations anymore after Brad had shown up unannounced a couple weeks ago. I knew they loved having her whenever they could. But if I wasn't scheduled to work Saturdays, I started to keep her with me. They watched her when I worked so they still had a lot of time together. However, if one of us could have a happy weekend, I'd prefer it be my baby girl. She didn't need to hear me moping and crying.

Me: *Sure. Would you like me to bring her over to your house?*

Marla: *Trent is coming over in a little bit. He said he could pick her up on his way if you're okay with that.*

While I wasn't too keen on seeing anyone given my emotional state, I figured I could hide my devastation from Trent much easier than I could from Marla. Marla's mothering senses were strong. No one could hide anything from her watchful eye. It was one of the many things that made her a wonderful mother.

Me: *That's fine with me.*

Marla: *He said he would be there in about an hour. Does that work?*

Me: *Yes, it does.*

"Hey, sweetie, you're going to spend the night with Grandma and Grandpa. How does that sound?" I asked my daughter who had climbed off my lap and was now inspecting our tree.

"Yay! Gramma's house!" she said enthusiastically as she started dancing around to the Christmas music I hadn't noticed was still playing.

I went into her room to pack an overnight bag. Then I went to the kitchen to make her a snack. I knew Marla would feed her dinner, but Stella had been going through a growth spurt and seemed to be hungry all the time.

While we waited for Trent to come pick her up, Stella and I started to watch a Disney movie together on the couch. Having to take care of Stella was helping keep my mind off of Kyle and the cuddles were soothing to my soul. Admittedly, I was worried about what would happen as soon as she left. I could still feel the pain in my chest and knew it was going to get worse when I didn't have anything to distract me.

A while later, I heard a knock at my door. I pushed myself up off the couch, the mental exhaustion from the day finally catching up with me. I opened the door and invited Trent to come in.

"Unky Trent!" Stella yelled as she slid off the couch and ran to him. He picked her up and hugged her tightly to him. At least Trent would always be a positive male role model in her life. The thought made me both happy and sad. I knew she would never feel the sting of abandonment from her doting uncle, but I wanted her to have Kyle in her life as well. He would have made an excellent father.

Trent looked at me and my face must have given me away. "Hey, what's wrong?" he asked, placing a comforting arm around me.

"Just a really bad day," I told him honestly.

"Where's Kyle?" he asked, looking around my apartment like he was expecting to see him. "He told me he was going to be over here all day."

That was enough to set off the waterworks. My soft cries soon turned into gasping sobs and I couldn't seem to stop.

"Oh shit, what happened?" Trent asked, pulling me into a hug.

"Your brother happened," I managed to get out, not hiding the venom in those three words.

"What do you mean?" he asked slowly. He pulled back, a hard look on his face. "What did Brad do this time?"

He placed Stella on the couch so she could continue watching her movie. Then he guided me over to the dining table so we could talk freely. Once I was able to speak through the sobs, I told him every embarrassing and humiliating thing about my fight with Kyle. I told him about Kyle finding the drugs in the storage closet and then the texts that Brad sent over when we questioned him about the drugs. I was so embarrassed sharing the details of my behavior from that night three years ago, but once I started I couldn't stop.

Once I was finished I couldn't look up at Trent. I was completely humiliated and the silence between us was making me even more uncomfortable. I was just about to stand up and go to my bedroom when Trent finally spoke.

"Simone, I'm so sorry," he said, placing his hand on mine. "I'm not excusing Kyle's behavior, and he should have stayed and talked things out with you, but you have to understand his childhood screwed him up more than he is willing to admit. Finding his mother after she had OD'd gave him serious trust issues. She had promised him that she was clean and he believed her whole-heartedly. This has less to do with you and more to do with what he's been through."

"I understand that. I really do," I said, wiping at my hot face. I felt like I'd been crying for hours. "But it's still painful knowing he didn't trust me enough to believe me when I told him it was a one-time thing. It hurts even more that he walked out on Stella."

"Just give him some time. I know he loves you. It's obvious to anyone who sees the two of you together. I'm sure he'll come around eventually," he urged, kissing me on the top of the head and squeezing my shoulders.

I wanted that to be true. Even though I was mad at Kyle for walking out, if he came over right now I would welcome him back in a heartbeat. I loved him that much. I'd give Kyle a second chance. Not just for Stella, but for me because this whole thing was messed up and it was Brad's doing. I had to remember that his goal was to destroy what I had with Kyle any way he could, probably just to spite me for messing up the easy life he had before I came into it.

Trent stood up from the table and walked back to the living room. "Hey, munchkin, you ready to go to Grandma and Grandpa's house?" he asked Stella.

"Yea," she answered, a little uncertain and looking back at me. Obviously I wasn't doing a good job of hiding my heartbreak from my daughter.

I gave her a weak smile. "Go get Mr. Animal, okay?"

With another uncertain look, she walked over to me, and gave me a hug when I pulled her into my arms. "Wuv you, Mama," she said so sweetly that I nearly started to cry again. But I didn't. I set her on the floor and she ran off to grab her favorite stuffed animal.

"Do me a favor," Trent said, turning his attention back to me. "Go out for a walk or something after I leave. I don't want you sitting around here crying. That isn't good for you. I'd take you with me to my parents', but you don't need the third degree from Mom and I think you need some time to yourself. Plus... Kyle might actually realize he's being an ass

301

and come back. Though it'd serve him right to find an empty apartment..."

I smiled up at him. It was nice to hear his anger on my behalf. "I may go out and get myself some dinner, but I can't promise I won't spend the night crying," I told him. "But I'll try, for you."

He sighed, shaking his head. "What a mess," he bemoaned. "Fucking Brad. I can't believe we share the same DNA." His grimaced then forced himself to calm down when Stella came back with Mr. Animal. "Well, if you need anything, please call or text me. I'll be here if you need me." He gave me a hard look until I gave him a nod of obedience. "Good." Then he picked Stella up and headed to my door. I picked up her bags and handed them to him, which he easily handled on top of an excited two-year-old toddler.

"Thank you, Trent," I said, and he smiled back at me. I gave him another kiss on the cheek and then kissed my daughter's face. I waved, and watched the two of them go down the stairs then closed the door behind them.

As soon as I sat down on the couch I heard my text alert go off again. Hoping it was Kyle, I grabbed it and turned it on only to see a text from Brad.

Brad: *Kyle deserved to know the real you. You're always trying to act better than everyone else. You both needed a reminder of your trashy past.*

That was a low blow. Brad knew that my background was a sore subject for me. During our relationship he often reminded me that I was unwanted and undesirable. I had worked hard, with the help of my therapist, to try to overcome the many terrible things I had been through in my childhood and marriage.

But now, sitting here by myself, I was reminded that no one would stick around forever. I was truly alone in this world except for my daughter. Yes, Brad's family was kind and treated me well, but if I didn't have Stella I'm not sure they would have stuck by my side.

A few minutes after Trent left, I went out to my favorite Mexican restaurant and got dinner to go. Unfortunately, once I got home, I realized I didn't have much of an appetite. Instead, I lay on my couch and turned on the television. It didn't matter what was on because I wasn't really paying attention to it. I could feel the tears streaming down my face. I didn't bother to wipe them away or make an effort to stop them. It was a waste of time anyway. Nothing was going to stop me from crying at this point. I grabbed my phone again and started to type out a message to Kyle. But then I thought if he wanted to talk to me, he would have reached out to me. He said he needed some time to think. I owed it to him to give him that time. I was so exhausted that I fell asleep on the couch.

Abruptly, I opened my eyes, feeling heavy and disoriented. I pushed myself up and looked around my apartment, seeing that it was dark. I had no idea how long I had been asleep. I looked out my sliding door and could see a hint of soft light coming over the horizon so I knew it was early in the morning. My throat was sore from my sobs, my nose was stuffy, and my eyes felt so swollen it hurt to open them all the way.

I got up off the couch and walked down the hallway to the bathroom. When I looked in the mirror I was horrified by my reflection. My mascara had made large tracks down my face. Not only were my eyes swollen, they were also red and I had ghastly dark circles under my eyes.

I hopped in the shower in an effort to clean up a bit and hoped it would make me feel a bit better. I washed my hair and took time rinsing the shampoo out. I let the hot water run over my head and down my face for several minutes while trying to clear my mind of any thoughts of Kyle.

I managed to get myself dressed and made some toast and coffee. I still wasn't hungry, but figured I needed to eat something since I had skipped dinner. Walking into the living room and seeing all the Christmas decorations we had worked on together made me start crying all over again. I really needed to get a grip. I was heartbroken that Kyle left me, but I was a strong woman and I had a daughter I needed to take care of. I would allow myself to mourn the loss of our relationship today while I was by myself but as soon as I had Stella back I was going to make an attempt to just focus on her.

I knew in my heart that it was unlikely that I could get over it that quickly, I just had to make an effort. Sitting around and crying over Kyle wasn't going to bring him back. He needed to figure things out on his own and decide if he wanted to continue a relationship with me.

Later that afternoon, I drove over to Jim and Marla's to pick up Stella. I was dreading going over there since I had no idea if Trent had shared anything with them regarding Kyle and me. I knocked on the door and waited for someone to answer.

The door opened and I made eye contact with the last person I expected to see today.

"Hey," Brad said as he pulled the door open for me to enter the house.

"What are you doing here?" I demanded bluntly, letting

my hatred for him shine through.

He had this awful Joker-like smile plastered on his face. "Actually, I was just leaving," he said as I pushed past him.

"Mama!" Stella shrieked when she saw me. I kneeled down as soon as she reached me and gave her a huge hug and kiss.

"I missed you, baby girl. Did you have fun with Grandma and Grandpa?" I asked.

"We had lots of fun," I heard Jim announce from the living room. "She picked out the best tree at the lot and we've spent all day decorating."

I gave him a small smile, feeling uncomfortable with Brad in the same room. I realized that Stella wasn't interacting with her father at all and I wondered if he'd even tried to spend any time with her while he had been here.

"Well, I'm taking off," Brad announced, speaking more to his dad than to me.

"Um… Brad can I talk to you for a minute before you leave?" I asked, hating to go back to that subservient Simone who was always timid and meek. But at least this time, I was determined to get answers.

"Make it quick," he said, checking his phone and effecting a bored air, "I have some people I'm meeting up with."

"Hey, Stella, let's go see if Grandma's cookies have cooled off," Jim said, removing Stella from the tense situation that was forming in the entryway.

"How long have those drugs been in the storage closet?" I demanded.

"No idea what you're talking about, Simone," he said, smirking.

"You've got to be kidding me, Brad! You know they weren't mine. When I caught you with Tiffany I saw the coke on the bedside table. You've obviously used since that night three years ago. Why can't you just be honest with me for once?!" I said, raising my voice. I didn't care if Jim and Marla heard. I was mad I'd never told them about this before.

His expression became ugly, his lips turning into a snarl as he spat out, "Why should I tell you anything? Just so you can use it against me later? You're just pissed off because Kyle found out the kind of behavior you're capable of and left you. I can't help it if he doesn't want to date a coke whore."

"Brad!" I heard Marla gasp from the doorway.

"I'm outta here," he said, not letting his mother say another word. He walked out the door without a backward glance.

I felt the tears prick at my eyes as I turned around to face Marla. "It's not true what he said, I swear!"

"Oh, sweetie..." Marla said, coming over and wrapping her arms around me. As soon as I was in her arms, the dam broke open and my tears soaked her shirt.

"I promise, I'm not doing drugs..." I trailed off. I didn't know what else to say. What if she didn't believe me? What if her and Jim believed Brad and thought Stella would be better off with them?

"Simone, look at me," Marla said placing both hands on the side of my face. "I believe you." Those three words were so powerful.

I was able to calm myself a little. "Everything is totally screwed up," I said tearfully, thankful I wasn't sobbing.

"And the worst part is I allowed another man to walk out of Stella's life. What kind of mother am I if I can't even protect her from the men I pick?"

"There is no excuse for Brad's behavior. He's hit rock bottom, from what we can tell," she said, still trying to calm me down. "Jim and I can only hope he gets help before things get worse. As far as things with Kyle, I have faith they will work out. I don't know what happened between the two of you, but I have never seen him look at someone the way he looks at you. He loves you and love can overcome a lot."

"Oh, Marla, I'm not sure love can overcome this. What he saw is most definitely a hard limit for him, and I'm not sure the truth is enough for him to be able to let it go," I said. I pulled back and tried to have more control over my emotions.

I went to pack up Stella's clothing and toys feeling the exhaustion of the last twenty-four hours wash over me. I wasn't sure why Brad had been over here and it wasn't my business. I could have asked his parents but, frankly, I didn't feel like talking anymore. I just wanted to get back to my apartment.

I drove Stella and myself back home, trying not to overthink everything and dwell on how my life had once again been turned upside down. Nothing lasts forever, I thought, especially for me.

Back inside the apartment, I spent the evening just snuggling with my baby on the couch feeling some happiness for the first time since Kyle walked out and Brad had managed to hurt me, once again.

After some mother-daughter bonding time, I gave her a bath and read her a story before putting her down for the night.

"I wuv you, Mama," she said sleepily. It's like she knew I needed to hear that on repeat, and it made me feel better. I tucked her in tight, glad she didn't seem to bothered by my emotional rollercoaster.

"I love you, too, sweetheart," I said, and kissed her on the forehead. "I'll see you in the morning." Then I walked out and closed the door behind me.

I went through my nighttime routine, washing my face, brushing my teeth, and changing into pajamas. All my movements were mechanical, like a robot with no thought, and I was glad to be operating on autopilot. I had to work tomorrow so Stella was going to spend the evening with Kayla. I re-packed her bag so I wouldn't have to do it in the morning. I climbed into bed around nine and looked at my phone again. I still hadn't heard from Kyle. Deciding I couldn't go to sleep without reaching out to him, I scrolled through my contacts to his name and sent him a text.

Me: *I miss you.*

That was all. I had so much more I wanted to say to him but that would have to do for tonight. I held onto my phone hoping to hear from him. I fell asleep with the phone next to me, but it never went off. I took that as confirmation he really was done with me.

Chapter 18

Kyle

$\mathcal{I}$t had been a week since I'd walked out of Simone's apartment, leaving a huge part of my heart behind. I was so torn. I knew those pictures were old and I really wanted to believe that she hadn't touched any drugs since then. But I had grown up with someone lying to me about that very thing and it was hard for me to separate the two situations in my head.

I was also having a hard time dealing with another thing those pictures showed. I knew she'd had sex with Brad, obviously they had a child together, but seeing photos of her in that state had messed with my head. I didn't peg her as the type of girl who would allow her picture to be taken while practically naked and engaged in those types of activities. I could tell by her eyes that she was high as fuck and I just couldn't handle seeing her like that. Unfortunately, every time I closed my eyes that's all I could see. Needless to say, I hadn't slept much these last few days and it was starting to affect my job.

Additionally, the tension in the office was making it awkward as hell for everybody. I could tell by the disapproving looks from Trent that he didn't agree with my decision to walk away from Simone. He was, however, smart enough to not confront me about it. We had been friends for so long that he knew when to give me my space. But I knew time was running out before he decided enough was enough and forced me to talk about things or kick my ass.

Avoiding Addie had been more difficult. As soon as she saw me on Monday morning she knew something terrible had happened. She had closed my door and forced me to share what had gone down. I didn't tell her all the details because I still felt a need to protect Simone. If by some miracle Simone and I worked things out, I didn't want anyone to look at her differently.

But I told her some things had come up between us, things that I was having a hard time dealing with, and that I just needed some time to think.

"I hope you didn't screw things up for good, Kyle," she said.

"Gee thanks," I replied sarcastically.

"Seriously!" she said, throwing her hands up in disgust. "Simone is so good for you, and you're good for her and Stella. I hate to see you throw away what could very easily be the best thing in your life."

I was happy that Addie believed Simone and Stella were good for me, but I wasn't convinced we were a perfect match. I also feared that my words and actions last weekend had completely ruined my chances with Simone. I knew I still had a ton of shit to work through without so many people in my face about it if I wanted to think about getting back with her.

I sat at my desk reading the text from Simone for probably the hundredth time since I had received it on Sunday.

I miss you.

Three simple words that both brought me joy and broke my heart. She hadn't sent any more texts since then and I couldn't blame her. I hadn't responded to that one so I was sure she thought I didn't care. It wasn't that. I still loved her, more than I could ever imagine loving anyone, but I was having a hard time getting my thoughts straight in my head. I planned on going to her once I worked things out. I just hoped I wasn't too late once I got my shit figured out. A part of me thought that with Simone knowing about my past and having similar experiences, she could help me sort through my own issues. But the shock of seeing those pictures had been a major setback. If she had been honest with me before I found the drugs I think we would have been able to move past it. But I wasn't completely sure, and now I'd broken her trust by leaving her. Leaving Stella. If I had stayed, and heard her out—would it have solved anything? I didn't know, and now I never would. After I left that afternoon I'd roamed the city, feeling lost and confused. I still felt that way.

I closed my eyes, leaning back in my seat. Normally, I could dive into my work and forget about everything else for a while, but now all I thought about was Simone. I hated going home and seeing evidence of the time her and Stella spent there. I'd even sat in Stella's room one night, recalling her playing and laughing in there as Simone and I looked on.

"Kyle!" I heard Trent yell from his office, the panic clear in his voice. I jumped out of my chair and ran to his office. As soon as I saw him I knew something was wrong. The look of complete shock and disbelief was all over his face as he slammed the phone down. "We've got to get to the hospital. My parents just called, Brad OD'd. Sounds like he went into cardiac arrest."

"Fuck!" I yelled, running back to my office to grab my car keys. There was no way I was going to let Trent drive right now.

"What's going on?" Addie asked from her desk.

"It's Brad. I'm driving Trent to the hospital. Can you handle things here?" I asked barely waiting for her answer.

"Of course, but call me from the hospital and let me know what's going on," she called out as I rushed past her back into Trent's office.

He was already grabbing his jacket and messenger bag. Once he had everything, we both went running out of the office to my car. I jumped into the driver's seat and started to pull out before he even had a chance to buckle up.

Trent kept looking at his phone. "I can't fucking believe this," he whispered.

"Who found him?" I asked, keeping focused and driving us as fast as possible to the hospital.

"It was my dad. He had a few things Brad wanted dropped off... I guess he went to Tiffany's apartment since they're back together and that's where he found Brad. I don't know anything else." He sighed, looking out his window. After a few more minutes he added, "I know he has fucked up a lot the last few years, but he's still my little brother. I can't lose him."

Sadly, I knew all too well what Trent was feeling right now. There was nothing I could say or do to take away his fear. I could just vow to be with him every step of the way. Trent, for all intents and purposes, was my brother and family was always there for each other.

I pulled into the parking lot of the hospital. Not seeing any parking spaces right away I drove to the drop zone and let Trent out. "I'll meet you in there. Go find your parents," I told him as I watched him run through the sliding doors and into the building.

I found a parking spot in the parking garage and hurried into the hospital. A sense of déjà vu washed over me but I pushed my own issues aside. This wasn't about me and I needed to be strong for Trent and his parents. I went directly to the emergency department's waiting room figuring that's where they would take Brad if he was, indeed having a heart attack. I saw Jim and Marla huddled in a back corner. Jim was comforting his wife who was crying into his shoulder. Trent was over at the reception desk trying to get any information he could from the woman there.

I went over and sat down on the other side of Jim and placed a hand on his back in an effort to lend any support I could. Trent came back over and sat down next to his mom, placing an arm around her but staring off, still in a daze.

"It sounds like they were able to stabilize him in the ambulance on the way here. We'll have to wait awhile for any more updates," Trent informed all of us.

I could hear a small sigh of relief come from Marla. Jim took the opportunity to fill us in on what happened earlier in the day. He had received a phone call from Brad and he said he sounded absolutely frantic about getting a box from the house. Jim had been able to locate the box in the garage and decided to take it over to Tiffany's house since Brad had made it sound like it was an urgent matter. When Jim got to the apartment, he knocked on the screen door. He could see in since the other door was open but didn't see anyone moving around. He called out and still didn't hear anybody. He was just about to return to his car when he heard a scream come from inside. He rushed in and followed the screams back to the bedroom where he saw Tiffany leaning over Brad who had collapsed on the floor. He had Tiffany call 9-1-1 and he started CPR on his son.

As Jim finished sharing with us what had happened, the

doors to the waiting room slid open. Tiffany walked in looking like a mess. She looked like she hadn't brushed her hair in a week and she was wearing some ratty sweatpants and an old sweatshirt.

"How is he?" she asked as she walked over to us.

"We aren't sure right now," Trent informed her in a tired voice. "Sounds like they got his heart going for now, but we don't know anything else."

No one offered for her to take a seat so she sat down next to Trent.

"We could be here for a while. Do you want to go home and get cleaned up?" Trent asked and I could tell he was already irritated by her presence.

"No, I'm going to stay until I know he's okay," she said.

Silence descended on the room, none of us really knowing what say. Since we were in for a long wait, I decided to text Addie.

Me: *At the hospital. Brad overdosed and had a heart attack. Sounds like they got him stabilized. Don't know anything else right now.*

Addie's response was immediate:

Addie: *OMG, what can I do to help?*

Me: *Will you call Erik and Ian? Trent needs as much support as he can get.*

Addie: *Of course. What about Simone? Has anyone told her yet?*

I had already thought about Simone but hadn't asked anyone yet if they had contacted her. I didn't know if it was a good idea. There wasn't anything she could do here but at the same time, he was Stella's father. She probably deserved to know.

"Has anyone contacted Simone?" I asked.

"Not yet," Jim whispered, shaking his head. I had never seen him this sad. In fact, I wasn't sure I'd ever seen him cry. "But we should definitely do that."

"I could have Addie text her," I suggested. "She's already calling Ian and Erik."

"That would be helpful," Marla agreed.

Me: *Could you text Simone as well?*

As soon as I sent the message, I realized I didn't want her getting that kind of news via text.

Me: *Never mind. I'm going to go tell her in person.*

This was not the way I wanted to come face to face with Simone since I left her but she couldn't be alone when she heard the news. If she wanted to come to the hospital I was going to be the one to drive her.

The drive to her apartment seemed to take double the amount of time it should have. Even so, when I arrived at her place I still had no idea how I was going to tell her about Brad.

I knocked on her door and could hear footsteps and then the deadbolt being unlocked. The look of surprise on her beautiful face broke my heart.

Her hair was up in a messy bun and she was in loose-fitting jeans and an oversized sweater. She looked exhausted, dark circles under eyes, and her nose was red. I stood there staring at her for several long seconds. She still looked absolutely stunning.

Looking at her physically hurt me because it reminded me of everything I had lost when I'd walked away from her. And for what? My self-pity and wallowing in it for a week? It was like a moment of clarity came over me. At just how much I missed her. Missed Stella. Being with them, in this apartment or at my condo. It was so obvious to me, standing before her, what a complete selfish ass I'd been.

I love you.

"Uh, hey," was all she could get out. I hated to see her struggle to even talk to me.

I miss you, too.

"Hi there," I said awkwardly. A dozen thoughts raced through my tired brain but right now, it wasn't about me or her or us. "Um..." I had no idea how to break this news so I just blurted it out. "There's been an emergency with Brad. It looks like he overdosed and had a heart attack."

She just stared at me in shock, not expecting me to say that. But she quickly snapped out of it.

"Is he..." she started, but her voice started to break. "Is he... still alive?"

"Yeah, he's at the hospital right now. I didn't want you to be alone when you found out. I also didn't want you to drive yourself if you wanted to go to the hospital," I added.

"I should go, but I don't want to take Stella. I can drive myself. Thank you for coming to tell me," she said and then started to shut the door.

I put my hand out to stop it from closing in my face. "I'm not leaving you alone," I informed her.

She stood her ground and I could see the determination on her face. "I need to find someone to watch Stella. It might be a little while before I can get out there. Really, I'm fine. You should be there for Jim and Marla — and for Trent," she said, not looking into my eyes.

I hated myself right then. Had I broken her so badly that she could barely stand to be in my presence? "Simone… please," I said softly. Whatever was in my voice must have touched her a little. Her expression wasn't as hard and closed off; still, she only gave a stiff nod and went back inside. She didn't open the door wider for me, but at least she hadn't slammed it in my face. It wouldn't have mattered. I would have just waited outside for her.

Kayla agreed to watch Stella so we both sat on the couch awkwardly waiting until she arrived. Stella had been napping and I wished she had been awake. Not only did I miss her mother terribly, I really missed spending time with her. I knew I wanted to be a father figure to her. Even now, if Brad finally saw this as a wakeup call and became an excellent father, I would still be there for Stella. A child could never have too many people who loved them.

We remained silent on the drive back to the hospital. Simone spent the entire ride looking out the passenger window. I wasn't sure if it was because of the situation or if she just didn't want to look at me. That hurt, making my stomach twist as though a knife was stuck in me. I couldn't handle the silent treatment anymore. I wanted to be of some sort of comfort to her. I wanted to start making up for my behavior, prove to her she could trust me. That I did love her. That she wouldn't be alone in this. And then I'd keep proving myself to her until she forgave me and realized I wasn't going away.

I placed my hand on hers, which had been resting on her leg. She flinched as soon as I touched her and that made what was left of my heart break just a little bit more. "Please, Kyle, I can't do this with you right now," she said quietly with her head still turned away from me. She pulled her hand away. That proverbial knife turned in me more.

"Honestly, I'm not trying to push anything right now, Simone," I said. "I just want to make sure you are okay. Whatever you need, I'll be there for you."

"*Now* you want to be there for me?" she asked harshly before taking a deep breath. "Never mind, don't answer that. I just want to get to the hospital."

I didn't want to upset her any more so I kept my mouth shut. For now. I deserved the silent treatment, her wrath and anger, her disappointment and mistrust—I knew that. But I was suddenly brimming with all these things I wanted to tell her, wanted to share with her. Beg for her forgiveness. I knew it wasn't the right time, but when was it ever the right time? Still, I just drove, gripping the wheel for dear life.

After a few more minutes of silence she asked, "How are Jim and Marla?"

I exhaled, glad to hear her voice and that she was talking to me. I didn't care what the topic was, just as long as she didn't keep shutting me out. "They seem to be doing okay." I chanced a look at her, but she averted my gaze. "Jim was the one who found Brad and he had to perform CPR. He probably saved his life."

She sighed, and fell back against her seat. She shook her

head. "Poor Jim. I can't imagine having to find your own child like that," she said sadly.

Now it was my turn to be silent. I knew how terrible it was to find someone you loved in that position. It had been much too late for any life-saving efforts in the case of my mother, but Brad at least had a chance. When I'd found her that day, she had been dead for several hours. The coroner report had determined that my mother had died just about an hour after Addie and I had left for the Thompsons' house. Truthfully, it was never easy, whatever age you were.

I pulled my car into the parking garage and we were able to find a spot near the stairs on the second level. I got out and started to make my way to Simone's side of the car so I could open the door for her, but she had gotten out before I got over there. She started toward the stairs and kept walking, not waiting for me.

I sped up so I could walk next to her once we were on the first level. I directed her to the emergency room's waiting area. As soon as she saw Jim and Marla, she ran over to them and hugged them tightly

Trent moved over to make space for Simone next to Marla and I went back to sit on the other side of Jim. "Where's Stella?" Jim asked.

"Kayla's babysitting at my apartment. I didn't think it was a good idea to bring her here," Simone answered. She looked pale but was composed.

"Has there been any update?" I asked.

"The doctor said we could probably see him soon. Right now they are limiting it to immediate family members," Trent answered. There was no emotion in his voice and he was in the phase of shock where he was just waiting for the other shoe to drop. The waiting was what made it worse.

As we sat in silence, I looked around the waiting room and noticed that Tiffany had left at some point while I had been gone. "Hey, where'd Tiffany go?" I asked.

I noticed Simone tense at the mention of the woman she had caught with Brad all those months ago.

"She got a text and said she had something to take care of. I'm not really expecting her to come back," Trent explained.

I wasn't surprised that Brad's occasional girlfriend would abandon him in his time of need. Based on their on-again, off-again status, it was clear their relationship wasn't built on solid ground. I could only hope that the fact his family was here, even when he had turned his back on them, would be some sort of wakeup call for him.

"I need to call my boss to let him know I won't be making it for my shift tonight. I'm going to step outside for just a moment," Simone said, grabbing her purse and heading out the sliding doors.

I couldn't help but watch her the entire time she was outside. I wanted so desperately to go wrap my arms around her and hold her tightly through this ordeal. I had fucked up badly and I wasn't sure I was ever going to be able to fix it.

After she hung up the phone, I saw her wave to someone just out of my line of sight. A moment later I saw Addie run up and give Simone a huge hug, followed by Erik and Ian. I assumed they all drove over together. The four of them walked into the waiting room and everyone began exchanging hugs with each other.

We sat around chatting about anything but Brad or being in the hospital for another hour before the doctor came out. He informed Jim and Marla that they could go back and see their son. The both released sighs of relief as they got up out of their chairs and followed the doctor through the doors and back to Brad's room.

After about thirty minutes, Jim came back out to get Trent so he could go visit with his brother. The five of us remained in the waiting room making small talk. About twenty minutes later, Jim, Marla, and Trent had all come back to the waiting room.

Brad wasn't completely out of the woods and the hospital staff wanted to limit the time with visitors to family only so he could rest. Since he was stable, Jim urged all of us to go home, get some rest, and come back tomorrow when we could actually visit with him. The three of them were going to stay for a little while longer.

I drove Simone home and she was just as quiet as she had been on the way to the hospital. "You can just pull up behind my car," she said when we pulled into the parking lot of her apartment complex. She was making it very clear that she didn't want me to come up, not even to walk her to the door. Even though it went against everything I was taught on how to treat a woman, I decided not to push the issue.

"Do you want me to pick you up on my way to the hospital tomorrow morning?" I asked, hoping she would at least let me do that for her.

"No, I'll be able to drive myself. Thank you for the ride today, though," she said as she got out of my car and closed the door behind her before I could say anything else. I stayed where I was so I could at least watch her walk to her door and make sure she got in okay.

She may not have wanted my help or even my company right now, which was painful to admit, but I was more determined than ever to get my girl back.

Chapter 19

Simone

*T*he next few days were a mix of working and spending time at the hospital with Brad's family. I wanted to be there for them like they had been there during my tough times. I brought Stella a couple times to spend an hour or so in the waiting room with Jim and Marla. Her visits seemed to brighten their spirits and I was happy to see it brought them some comfort.

I had received a text this morning from Trent telling me that Brad was asking to see me. I had no idea what he wanted to talk to me about, but I was willing to go in and give him a chance to say what he needed to. Trent mentioned that he was going to lunch with his parents to discuss what their next steps were in helping Brad so I figured that would be a good time for me to go see him.

I looked in the waiting room to see if anyone was still in there, but it was empty. I walked down the long, bright hallway to Brad's room and stopped just shy of the door. His room was private, just his bed in the middle of the open space. Brad was lying in the bed with his head turned so he could look out the window that overlooked the busy roadway below. The television was turned off and the only sound was coming from the various medical equipment set up to monitor his vital signs. It was odd to see someone his age and who had appeared relatively healthy hooked up to machines and looking so frail and weak in a hospital bed. The drugs had clearly done a number on him.

I walked in, the sound of my footsteps causing him to turn and look at me. "Trent said you were asking to see me," I said, but it came out a bit harsher than I meant for it to.

"I was," Brad responded, sounding tired and weak. "I wanted to apologize."

I didn't know what to expect when I walked in, but an apology wasn't it. "Okay…" I paused, letting his words sink in. "What did you want to apologize for?" I asked. The guard I'd put up when it came to Brad was still firmly in place. I wasn't sure I'd ever let it down when I was around him.

"Well, for starters, I should have been spending more time with Stella. I'm sorry that I bailed on our daughter," he said. I couldn't believe it and my immediate reaction was I shouldn't, but I could actually detect some remorse in his voice and expression. "That wasn't fair to either of you. I'm going to rehab and I hope when I'm done, you'll let me spend some time with her."

"I've never once tried to keep her from you," I pointed out. Brad may be contrite now, but I had to remember that he could change in an instant. I had seen it before. I wasn't going to put my daughter in a situation where he could disappoint her again. "And now that I have confirmation of your drug use, it's going to be a while before I can ever trust you with her, especially alone. If you show that you're serious about getting clean, then we can talk about you visiting her at your parents' house with them supervising."

"That's fair," he agreed, nodding.

"It doesn't matter whether it's fair or not. You really fucked up and now you have to face the consequences of your choices," I said, hoping to God he was actually listening to what I said. I checked my phone, and then glanced at Brad. "Is there anything else you wanted to say? I need to go get Stella."

"Where is she?" he asked.

"She's with Kayla. She's been helping out a lot since your overdose." Brad flinched when I said 'overdose'. But I wasn't going to sugar-coat things for him anymore. I never felt like I could speak my mind with him before, and I was done with that. If he was truly sorry and wanted to make things better, then it was going to be on my terms and my terms were based on what I thought was best for Stella. "Anything else?" I asked, already heading toward the door.

"I'm sorry for sending Kyle those pictures," he said, stopping me in my tracks.

"Why wasn't I aware that you had taken them in the first place?" I asked, moving back toward his bedside.

"I don't know. I was an asshole for taking them. We were both high as fuck that night. I guess I thought it was fun at the time," he said, actually looking remorseful.

That'd be a first.

Truthfully, this new Brad was strange. I also believed him, which was even stranger. "Why did you send them to Kyle?"

He sighed, resting his head back. "I don't know," he whispered. Brad showing any emotion, other than anger, was rare. It also didn't soften my resolve. I was still going to demand that he respect me, if anything, as the mother of his child. "I was angry at you, my brother, my parents, just everybody. Every time I talked to my mom or dad, they would lecture me on how I needed to step up as a parent. Then they would go on and on about how you were doing a great job. Fuck, even Addie thinks you're wonderful and she should have hated you. I was tired of every one seeing me as a fuck-up and seeing you as this perfect mother."

"It's not my fault that you made those choices or felt that way. You know, I had a night of really bad choices, but it was just *one* night. I've worked my ass off to be a good mom, and however misguided I was, I tried really hard to be a good wife to you. You had to know that those pictures were going to be a deal-breaker for Kyle. You wanted to hurt me so badly that you used the one thing Kyle couldn't handle to get him to leave me."

"I'm sorry," he said again, and I could hear the sincerity in his voice but I was still angry. I had lost so much because of the crappy choices Brad made.

"Well, sorry isn't going to give me back the man I love, now is it?" I gritted out, letting my anger get the best of me.

In the past, any time I showed emotion, it would piss Brad off, but that didn't happen this time. "You love him?" he asked. There wasn't anger in his tone just general curiosity and maybe a little surprise.

"It's really none of your business and it doesn't even matter anymore. He made it very clear he wants nothing to do with me, so thank you for that." I couldn't have this conversation with him any longer. I felt like the walls were closing in on me, I had to get out of there.

I stepped out of the room and turned to my right just to see Kyle standing right there by the door.

"Whoa, you okay?" he asked, placing both his hands on my shoulders. I looked up into his gorgeous green eyes and I felt like I couldn't breathe. I was already frazzled from my conversation with Brad. I couldn't deal with Kyle on top of it. A girl could only handle so much at once. I broke out of his grasp but immediately missed the warmth of his hands on me. I had no idea how much of our conversation he'd overheard and I didn't want to ask. I could feel the tears streaming down my face. I just needed to get out of there.

"Hey, talk to me," he implored.

"I need to go," I said as the sobs started to break free. Scared he was going to reach out for me again, I started to run down the hallway.

I didn't stop running until I was safely in my car. That's when I let my sobs take over. I felt like I was hyperventilating so I made myself take some deep breaths like I learned in my childbirth classes. Once my breathing evened out I started up my car and drove out of the parking garage. I still felt tears rolling down my face, but at least I wasn't hysterical anymore.

I took city streets to Kayla's house instead of the freeway. I wanted a little more time to compose myself before I picked Stella up. As I pulled into Kayla's driveway, I heard a notification alert on my phone. I decided to ignore it and go in to hug my daughter instead. Seeing Stella immediately brightened my spirit. My relationship with her father may have been difficult, but I wouldn't change anything in my past because it had brought me the greatest gift... her.

"Thanks for watching Stella, again," I told Kayla. I was emotionally wrecked. Kayla just smiled and hugged me. "I don't know how I would have made it through this week without your help. Hell, not just this week, you've been a lifesaver for several months now."

"Don't worry about it," she said, smiling. "You know I adore Stella and I would do anything to help you out."

I gave her another hug and took Stella out to the car. Once I had her buckled in I decided to take her out for lunch. After lunch we went to play at the park near our apartment, where she tired herself out by running around nonstop. As long as I stayed busy with her I couldn't think about everything else going on in my life.

She fell asleep on the way home and I managed to carry her up to her room and put her in bed without waking her. I didn't have to work tonight so I thought I would take advantage of the quiet time and catch up on some reading.

Then I remembered that I never read my text from earlier. I grabbed my phone, knowing in my gut who it was from.

Kyle: *Please let me know you made it home. You ran out of here so quickly, I'm worried about you. Please call me. We really need to talk.*

I didn't know how to respond to his message. It warmed my heart to know he still worried about me, but was I ready to talk to him? Part of me wanted to hear his voice so badly, talk through things, and move forward. But the other part was scared that after talking, he would still decide he didn't want to be with me, breaking my heart all over again.

A knock at the door broke me out of my depressing thoughts. I looked out the window and saw Kyle's car down in the parking lot. I stood there for a couple minutes contemplating what to do.

"Simone, please let me in. I heard you walking around in there," he called out, sounding defeated.

I took a deep breath. I wasn't going to be a coward about this. This conversation with him was bound to happen, sooner or later. I opened the door and moved to the side silently giving him permission to enter. He moved past me and just the slight brush of our arms brought goosebumps to my skin. He walked to the couch and sat down, looking like he belonged there. Or maybe that was my own thoughts and desires telling me he belonged here with me.

"You didn't answer my text," he stated unhappily.

"I just read it a couple minutes ago, and then you knocked on the door," I explained while still standing by the door with my arms crossed in front of me.

"I can't do this anymore, Simone," he started.

I blanched, not expecting him to be so blunt. "Then why waste your time coming over here to talk?!" I shouted, throwing my hands up in the air. I couldn't bear to hear him rehash all the reasons we couldn't be together. "You saw pictures of me doing something that's a deal-breaker for you. I can't go back in the past and change it. I should have told you, but this is *why* I didn't." I was crying now and my emotions were raw.

"Babe, stop," he said, exasperated. "That's not what I'm saying."

I stopped talking and just stood there staring at him through my tears.

"Could you please sit down?" he asked. I took a moment to study his face and I could see the same heartbreak I had been feeling staring back at me.

I sat down at the other end of the couch and turned to face him while wiping at my face. "Okay, so what are you saying?" I asked, still unsure why he was here.

"Like I said, I can't do this anymore. I made a huge mistake walking out on you when Brad sent those pictures. I let my past control my thoughts rather than use common sense. It was obvious those pictures were old. It didn't help my ego to see you in a compromising position with another man. My pride took a hit and I took it out on you. The issues with my mom and my childhood shouldn't have been applied to this situation. Instead of being mature about it, I refused to deal with it and pushed you away. I'm sorry." He paused to take a deep breath. "I'm so very sorry that I hurt you. I love you so much and it kills me that I've caused you pain…" His voice faltered at the end of his speech.

I sat there in silence for a few seconds. I could feel a couple tears slip free and Kyle moved closer to me so he could wipe them away.

"Don't cry, babe. I know I don't deserve a second chance, but if you give me one I will prove to you that I will always listen to you and be there for you and Stella," he said, his voice a near-whisper. I could see his eyes tearing up too, and I knew he meant every word.

I was overcome with waves of emotion and incapable of forming any words so I leaned forward and kissed him gently. The kiss took him by surprise, but he quickly returned it, filling his kiss with so much love and passion that I knew everything he had just said was true.

Eventually, I pulled away from him. "I love you, too. I've missed you so much. Watching you walk away was beyond painful. I felt like I had finally found everything I had been looking for and you just… left. Please promise me that you'll talk to me if something upsets you, because I can promise you I will never do anything to intentionally hurt you."

"I will never leave you or Stella again, I can promise you that. I'm here for the long haul. You both mean the world to me," he said hoarsely, holding me hard against him. "I've barely been able to function without the two of you."

We continued to talk a little, which eventually led to us making out on my couch, until I heard Stella start to wake up. I reluctantly broke away from Kyle and went into the bedroom to get her. After changing her diaper the two of us made our way back out to the living room. The minute she saw Kyle sitting on the couch, she ran full speed into his open arms.

"Ky, you're here!" she shouted. "I missed you."

"Oh, baby girl, I missed you, too," he said, tears rolling down his cheeks. The fact that I found a man that not only loved me but also loved my daughter in equal measure was an answer to all my prayers. I knew then, watching the two of them embracing each other, that this was my happily ever after.

Epilogue

Kyle

Ten Months Later

"*Ky*, I'm hungry!" Stella shouted as she jumped onto our bed, effectively waking me up. I didn't think I'd slept past seven in the six months since Simone and Stella moved in. I had never been a morning person, but even the early wakeup calls didn't make me regret asking the two of them to live with me.

I had wanted them to move in with me shortly after we got back together, but walking away like I did had hurt Simone more than I'd even realized. I had to work hard to earn back her trust before she would consider taking such a huge step. I couldn't blame her. Almost everyone in her life had abandoned her and she worked hard every day learning to trust those of us who loved her.

"Let's go make breakfast while we let your mama sleep," I suggested, climbing out of bed and carrying Stella down to the kitchen.

It was Saturday and I had a whole day planned for Simone and me. First, she was going to drop Stella off at Jim and Marla's for Brad's visitation. After his overdose, Brad entered a ninety-day, inpatient rehab facility. He was lucky to have the support of his family and I think it was one of the largest factors in helping him with his recovery. Once he completed the program, he moved back in with his parents and continued participating in drug treatment classes.

I still wasn't his biggest fan, but I could see that he was making an effort, especially when it came to Stella. It would be a long time before we ever trusted him with her by himself, but for now, our arrangement was working.

While she was gone, I was going to get everything ready for our 'beach date'. Simone's birthday was coming up in a couple days so we were having our own private celebration today. I was hoping it would be her most memorable birthday yet.

"What's going on down here?" Simone asked as she walked down the stairs into the kitchen. Even in a robe and her hair a mess, I thought my girl was the most beautiful woman in the world.

"We're making pancakes," Stella announced from where she was kneeling on the barstool, stirring the batter I had put in front of her.

Simone walked over to her daughter and placed a kiss on the top of her head before meeting me by the stove and to give me my morning kiss as well. I loved that we had settled into a routine. When I bought this house a couple years ago, the idea of a family filling it seemed like a distant dream. I never expected it to happen so soon. Now I woke up every morning to the faces of the people I loved more than anything in the world. I couldn't imagine my life any other way.

After breakfast, the girls finished getting ready and headed out. As soon as they left I started making the lunch we would be eating on the beach. It was early October, so it wouldn't be too crowded out there today. The forecast was calling for sunny skies with temperatures in the upper sixties.

I made a simple cold pasta salad and prepared a cheese and cracker platter. I packed up the food, along with some water and a bottle of champagne and glasses into the picnic basket I had purchased recently.

I ran upstairs and took a shower knowing I only had a little bit of time before Simone would be back. I changed into a pair of black cargo shorts and a gray T-shirt. We were going to be sitting on the sand so I wanted to be comfortable. As I came back downstairs I heard the garage door open and saw Simone walk in.

"Are you ready to go?" I asked, picking up everything we needed off the counter. I hadn't told her what we were doing today, but she could probably guess by the basket and huge blanket I was carrying.

"Sure," she said, eyeing everything in my arms. "I guess I'm dressed okay?"

I looked her up and down in her blue maxi dress and cardigan. "You look perfect," I told her honestly.

I held her hand as we walked down to the sand. We found a perfect spot away from the few other beachgoers. I spread the blanket out for us and sat with Simone between my outstretched legs.

I pulled a small portable speaker from the basket and started the special playlist I had made for today. The first song was the one that had been playing at the club when we had kissed out on the dance floor the night of her birthday.

We opened up the food and snacked on that for a little bit while the songs continued, each of them holding special meaning for us. I had never felt so much peace in my life as I did now holding the love of my life in my arms, just looking out at the water.

Finally the moment I had been anticipating was here. Train's "Marry Me" started playing in the background. I don't know if Simone noticed right away so I remained quiet just listening to the music. When the song came to an end, I gently turned Simone around to face me. When I looked into her eyes I could already see them glistening with tears.

I wasn't kneeling in front of her, but our position felt more intimate this way. I wanted to be able to continue holding her when I laid my heart out to her.

"Simone, I love you. Being with you has been the happiest time of my life. I can't imagine my life without you or Stella. I want to be the man you both can depend on. The man who will protect you and never let you go. The one who will love you for the rest of our lives." I paused, having rehearsed this speech, wanting it to be perfect when I delivered each line. "Will you marry me?"

I opened the black velvet box I'd had in my pocket so she could see the diamond ring I'd picked out. She was quiet for a few moments but then her eyes met mine and I could see the love and joy I had for her reflected back at me.

"Of course I'll marry you," she said, placing her hands on both sides of my face, kissing me. She then pulled back so I could put the ring on her finger. "I love you, Kyle."

I continued to kiss her, hoping she could feel every ounce of love I was putting into it.

Falling for Simone may have been unexpected, but it was the best thing to ever happen to me.

The End

Author's Note

Making the decision to move forward with publishing this book was both an exciting and scary undertaking. The amount of support and encouragement I received throughout this entire process was truly inspiring. I am eternally grateful to all of you.

To my amazing husband, there is no way I could have done any of this without you. You kept everything going when I would lock myself away in my room to write. The kids and I are extremely lucky to have you. I love you!

William, Madalyn, Gina, Genevieve, and Michael, you are the best kids a mom could ask for. And even though you aren't allowed to read this book, I hope I have taught you that it's never too late to chase your dreams.

Mom, thank you for being my biggest cheerleader. It's because of you that I discovered my love of reading. Dad, thank you for giving up your spot at the table so I could come over and write when I needed a quiet spot to focus. You put up with Mom and me talking nonstop about book ideas. Love you both!

To Carolyn, my awesome mentor. I will never be able to express how appreciative I am to you for all the guidance you have provided. Thank you for always being there to answer my questions and for keeping me motivated.

My editor, Katie, thank you for taking a chance on me and caring about my story and characters. This whole process was scary but you made it so much better.

Tabitha, my partner in crime. Thank you for being the first person to read *Falling for the Unexpected* and encouraging me to continue. Your friendship means more to me than you'll ever know. I'm so glad you've become such a big part of my life.

Meagan, who would have thought a chance meeting at a book signing would've sparked such a meaningful friendship? Thank you for always being there for me to bounce ideas off of, give me feedback, and provide me with encouragement when I'm just not feeling it.

BookSmacked Promotions, bloggers, and reviewers, thank you for all you have done to spread the word about *Falling for the Unexpected.*

To the readers, thank you for taking a chance on a new author. I hoped you enjoyed reading this story as much as I enjoyed telling it.

Playlist

Mirrors – Justin Timberlake

Two Weeks – All That Remains

Radioactive – Imagine Dragons

Home – Three Days Grace

So Far Away – Staind

Painkiller – Three Days Grace

Just Like You – Three Days Grace

This Is What You Came For (feat. Rihanna)– Calvin Harris

Shape Of You – Ed Sheeran

Cake By The Ocean – DNCE

The High Road – Three Days Grace

Marry Me – Train

About The Author

Rachel lives in the San Francisco Bay Area with her husband, five children, two dogs, two cats, and a gecko. Whenever she has some free time you'll find her with a book in her hands. She never believed she was the creative type until she sat down one day and started plotting out a story that wouldn't leave her head. From there, the ideas continued to flow. It was then that she found her outlet and she hasn't stopped since.

Falling for the Unexpected is her debut novel.

Follow Rachel here and get updates on future projects:

Facebook: www.facebook.com/rachellynadams

Twitter: @rachellynadams2

Email: rachellynadamsauthor@gmail.com